SO-AXJ-472

JONAS
AND
SALLY

JONAS
AND
SALLY

—— A NOVEL BY ——
RICH FOSS

Good Books®

Intercourse, PA 17534

Acknowledgments

Deep gratitude to all my brothers and sisters at Plow Creek Fellowship who made my summer 1993 sabbatical from PCF leadership possible so that I could complete this story. Each of you have touched me with your stories and love and I am privileged to be a living stone with you.

Special thanks to Jim Monterastelli and Jack Domagall who made possible my leave of absence from Horizon House at the same time.

Appreciation to Julie Marcum of the Tiskilwa Library for all the books through inter-library loan. Also to Phil Martin of the Wisconsin Folk Museum for pointing to historical sources on commercial fishing in the Great Lakes and for supplying the music. Also to Geraldine Strey of the Wisconsin Historical Society Library for the bibliography and articles on commercial fishing in Lake Michigan. Also the Great Lakes Fishery Commission supplied research materials. Without the help of each of you I wouldn't know about the life of a commercial fisherman on Lake Michigan in 1932. Any errors are mine.

Thanks to Anne Stewart for comments on the early chapters, to Sarah for reading the first draft and making invaluable comments that greatly improved the second draft, and to Rick Reha for proofing the second draft. Thanks to Carey Carlson, Mark Horwath, Ed Johnson, Mark Stahnke, and the Associated Mennonite Biblical Seminary library for the use of your computers.

Songs played at the engagement and wedding dances can be heard on *Across the Fields, Traditional Norwegian-American Music From Wisconsin, Volume 1,* Folklore Village Farm, Inc., 1987.

Finally, there wouldn't be a story without you, Creator and Restorer of the years lost to the swarming locust.

Cover art by Stan Miller
Desgin by Dawn J. Ranck

JONAS AND SALLY
© 1994, 2000 by Plow Creek Fellowship, Inc.
First published 1994.
REVISED EDITION, 2000.
International Standard Book Number: 1-56148-305-2, paperback
International Standard Book Number: 1-56148-128-9, hardcover
Library of Congress Catalog Card Number: 94-27871

All rights reserved. Printed in the United States of America.
No part of this book may be reproduced in any manner,
except for brief quotations in critical articles or reviews, without permission.

Library of Congress Cataloging-in-Publication Data

Foss, Rich.,
        Jonas and Sally : a novel / by Rich Foss.
        p. cm.
        1. Man-woman relationshiops--Lake Michigan Region-- Fiction.
I. Title.
PS3556.07554J66   1994
813'.54--dc20   94-27871
                                            CIP

To my wife,
Sarah,
for your passion, honesty, and love.

And to my children,
Hannah, Heidi, and Jon;
I love being family with you.

1.

The tug plowed through the Lake Michigan night, carrying Jonas and Sally to their honeymoon and her father to jail. The water slapped against the tug. Jonas and Sally huddled under a slicker at the bow to keep dry from the rolling waves. Gradually the sprays stopped, the lake settling down after the storm. Jonas peered out at the stars over the pilothouse.

Stars are known by their families. He remembered his mother telling him that when he was twelve. That was the year his father added a new dormer to their house. Jonas' two younger brothers, who shared the new room with him, were asleep, but he was awake when his mother came into the darkened room to say good-night. She walked to the new window, then called to him to come and look at the stars. As he stood next to her, she began to tell him about the stars. Soon, even though it was late fall and cold in Wisconsin, she opened the window. They leaned and twisted out the window while she pointed out the Little Dipper, the Big Dipper, and other groupings of stars. It was then that she told him that the stars are known by their families. Jonas had not known that his mother knew anything about the stars. Now nearly nine years later, as he leaned next to Sally on the tug deck, he remembered something else about that night: the warmth of his mother's side as they leaned out the window.

Jonas looked up at the pilothouse. He could make out Daniel's dark shape at the wheel. Her father must be at the stern. Jonas couldn't imagine what her father was thinking. He was probably glad to escape the island, but what would he be thinking about the deputy sheriff who awaited them when they docked?

Jonas leaned against Sally. He wanted to think of something more pleasant like the Sunday the spring before when he met her. It was late April 1932 and he had preached to three people on the beach. Two women and a man. He sat on the Norsk Island beach with his back to Little Oslo, thinking about the huge crowds that pressed to hear Jesus. Once Jesus had borrowed Peter's boat and spoke from out on the lake, using the lake to carry his voice. Jonas knew he would never have a crowd like that on this island. One of the women who listened to Jonas preach had come to hear him for the first time. The other woman was deaf. For twenty minutes he preached Jesus as the light of the world. Jonas, who loved the stars, told his tiny congregation that the stars are known by their families. Then he invited them to become part of the family of God.

Before preaching he told the story of Moses in the bulrushes to half a dozen children, but they wandered off when he started talking about the stars. When he finished preaching, the three shook his hand and went home. Jonas was twenty years old, a preacher and hired man on this small island in Lake Michigan for two weeks.

He clutched his Bible and watched the waves in Rock Point Harbor. Was that a child crying? The waves sparkled and rolled in from the west under the late morning sun. Then the sound again. And again. Jonas went looking for a child. He found her sitting on the porch of a cabin. A little girl of about four.

"Why are you crying?"

"My mama won't get up and play with me."

Jonas peered through the screen door. The smell of stale beer. A loft with a ladder leading up to it. Below the loft, a bedroom with a woman asleep on a single bed next to a pedal sewing machine. Jonas quickly looked away.

"I'll play with you," he offered. He missed his younger brothers and sisters.

"What can you play?"

"Anything you want."

They played in the beach sand, building cabins, catching imaginary fish, and storing them in fish houses. They played in the waves. They hunted shells.

Suddenly her mother stood beside them on the beach, wearing a tattered, quilted blue robe. "Samantha, come with me right this minute. What is he doing with you? You are never to be with someone I don't know." The woman pulled the child so sharply by the arm, she began to cry. The mother glared at Jonas. He stared at her eyes. Once he had seen northern lights as brilliantly green as her eyes. "Did he hurt you?" she asked looking down at the girl.

"No, Mama, he played nice," sobbed the little girl. The woman's glare moved back to Jonas.

"I played nice," he said, holding his palms up.

Samantha grew braver. "We made sand cabins (sniffle) and catched fishes (sniffle) and he found me a pretty shell (sniffle)." She opened the hand that still clutched the shell. All eyes turned to the shell, glinting in the sunlight.

"I'm glad he was nice to you," she said, her voice softening. She touched the child's cheek.

"So," she looked at Jonas, "you are the new preacher. Well, whether you are or not, don't ever do that again . . . " Her voice dropped and she covered her eyes with her hand. "Scared me half to death, taking Samantha while I was sleeping," she muttered.

Samantha was drying her tears with the back of her fists.

"Is it really morning? Please, tell me it's not morning," the woman ran her fingers through her thin, tangled blonde hair.

"It's morning, Mama," Samantha said, finished with drying her tears. She turned hopefully to her mother.

"Please, Samantha, make it night again. I want to go back to sleep."

"Okay, Mama," said Samantha, brightly. The woman burst out laughing, then grabbed her head with both hands. "Ohhhh, it hurts to laugh." The woman didn't look much older than Jonas.

Letting go of her head she dared him, "So, you are Jonas the preacher."

"I . . . " Jonas tried to think of something to say. All that came out was " . . . and a hired man."

"Jonas, the boy preacher." She brushed the hair from her eyes. "Daniel and Theresa and Philena have been telling me about you." Daniel was the captain of a fishing tug that Jonas worked on a couple of times. Theresa and Philena were part of the crew. Samantha let go of her mama's robe and took a step away, keeping an eye on her mama to see if she would be scolded again.

"You don't look like I expected," the woman said, eyeing Jonas.

"What am I supposed to look like?" asked Jonas, finally finding his tongue.

"I don't know," she said, again moving strands of blonde hair out of her eyes. "Impressive, I guess. Maybe huge. When they told me that Brawn started crying and told you all about his daddy going down . . . and Daniel says you have the makings of a captain . . . I thought you were going to be impressive, not just some skinny kid with freckles and red hair."

"I didn't think I looked that bad," flared Jonas.

"I don't mean you look ugly." Then for the first time she smiled at Jonas, her eyes turning a softer shade of green. "What am I saying? You look fine. Just different than I expected." She shook her head. "This headache is making me say crazy things. Let me put it this way. Another time of day you might be really good-looking."

"I'm glad you don't think I'm ugly," said Jonas, smiling tentatively in return. "My mother used to get bad headaches," he said, remembering. "One thing that helped was when my dad or I would rub her neck. It helped her a lot."

"Well, I don't have anyone to rub my neck."

Jonas blushed. He hoped she didn't think he was offering to rub her neck. He wished he had kept his mouth shut. Then it came back to him what his dad did for a headache. "My dad's cure for headaches was to go float in the pond on his back. He used to say he could shut out the world, and the pond drained the headache right out of him."

"If I tried that," she said sarcastically, looking at the harbor, "the water would freeze my headache out . . . now if you'll forgive us. I need some coffee. And then I must go to work." She recaptured Samantha and left, pulling the little girl after her. Samantha turned back, waving.

"Lady," Jonas called after her, "wait. You know my name but I don't know yours." He believed as a preacher he should learn the names of all the people in Little Oslo.

She stopped, her back still to him. Then she turned and looked at him. "Did you say, 'lady?'" He nodded. She paused a long time as if she were struggling over something. He thought a tear appeared in her eye like a drop of water on a lily pad. She shook her head, shrugged her shoulders, and said, "I'm Sally." Then she walked away with Samantha. Puzzled, Jonas watched them until they disappeared into their cabin.

2.

Jonas wrote his first letter home, telling his family and church that he had preached two Sundays in a row. Then he decided to explore part of the island, walking south along the shoreline. Daniel had told him that the island was five miles long and two miles across at the widest point. When the land became more and more marshy he left the shore, heading inland through the scrub pine bordering the marsh. He swatted fierce mosquitoes, kept watch for sinkholes, and dodged head-level pine limbs. Finally he reached the other side where breezes kept the mosquitoes at bay and the terrain was easier for walking. He headed north. Eventually he came to a bay with another settlement of a dozen cabins. This was the East Side, the other small fishing village on the island.

Three kids—eight to ten years old—spotted him. "Who are you?" they sang out. "Bye preacher, bye preacher," they chorused as he moved north out of their circle.

Norsk Island's northern tip grew giant pines and threw up a rocky border. Jonas scaled the bluffs and dodged boulders along the shore. By the time he circled the island back to Little Oslo it was supper-time. Sally and Samantha were digging clams. "Could you teach me how to dig clams?" he asked, looking for an opening with the woman.

Sally stared at him. A half smile formed on her lips. "Are you fast enough?" she asked.

"Fast enough?"

"Clams are quick as rabbits. You have to be fast to dig them."

"I was quick enough to catch little pigs and get them away from the sows before they got me."

"Get yourself a shovel and bucket and I'll teach you," she said with a tilt of her head. She sent him to Daniel's gear shack to find the equipment.

When Sally showed him how to dig for clams, he soon saw that he was plenty fast enough. "Rabbits must move pretty slow on this island," he ventured.

"Yes," she said with a laugh, "about as fast as clams."

"How's your headache?" he asked as they dug.

"Better. Nothing like a little coffee to get me feeling civilized again."

Jonas had about half a dozen clams when Sally finished. "How are you going to cook yours?" she asked.

"I think I'll build a fire on the beach and make some soup with them."

"Oh, I haven't eaten clam soup by a fire on the beach since I was Samantha's size. That first season we came to the island we ate outside while Daddy was building our cabin."

"Let's eat on the beach," squealed Samantha.

"Join me," said Jonas.

"How many clams have you dug?" asked Sally.

"Half a dozen."

"Tell you what. You give me your clams and, while you build

the fire, I'll throw your clams and some potatoes into a pot with ours. We'll cook them all together over the fire."

Jonas handed her his clams. He noticed that she was wearing a long, light green dress that contrasted with her deep green eyes. She was very slender, and she had washed and combed her shoulder-length, blonde hair. She took the clams. "May I help Jonas build the fire?" asked Samantha.

"No," said Sally.

"Please, Mama."

Sally paused, looking at Samantha and then at Jonas. "Where will you be getting the wood?"

"There's wood by Daniel's gear shack that he lets me use for cooking. I'll bring it over here for the fire." Sally looked the hundred yards down the beach to the gear shack.

"Okay, Samantha."

"Yippee!" squealed Samantha. She grabbed Jonas' hand, tugging at him.

"I'll be keeping my eye on you," Sally warned. Jonas assumed she was addressing Samantha, but when he glanced at her she was looking at him.

He felt a flicker of uneasiness. "I'll get the fire going," he said.

He built the fire and Sally made the soup. When they finished eating, Samantha wandered off in search of more shells. "What's that book you have with you?" asked Sally.

"A Bible," Jonas said.

"Do you carry it with you everywhere?"

"Yes, I usually do. Except when I set it down someplace and can't remember where I put it. If I have it with me, I can read it when I have a minute."

"What does the Good Book have to say today?"

"What about?"

"Married love," she said, a challenge in her voice.

Jonas swallowed. When he first met her that morning, she seemed edgy. He couldn't imagine what she'd say next. Then this evening she seemed easygoing in her teasing. Now she asked him about a topic he had never talked about with anyone, let alone a woman. It *was* something he had thought about. In fact, he had combed the Bible to see what it had to say. He flipped open the book. *But from the beginning of creation God made them male and female. For this cause shall a man leave his father and mother and cleave to his wife; And the twain shall be one flesh: so then they are no more twain, but one flesh. What therefore God hath joined together, let no man put asunder.* Mark 10:6-9.

"Do you see a husband around here?" she asked.

Jonas looked around, then felt his face redden when he realized he was looking for a husband who didn't exist. The fire was dying down. He thought of jumping up and putting out the fire and leaving. He should not be having this conversation. "No," he said.

"What does that Good Book have to do with me then?" She was smiling but her eyes weren't. They had deepened to a green like the sky before a thunderstorm.

"That was God's intention."

"What was God's intention?"

"That a man and woman marry and be one from then on."

"I guess Samantha's father and I were asunder before we were one." She was looking at him hard, as if daring him to speak. He didn't speak. She continued, "He forced himself on me and I bet that book doesn't say a thing about that." When she said "forced" she sounded like she was spitting.

Jonas' mind went blank. God, what could he say to her? He didn't know about that.

"My dad was always preaching the Bible," she said angrily. "'Wives, submit to your husbands. Children, obey your parents. Do as I say or God will leave you behind at the Second Coming.' So you read to me that *what God has joined together, let no man put asunder*. But what about a man forcing himself on a woman? What does the Good Book say about rape, Preacher?"

Jonas had to say something. "*Eloi, Eloi, lama sabachthani?*" he said.

"What?" she asked.

"*Eloi, Eloi, lama sabachthani?*" It means, 'My God, my

God, why hast thou forsaken me?'"

"Why do you say that?"

"You asked me what the Bible has to say about a man forcing himself on a woman. It was the first thing that came to my mind."

"The Bible says that?"

"Yes, Jesus cried out with a loud voice, *'Eloi, Eloi, lama sabachthani?'* He cried out when he was dying on the cross."

"What does that have to do with a man forcing himself on a woman?"

"They took his clothes off him. They nailed him to the cross with his arms out like this," he said. He held his arms out.

"Teach me to say that," she insisted, her eyes flashing.

"*Eloi, Eloi, lama sabachthani?*" he asked.

"Yes," she said, her voice low. Jonas was taken back, but he didn't know what else to do so he taught her.

"You better take Samantha over to Alice's," she directed. Something in her tone made Jonas decide not to question her. Sally picked up the pot and their bowls and spoons and headed toward her cabin. Jonas put out the fire and led Samantha toward Alice and Daniel's cabin.

"*Eloi, Eloi, lama sabachthani?!*" He turned. She was in her cabin. She cried out again, "*Eloi, Eloi, lama sabachthani?!*" Then he heard her break into sobs.

Samantha started to cry and turn back to the cabin. Jonas picked her up and walked along the path. "You can't take care of your mama," he said. "God is listening to her. Your mama asked me to take you to Alice's." He clung to Samantha. "God, I hope you are listening," he breathed.

3.

The next day Daniel told Jonas he could use an extra hand on his crew for the day. Daniel was a small, wiry man in his early sixties with a salt and pepper beard and white hair that curled out from under the back of his cap. Having emigrated from Norway when he was fourteen, he spoke with a strong Norwegian accent with its unexpected high, flat waves.

Two weeks had passed since Jonas boarded the *Lillian* for passage to Norsk. The steamship *Lillian* made a daily trip from the mainland to Norsk Island to deliver mail, food, goods, and an occasional passenger, and also to pick up fish from the island fishermen. Jonas arrived on the island carrying his clothes in a battered old suitcase and a hammock slung over his shoulder. The first thing he did was ask about work. Someone pointed him to Daniel, who had just hurt his back driving spiles. He might need an extra hand.

Jonas had approached the small man. "Ya, what brings you to this island then?" Daniel asked Jonas in his surprisingly gruff voice.

"I want to be a preacher here."

"A preacher, ya?" Daniel said, eyeing the skinny, twenty-year-old kid in front of him. "There's no church on the island."

"I'll start without one."

"Ya, preaching with no church won't put fish on the table."

"That's why I'm looking for work. I'll be a hired man, too."

"What can you do?"

"I grew up on a farm. I know all the work there is to do on a farm."

"There's no farming on this island."

"I can learn whatever needs to be done."

"Ya, fishing, that's what we do. A little tourist business, too."

"Then I'll learn whatever needs to be done."

Daniel took off his cap, scratched his head with the hand that held the cap, put the cap back on, and growled, "Start by giving Brawn a hand getting those spiles into the lake. We need to tow them out and drive them. Brawn's the big one." He pointed to a huge redhead a little older than Jonas who was standing with several other men next to a pile of tamarack, oak, and white ash. Some of the tamarack had been spliced to oak or white ash. Jonas had his first job on the island.

"What are spiles used for?" Jonas asked Brawn as they levered the spiles into the lake.

"Drive'm into the lake to hold the pot nets in place."

"How do pot nets work?"

"Pots are like corrals. Mouth of the corral, the pot has wings, nets that stand upright just like a fence and extend out. Long wings. Fish swims into the inside of a wing. Turns one way, he swims free; turns the other way, he swims into the pot. Once they're in the pot they usually don't find the mouth to swim back out."

Jonas thought he understood.

They drove the spiles into the lake like fence posts, using an apparatus on the barge.

Later as Daniel guided the spile-driving barge back to the island, he called Jonas over to him. "Ya, we could use a preacher on the island."

"Thank you, sir," said Jonas.

"Nay, don't thank me," Daniel said. "Being a preacher will cost you plenty."

"But I don't have anything to pay."

"Ya." He paused a long time. "No doubt the cost will be in tears."

"Tears?"

"Ya, you will come to love the island and its people, starting with us," waving his hand to encompass his barge and crew. "And that will break your heart a few times. Preachers, they have to love, you know, and you can't love without your heart getting broken a few times."

"Are you a preacher?" Jonas asked, wanting to know what he was getting into.

"Nay, I am no preacher. Ya, they ask me to do the funerals and weddings on the island. But I am a fisherman, not a preacher." Gesturing to the lake he went on, "Ya, the cost of fishing is the cost of the lake. No fisherman knows what the

lake wants when he sets out in the morning, but he knows he will pay. No preacher knows the cost of opening his mouth . . . "
His voice trailed off as he concentrated on guiding the barge in to Rock Point Harbor. "Now," he said, dismissing Jonas, "help Brawn tie the lines to the dock."

Although Jonas grew up on a farm well inland from Lake Michigan and had never fished any place bigger than a pond, he came willing to learn and able to work. Daniel hired him for a second day. The nets were bringing in more fish than usual and Daniel could use an extra hand.

Late in the morning after the pot nets had been pulled and the fish scooped into the hold, Daniel put Jonas to work cleaning fish. Philena taught him to gut the trout. A woman in her late thirties, Philena had graying hair tied back in a blue kerchief and a smooth face with only the smallest trace of wrinkles by her pale blue eyes. She and her twenty-one-year-old daughter, Theresa, were part of Daniel's crew. Jonas stood with them at a slippery, scaly table on the boat cleaning fish. Philena held a thrashing fish on the table. A knife in her hands flashed in the sun, then deftly sliced through the fish. She tossed the guts into a barrel and packed the cleaned fish into a box with ice.

Jonas tried to imitate her motions. First the trout slipped out of his grasp and landed on the deck. He hastily dove for it, trapping it up against the gunwale. Philena's laughter rang out on the boat. When he cut the fish, his cut veered off at an angle. Philena slowed down and showed him each motion in sequence. After several tries he began to succeed. Slowly through the morning he progressed, but he would never be as quick as she was. He concentrated on cleaning fish; Philena and Theresa chitchatted.

That afternoon, for the first time since leaving home, he began to feel lonesome. He remembered stopping at the top of the hill the day he left, looking down into the valley at the farm. His mother and father and younger brothers and sisters stood there watching him go. He waved. They waved back. He thought about his three-mile walk to catch the train. His church had taken up a collection to pay for his ticket.

In the late afternoon as Daniel headed the tug back to the island, Philena asked, "When did God tell you to be a preacher?"

"When I was nine years old."

"You knew about the island then?"

"No, I just knew that God wanted me to be preacher."

"How old are you now?"

"Twenty."

"How did you know about this island?"

"About a month ago I dreamed about it. In the dream I saw the island. And I heard a voice say, *'This is the place for you to preach.'* The farm I grew up on was in the middle of Wisconsin so I knew about this big lake. But I didn't know about Norsk Island. After the dream I asked around about the island. One man had heard of the island. He said fishermen lived on it. I knew the island in my dream and the island on the lake were the same, so as soon as I could, I left home to come here to preach. We were about to start spring planting, but I left.

"I have heard there is another island many miles north of here," she said. "How do you know you were supposed to come here and not there?"

"I didn't know there was another island, but now that I am here, I'm sure I'm at the right place."

"You are so young," she said. Jonas thought she sounded sad. He didn't understand why.

Philena wiped her hand on her apron and pushed a wisp of hair out of her face and back under her kerchief. "I once had a mission from God," she said.

"You did?"

"Yes. When I was seventeen a young man came to work on this island. I fell in love with him. My mission was to love him. It was fun. We got married. We had Theresa." She cleaned a fish, packed it, and stood at the table with the soft look of a woman remembering happy times.

"What made it a mission?"

"*Who*," she said, correcting him. "*Who* made it a mission? God did."

"Was something wrong with him?"

"With God?" she said, looking at him puzzled.

"No, your husband."

"Oh," she laughed. Her face lit up. "No, nothing was wrong with him. He was a handsome, healthy man who loved to laugh and tell jokes and stories. It was fun to love him. Every night I thanked God for such a man, for such a mission. He could snort like a bull. Strong, oh, he was strong."

"And your mission was to love him?" Jonas had never heard of such a mission. He had heard of preaching and evangelism and the mission field, but this?

"Yes," she said, winking at him. "At first I was afraid I was making up something so good, such a wonderful mission. But when I told my mother she said, 'God didn't call you to be a nun, Philena.' So I took up my mission with Gresig. Theresa was born. Then I started having miscarriages. After awhile I came to understand that my mission really was Gresig, not a lot of children."

"I still don't see what made it a mission," Jonas said.

"You are young," she said with a smile. "You have much to learn." She scraped her knife onto the table. She never stopped cleaning as she talked.

"What can I compare my mission to?" she thought, wiping her hands on her apron and resuming scaling.

"Daniel's mission is the tug. Watch him. You will always see him taking care of this tug. His mission isn't fishing. His mission is a tug that always tugs the best. He does many things in life—supervises a crew, delivers a lot of fish—but his mission is this tug. You can tell by the way he watches the tug and touches it.

"My mission was Gresig. I watched him, touched him. He became a much better man. Stronger. Gentler." She laughed. "Funnier. Sadder. All the good things about being a man."

She leaned quietly against the cleaning table. She had finished cleaning her last fish.

"It's a shame he died," Jonas said, cleaning his last fish. He knew that she was a widow. Hank, a lean, silent member of the crew, closed the last fish box and stacked it with the rest.

"Yes, it has seemed that way to me, too. For a long time I thought it was a mistake. I still think his death was a mistake. God wanted him alive. God doesn't make mistakes, but this world is full of them. God works with mistakes. When Gresig died I learned something about missions. Something that it would be good for you to know, even if you have to learn it later. Missions change, but God never does. Missions don't last forever; they change."

"What is your mission now?"

"My mission is to be messy."

"Messy?"

"Do you know that I grew the first big potatoes on the island?" Jonas didn't know. "I brought topsoil over from the mainland, a little bit on every trip from the mainland. I'm always asking other people to bring some, too. The island doesn't seem to grow much but moss, pines, and a bit of grass.

"I'm like the soil I brought over. On the mainland it was rich and grew lots of stuff. Then I dug it up and carried it over to the island and nothing but weeds grew in it. I just kept adding to it. It was a mess. But eventually I had enough dirt and I ended the mess. I hacked down the weeds, turned over the soil, planted the potatoes, and now the island grows potatoes as big as the mainland.

"Some day," she continued, "my mess will straighten out for awhile. God will grow some new potatoes in me."

4.

In good weather Jonas slept in his hammock on the deck of Daniel's tug. The stars drew him. Wrapped in a wool blanket he lay searching for familiar stars like the Big Dipper and

Orion, the boat gently rocking, the soothing water lapping against boats and shore, until he faded to sleep.

One night Jonas wakened to a woman crying. It was Sally sitting at his feet. He sat up in the hammock, pulling his feet under him, making sure he was covered by the blanket.

"Don't send me away," she pleaded.

"I won't."

She continued to cry quietly. He hugged his knees. The lake was restless, with more of a southerly breeze than usual. The tug rose and fell at its mooring. Boats bumped against the dock. Clouds crowded together to block out the stars.

Still she cried. He wiped the sleep from his eyes. God, what was he to say to this woman? The wind changed to the southeast and the clouds covered the stars when she spoke. "Jonas, I screamed those words, *Eloi, Eloi lama sabachthani?!* until I couldn't . . . until I was wore out. At first it felt good to scream. It felt so good to sob my heart out. I began to feel clean for the first time. When you brought Samantha back I felt like a boat that had come through a great storm to find shelter in a small bay. But then tonight in the middle of the night I woke up and my pillow was wet. I was crying again. I felt empty. As empty as a cat dish licked clean. I felt nothing. I wanted to feel something. There has to be something more. I thought of you. So I came. What am I missing?"

"After Jesus cried out, he died," said Jonas quietly, searching for familiar landmarks among the stories of the Bible. "They buried him. He was dead. He was as empty as you feel. He was a body in the grave. He was nothing. For three days. You will feel empty for three days."

"What happened after three days?"

"His Father in heaven raised him from the dead."

"Will the same thing happen to me?"

"Jesus will touch you."

"I swore that I would never let a man touch me again."

"I need to think," Jonas said, reaching for his pants hanging on the rope of the hammock. He struggled into them under the wool blanket. He started to walk across the deck.

"You will be back?" she said anxiously.

"Yes." He vaulted over the edge of the tug, landing waist-deep in the frigid water. He dived and swam under the water, opening his eyes. He could see nothing. He swam further. When his lungs cried for air he surfaced and gulped. He treaded water and looked at the dim outline of the boats at the dock. He swam back to the dock. Standing in the water he rested his hands on the dock, bracing himself against the waves. He thought of Peter jumping out of the boat and wading to shore to talk to Jesus who had been dead but was now cooking fish over a fire.

He pulled himself onto the dock and then into the boat. As he stood on the deck dripping water, shivering, she said, "I am so empty. I . . . I . . . I am ready for Jesus to touch me."

"Jesus waited three days for his Father to raise him from the dead. You will have to wait, too."

"How long?" she said plaintively.

"I don't know. I hope not more than three days." He sat on the railing. "I hope not more than three days."

"It's already been more than three days." Jonas didn't say anything. "I have to wait some more?" she said.

"I think so. Jesus had to wait."

She sighed, "I will wait. Thank you," she said as she left. Shortly the breeze picked up and the first thunder sounded in the distance. He wished she didn't have to wait. He wondered why she had thanked him.

He went along the shore to a big boulder. He wanted to be a preacher who would say what God would say. It was hard to say: wait. Island boys used the rock to dive fifteen feet into a deep pool. He took a deep breath, leaped off the rock, relaxed his body, and plummeted deep into the lake. He did not move a muscle. The water was cold, but he felt like his skin was wrapping him in warmth. His descent came to a stop. Slowly he began to rise. He waited for God to bring him to the surface.

Then he hurried out of the lake to escape the lightning. Retrieving his hammock he went to Daniel's gear shack to sleep the rest of the night, the rain drumming on the roof.

5.

Jonas' reputation in Little Oslo as one with an uncanny power to open hearts had its beginning the first time he worked with Daniel's crew. Before dawn they headed for the fishing grounds, Jonas sitting next to Brawn, both of them wearing slickers to keep dry in the spray. Brawn's giant face was perpetually red, burned again and again by the sun.

Jonas had worked with him earlier, driving spiles for the pot nets. Brawn maintained a brooding silence that day, breaking it only to issue directions to Jonas or the other workers. Now they sat together, Brawn as silent as a bird at night.

Finally Jonas started, "How did you get into the fishing business?"

"My dad."

"Is Daniel your father?"

"No."

"How long you been fishing?"

"Seven years."

"What's the worst time you had fishing?"

Jonas sensed him looking at him for a long time in the darkness. Jonas wondered if he was angry. Was he going to tell him to shut up? Throw him overboard? Brawn stopped working on the net he was fixing. Should Jonas tell him he didn't need to answer?

"Last summer," Brawn said. He paused. Jonas saw the darkness in the east paling. "Big storm. Struck quicker than a rattlesnake. Dad didn't have time to turn the tug into the waves. We were next to a spile so I grabbed it to keep us from swamping. It was the only thing I could think of doing. I'm the strongest. I wasn't gonna let that storm get the best of us." He shook his head. "Dumb. The spile snapped and I went overboard still hugging it. I thought I was a goner. A strong man ain't nothin' in this lake." He went back to silence.

"What happened?"

"Bobbed around in the water for a long time. Maybe two hours. I was just trying to breathe. I didn't expect to live. Finally the storm petered out and I was still breathing. That was a great feeling." He chuckled. "Great feeling. I figured if I was still bobbing and the storm was over, I had a chance. Looked around. I couldn't see the shore. Sun came out a couple of hours before it set, so I knew which way to head. Let go of the broken spile and started swimming. I was worried I wouldn't make it to shore before it got dark. Longest swim I ever made. Stars were coming out when I finally hit shore."

Brawn's voice was very somber. He didn't act like a man who had just told a miraculous story of survival.

"I was the only one who made it," he said.

"Who else was on the boat?" Jonas finally asked.

"My dad and brother and another crew member. It took me a day to find out. I washed up on the shore of the mainland. Another fishing boat told me they never came home."

They went back to silence. Death, the silencer, thought Jonas.

The east sky was lighter. Jonas turned to look at Brawn. Tears, silent tears, were making rivulets down his ruddy cheeks. He was blinking. Jesus, prayed Jonas, can you touch this broken giant of a man? What can I do? If I mess up and get him mad, he could throw me overboard like a twig.

"There was once a man named Peter, a giant of a man," Jonas said. "He worked for a man called Jesus. Before he worked for Jesus he worked for his dad. He and his dad and brothers were fishermen. But he and his brother left his dad to work for Jesus. Jesus was like a politician. He talked real good and crowds would bunch up to listen to him. Peter and his brother and some others traveled with him." He paused. Where was he going with this story? What did it have to do with Brawn?

"Peter really looked up to Jesus," he continued. "He was a man whom Peter could admire. Jesus would take on the high and mighty in a debate, and in minutes he'd have 'em silenced, in awe of what he'd said. He could touch people and heal them. That drew the crowds too. He'd tell the best stories Peter had ever heard. Then Jesus began to tell Peter and the others that he was about to be killed."

Brawn began to sob. Loudly. Great gasping sobs that shook his huge frame. Jonas glanced around in the faint light of dawn at the rest of the crew. They had arrived at the fishing grounds. Daniel cut the engine and walked out of the pilothouse. He made his way to them, stepped past Jonas, and crouched beside Brawn, putting his arm around Brawn, looking small and old beside him. Brawn cried louder.

Finally, between gasps and sobs, he said, "My dad said I was going to have to get along without him." Daniel nodded. "He told me I was strong and a good fisherman. That I could make it without him." He sobbed some more. "He told me that the day before the storm." When he quieted down he said, "But I didn't want to make it without him. I'm not that strong. That spile broke even when I tried to hold it to save us. It broke off in my arms." He was crying more quietly.

"Ya, Brawn's been talking more in the last fifteen minutes than in the last year," said Daniel gruffly to Jonas. "Ya, Brawn, you got good reason to cry," Daniel said, patting his huge shoulder.

They went back to work. Later Brawn pulled in the gill net and Philena, Theresa, and Jonas picked fish and tossed them into the holding tank.

"What happened after he told Peter he was gonna die?" Brawn said.

"Soldiers came and killed him."

Tears came to Brawn's eyes again, the muscles in his arms bulging as he pulled the nets. "Just like my dad." Jonas nodded. "What happened to Peter?" Brawn asked.

"He went back to fishing."

"Just like me."

"But that wasn't the end of the story. Jesus came back to life and visited Peter when Peter was fishing."

"My dad never came back. My brother never came back. They are still in this lake some place." Jonas and Brawn looked at the lake in the early morning light, a dark, shimmering surface covering great secrets. Perhaps they were right over Brawn's dad's body. "What happened then?" Brawn asked.

"Jesus talked to Peter and the others and told them they were going to have to carry on without him. Then he went to heaven."

"I know about carrying on," Brawn said.

"But Jesus said he would not leave them alone. They were to carry on everything that Jesus taught them, and Jesus would ask his Father to send the Holy Ghost to help them."

"Holy what?"

"Holy Ghost."

"What's that?"

"After your dad died, did you ever have a feeling of his presence?"

"Once or twice. Once when I was being tossed on the waves like a cork during the storm. It was like his voice saying, 'You are the strongest, Brawn. You are going to make it.'"

"The Holy Ghost is like that. He's God's presence that can tell us things we could never know by ourselves and help us do things we could never do by ourselves. He helped Peter and he's been helping people ever since to carry on what Jesus taught."

"I could use some help carrying on like Dad taught," he said. They worked silently. "Tell me more about Jesus. He sounds like my dad." Jonas told him lots, starting with how he was born in a barn. Brawn kept interrupting him with stories about his dad and brother.

Jonas didn't mind.

6.

When Daniel or one of the other fishermen didn't have work for Jonas, he took other jobs. One day he pitched manure out of Old Lady Bills' henhouse and spread it on her garden.

The job didn't take much concentration, and Jonas found himself thinking about manure. Every critter has his manure. Put him in a house and you collect manure. Somebody has to do something with the manure. It might as well be him.

Then he noticed something in the manure. He leaned against the pitchfork and looked more closely. It was a small, rusted metal box. He picked it up and pried it open. It was filled with silver dollars. Money in the manure. He counted it: 97 pieces. He put them on the ledge and went back to pitching manure.

Later he stirred the earth and manure together in Old Lady Bills' flower gardens. He knew Old Lady Bills would be glad if he just spread it on the garden, but it would be better mixed together. So he mixed it.

It was supper-time when he finished. Old Lady Bills invited him for supper. Before he went in to eat, he washed the box of coins and left them on the porch. When they were finished eating, he brought the coins in and gave them to Old Lady Bills, telling her where he found them. She looked at the box for a long time. Then she looked at him. She smiled. "I can't believe it. My husband never trusted banks. But I didn't know he was using the chicken barn as his bank. I suspected he was keeping some money on the side." She shook her head. "What good is it to me now?" she kept on going. "My husband is dead. He provided for me before he died. Soon I will be dead." She was speaking as if to herself. "We could have used it when we were both young and well. I always wanted to go on a trip back to the Old Country. But Hans said we couldn't afford it. So we didn't go. We stayed. Hans died. I am too old to travel. This could have taken us to the Old Country."

She talked on about her husband and the boatbuilding business and the Old Country. Dusk came. She lit a lantern and still she talked.

Finally she took Jonas' hand and pressed the box of coins into it. Holding his hand she said, "You are young. You take this money. You take this box . . . " She stopped, sounding puzzled. "I was going to tell you to go to the Old Country with it, but now I don't know what you should do with it. Just take it." She released his hand, leaving the box.

That night he went to sleep to the gentle rocking of Daniel's tug, wondering what it meant to be a preacher and a hired man with a box of silver dollars.

7.

Two days later Jonas gave away some of the silver dollars. He had just read the story of the rich young man whom Jesus told to sell all he had, give what he earned to the poor, and follow him.

That day he was working with Daniel. Daniel had his boat in dry dock, and they were cleaning and repairing the hull. "Who's the poorest man on the island?" Jonas asked.

"Ya, that would be Jackson," Daniel said.

"Who's he?"

"Oh, he's a man of about forty-five. He hasn't got any legs. He froze them off one winter. He got drunk and passed out on his way home. He was lucky he was wearing good mittens; otherwise he might have lost his hands, too. He paints pictures and sells them to the tourists, but he doesn't make much at that. People help him out."

That night Jonas went to visit him. Jackson was sitting on a chair painting a picture of ducks flying above the lake. He had graying hair and a wispy beard. His face was ruddy. Jonas brought him some fish.

"I've never seen you before," Jackson grunted. When he spoke Jonas caught a glimpse of a silver tooth.

"I'm new here." They exchanged names. Jonas offered to cook up the fish for him.

"I wasn't planning to eat them raw," Jackson said.

They ate the fish at a makeshift table made out of two planks on two sawhorses. "Tell me about yourself," Jackson said. So Jonas told him some things.

"I don't want you preaching at me, so if you have that in mind, you can leave right now."

"I won't preach unless you ask for it," said Jonas.

"I'm not asking."

While they were eating, Jackson found five silver dollars in the mouth of his fish. He didn't say anything, just slipped them into his shirt pocket and went on eating. When they were done eating, he said Jonas should come back the next day because he could use a hired man for awhile.

Jonas wasn't sure he could come back the next day. Daniel might need him, but when he could come back, he would.

8.

Jonas was sitting on the deck at dawn the next morning, waiting for Daniel and the rest of the crew to arrive, when Sally came out of her cabin and walked down to the boat. She sat down beside him. "I have been empty more than three days," she said.

He reached out and held her hand, silent in the presence of her sadness, waiting for God.

"Isn't there some other word you can give me from the Bible? *Eloi, Eloi, lama sabachthani* helped, but I need something more."

He shook his head. "I feel like a little boy. There is so much I do not know."

"But you knew what to say to me last time."

"Not me. The Holy Ghost. I didn't know what to say."

"Well, get the Holy Ghost to say something more."

"He speaks when he wants. I don't make him speak."

"What am I to do then?" She sounded so forlorn. He squeezed her hand and waited for the Holy Ghost.

"I had a dream last night," she said. "I just remembered it. I dreamed that I was sitting astride a log drifting down a river. The log didn't roll; I kept wondering why I didn't tip over.

Then I wanted to get ashore because I was coming to the mouth of the river. I didn't want to drift into the lake. But I was afraid to try paddling toward shore because I thought the log might roll. I was getting closer and closer to the lake and more and more scared. I couldn't move. That's when I woke up."

"Now I have something to say," Jonas said. "I think you are ready to be baptized."

"Baptized? What's that?"

"It's going out into the lake and letting someone dunk you under the water in the name of the Father, Son, and Holy Ghost. It's a way to let people know that you have decided to follow Jesus."

"I could never let anyone touch me in the water," she said sharply.

"Why?"

"I was swimming when he forced himself on me."

They sat in a cold silence. The only warmth he felt was her hand that he still held. The gulls wheeled and screamed and glinted in the morning light.

Jonas suddenly felt angry. "I'd like to drown whoever it was," he said. "I know that's not very godly of me . . . "

"I've dreamed that I was holding his head under the water trying to drown him. I always wake up before he's dead."

"I thought the Holy Ghost told me you were ready to be baptized . . . but maybe I didn't hear right."

"Why the dunking under water?"

"It's like dying with Jesus and rising with him. The dunking is the dying; the coming up out of the water is the rising from the dead. You come up a new person. The person who dunks you helps you stand up."

"I would like to do that."

"You would?"

"I can't bear the thought of it, but I want to so bad."

She let go of his hand and wiped tears from her eyes on the back of her blouse sleeve. Daniel came out of his cabin and headed toward the dock. "Is it really possible for me to go back to the water and come up a new woman?" she asked.

"Yes."

She walked back to her cabin. Jonas' hand stayed warm for a long time after she left. He had never held a woman's hand before.

9.

That afternoon on the way home from a day of fishing, Daniel was at the wheel. He called Jonas to him. "Ya, you done well today," he said.

"Thank you. I enjoyed the work."

"Ya, a question has been bothering me then. Maybe I have some advice for you, too."

Jonas waited.

"Ya, the question. Do you know Jesus?"

"I know him," said a startled Jonas. "You hear me preach every Sunday."

"When I had been running my own boat for a year, an old captain asked, 'Dan'l, do you know this lake?' 'Ya, I do,' I said. 'Dan'l,' he replied, 'let me tell you a story. There was a man who fished these waters for forty years. He was the best. A friend of the fish. He knew the fish and he knew the water and he never came home empty-handed. Or almost never. Then one day he got too old and his son took over. His son caught lots of fish just like his dad for a few days. Then he began to catch fewer and fewer, even though he tried to fish the same spots as his dad. Finally he went to his dad and said 'Dad, what am I doing wrong?' The old man looked at him, 'All these years in the boat with me and you were watching me and not the lake. You don't know the lake. You will have to learn the lake like I did.'

"He begged his father to come back with him and teach him the lake. The old man said, 'I cannot. I no longer know the lake. I have been gone from the lake for a month. The lake will have changed too much. I am a stranger to the lake.'

"'What am I to do?' asked the son. His father said, 'Son, you have many years to get to know the lake. Many years to become friends with the fish and the water. Go.'

"His son went. The old man said to himself, 'He is sad now, but he will learn the lake and he will know it every day for many years. Now that is good.'"

Daniel looked up. Jonas followed his gaze. He tried to understand what Daniel was telling him. "I don't understand the connection between your story and your question," Jonas said.

"Ya, God has made you a preacher," said Daniel. "It's plain to see. But like a captain you will have to get to know the lake all by your lonesome every day."

Jonas thought he understood. Jesus was like the lake. Life was like the lake. Every day he was to get to know life and Jesus.

"I love this tug," said Daniel, patting the wheel. "It keeps me safe and other people safe. But no boat can save you if you don't pay attention to the lake every day. Ya, that's my advice. Keep your boat in good shape and know the lake." Daniel stood at the wheel guiding the tug through the great lake. As they stood there in silence Jonas began to think of Sally. He remembered the warmth of her hand.

"What do you think of marriage, Daniel?"

"Ya, marriage is honorable in all and the bed undefiled. Ya, you ought to get married."

"Why?"

"Nay, you always have questions, don't you," he said with a smile. He thought for awhile. "Ya, here's a good reason. You got to learn how to be a captain to those close to you. A captain is no good unless he knows how to captain someone who is close to him. No one is closer than a wife. No one is harder to captain. But if you can captain a family, then you got a chance to captain anyone."

"You keep talking as if I'm going to be a captain. I'm a preacher."

Daniel put his hand on Jonas' shoulder. "Ya, I know you are a preacher. God makes trees out of wood. He don't make flowers out of iron. You are like a tree that's been growing twenty years. You've been growing in the shape of a preacher for twenty years. But you can learn something from an old man like me. A preacher does more than preach, just like a captain does more than give orders. A captain must know his crew and be a captain to every man. A preacher must know every man, woman, and child on his crew and be a preacher for each one." Daniel squeezed his shoulder and let go.

"Is that the only reason to get married?" Jonas asked.

"Have you ever climbed a hill and dropped a ball from the top?"

"No."

He was smiling now. "Well, think what would happen if you did." He looked across the water, then back at Jonas. He laughed. "God gave you balls and those balls were made to roll. Ya, the bed is undefiled." He snorted. "You are getting a little red around the ears, Jonas."

"I never talked to anyone about these things," stammered Jonas, glancing around to see if any of the crew was listening. No one seemed to be. Despite his embarrassment he wanted to know more. "But why should a woman get married?"

"Ya, it's good for a fellow your age to know some of these things. God made woman to roll, too."

"He did? I thought they were different."

"They aren't built like a man, but inside they like the same things as a man. Mostly the same. Now here's another reason for marriage, too," he said, changing the topic. Jonas wondered what "mostly the same" meant.

"In the winter-time, you know," Daniel continued, "when I can't be out on the lake, I get owly. I'm a captain. Take me away from the lake too long and I get miserable. Being married is something like that. Man and woman can't stand to be alone. A few can, but almost everybody marries. Why? I'm not complete unless I'm on the lake. Ya, a woman isn't complete alone. Same thing with a man. It isn't that marriage makes you complete. But for most everybody, it's the right direction. For a man, being with a woman is moving toward someone. Same thing for a woman being with a man. You're moving toward someone deep inside you that needs someone outside you in the biggest way."

10.

Jackson hired Jonas to build him a chair on wheels. It had to be a chair Jackson could move with his hands. Jonas fiddled around for a day before he came up with an idea that might work. Three wheels. Two large, front wheels level with a seat built on an axle—Jackson could roll these two wheels with his hands to move the chair—and one small wheel in the back that could swivel. It took another three days to build it. He got the big wheels off a cart from Old Lady Bills. The small one he got off a broken-down wagon of Daniel's.

Jackson did a lot of pleased grunting when he could get around his house in the finished chair.

Then he had Jonas clear a path big enough for the chair between his cabin and the main path. Next he asked Jonas to remove his cupboards and re-hang them lower to the floor so that he could reach into them from his chair. When Jonas opened one of the cupboards, he found a fiddle. Jonas asked him if he played it, and he grunted that he did. But when Jonas asked him to play a tune, he said, "I'm not feeling inclined."

Then he had Jonas hack out a small plot for a garden next to his cabin. Late one afternoon, Sally and Samantha came to help. Sally worked for Daniel's wife Alice who ran a small resort of five cabins. She had finished cleaning for the day and needed a break. Jackson wheeled his chair out and dazzled Samantha with mouth sounds. He imitated birds and animals and then scooped up a root and turned it into a puppet, holding a lively conversation with it.

Jonas had cleared the trees and was pulling out roots. Sally joined in digging roots and tossing them on the pile at the edge of the cleared area. Jonas stole glances at her. She stole glances at him. Her eyes were light green like a new leaf in spring. Their eyes met for a moment and Jonas smiled shyly, and then they both quickly looked back at the roots. Once Sally was straining at a big, stubborn root and Jonas offered to help. They both pulled. Suddenly the root let go and they tumbled backward onto the ground. The six-foot root flew into the air and landed on them.

"Are you hurt?" asked Jonas anxiously, looking over at Sally who lay beside him. The larger end of the root had landed on her.

"No," she laughed as she started to push the root off them. "I wondered if that was going to happen when we were both pulling on it."

"Here, let me move that," said Jonas, still sitting on the ground as he grabbed the root.

"Mine," said Sally, sitting and pulling it in her direction. Jonas stared at her in surprise but didn't let go. "Mine," she repeated, sober-faced but with a lightness in her eyes, and pulled.

"Mine," laughed Jonas and began to pull.

"Mine," said Sally, bracing a foot against Jonas for leverage as she pulled. Laughing, Jonas slipped away from her foot and jumped up, still with a firm grip on the long root.

"Ours," he said, repeating what his mother said when she was trying to teach him and his brothers and sisters not to quarrel. He pulled steadily on the root, which she still gripped, and lifted her to a standing position. "Let's put it on the pile together."

"Mine," she insisted, her mouth in an exaggerated pout, still tugging at the root.

"Yours," said Jonas, releasing the root with a bow.

"Ours," said Sally, offering an end of the root. He accepted and, stumbling, laughing, and bumping into each other, they carried the root and threw it onto the pile. When Jonas turned back from the pile he saw that Samantha had stopped playing with Jackson and was watching them with a tentative smile.

11.

The next morning when they were ready to plant, Jonas asked Jackson if vegetables would grow. Philena had brought topsoil from the mainland to grow potatoes. Jackson said he had a plan. He had Jonas spend the morning collecting moss and mixing it into the soil of the garden. Moss makes things grow, he said.

In the afternoon they planted, keeping the rows far enough apart so that Jackson could move his wheelchair in between. But soon he was out of his chair, dragging himself along, planting beets, radishes, carrots, corn, tomatoes, and lettuce.

Every day Jackson seemed to drink less and look healthier. As they finished the planting he said to Jonas, "When I was a boy my mother used to garden. When I was eight she gave me a little corner of the garden for my own. I planted beets because I loved pickled beets. But soon I lost interest and the weeds proliferated. My mother kept the rest of the garden weedless, but mine soon became a weed patch. She never said anything to me, but whenever I saw those weeds, I felt pangs of guilt. I would pull a few weeds, but it was too overwhelming. That fall there were only enough beets for three pints of pickles.

"She let me have my corner of the garden the next spring and the next spring for five years in a row. Every year, sooner or later, I let it go to weeds.

"Then one day when I was thirteen, I overheard my father and mother talking. He told her she should not give me any of the garden since I just let it go to weeds. But my mother said that one day I would not let the weeds conquer me.

"She believed in me," he said with a catch in his voice. He looked over at Jonas digging. Jonas thought he might cry. He went back to forming the earth with his hands.

"That summer I weeded every day for the first half of the summer. The longest stretch of weeding I ever did. Then I began to let it slide. One morning I saw my mother heading out the door and I knew she was headed for the garden. I stopped her. 'How do you do it, mother?'

"She knew what I was talking about. 'Three things,' she said. 'Every day before I go to the garden I think of the straight rows of jars I will have on the shelves this winter. Then I think about every vegetable at its finest. I imagine pulling up an eight-inch carrot. Or coming out in the morning and seeing the slanted rays of the sun on an orange pumpkin. Or a potato bigger than my palm. I imagine pulling weeds away to get a better look at these vegetables. Then I go out and weed that day. Afterwards, I always stop long enough to admire the clean, straight rows of vegetables before I go back to the house.'

"I haven't thought about that summer for a long time. It was the first summer I conquered the weeds." He paused, looking away from Jonas. "And the last, too."

When they finished the planting, he pulled himself up into his chair at the end of the garden and looked at the stakes that outlined the rows they had just planted. "It's been a long time since I've had straight rows in my life," he said.

He gave Jonas three silver coins for his work.

12.

The morning after finishing the job for Jackson, Jonas worked on Daniel's crew. Philena was sick that day, so Daniel had Jonas clean fish with Theresa. It was the first time he had worked alone with her.

She had short, dark hair, a small face, and eyes that took in everything. She told him about the fish in the lake, explaining which fish were found at which locations and depths in the lake. She told him about the lake at different seasons of the year. While she talked and her knife flashed in the sun, she watched the gulls that swooped, waiting to catch the fish guts she occasionally threw overboard. She watched the men handling the nets, the fish, and the wheel.

In the afternoon she said to him, "I have read the Bible, but I don't understand it. It seems like looking through the fog most of the time. Everyone says the Bible is the Good Book, but no one spends much time reading it. Not even my mom."

"Did you read anything that you liked?" he asked.

"There is one story about Jesus that I like. It's the one about the woman at the well. She works and talks to Jesus. I'm the only girl I know who works on the water. Look at the water," she said. He looked. The swells were small and constant in the stillness of the early afternoon. "Do you see it?" she asked. He could see that she was seeing something that moved her deeply and wanted him to see it too.

"I don't know," he said, looking to see where she was looking. There were waves, endless waves chasing each other, sunlight dancing off them. There were birds wheeling over the water. There were cumulus clouds over the hint of a shoreline in the distance.

"Do you see it?" she implored.

Puzzled, Jonas told her what he saw: the water, the birds, the clouds, the land. She was disappointed. Obviously he was missing something. "What am I supposed to see?" he asked.

"I see the beginning of the deep," she said. He looked at the water and wondered how many feet deep it was. "I see the beginning of the deep," she continued. "I like to be on the water because it is as close to the deep as I can get. When I was a little girl, I swam. I opened my eyes under water and I saw fish. I saw life under the water. I wanted to stay under the water forever, but I couldn't, of course. Then I realized that by swimming I would always be near the shore, but by fishing I could be close to the deep, deep water. So I asked my dad to teach me to fish so I could go with him. He taught me when I was twelve. When I was thirteen, he died. My mother had to support us, so she took up fishing. 'If you can do it, I can do it,' she said. Daniel took us onto his crew. Now every day I am close to the deep."

"What does the deep have to do with the woman at the well?" Jonas said.

"She sent her bucket deep into the earth to draw water. I know she was looking for something deep. But there was nothing deep in her life but the well."

"What do you mean . . . 'nothing deep in her life'?"

"She had five husbands, and the man she was living with was not her husband."

Jonas was puzzled.

"She must have been hurt once and never went deep again."

It still didn't make sense to him.

"I lost my daddy to the lake in a bad storm. At first I couldn't cry. At first I couldn't look at the lake. I hated boats and fishing. One day Daniel came to see me. He had worked with Dad a lot. At first I wouldn't talk to him. My mother told Daniel to wait while she went for a walk with me. On the walk she told me the story of the woman at the well. She told me that when the woman lost her first husband, she never felt anything deep again. I realized that I lost my dad and the deep of the lake at the same time. When she said that, I started to cry. I cried and cried. Finally I told her that I had lost my dad and the deep all at the same time. She told me that I had lost my dad, but that I didn't need to lose the deep. I cried some more.

"Finally we walked back home. Daniel was still there. 'Theresa, I come to ask you to work on my boat,' he said. I burst out crying again. He said, 'Nay, if you don't want to . . . ' 'I think she wants to,' my Mom said. We all sat there and I cried until I could finally say yes to Daniel."

Theresa did not have tears in her eyes. Her voice caught a couple of times, but no tears.

"Later," Theresa continued, "I asked my mom to show me the story of the woman at the well in the Good Book. She showed me, and I saw that Jesus told her he was the living water. I knew he was talking about the deep. I knew he was as deep as this lake and as full of life as this lake. Also, I knew he was as dangerous as this lake.

"This lake, I love it. It took my daddy, but I love it. How can a girl love a lake that stole her daddy?" She looked at Jonas and repeated the question. "How can a girl love a lake that stole her daddy?" Her question netted him. He struggled.

"I don't know," he stammered.

"Find out in the Bible and tell me," she said. "There must be a story that tells."

They kept cutting the fish, tossing the guts into the barrel, and listening to the creak of the windlasses as the others cranked up the pot nets.

13.

Late in the afternoon Jonas stood on the aft of the deck as they headed back to the island. He tried to think of a story in the Bible that answered Theresa's question, but he was tired and couldn't think of any. Daniel was at the wheel. The rest of the crew scattered about the boat to the favorite spots each went to at the end of a day.

Jonas turned and looked starboard. Still a mile to Rock Point Harbor. As soon as they docked and had the fish stored, he was going to Sally's for supper. He imagined himself and Sally strolling along the beach after supper. More and more he wanted to be with her.

In the distance he saw spiles from another fisherman's pot nets poking up out of the water like fence posts. They reminded him of the farm. Once he had carried his baby brother across a field of wheat that looked like an amber sea at dusk. The neighbor's fence line poked up beyond the sea of grain. He was eleven at the time and had been left at home to care for his younger brothers and sisters while his mama took his dad supper out in the field.

A half hour after she left, his baby brother, Joel, started to cry. Nothing would comfort him. He put his ten-year-old brother in charge of the others, sat his baby brother on his hip, and threaded his way around the wheat field to bring him to their mama. As he walked, Joel quit crying. But if Jonas stopped, he'd cry again, so he kept a steady pace. He and his dad and two younger brothers had been tying shocks. He and his brothers had been sent home to eat while their mama took supper to their dad. As he neared the part they had cut and shocked, he wondered why he couldn't see his parents. He was about to call out when he saw his dad stand up from the opposite side of a patch of standing wheat. He seemed to be pulling up his pants. Then he reached down and helped Jonas' mama to her feet. She saw Jonas and the baby.

"What are you doing here?" she exclaimed.

"The baby wouldn't stop crying."

"He's not crying now," his mama said.

"He stopped when I was walking."

"How long have you been here?" his dad asked.

"I . . . I just came," stammered Jonas.

"You just saw us?"

"I didn't know where you were. I was just going to yell for you." His parents were facing him across twenty-five feet of standing wheat.

His father said something to his mother that Jonas could not hear, and they both laughed. Then they walked hand in hand around the end of the wheat.

"What did you say over there, Dad?" asked Jonas as his mama took the baby from him.

"When?"

"Just now when I said I was going to yell for you."

"Just a little love talk to your mama," he said with a laugh as he patted her on the butt. His mama and daddy laughed as they looked at each other. Jonas wished he knew what that look meant. "Now, Jonas," said his dad, "give me a hand with this wheat and let's see if we can get the stuff that's cut done tonight."

Jonas had spent several days trying to puzzle out why his dad would be pulling up his pants and why his parents seemed so happy. Now as he looked past the widening V of the wake of Daniel's tug to the distant spiles, he wondered if he would ever pat Sally on the butt. He wondered if Sally would laugh like his mama had. He sure hoped so.

14.

Jonas spent so much time with Sally in the last two weeks of May that he began thinking about marrying her. The very idea frightened him. He wrote a letter home to his family and church saying he was witnessing to a man with a drinking problem. He added that he had led a young woman to the Lord. He asked for prayer. He felt a little better after writing the letter, but he still didn't know about marriage, and he couldn't imagine how to ask her to marry him.

He was lying in his hammock thinking about this early one morning when Sally slipped onto the tug. He didn't hear her. When he sensed someone's presence, he opened his eyes and there she was.

Her eyes were shining. "Last night Daniel laid hands on me and prayed for me." Jonas wasn't sure he liked that, but he shrugged off the thought. "There was a beautiful sunset last night. My baby was in bed so I came out and sat on the beach and looked at the sunset and cried and cried. It was at a sunset that I was forced.

"Daniel came along and saw me crying. He knew what I was crying about. I don't know how he knew. He just knew. When he saw me crying, he sat down beside me and didn't say anything. He watched the sunset with me. I couldn't stop crying. I started wishing he'd hold me. Not hold me like a boyfriend, but like a daddy. When I was a little girl on the East Side, there was a girl there who got jilted. The day of the wedding her fiancé took off and never came back. She comes to the wedding in her pure, white dress, and her man never shows. Everybody waits and wonders. After awhile the tears start to come down her cheeks. Her daddy gets up and walks over to her, sits down, and puts his arm around her. She turns and buries her face in his chest and starts to wail. Her daddy holds her for a long time while she cries her heart out. I thought about her as I was sitting there next to Daniel.

"Then he put his hand on my shoulder and I turned my

head into his chest and cried up a storm. He held my head.

"When I was all cried out, I sat up and wondered if I had done anything wrong. I didn't think I had, but I was mad at myself for being such a baby.

"He took my head in his hands and real gentle turned my face toward him. 'I lay my hands on you like they tell us in the Bible to do when people need healing.' Then he put a hand on my head and looked up at the sky. The stars had come out by then. 'Sally's Father in heaven, hallowed be thy name, thy kingdom come in Sally's life, thy will be done in her life as in heaven. Give Sally her daily bread. Forgive her debts as she forgives her debtors. Lead her not into temptation but deliver her from evil. For thine is the kingdom and the power and the glory forever in Sally's life. Amen.'

"Isn't that a beautiful prayer? He went home, and I got up and walked home like I was walking on water. I couldn't believe how good I felt. It was beautiful," she said dreamily. She had her eyes closed, a smile on her face, remembering.

Then God said, *Jonas, Sally is the one for you to marry.*

But she is thinking about Daniel, not me, he protested silently.

Sally is the one.

Jonas watched her smile and remember. *Sally is the one. Sally is the one. Sally is the one.* The words repeated with the rhythm of the waves lapping against the boat.

Jonas listened but did not repeat what he heard to Sally, because he was too scared.

15.

Jonas was getting off Daniel's boat when he noticed Jackson in his chair stuck in the sand up the beach. "This chair can go lots of places," he said when Jonas got to him, "but it is not worth a sunken ship in sand."

"Where are you headed?" Jonas asked.

"To the lake," he snorted. "What does it look like?"

Crouching in front of him, Jonas half rolled the wheels of his chair, half skidded them through the sand until they reached the lake's edge. "Don't stop now," Jackson said. Jonas continued backwards until the cold waves washed against his back and reached the seat of the chair. He stood up and stepped aside so that Jackson faced the waves of the lake. Tears began to form in Jackson's eyes as he looked out over the water. He was hanging on to the chair to keep from floating away.

Even though the lake was cold, he grinned at Jonas, his silver tooth flashing in the western sun. "Damn," he said, "it has been a long time since I have been in this lake." He kept repeating it like a chant, and the tears came out of his eyes in waves.

"I always thought," he finally said, "I deserved to lose my legs. After all, I was inebriated. Now that I have this chair you made for me, I've gone places I haven't been for ages. I never thought I'd be in the lake again. Damn it, I don't deserve this," he said with a new wave of tears. "I even drank again last night after being off the bottle for two weeks. But I am in this damn lake. Who would believe it?"

Then a big wave swept over his head. Jonas jumped to rescue him, but when the wave passed, he hadn't budged. Jackson let out a joyous bellow. "This lake always was a sassy lady. That is what I like, a sassy lady, and here she comes." Another wave swept over him.

16.

Jackson hired Jonas to rebuild the roof of his house. The job took Jonas days, and each day Jackson's breath smelled of wine or beer earlier in the day.

Jonas wrote a letter home to his family and church, reporting about the man with a drinking problem. He had stopped drinking for awhile, but now he was drinking again.

Jonas admitted to being discouraged and asked for prayer. He also asked for prayer about a wife.

On the last day of the job, Jackson gave him some advice. Jackson was sitting in his wheelchair while Jonas sat on a stump outside the cabin. They were eating baked fish with their fingers. Jackson kept uncorking the bottle he had on his lap every so often and taking a drink. Jackson was the kind of fellow that, even though he drank, got you talking, and you ended up surprising yourself with what you said. Jonas tried to keep out of range of his breath, but still he told him many things.

"Son," Jackson said, "I can see a problem on the horizon for you." Jonas waited. "You are going to marry Sally. That is not the problem. The problem is you are about to get hit hard by the power of sin." Jonas frowned. What was he talking about?

"Many years ago I lived in a town that was hit by a tornado. It hit the school. I lost my younger brother. The town was never the same. People cried. People got mad. People started blaming each other. My folks and I finally left. But five years later I went back. I could not stay away. I went to the place where the school stood and I cried. You see, I had been playing hooky that day with three of my friends. We were off sharing a bottle of wine. We lived. Most of the rest of the school died. We were the bad kids of the school and we lived. It did not make sense.

"You see, when something big and bad happens to you, it can freeze something inside you. I went away from that town thinking the only way for me to live was to keep on being bad. For five years I was frozen with that idea. I was bad. I made myself and a lot of other people miserable. But when I stood by that school five years later and cried, something started letting loose in me. I fell on the ground and beat it with my fists and cried. I didn't know why I was throwing a fit. I just did it.

"Another way to say it is that when something bad happens to you, you build your life around it. Sally has built her life around being raped. It's hard to be a husband to someone like that."

"So you don't think I should marry her?"

"No, I think you should." He smiled, threw away the last of his fish bones, and wheeled closer to Jonas. "But you shouldn't be surprised when you get gravel in your teeth."

Jonas looked at Jackson's silver tooth. He stood up and began to inch backward out of the range of his breath. He was doubtful, but, just in case Jackson was right, he wanted to know more. "How can I make things better for Sally?"

"You told me that God has told you to marry Sally. You will need his help," he said, following Jonas.

"You act like I shouldn't marry Sally, but you tell me to go ahead," said Jonas, backpedaling.

"I know the power of sin," Jackson said, following him, "but there is a greater power. Think of it this way. You are rebuilding my roof because the original was too flat. I built the original with too low a pitch because I built the cabin under a tree with a limb I was taking into consideration. I liked the idea of a cabin snug under a pine. For years I've paid for my foolishness by needing to have the roof patched. Not enough pitch caused it to leak easily. There are many good things about this house and its location. But I have had to repair the roof often and now I'm having it rebuilt.

"You and Sally are going to get leaks in your roof. But the two of you can put up with the leaks if there are other good things about your house. And there will be. So you can put up with the leaks and the repairs, and maybe someday God will help you put on a new roof."

A squirrel scampered over the limb of a nearby tree. They stopped to watch the squirrel.

Jonas moved back again. Jackson continued, "At times I've felt like a squirrel—little, easily hurt, hoarding nuts for winter, ever on the alert for enemies. You may not believe this, but I found God and goodness while I was throwing a fit on the ground where the old school used to be. But I lost him after awhile. Or he lost me. Do not lose Sally. Do not lose God. It is sad to be lost." He seemed near tears. He uncorked the bottle and took a drink.

"If you turn to God, he will accept you back," said Jonas.

"Do not preach. You promised." Jackson took a pull on the bottle he now kept on his wheelchair.

Jonas looked up at the roof. It was time to put the finishing touches on it. He was definitely out of range of Jackson's breath up there.

On the roof he wondered if marriages needed repairs as often as houses did. When he was done, Jackson paid him another two silver coins. When Jonas left, he put the two coins in the garden; one by the lettuce and the other by the carrots.

17.

It was night and Jonas lay awake under the stars and a crescent-shaped moon. What was he doing on this island? Daniel came to worship on Sunday and brought Alice, his deaf wife. Old Lady Bills came now. Philena came. Sally came. Others had come once or twice and then no more. The children came for his Bible stories. Jackson had never come even once and, although he had given up drinking for awhile, he was now drinking as much as when Jonas first met him. It was the beginning of June. If he were back home he'd be enjoying the scent of alfalfa hay instead of the daily smell of fish. That night he was doubting everything. Did he make up the call to come to this island?

He couldn't sleep, so he walked along the shore. He listened to the waves. There was a lamp lit in Sally's cabin. She answered his knock. "I can't sleep," he said.

"Samantha woke up from a bad dream. She's finally sleeping soundly. Let's listen to the waves."

They sat side by side on the damp sand. They were silent, but the lake spoke continuously. Something about the sound wet Jonas' eyes. Sally leaned against him. He slipped his arm around her. The touch brought tears. He was so far from home.

Ask her to marry you.

What?

Ask her to marry you.

It must be the voice of God. It scared him. His tears dried up. He felt cold. Sally felt warm. Since the first time he thought God had told him to marry Sally, he had been with her several times, but he had never brought it up. The sound of the lake suddenly seemed distant compared to his heart beating. Did she know what he was thinking? What would she say if he got the words out of his mouth?

Ask her to marry you.

He began to shiver.

"Do you want to go back in?" she asked.

"No." She put her arm around him and squeezed. Then she rubbed his back as if she were trying to rub out the cold. She scooted close to him, her leg pressing against his. Still he shivered. His teeth started to chatter.

"Will you marry me?" he said between chattering teeth.

"What?" Her hand stopped rubbing.

He clenched his teeth to stop the chattering. "Will you marry me?" he said between his clenched teeth.

"I can't understand what you're saying."

He opened his mouth. "Will you marry me?" His teeth went wild with chattering.

She said something. He couldn't understand over the sound of his teeth.

"What?"

"You want me to marry you?" she said directly into his ear.

He gritted his teeth to stop the chattering. He nodded his head. He was afraid to look at her. She put her mouth up to his ear. Then she drew back. Oh no, he thought. What was she thinking? Again she put her mouth to her ear. "I want to marry you, Jonas."

"You do?" he shouted, forgetting about chattering. "You really want to marry me?"

"Yes, Jonas."

He hugged her very hard. "Sally, I have been so far away from home. But now you will be my home. God, thank you.

Sally!" he shouted into the sound of the waves, "I love you!" Her clear laughter rang out over the waves.

"Jonas, I love you too!"

They lay back and she held his head to her chest. She was so warm. Slowly he warmed up. He could not remember anyone so warm. His desire for her began to stir. He moved so that he could kiss her. Her lips were warm and moist and eager. Oh, this is good, he thought.

Enough for tonight.

No.

Enough for tonight.

He groaned. That broke the spell. They sat up, then stood. Then she was in his arms, again their lips seeking each other. I never knew what this was like, Jonas thought. They kissed for a long time. It seemed like the middle of the night when they walked back to her cabin.

"Ask me again," she said at the cabin door.

"Sally, will you marry me?"

"Jonas, I will marry you!" she whispered in his ear. His spine still tingled from her breath as he walked back to Daniel's boat.

18.

"I want to be baptized before we announce our engagement," Sally said the next evening. They were sitting in her cabin. A storm was brewing outside.

He squeezed her hand. "I would be deeply blessed to baptize you."

"It can't be you," she said.

Lightning flashed, followed by an instant clap of thunder. Both of them flinched. "Why not?"

"I don't know. It can't be you. The last time I was in the lake I was dragged out and forced. It can't be you." The rain began, first a few drops on the roof, but soon it became a din.

"Please understand."

She's right.

She is? But it should be me. I am going to marry her. I ought to baptize her, he protested silently.

She's right.

Jonas stood up and went to the door, opened it, and watched the sheets of rain. He wanted her all to himself. He should baptize her.

She's right.

She came and stood beside him. "Please," she said, "shut the door. You're getting the floor wet."

She's right.

He shut the door, walked over to the rag bag, picked out a rag, went back to the door, and wiped up the floor.

"Okay, someone else can baptize you. I don't understand, but I guess you're right." She hugged him. "I can talk to Philena to see if she would baptize you. She's a believer."

"It has to be a man."

He walked to the window, his back to her. Through the rain streaking down the window he could see lightning far out on the lake. This was too much. Not him. Another man.

She's right.

"Why?"

"I don't know. I just know it has to be a man. Jonas, please don't be so jealous. I don't like the idea of going into a lake with a man. I hate the idea. But I think God wants me to be baptized by a man."

She's right.

To the north another streak of lightning ripped through to the island. Are you trying to tear us apart even before we're married? Jonas wanted to ask God.

No, I am bringing you together.

Who is this man you have in mind? Daniel, I suppose, remembering her telling him about Daniel sitting on the beach with his arm around her.

Yes.

Daniel?! Jonas' breath fogged the window. He reached up

and slowly, absently, lettered "Jesus" in the mist.

"I could ask Daniel," he said. "He's a good man. He's a believer."

"I am really scared of getting into the water with him," she said.

"Is there someone else?"

"No, I think Daniel is the right man. I thought of him even before you mentioned him. You know I lived with Alice and him for awhile around the time I had Samantha. I kind of trust him. Maybe he could marry us, too."

"He is a good captain."

She pulled him gently away from the window so that he faced her. "Do you understand, Jonas?" she implored.

"No, Sally, I do not understand. I think it would be the most wonderful thing in the world for me to baptize you and then marry you. But God doesn't think that way."

"He doesn't?" she asked, brightening.

"No, you're right. It should be a man other than me. You think like God." He smiled at her, knowing she would be happy to hear she thought like God. His smile faded. "Maybe some day I will understand. But I don't have to understand to know that I love you." He took her in his arms, hiding his face in her blonde hair.

Early the next morning Jonas wrote home to his family and church, telling them that God had answered their prayers regarding a wife. He mentioned that she had recently come to the Lord and had a wonderful four-year-old daughter. He also urged them to keep praying for the man with a drinking problem.

19.

The day of Sally's baptism Jonas stood on the beach with a handful of people. Sally told them that she believed in Jesus. She said that she was afraid of the lake, but Jesus said to be baptized, so she was going to be baptized.

Daniel read the story of Jesus' baptism. On this day there were no doves, only gulls squawking overhead. Daniel and Sally waded into the surf. Tears on Sally's face glistened in the Sunday morning sunlight. Jonas thought of his mother crying when his younger brother died. He must have been five or six. She was sitting on her bed. He asked her what was wrong. She told him that the day before she had had a baby, a brother for Jonas, but that he was dead when he was born.

When Daniel and Sally were waist-deep, they stopped. Daniel said something to Sally that Jonas couldn't hear. She plugged her nose with her left hand. Daniel took her right arm with his right arm and, with his left hand supporting her back, he lowered her into the lake, calling out for all to hear, "I baptize you in the name of the Father and of the Son and of the Holy Ghost." She disappeared under the water.

Jonas remembered his baby brother being buried. He didn't remember the funeral. Only finding his mother crying, and then the burial. He remembered other funerals, so he was sure there had been a funeral first. No one had told him that they were going to put the little box that held his brother into the ground and cover it up. When the farmers started to shovel in the dirt on top of the box, Jonas cried out and grabbed the shovel of the nearest man. His dad gently picked him up and explained that his brother was in heaven; only his body was in the box. He said that putting dirt over the box was like putting a blanket over his baby brother so that he would be snug until Jesus raised him up. Then he offered a shovel to Jonas so he could help cover up his brother.

Jonas squirmed away from the shovel. He cried as the men kept shoveling. But he also wanted to cover his brother. Finally his dad set him down, and he scooped a shovel full of dirt onto the grave. He kept shoveling with the farmers until the last of the dirt was heaped over the grave. He had not wanted to let go of the shovel, so his father carried him home while he clutched the shovel.

Daniel lifted Sally up, and while the water was still running off her, he tousled her hair. She laughed, her laughter piercing Jonas' heart. Daniel took her hand and led her ashore. She left him and came to Jonas and flung herself into his arms.

"Jonas, we can plan the engagement party now," she whispered into his ear. He held her, letting the cold water soak into him.

20.

That night Jonas asked Daniel if he could use him fishing the next day.

The next morning he volunteered to pull the nets. By mid-morning his hands were raw. Daniel wanted to assign him another job but he refused.

Jonas didn't know what he was looking for, but he found himself searching for something every time the net surfaced. There were fish, lots of fish, but that didn't seem to be what he was looking for. The day was hot, the sky heavy and gray, and the lake dark.

That afternoon as they returned across the lake, Jonas' hands burned. The work was done, and he stood on the prow, still searching the lake. Daniel gave the wheel to Theresa and came and stood beside him. "Ya, so what are you looking for then?" Daniel asked.

"I don't know."

"A captain should always know what he is looking for."

"I am not a captain."

"You are as close to a captain as our church has got."

Jonas sighed deeply. "It is such a small church."

"Ya, it is a small island. Did not Jesus say, 'Where two or three are gathered in my name, there I am in their midst'?" Jonas was silent. "So you are being stubborn I see. You worked your hands raw today," Daniel said. Jonas was silent.

"When you refused to do a different job," Daniel continued,

"I thought, I wonder why he wants his hands raw."

Still Jonas was silent. He stood with his legs slightly apart, using his toes to keep his balance with the rise and fall of the boat, staring at the dark lake.

"Ya, there is something you want to hold with your hands that you can't get hold of."

"I want to hold Sally in the lake." Jonas was surprised at his words and wave of feelings.

"I thought so."

"You did?"

"I saw the pain in your eyes when you asked me to baptize her."

"I was obeying God."

"Ya."

"Sally was so filled with joy when she rose up out of the lake."

"It hurt to be on the shore, right?"

"I guess it did."

"Ya, I think you should jump into the lake right now," Daniel said.

For the first time since they began talking, Jonas looked at him. Daniel was looking over the gunwale, smiling.

Jonas shed his shoes, socks, and shirt swiftly and leaped overboard. He plunged beneath the water, the cold stinging his hands. When he came to the surface a life preserver splashed beside him. He crooked an arm over it and let it pull him through the dark water. Out of the corner of his eye he saw a movement. A splash. A moment later Daniel surfaced beside him.

"This lake is an old one," he said. "It's older than the hills or you or me." That's all he said. For fifteen minutes the boat pulled them through the lake beneath the sultry, gray sky.

After Brawn pulled them back on board, they dried themselves and dressed. When Jonas looked over the prow he could see the island.

"Ya, the lake has been here for a long time," said Daniel. "It will still be here, you know, when you and Sally need it."

21.

They unloaded the fish, cleaned the boat, and readied everything for the next morning. Brawn invited Jonas to his house for supper.

After supper they sat around the table talking. Brawn's mother was there, as well as his two younger sisters and younger brother. Brawn's mother was telling stories about when Brawn was a little boy. Jonas had a hard time imagining Brawn as a little boy. Brawn was a good six inches taller than Jonas and had arms twice as big. One day, according to his mom, when Brawn was playing in the nets by himself, he got tangled up in them. No matter how hard he struggled, he couldn't get loose. So he simply waited for someone to come along and help.

Brawn's mother looked at her oldest son across the table and laughed, "You were so wise for your age. You waited patiently until your dad came along and said, 'Brawn, get out of those nets. Look how you've tangled them up.'

"'I'm stuck, Dad,' Brawn said, calm as could be. So his dad rescued him. Brawn came home and told me what happened. I said, 'Weren't you afraid?' 'No, I knew Daddy would come,' he says. 'What did you think about while you were waiting?' I asked. 'I watched the birds breaking clams on the rocks,' he said. 'You weren't scared?' I asked again. 'No, Mama, I just knew I had to wait. And I was right.'"

That day the *Lillian* brought a letter from his mother. Usually they were a journal of family events with only a line or two in answer to his letters. This letter began:

You didn't say when you are getting married. I hope you bring this girl home to meet your family. I hope you know what you are doing. You have been gone barely two months. That's awful fast to meet somebody and know for sure she's the one.

Jonas smiled. He was sure he knew what he was doing. He had heard God.

The letter went on to tell about what food she was taking to the annual Sunday school picnic and all about Janey being stung by hornets when she was playing in the woods.

22.

Their little girl was in bed. Soon to be *their* little girl. When Sally and Jonas married, he would have a daughter. He and Sally sat on benches at right angles to each other at the corner of the table in Sally's cabin, watching the sun set through the window.

At the very point the horizon closed its eyelid on the sun Sally said, "Tonight I want to tell you about it. We can't announce our engagement until I tell you."

"Another wait?" protested Jonas. "You said that we couldn't announce our engagement until you were baptized. Now you've been baptized," said Jonas.

"I know I said that, but I wasn't thinking. You have to know about my past before we announce the engagement."

"Your past? Is there more?" He shivered at the seriousness of her voice.

"About who forced himself on me."

"I thought it was a stranger?"

"That's what I told everybody."

He took a deep breath. So it was somebody she knew. He leaned across the corner of the table toward her. "I'm ready."

"It was my daddy."

"What?"

There was a long silence. He searched her face. It was frozen. She didn't look at him. Her face was toward the window and the lake. He looked at the lake, the gulls wheeling over it, the gentle waves, the setting sun. There was a mistake. He didn't hear right. It couldn't be. But she would know.

Wouldn't she? He looked at her face again. Frozen. As motionless as death. He hadn't heard right.

"What did you say?" he asked.

He waited for her to speak. She did not. He began to smooth out the tablecloth. Waiting. Please speak, he silently begged, please speak. The cloth was as smooth as a chalkboard. "Did you say 'my daddy'?" he whispered.

"You don't believe me?" she said flatly and lapsed into silence.

"I believe you," he said. "I believe you. I mean, it's hard to believe, but if you say it happened, I am sure it happened. It's just that I never . . . I mean, I don't know . . . I mean . . . ." He fell silent.

Finally he whispered, "Your daddy?" He scooted his bench next to hers and, half sitting on hers, half his, put his arm around her and laid his head on her shoulder. But she was stiff and as distant as his own mother across miles of lake and land. "Your daddy," he whispered, sitting up.

"I have never told anyone the truth," she said. "I pretended it was a stranger."

"Sally, I love you anyway." He felt sick.

"I want to tell you all about it tonight."

He moved around, trying to find a more comfortable way to sit on the bench. He looked at her in the fading light coming through the window. "I will listen," he said. He did not want to listen. God, how could he listen? "I am ready," he said. He would listen.

"It might take me awhile," she said in a small voice.

"You can take all night," he said, forcing himself to speak softly. There was a long silence. In that silence he slowly, absently wrote with his finger on the smooth cloth, "Daddy." When he realized what he had spelled he glanced at Sally, hoping she hadn't noticed what he had spelled. She was sitting, staring through the window at the lake, as still and unseeing as a snow sculpture in twilight. He smoothed the cloth with the palm of his hand, as if removing what he had spelled. After awhile he wondered if he should light a lamp.

It was almost dark when she spoke. And then a full moon lifted its head and peered at them through the pines, casting a faint light through the east window of the cabin. "My daddy loved me when I was a little girl. He played with me. One day I remember him giving me and my two brothers piggyback rides. Another day he told me that I had nice hair. When I started cooking, he always praised my food. I made the best soup. Then sometimes he would touch me in ways that felt bad. And sometimes he made me touch him. Not too often, but sometimes. I hated it. I liked playing with him when we weren't alone. He was nice to me. He would play games with us kids. But if we were alone, I knew he would start doing bad stuff. So I tried not to be alone with him. I tried, but he'd still get me alone sometimes." She sounded like a little girl reciting.

"Sometimes I thought my mother did not like my daddy. She always called him no-good. My brothers worked with him on the boats, but my mother never let me go on the boats with my daddy. 'Boats are no place for a girl,' she'd say. 'You stay and help me.' I stayed in and helped her, and, when I didn't help her, she insisted that I learn a 'womanly trade,' as she called it. She didn't care what I learned, as long as it made it possible for me to support myself if I needed to. I tried different things, and that's how I came to learn to sew.

"When I got to be older, Daddy stopped bothering me. He just stopped. I thought it was because I was older."

Jonas' mouth was dry. "Didn't you tell your mom?"

"One time when I was little, I told her I didn't like it when Daddy made me feel bad. She slapped me and told me I had to learn to behave better."

"Behave better?" sputtered Jonas.

"For a long time I tried to figure out how I could behave better so Daddy wouldn't do bad stuff when he got me alone. I never could figure it out."

"Maybe she thought you were talking about how he made you feel bad when he spanked you?"

"Maybe." She spoke so softly that Jonas could barely hear her. He fidgeted on the bench. This was hard to listen to.

"Do you want me to go on?"

He nodded and tried to sit still.

"I never had many girlfriends, so I liked to go swimming by myself. Mother let me go swimming. She liked swimming herself, so she thought that was fine.

"When I was sixteen, a boy started to like me. He would stop by our house and visit when I was hanging out the wash. Or he would go for walks with me. It was okay with my mother. But one day my daddy came home from fishing and he saw the boy, and he started to scream at me and the boy. The boy left. I don't know why he was screaming at me. I didn't say anything. He said he didn't approve of that boy and he didn't want me sneaking off with him either. I was not to see the boy anymore. Then he said what he usually said when he knew us kids didn't agree with what he was saying: 'Children obey your parents.'

"I did sneak off with the boy. I was tired of Daddy telling me what to do. Daddy was wrong. The boy was a nice boy. He and I didn't do much but talk. He told me all about how he was going to settle on the mainland and be a farmer. He did chores for a dairy farmer over the winter months when he was on the mainland.

"Then one time just before supper, I went for a swim."

She stopped talking. Jonas slid his hand across the tablecloth, smoothing it over and over again. He waited. Please tell me, he thought. He didn't want to know, but he wanted her to tell him quickly. *What is done in darkness will be brought to light.* He wanted to know the truth. He hated what she was telling him. Please tell me, he implored silently. But he said nothing as he waited. Darkness had set in, but the moon was shimmering on the lake. The moon was a cold light. Finally he touched her arm. She jumped. Her arm was cold. "I didn't mean to scare you," he said.

"I know," she said. He thought of their little girl, and he listened for any sound from her loft. There was no sound.

"I was swimming when Daddy and my brothers came home from fishing. Daddy seemed so happy to see me. He joked about his little girl being a mermaid. When he and my brothers were done cleaning out the *Tamarack*, Daddy's boat, my brothers went home. Daddy said he felt like swimming. He took off his shoes and shirt and dived off the boat. At first I felt funny. I had never swum alone with Daddy, but he laughed and dived and swam. He said he was a better swimmer than I was, and he wanted to race me. We raced to the next dock and I won. He laughed and said his little girl was as quick as a fish. He said if I gave him ten yards, he could beat me to the first buoy. We raced again and I still beat him. He laughed, but it wasn't a happy laugh. He clung to the buoy to catch his breath. I was treading water a little ways away.

"Suddenly he lunged and grabbed me, his arms trapping my whole body. We both went under. He let go of me except for my arm. We came to the surface. 'See,' he said, 'I can still catch you. You may not obey me anymore, but I can catch you. I know you've been seeing that boy behind my back.' I tried to pull away, but he wouldn't let me go. I saw his eyes; they scared me. 'Daddy,' I said, 'please, Daddy, let me go.' Instead he pulled me to him and pushed his hand . . . " she stopped.

She began to shake. Jonas slid onto her bench and put his arm around her, pulling her close to him. She was cold. She moved away from him. "Don't," she said. "I can't have you touching me. Just let me talk." He dropped his arm and hurt his hand on the back of the bench. He slid partway back onto his bench.

"I want to help you," he said.

"Just let me talk."

He hated to think what she was going to say next.

"He grabbed me between the legs. I started to scream, but he dunked my head under the water. I thought I was going to drown. He let my head come up. I coughed and coughed and coughed. He said, 'Don't try screaming again, little girl. You will obey me. I have to do this.' He kept his hand there, squeezing me and hurting me. Then he started to swim to shore, dragging me with him. I was so scared.

"But he didn't swim straight to shore. He began to swim

towards a place where the woods come close to the shore. I tried to get away, but he was so quick and strong. He caught me and slapped me." There was a long silence. Jonas wondered if she was crying; he couldn't tell in the moonlight. He sat a little ways from her and did not touch her and did not leave, but waited. Jesus, he prayed, Jesus. He thought of Jesus alone in the garden, the disciples asleep. He turned and looked out the east window at the moon. He wondered if it was a cloudy night when Jesus was in the garden and if the same moon shone on Jesus and the disciples. He wished he could go to sleep. Jesus, help me listen.

"When he was close to the trees," she continued, her voice sounding dead, "he pulled me towards shore. He kept one hand over my mouth and carried me into the woods. He laid me down. He kept touching my breasts. Then he took off his shorts and stuffed them into my mouth. I couldn't scream. I couldn't move. Then he . . . he . . . had his way with me."

She was silent for a long time. In the distance there was an owl. "Who, who, who," it moaned. Jonas wished he were an owl. He wished he were a wolf howling at the cold light of the moon. He imagined being a wolf and leaping at the throat of Sally's daddy. He shook his head. He shouldn't think such thoughts. He would sit there even if he had to sit there all night. They sat for a long time.

"When he left me he said, 'Don't tell your mother, little girl. She will never, ever believe you. Don't ever tell anyone, or else.' I thought he would kill me if I ever told anyone. I fell asleep in the woods that night. In the morning I was wet with dew. When I came home the next day, my mother hit me in the face. She thought I had spent the night with my boyfriend. At first I didn't tell her any different. Mama was yelling about me and this boyfriend. Daddy winked at me. I have never looked at his face since. Do you think it is wrong that I sometimes think about killing him, Jonas?"

"No, I think it is fine. I mean, maybe not fine, but I understand you thinking about killing your daddy. I could think about killing him."

"Jonas, do you still love me?"

"Yes, I love you."

"Jonas, sometimes I don't feel like a woman."

"You are a woman. You are a mother."

"I am a mother. Sometimes I wonder if Samantha will ever know how she came to be . . . who her daddy is."

"I am going to be her daddy."

"Jonas, I love you." She turned to him and they clung to each other. Faintly he could hear wave after wave hit the shore, and he wanted to cling to her forever.

After awhile Jonas went back to his hammock on the *Edna* and spent the longest night of his life. He never slept.

23.

The following day Jonas went with Daniel and a group of men to cut trees for next year's spiles. At lunchtime Daniel told Jonas to bring his sandwich and come with him—he wanted to talk with Jonas.

Jonas hurried after Daniel, who kept up a spry pace as he wound his way through the trees and down to the beach.

"Ya, something happened," Daniel spoke loudly to be heard against the lake pounding the shore.

"What?"

"Something happened to you. You look like someone who's been chased by a ghost, you know. Ya, you need to tell someone. I thought you might tell me."

"How did you know?"

"You been so white all morning you don't have any freckles left. You look like a man who has seen death or something like that."

"It's like I have," Jonas said, starting to sob. Daniel looped an arm around him. "Someone didn't actually die, but it's like they did," Jonas choked out. He cried more. "Sally told me . . ." he wished he could stop crying, " . . .

who forced her . . . how it happened."

"Uffda, Jonas," Daniel said, giving Jonas a sympathetic squeeze. Then he sounded angry when he said, "Nay doggone! Some no-good bum did it, I'm sure!" said Daniel. Jonas stopped sobbing, but his tears still flowed. He had never seen Daniel angry. "Nay, no wonder you are walking around like death is chasing you. The bum. Nay doggone." Daniel dropped his arm from around Jonas and kicked the sand on the beach. "What are you doing about it then?"

"I don't know what to do. I've been in a daze ever since she told me. I love her. I don't know what to do."

"Son of a bitch! Pardon me. The no-good bum, I mean! Whoever did this is lower than scum." He paused for a long time, shaking his head. "Let me get ahold of myself." He picked up a piece of driftwood and began to turn it over in his hands.

"The worst thing," he said, "that can happen to a woman has happened to yours. When a man's woman gets raped, it hits him square in the gut. Ya, to be even more truthful, it hits him square in the balls. Ya, it really knocks a man for a loop." He drove the point of the driftwood into the sand. "Tell me what happened."

"You mean what Sally told me?"

"Ya."

"I don't know if I should."

"Well, why not?"

"It's so evil and I don't think I should tell who unless Sally says I can."

"Tell me what you can then."

"I get sick thinking about it. I'm not sure God wants me to think about something so evil. I think I should think about what is pure and good and undefiled."

"You being a preacher, you know the Bible." Daniel pulled the point of the driftwood out of the sand.

"Yes," Jonas said, wondering what was coming next.

"I have read the Bible. One of the wickedest stories in the Bible is Jesus' death." Daniel spoke fiercely. "Ya, it's ugly. But then the Bible tells it in gory detail, not once, but four times. Jesus got the bad part of his story told four times. Why? Ya, because it was the truth. It really happened to him. Sometimes the truth has got to be dragged into the light even if it is so ugly it makes us sick." He stabbed the driftwood back into the sand.

Then he spoke more quietly. "Ya, it's a hard story to tell. But Jesus didn't stay in the grave, you know. He kicked the stone aside and walked around and talked to people. If that hadn't happened, it would have been just another ugly story." His voice was rising. "I don't want Sally's story to be just another ugly story. I don't think Jesus does either. So let Jesus have the story."

"What do you mean—let him have the story?"

"Tell it to him. Let him become part of it."

"I don't know how to let him become part of this story."

"For starts, tell me the story. Jesus will be listening."

So Jonas told the story. Except he didn't tell him who. He only said it was someone she knew. He had to force himself to speak. Each word tasted like bile. He nearly threw up when he told how the man stuffed his underwear into her mouth.

When he finished, he stared out at the lake. He watched wave after wave break against the shore. He sensed Daniel's head turn away from him. Crack! Jonas looked. Daniel had broken the driftwood over his knee. Then he knelt and leaned the two pieces of driftwood up against each other. He patted sand around the base of each so that they stood. "Ya, your woman was brave to tell you the truth. You got a backbone for the truth, I see. Truth should always be honored." He wrote "honored" in the sand. He stood up, reached out, and put his hand on Jonas' shoulder. "Ya, the truth is sometimes awful," he said. Tears formed in Jonas' eyes. "I got awe in my heart then. Your woman speaks the truth and you hear it. Nay," he said, shaking his head, "that's no small thing. The two of you leaning into each other, standing in the light."

Eventually he took his hand off Jonas' shoulder. "Ya, it is time for us to get back to the crew, and it is time for you to cut down a tree." They wound their way back through the woods to where the crew was finishing their lunch.

24.

Daniel gave instructions to the crew, and then he led Jonas a quarter of a mile through the trees to a stand of tamaracks. He stopped.

"Nay doggone," he said, leaning up against a tree. "Once years ago I saw a man hit his twelve-year-old daughter," he said. "He hit her really hard with his fist, gave her a bad black eye. Seeing him do that, something jarred loose in me. I hit him, and he went down like he had been poleaxed. He lay there on the ground, and his daughter fell on him, crying and hugging him. I think she thought I killed him. I thought I might have, too, but I checked and his ticker was still ticking. I told her he'd come around pretty soon. She begged me to leave then. I didn't think that was a good idea because there was no telling what he'd do with her when he came around. But she got mad and started clawing at me. So I went. Ya, I looked back and she was holding his head and he was trying to sit up. There was no sense to it; I saved the daughter, and yet she was holding him like he was a wounded pup when I left.

"Years later I told Philena about it. She said, 'Vengeance is never simple. Vengeance twists and turns back on you like a snake. Vengeance is best left to God. *Vengeance is mine, saith the Lord*.'" He studied the bark of the tamarack he was leaning against. "Ya, I've given a lot of thought to what she said and I agree: vengeance is best left to God.

"But anger, that's another thing. Anger is a fit thing for people who've been hurt. Truth demands that a hurt person gets mad then. Sally is hurting. She's bound to be mad. And you're hurting, too, boy. So I think you oughta take out your anger on a tree. Otherwise you'll take it out on somebody else.

The bum who did it. Sally. Yourself. Who knows? Ya, and while you're chopping that tree, let the truth be known." He handed Jonas the ax.

"I don't know what to do," said Jonas, feeling confused.

"Ya, you're looking like a tornado went through you. You're a little scattered, but we'll bring you back together again. Sally needs you together again. Ya, she needs you; otherwise she never would've told you this thing. You go now and find a tree."

Automatically Jonas looked up to see the tops of the trees for an opening where a tree could be felled without hanging it up on another tree. He had felled many trees on their farm when he was a boy. He saw an opening. He saw a tree that he could fell through the opening. He went over to it.

"Will this do?" he asked Daniel, looking at the tree.

"Ya, I'll be back," Daniel said. "You need time alone with the tree. But do not start cutting until I am back." He disappeared.

Jonas looked at the trunk of the tree. It was a very tall tamarack, amazingly tall for a tree that had a twelve- to fourteen-inch trunk. He looked at the bit of the ax, felt the blade with his thumb. It was sharp enough. He would have to make a deep notch in exactly the right place to fell it in the opening. He ran his hand over the rough bark. What did this tree have to do with Sally? He was supposed to be angry at this tree? This tree had done nothing wrong. He was supposed to tell the truth as he cut it down? The truth was that this tree had nothing to do with what had happened to Sally.

He leaned against the tree, using it for support, looking up at the path for the tree when it fell. Truth. What was the truth regarding Sally? The truth was that her daddy had betrayed her. The truth was that he had treated her like no man should ever treat a woman, let alone a daughter. The truth was that he deserved to die for what he had done. Suddenly Jonas turned and pounded his fists against the tree, "My God, my God, why did you let it happen?" Tears blurred his eyes as he struck the tree.

Daniel touched his shoulder. There was sorrow in his eyes. "Ya, you are ready now," he said.

Jonas looked at the opening between the trees and at the trunk and gave a final check of the place and angle for the notch. "You should never have laid a hand on her the way you did," Jonas said, and sank the bit at an angle through the bark and into the flesh of the tree. "You were wrong," he said louder and brought the bit straight in at the bottom of the angle he had cut. A chip flew out. "You deserve to die!" he cried, the bit slicing at an angle again. "My God, you should have stopped him," the ax came in level. Chip. Jonas had to stop and clear the tears from his eyes. Slice. "You crushed my woman!" Chip. "I wish I could stuff your underwear down your throat!" Slice. "I hate you!" Chip. "I wish I could gouge your eye out that you used to wink at her!" Slice. "My God! My God! Why did you forsake her!" Chip. "I wish I could bury this bit in you!" Slice. "My God, I don't know what to do to make it right!" Chip. "Sally!" Slice. "Jesus!" Chip. The notch in the tree deepened.

He said many more things. Finally the tree tottered. He gave it a push with his shoulder, and it fell in the path between the rest of the trees with a swoosh and a resounding, snapping, crunching thud. He dropped the ax and fell on his knees and clung to the stump and cried. And cried. He did not think he would ever stop crying.

Finally Daniel said that he must gather up the chips. He did not ask why. After taking off his shirt to use as a basket, he crawled around on his hands and knees, half blinded by tears, and gathered up all the chips.

Daniel led him to the lake and into the lake. When the water was up to their waists, Daniel took the shirt, cradled the chips in it, and told Jonas he must throw the chips one at a time into the lake. Jonas took the chips one at a time and threw them out into the lake. By the time he finished, some of the first ones were washing back toward them.

Back on shore Jonas put on his shirt, and they walked silently back to the rest of the crew.

25.

Sally and Jonas were cleaning. Sally had the afternoon off from the resort where she worked, and she said the cabin needed a complete cleaning. Jonas didn't ask why. He simply began to help her as she took everything out of the house but the wood stove. Samantha played among the beds, table, sewing machine, loom, chest of drawers, dishes, kettles, decorations, and clothes.

They washed the blankets, quilts, sheets, and winter clothes and hung them up to dry. Then they scrubbed the cupboards and walls side by side, using water from the same bucket. She scrubbed the outside of the stove; Jonas worked and worked on the oven. Then they washed the floors. They worked silently, speaking only when moving from one task to another, avoiding each other's eyes.

When they completed both rooms and the loft, Jonas thought they were done, but Sally said they still had to wash the ceilings. Earlier they had swept them. They stopped for supper and then stood on borrowed ladders, straining their necks, and cleaning the ceilings of flyspecks and grime from corner to corner, room to room to loft.

Then they went out and washed the furniture and kettles and decorations. When they finished with the cleaning, they carried each item back in and put it in its place. The last thing they did was make the beds. Sally slept on a single bed, while Samantha slept on a cot in the loft. Jonas would have to make a double bed for him and Sally. This thought was one of many that Jonas did not speak.

That night after Samantha was asleep, he and Sally sat on benches next to the table. A single lamp burned. "Maybe I should not have told you," Sally said, her face turned from him.

"No, you did the right thing."

"We act like strangers."

"I don't know what to say."

"Do you still want to marry me?"

"Yes, more than ever."

She turned her head and looked at him. "Why?"

"I don't know why. I just know deep within me that I want to marry you."

"It doesn't matter what happened to me?"

"Oh, it matters. It matters so much ... but I still want to marry you." There was a long silence. He knew she was looking at him, but he had not looked at her yet. "Do you want to marry me?" he asked.

"I am so scared, Jonas, but I want to marry you."

"You do?"

"Yes."

He did not understand why tears welled up in his eyes. He looked at her. They reached for each other, sliding their benches close together, holding each other.

After awhile they parted and he said, "Sally, I have to tell you something." She waited, her eyes afraid. "I told Daniel what you told me." Her eyes widened. He hurried on. "I didn't tell who did it. Daniel knew that something had happened to me. Something like death. So he took me aside and asked me about it and I told him. It came pouring out of me like water from an overturned bucket. I didn't think that you might not want me to tell. I'm sorry." The rush of words stopped. Sally was silent for a very long time, not looking at him.

"I trusted you when I told you, Jonas," she said, looking at him. He swallowed and waited. *"Trust in the Lord with all thy heart and lean not on thine own understanding; in all thy ways acknowledge him and he shall direct thy paths.* You taught me that. I don't think you could know how much trust it took to tell you. I knew you might leave me." She paused. "But what did he say when you told him?"

"At first," Jonas said, "I said it was too evil. I shouldn't tell. But he said that Jesus getting killed was evil, and yet his story got told four times in gory detail in the Bible. He told me that I should tell the story and let Jesus become part of it. So I told

him. When I finished telling him, he was angry. He kept
calling the man who did it a 'no-good son of a bitch.' He also
said that he honored you and me for telling the truth."

"What did he mean 'let Jesus become part of the story'?"

"I don't know."

"I like it," she said. "It's what I want. I want Jesus to
become part of my story. What happened next?"

"I'm ashamed to tell you what happened next." He could
see the fear flicker across her face. "But I will. I told him at
lunch, and after lunch he took me out to a stand of tamaracks
and told me to cut one down. He said to tell the truth to the
tree as I cut it down. I can't believe what happened. I said
terrible things." Jonas fell silent, wishing he did not have to
repeat what he said, afraid of what Sally would think, afraid
of being condemned by God, afraid that repeating what he had
said would make matters worse.

"What happened?"

"I started chopping the tree down, and with every chop of
the tree I said things." He couldn't bring himself to repeat
what things. "I said bad things. Things I have never said in
my life before." She reached out and held his hand.

Finally he blurted out the worst things. "I said I wished I
could stuff his underwear down his throat. I wished I could
gouge the eye out that he used to wink at you. I wished I could
sink the ax into him. That I didn't understand why God had
forsaken you." Jonas bowed his head in humiliation. "I said
nothing that came from faith," he said, shaking his head sadly.

Sally started to laugh. At first it was a giggle that she tried
to smother. Soon it was an outright laugh. Jonas looked at her
in amazement. He began to smile even though he was puzzled.
Finally he was chuckling too. "What's so funny?" he asked.
She laughed and laughed.

"You said those things?" she choked out and laughed more
when he nodded.

"What's so funny?"

"Those things you said were wonderful." More laughter.

"They were?"

"You said things that I hadn't even thought of saying." Her face crumpled and tears began to flow like water over moss-covered rocks. She threw herself on his lap, clinging to him. Half laughing, half crying, she kept saying, "I can't believe you said those things." He held her. He prayed, feeling confused.

"You're glad I said those things?"

"Oh, yes!" she exclaimed. "Jonas!" It was almost a wail. "Jonas, I have so many things to say. I feel like I have a nor'easter in me that would wipe out this whole island if I began to say what's in me. But, Jonas, I want to say it. I want someone to listen to me." Abruptly she stopped. "Did Daniel hear what you said?" He nodded. "Good. I'm glad he listened. Oh, Jonas!" she wailed. "I thought when I cried, 'My God! My God! Why did you forsake me?' that I was over this. Jonas, when will this ever be done?" She grabbed him by the shoulders and shook him. "When will this be done?" She stopped shaking him and clung to him.

"I don't know. I don't know." Jonas began to rock her. Touching her hair. Rocking her. He prayed aloud. *"I cry aloud to God, aloud to God that he may hear me. In the day of my trouble I seek the Lord; in the night my hand is stretched out without wearying; my soul refuses to be comforted."* He squeezed her.

"I think of God, and I moan," he prayed. *"I meditate, and my spirit faints. Thou dost hold my eyelids from closing; I am so troubled that I cannot speak."* He lifted some of her hair, blonde and fine, and let it fall from his fingers.

"I consider the days of old, I remember the years long ago. I commune with my heart in the night; I meditate and search my spirit. Will the Lord spurn forever, and never again be favorable? His steadfast love forever ceased? Are his promises at an end for all time? Has God forgotten to be gracious? Has his anger shut up his compassion? And I say, It is my grief that the right hand of the Most High has changed." Tears dropped from his eyes onto her hair. He kissed her hair that was wet with his salty tears.

"I will call to mind the deeds of the Lord; yea, I will remember thy wonders of old. I will meditate on all thy work and muse on thy mighty deeds. Thy way, O God, is holy. What God is great like our God? Thou art the God that workest wonders, who hast manifested thy might among the peoples." He traced lightly with his fingertips the outline of Sally's arm, shoulder, hair, cheek, chin, and throat.

"When the waters saw thee, O God, when the waters saw thee, they were afraid; yea, the deep trembled. The clouds poured out water; the skies gave forth thunder; the arrows flashed on every side. The crash of thy thunder was in the whirlwind; the lightning lighted up the world; the earth trembled and shook." Sally sighed and nestled her head against his shoulder and neck. *"Thy way was through the sea, thy path through the great waters; yet thy footprints were unseen. Thou didst lead thy people like a flock by the hand of Moses and Aaron.* I pray this in the name of the Father, the Son, and the Holy Ghost. Amen." He held her quietly.

Sally fell asleep. Jonas lifted her gently, carried her to her bed, tucked her into her fresh smelling sheets and blanket. He turned down the lamp and made his way to his hammock on Daniel's boat.

26.

Philena and Jonas made trip after trip from the *Edna* to her garden carrying loads of topsoil. When they had dumped the last tub, Philena got down on her knees and, using her hands, began to level out the soil. Jonas started helping her, using a shovel.

"No, use your hands," she said. He set the shovel aside, knelt down, and began smoothing out the ground with his hands. The soil was moist, filled with living and decaying vegetation and worms. "I think we should use our hands so that we can be tender with the life in the soil. I use a shovel to dig it up because I can't dig it with my hands, but I can spread it with my hands." She cleared her throat. "You've been quiet lately," she said.

He couldn't think of anything to say. He didn't want to talk about Sally. About force. About her daddy. He did not want to talk about it.

"That's okay," she said. "It's okay to be quiet." She sat back on her haunches and began to slowly work out a quack grass root from a clump of dirt. Jonas kept moving the soil with his hands.

"Maybe you're missing your home," she said, tossing aside the quack grass root and putting the dirt in its place. "You're awful young to strike out on your own. I remember when I left home. I left my parents when I got married. I was sixteen and didn't know much of anything about life. Or being married. Then I had a baby a year after we were married. Theresa. Six weeks after she was born I got sick. I thought I was gonna die, I was so sick. I couldn't eat anything and I puked up everything. I hurt like I was a ball of fire. And Theresa was hungry. Our neighbor lady told me I should put on hot packs and wait it out. Theresa would be feeding and I'd be sitting there bawling my head off. I'd be sitting there crying for my mama. I wanted to go home so bad. Here I was with my own baby, my own man, my own house, but I wanted to go home so bad. But my baby needed me. She couldn't live without me but, oh, the pain."

Jonas was only half listening to Philena. He looked at the soil they were leveling out. He remembered how Philena had told him that her mission from God was to be a mess. A mess like soil lying fallow, waiting to grow potatoes. He was becoming a mess himself. Sudden urges to get away from this island where a daddy could force himself on his daughter swooped into his mind like a shrill magpie. He pushed these thoughts aside, but they kept coming back. He was beginning to wonder what he was doing on the island. He had come to the island knowing that he was called here to be a preacher and a hired man. He had been so sure of marrying Sally when she said yes to him. Now he was becoming more uncertain all the time. Should he tell Philena? Should he tell Daniel? What did God have in mind?

"I remember," Philena was saying when Jonas next heard her, "one particular day thinking I couldn't keep going. I laid Theresa down and went out of the house and looked at the road that led home. Theresa started to cry. She must have known something was the matter. I walked out to the road and looked down it as far as I could see. I could imagine every twist and turn of the road between there and my home. I imagined walking up to the door of our house and seeing my mother come to greet me. She'd be happy to see me, but when she found out I left my baby she would send me home. I felt so bad standing on that road wanting to go home and not being able to. Finally I went back in, picked up Theresa and comforted her. When I was looking her in the face, she gave me the first smile she ever gave me."

Jonas had supper at Philena's that night. After supper he went out and sat under a tree and thought about going home.

27.

After worship on Sunday, Jonas spent the day wandering the island. He made his way north along the shoreline until the beach gave rise to a steep, rocky incline. It looked hard to climb, so he headed inland through scrub pine trees that clung to the rocky soil and then on into larger pines. Half a mile through the woods he came to a small meadow. He sat down in the meadow. He wrote a letter to his family and church, telling them that he was going through a trial and asking for prayer. For his mother he added that a wedding date had not been set.

Was he really called by God to this island? Was he really called by God to marry Sally? For days he had been feeling empty. After he had preached that morning, Daniel had taken him aside and told him that he thought he ought to preach on something else besides the way of salvation. After all, as he pointed out, everyone who came to hear him preach was already saved. It was true. Philena, Theresa, Daniel, his wife Alice who was deaf, Old Lady Bill, and Sally were the only ones who came regularly. Daniel had spoken very kindly, but Jonas went away from the conversation forlorn. It seemed a long time since God had spoken to him. He couldn't think of anything else to preach about. Was God's silence a sign he had wandered from his presence? Hadn't someone said there was another island in the lake further north still? Maybe he had come to the wrong island. He fell asleep.

He dreamed he was trying to climb a huge cliff. The face of the cliff was dotted with scrub pines. He was trying to make his way up the cliff by using the pines as handholds and footholds. He was so afraid that the pines were going to give way. He was sure they did not have deep enough roots. He looked down. Beneath the cliff was a broiling sea. He was sure there were rocks beneath the sea that would crush him if he fell. He was a very long way from the top. It began to rain, making the cliff slick and the pines slippery to hold. He saw just above him a pine that looked sturdier. If he could only get to that pine. Suddenly he was surprised to find the tree within grasp. He grabbed it and slowly its root began to give way. I'm going to fall, he thought.

He woke up. For a moment he was frantic, thinking he had fallen since he was lying on the ground. Then he realized it was a dream.

28.

The night after his cliff dream he had another dream. In this dream he saw a different island with people on the shore beckoning to him. When he awoke he was certain the dream was a sign that he was on the wrong island. Norsk Island was not where God had called him. God had a new island for him, an island of great promise.

At first he was scared and didn't tell anyone about the dream. He hid it in his heart that day as he pulled nets and picked fish on the *Edna,* and it grew like a dandelion. By the evening when they had docked it was a lively, bright, yellow feeling. Still he didn't tell anyone. Just in case. He would sleep one more night to see if it lasted before he started saying good-bye and preparing to move.

That night he brought fish to Jackson and stayed for supper. After supper Jackson pushed himself away from the table and stared at Jonas. Jonas began to feel uneasy. "What?" he said irritably, staring back at Jackson.

"What, I am wondering," Jackson said, "is going on with you?"

"Nothing," Jonas said, shrugging his shoulders.

"Nothing?" Jackson said, doubtfully. "For days, whenever I've seen you, you've been glum. Hardly a word out of you. And now tonight you're still not talking, but you keep humming."

"I've been humming?"

"Ever since you got here."

"I guess I'm feeling better about life."

"I don't recall hearing what soured you on life."

"I'm feeling better and when I'm ready to talk about it, I will."

"Okay," Jackson sighed. Looking at Jonas he said, "You know what you remind me of?" He didn't wait for an answer. "You remind me of a fellow who's been dry for a long time and has just decided to go to town to wet his lips. At that point one definitely starts feeling better about life."

Jonas looked back at him. "I don't drink," he said flatly.

"I'm just telling you what you remind me of."

"It's nothing like that," Jonas said emphatically. He suddenly felt cold. He said to himself, It's nothing like that. Is it? He fought a feeling of dread. Jackson was tempting him to doubt his dream. It was a bigger island. More people to tell about salvation. People who didn't do disgusting things with their daughters.

Jackson wheeled over to the cupboard and got his jug of wine.

People who didn't drink. People who didn't tempt preachers to doubt. People who didn't act like sourpusses. People who wanted to hear good news.

"I remember one time when I had been dry for three years," Jackson began. "I was in seminary studying to be an Episcopal priest and I was feeling better about life, and then life took a nasty turn as life is apt to do from time to time. I was in love. Yes, Jonas, once upon a time I was in love. A wonderful woman." He stared at the jug, remembering. He lifted his eyes and looked at Jonas. "We were engaged." He dropped his eyes, "And then she fell out of love with me. Two months before I was to graduate and two weeks after I found out I was assigned to an Indian reservation, she told me.

"I was full of myself then. I decided to be a saint. I graciously said good-bye to the woman and she promptly fell in love with my best friend. I gave them my blessing. Very saintly of me. A few days before graduation a classmate let slip that my fiancée and best friend had begun 'seeing' each other six months before she broke up with me. Still, I was the saint. I was so full of myself. After all, I was being sent to minister to the Indians. Graduation night I listened to my best friend give the valedictory address. I can't remember what he said because, as he started to speak, I suddenly knew that before the night was over I was gonna have a drink." He raised his jug and sloshed it back and forth. "Immediately I was happy. For several days I had been giving my former fiancée and former best friend a cold shoulder. But that evening I was very warm and cordial with them. It was a great evening of congratulations, best wishes, socializing. When it was over I went to the nearest bar and drank until I passed out."

Jackson lifted the jug and took a drink. He looked at Jonas and shook his head. "There's nothing quite like the guilt you feel when you wake up the next morning and realize that your sweet dream," he raised the jug and sloshed the wine back and forth, "is a long, swift descent into a boiling sea that will drown you."

Jonas stared uneasily at Jackson who hung his head. "Can't you just get ahold of yourself?"

"So," Jackson snorted, ignoring his innocence, "that's what your secret cheer makes me think about."

Well, I'm not gonna do anything wrong, Jonas insisted to himself as he walked back along the dark beach. He lay down in his hammock and tried to get back that bright feeling.

29.

Jonas got back his bright feeling, and a few days later a gentle breeze tossed up small waves as he left on Daniel's boat to follow the dream.

Sally was angry when Jonas said he was leaving. When he told her that as soon as he found the right island he would come back for her, she told him not to bother. He said he would come because he was still sure God wanted him to marry her.

Daniel was headed to the mainland anyway and reluctantly agreed to give him passage. Jonas was determined to come back after he found the right island to let them know that God did not make mistakes.

The island in his dream looked bigger than the one he was leaving. There were more people on it. And the people were waiting for him. They must be waiting eagerly to hear about God.

Now as he stood at the gunwale in the prow he thought about his journey ahead. In a couple of hours he would be on the mainland. From there he was going to journey north. He was sure the island was to the north. He had money to pay his passage to the bigger island since he still had some of the silver dollars from Old Lady Bills, plus money from wages. On the island he had just left, only six people besides the children joined him for worship on Sunday morning. He was sure everybody would come when he was on the right island.

"Jonas, this wind is picking up. We could be in for a nasty one," Daniel said, his gruff voice raised. Jonas suddenly became aware of the heaving of the boat and the wind gusts.

Jonas was starting to have second thoughts about marrying Sally. After all, he had made a mistake about which island he was called to. Maybe he had made a mistake about Sally, too. He tried to recall the dream. Had there been a woman among the crowd on the beach who was waiting for him?

It would be sad saying good-bye to Samantha, but that's what he would do. When God calls a man he must be ready to say good-bye to all. For some reason Jackson's words came back to him. "I was a saint. I was so full of myself." Jonas blinked, irritated at Jackson's voice in his mind.

Lightning ripped the sky to the north. In the instant of the lightning God spoke: *Jonas, you are running away."*

Crash! The most deafening clap of thunder he had ever heard.

The roar of the wind and the lake cut through his thoughts. He looked up. A huge wave was descending on Daniel's tug.

He heard Brawn yell behind him and he turned to listen. The wave crashed over the deck and swept him up in its furious arms. It carried him where it willed. It carried him and carried him.

His lungs screamed for air. I'm going to die, he thought. His head shot out of the lake. He gulped air. The lake covered him again. Screaming lungs. Air. The lake covering him. Air. Lake.

Once when he hit the air he saw a plank. The *Edna* splintered, he thought. He grabbed the plank with one arm. The lake tried to tear it from him. He held on crying, "Jesus, save me!" Jonas got hold of the plank with his other arm. He prayed, sure he was in his watery grave.

"Oh, God," he sobbed, "you've thrown me into the heart of this lake. I am completely done, your waves washing over me. Will I ever see your island again?"

The waves were huge, hurling him first toward heaven and

then toward the pit. One moment he was nearly airborne; the next, water swamped his throat. Then he swirled deep in the abyss of the lake.

Once a lake weed wrapped itself around his head as the waves plunged him to the roots of a canyon in the lake. He was sure he'd be counted among all the bodies the lake had claimed.

But he looped a leg over the plank and clung to it and was lifted from the lake over and over again. He discovered that even when he was under the lake, when his lungs screamed for air, he thought of God. He didn't know how long he was buried by the lake and raised again and again. Always clinging to the plank. "Jesus, I have taken the long, swift plunge into guilt."

Finally the lake began to relent. And as the waves carried him, he wondered if the island he saw in the dream was only a wish, instead. "I will return to my God and my island," he shouted to the sky. "I will sacrifice my wishes; I will live the promise I made when I left my home. Sally, Samantha, Daniel, here I come!"

Oh God, he suddenly thought, what if Daniel and the crew are dead. "Please, God. If they are, I should be, too." He laid his head on the plank. "Please, God."

When he lifted his head the sun had broken through low in the west. He had spent most of the day in the water. He looked east and was shocked: the waves were driving him against the face of the cliff at the northwest end of the island. The treacherous reef was only a hundred yards away. He tried to paddle south, but the waves insisted on carrying him toward the cliff. "Jesus! Did you save me only to dash me against the rocks?" He paddled furiously, futilely. He expected any moment to smash against rocks hidden beneath the surface.

Then an undercurrent suddenly sucked him beneath the lake, tearing the plank from his hands. "Jesus, did you save me from the storm to dash me against the rocks?"

But the undercurrent spit him up in an eddy twenty-five

feet from the beach. He swam to the shore and crawled onto the island. He was exhausted. All he could do was think how little faith he had and wonder where deliverance came from. He fell asleep as he crawled out of the deep.

30.

Jonas wakened during the night and began to trek back along the shore toward the west settlement. The moon was out, its reflection dancing on the waves beside him.

Daniel's tug was at the dock. Blessed be the name of the Lord, he breathed. He found his hammock.

It was still damp, but he was so tired that he lay down in it anyway. He let the *Edna* rock him to sleep.

"Jonas!" He opened his eyes. Brawn was staring at him. "We thought you were a goner," he said. Then he disappeared. Dawn was pale and pink. Jonas fell back to sleep.

The next time he woke there were a dozen people gathered around the hammock. He pulled himself into a sitting position.

"How'd you get here then?" asked Daniel.

"I got washed ashore by the cliff up north."

"Washed ashore?" said Theresa.

"Yeah," he said, rubbing his eyes.

"You were washed overboard miles out," Brawn said.

"I hung on to a plank. I thought the plank meant the *Edna* had broken up."

"You are one lucky lad," said Philena.

"God had mercy on me. I guess I was running away. I believe now that I do belong on this island. I think I'm here to stay."

There didn't seem much more to say. Everyone stared at him for awhile and then started to leave.

"Sally," Jonas called. She stopped, waiting a few feet away on the dock but not returning. The others kept going.

"Aren't you glad I'm back?"

"Yes," she said.

"You don't sound very glad."

"It doesn't really matter."

"What do you mean?"

"I don't trust you anymore."

"Don't trust me?" He stood up and vaulted over the gunwale.

She held up her hand to stop him. "You told me that God sent you on a mission to this island. I was a part of that mission. Then you told me God called you to another island. You left me. Now you come back and tell me that God wants you to stay here. What am I to believe?"

"I made a mistake."

"It's not that easy, Jonas." She turned and left without looking back.

31.

Jonas was miserable. Sally wouldn't have him back. "You left me," she had said. "You can stay left." She wasn't going to trust him again.

He worked all day with Daniel's crew, making repairs to the damages done by the storm. That evening he was walking alone when he ran into Jackson. His wheelchair was stuck on a root. Jackson was cursing in a slurred voice and trying to get the chair to move.

"Oh, Jackson, you're drunk."

"I am," he said, swaying on the chair as he gazed at Jonas. "Oh, it's you. The damn chair you made quit on me. It will not budge."

"Here, I'll help you get home." Jonas wiggled on the chair, loosening it from the root. Then he pulled on the chair until he got him back to his cabin. He lit a lantern.

"Son," Jackson said waving the bottle he clutched, "you are good. Join me for a drink."

"I don't drink. Wine is a mocker and strong drink is raging . . ."

"That, son, is why I drink," he said.

"I'll help you to bed."

"No, you listen. I got some-," he took a swig, "-thing to say."

Jonas sat down on a bench and waited.

"I just saw a turtle . . ." Jackson lost his train of thought. Regained it. "Tonight, I saw a turtle. I tried to pet it. It bit me." He held up a swollen index finger on his left hand. "Life is always biting at me," he started to cry. When he stopped, he wiped his eyes on his sleeve and took another drink. His Adam's apple pumped it into his gut. "Your turn," he said. "You tell me your troubles."

"Sally doesn't want to marry me."

"That's sad." Jackson started to cry again.

"I was thinking God was calling me to another island. But he sent me back here. Now that I'm back, Sally won't have me back."

"That's sad," Jackson blubbered. "You need a drink." He wagged his bottle.

"I need something."

"Pray," Jackson said, wiping his eyes on his sleeve.

"What?"

"You do not want a drink, you should pray," he slurred.

"I don't feel like praying."

"I will pray."

Before Jonas could stop him he started, "Unto thee, O Lord, do I lift the soul of this lad . . . "

He prayed on. Jonas bowed his head, wondering if it was blasphemy to have a drunk pray for you.

"Remember not the sins of his youth, nor his trans . . . Hold it, God, I will get it right . . . *trans . . . gressions: according to thy mercy remember thou him for thy goodness sake . . . "*

Jonas' transgressions welled up within him. He had run away from God. He had run away from the island and the people God had sent him to. He had told the people that God was sending him to another island. He had put words in God's mouth; the wrong words. Would God ever forgive him?

Jackson took another swig and prayed on, his voice becoming clearer. *"The meek will he guide in his judgment: and the meek will he teach his way . . ."*

Teach me, Jonas prayed.

"For thy name's sake, O Lord, pardon his iniquity which is great . . ."

Pardon me, Jonas implored.

"His soul shall dwell at ease; and his seed shall inherit the earth . . ."

Jonas sighed deeply, pardon easing through him.

"His eyes are ever toward thee, Lord; for you shall pluck his feet out of the net . . ."

Jonas could feel his feet being freed from the net as hands stronger than Brawn's lifted him.

"Let integrity and uprightness preserve him; for he waits on thee. Redeem Israel, O God, out of all his troubles."

Jonas sat there and let the prayer circulate through his body. God and all of him listened to the prayer. After awhile Jonas opened his eyes. Jackson had fallen asleep. He wheeled him over to his bed and helped him in. Jackson kept mumbling his thanks. When he finished putting Jackson to bed, Jonas went back to the *Edna* to sleep.

32.

Jonas worked a second day with Daniel and his crew, repairing the pot nets and gill nets that had been damaged in the storm. Sally didn't want anything to do with him. He was in a daze.

He ate supper with Philena and Theresa. Maybe Theresa will have me, he thought, as he ate trout. He didn't want Theresa. He wanted Sally. No, more than anything, he wanted God's will. But what was his will? This island was his will. But what about him and Sally? Was it his will or not that they marry?

Theresa went to visit Brawn after supper.

"You're quiet tonight," said Philena when they finished the dishes. "I would think a man who had his life saved like you did would be full of life."

"Sally doesn't want to have me back, and no one else seems that excited to see me either."

Philena lit a lantern and motioned for him to sit down. "Did she tell you why?" She opened a cedar chest, brought out needle and thread, and sat down and began to repair a dress.

"She says she can't trust me anymore."

She stitched for several minutes. "Do you know what it does to a woman's ability to trust when a man forces himself on her?"

"I didn't force myself on her," he protested, shocked.

"I know you didn't, Jonas." She looked up from her sewing with a smile. "But a woman like Sally has good reason to not trust any man."

"Do you know who raped her?" This was only the second time he used the word. He cringed when he said it. Sally never used it; she always said "forced." For some reason he wanted to use the word "rape." Maybe it was because he felt bad and "rape" was a bad word.

"No," she said. "I never did believe her story that it was a stranger. There are no strangers on this island. There are a few tourists, but they always stay at least a week since Alice only rents out the cabins by the week. But I'm sure she has her reasons for not telling. It doesn't matter. Whoever it was would hurt her trust in men."

"She told me who raped her."

"When did she tell you?"

"About a week ago."

"That's why you decided to leave," she said thoughtfully.

"No," he protested. "I thought God was calling me to another island."

"After yesterday's storm you changed your mind."

"That's because God made it clear I was running away."

"What were you running away from?"

"I don't know. This island, I guess . . . " he stopped. Guilt slipped into him like a fish hook. "Maybe I was running away from Sally." He put his head in his hands. "She's right not to have me back."

Philena came over and put her hand on his shoulder. He couldn't believe it. He had run away from Sally when she needed him most. God have mercy. He didn't mean to. He felt a wave of anger surge up within him. Her daddy! He had raped her. What could he, Jonas, do?

"Jonas, you did not rape her. She will sometimes act as if you are the man who did, but I know that you are not."

"What can I do to make up for it?"

"Forty days of kindness."

"What?"

"Show Sally forty days of kindness."

"How?"

"I'm sure you can think of ways to show her at least one kindness each day for forty days."

"She doesn't even want to see me."

She stepped back. "Lift up your head, Jonas." He lifted it up. She leaned against the kitchen counter and looked at him. "You are so young, Jonas, but you are learning. Sally is very fortunate to have you."

"How can you say that after what I did?"

"Jesus was fortunate to have Peter as his disciple, even though Peter denied him three times and then went out and wept bitterly. Jesus was fortunate because Peter came back to him. Sally is fortunate because you've come back to her."

"But she doesn't even want to see me."

"She will if you come back to her."

"I already have come back."

"Sally will need time to see if you are really back."

"I am," Jonas said.

"If you are, and I think you are, Sally will see it."

Jonas watched the flame flicker in the lamp. He was back, and he was never going to leave until God dragged him off the island.

"Jonas?" said Philena, softly. Jonas looked at her. She was still leaning against the counter. "You said that the people of the island did not seem excited to see you back?" Jonas nodded. "I won't speak for others, but I was sad to see you leave. You have been an enthusiastic preacher. I know not many people come Sundays, but you are important to those of us who come. You are so young and full of hope and excitement about following God. I remember the first time I heard you preach. You talked about Jesus as the light of the world. You made me feel God's love was shining over Norsk Island. When you preach you always make sure that Alice can read your lips, and you know right away when she can't and you wait until Daniel can interpret for her. And then when you started spending time with Sally, she was happy. Much happier than she has ever been since she came to Little Oslo. And when she began to smile, all of us in Little Oslo smiled with her. We didn't make a big thing of it, but we smiled."

She looked at Jonas with sad eyes, "What were we to think when you announced that God had called you to another island? We had never had a preacher before. You showed up telling us God had sent you. And it sure seemed to me like he had. Then just like that you are gone. There was going to be no more worship. No more preaching. And Sally staying in her cabin. The one time I did see her come out, she looked so sad I wanted to cry." Jonas blinked back tears. He knew what she was saying was true.

"When you left on the boat before the storm," she went on, "I was angry. You were leaving us just like that." She snapped her finger. "I thought you were being young and foolish, but that didn't make me feel any better. So when you showed up asleep on Daniel's tug the morning after the storm, it was a mixed blessing. I was amazed and glad that you were alive. I thought your foolishness had gotten you killed. But I was still mad that you left in the first place. Others feel the same way—glad that you're back, but still a little mad that you left in the first place."

"What can I do about it?" asked Jonas.

"You are a preacher. I'm sure God will tell you what to do."

"After being so wrong, I'm afraid I'll be wrong again."

"He brought you back here rather miraculously and made it clear that you are to stay here, right?"

"Yes."

"Then he has not lost his ability to speak to you. Not only is Sally fortunate to have you back, but I think the rest of us will be blessed as well. Now go. I'm tired."

Jonas left. He was warmed by Philena's words. He wanted it to be good that he was back. He walked through the darkness past Sally's cabin. No act of kindness that he could do for her came to mind. Tomorrow, he thought.

In the morning he wrote a letter to his family and church, telling them that he had been through a great trial and the Lord had delivered him. He debated a long time about whether to tell them about getting swept off the boat. His mother would worry. But finally he told them that he had been running away from the island when he got swept overboard in a storm, but the Lord had saved him from the lake. Then he asked them to pray that he would find good ways to love the people of the island.

33.

The following Sunday Jonas preached his first sermon on something other than salvation. It was also his shortest sermon. He had second thoughts because Brawn showed up. Maybe he was supposed to show Brawn how to be saved. But he didn't consider that for very long. God had already told him what to preach on, and who knew what God might do if he refused to do as he had been told. The last time he strayed, God swept him overboard.

When they finished singing, he sat on the beach facing those who had come and said, "Today I have a confession." It was at that moment that he realized Sally had not come to worship. He had been so worried about what he was going to say that he hadn't noticed her missing. "John 1:9 says, *If we confess our sins, he is faithful and just to forgive us our sins and to cleanse us from all unrighteousness.*

"Today I have a confession," he said again, and deep feelings welled up within him and he had to stop for tears. Finally he continued on in a broken voice, "I have sinned against God and against you," he said looking at Daniel, Alice, Philena, and Brawn. And I have especially sinned against Sally, he thought. "I told you that God called me to another island. I ran away from this island. I ran away from you. I ran away from God. I thought I was doing God's will, but I wasn't. I was full of myself." He stood in silence, the tears running down his freckled cheeks. "When that huge wave swept me off Daniel's tug," he said, his voice stronger, "God told me that I was running away from him. As the lake covered me I thought I was going to die. But I cried out to God and he heard me. He saved me. Over and over again, just when I thought my lungs were going to burst, I would come to the surface. All I tried to do was keep my head above water, and many times I couldn't do that. But while I was trying to keep from drowning, God was carrying me miles through the lake back to this island.

"While I was in the lake all those hours clinging to a plank, I begged God for mercy. I began to see that I was running away from here, and so from him, too. And he showed me mercy and brought me back to this island. He forgave me."

Jonas stopped. A fresh wave of tears swept through him. "Now I confess that I sinned against each of you when I left." More tears. He struggled through them and said, "I am back. Please forgive me." Then he bowed his head and let the tears flow.

Daniel was suddenly standing beside him with his hand on his shoulder. "Ya, I forgive you," he said. There was a chorus of "I forgive you" from the others. Then Daniel sat down beside him and touched Jonas' chin until Jonas lifted his head and looked through his tears at Daniel. "Jonas," said Daniel, "everyone of the disciples ran away from Jesus when he was arrested. Ya, and everyone of them came back except Judas. And Jesus took them back. He took them back because he loved them. Besides, he had work for them to do, too, then." Daniel thumped Jonas on the back and said, "Ya, you got some work here to do then."

"Thank you," was all Jonas could manage.

Later as they were parting, Philena smiled at him and told him that he had done his best preaching that day. When they were gone he sat on the beach, thankful to be forgiven, but sad that Sally had not come.

34.

Brawn and Jonas leaned against the gunwale of the *Edna* heading toward home. Brawn's huge frame was relaxed. During the day his muscles bulged again and again while he worked the nets. He could do the work of two men when it came to lifting.

"Brawn, have you ever beat anyone up?" Jonas asked.

"Humph," he snorted. Theresa came over and joined them against the rail. "Humph," he snorted again. "All the time I was growing up I was a runt," he said. "I couldn't fight my way out of three foot of water. Kids picked on me all the time. I'd never fight.

"Then when I was thirteen and on the mainland I got into my first fight. It was after school. There was this kid that lived by the school who wasn't right. He was five years old and he couldn't talk. He made noises, but no one could understand what he was saying. He was a runt like me, but he was a fighter. Somebody twice his age would give him a shove, and he'd lay into them for all he was worth. He acted like he wouldn't take nothin' from nobody. Course, he had to take something from everybody 'cause he was so small.

"One day I'm heading home from school. Some guys older than me are standing on the street corner mocking this little kid, making nonsense sounds. He piles into them with his tiny fists and they laugh, pick him up, and start throwing him back and forth between them like a twenty-five pound sack of potatoes. They set him down, and he starts swinging again.

"He gets lucky on one of his swings and bloodies Burt's nose. Burt's the biggest one in the bunch. I know the kid's in trouble now. Burt's tormented me lots of times. The brute hits the little kid in the face and breaks his nose and bloodies it all up. Then Burt throws the kid to one of his buddies. They start throwing him back and forth. The kid is making these high-pitched squealing noises. It's his way of crying. They keep laughing and tossing him. Finally one of the guys stops throwing the kid. He holds a cloth on the little kid's nose until the bleeding stops. The kid quiets down. But then Burt comes over, grabs both the kid's feet in one hand, holds the kid upside down, and shakes him until the little guy's nose starts bleeding again.

"I'm watching all this from a distance. I feel sick. Burt holds a cloth on the kid's nose until it stops bleeding again, then shakes him upside down until the bleeding starts again. All the time the bastard's laughing and making jokes about stuffing the kid like a squirrel to mount on his wall after he drains all his blood out.

"I can't take it anymore. 'Stop it!' I yell.

"Everyone looks at me. 'What did you say, scrawny Brawny?' Burt asks. 'Stop it!' I scream. I'm scared. 'You want me to stop, scrawny Brawny, come and tell me to my face,' he says.

"I walk toward him, knowing he's gonna beat me up. I never walked toward somebody who's gonna beat me up before. I always ran. Lots of times I got caught, but I always ran. Now I'm walking toward Burt who's ten times bigger than me. As I walk toward him, he sets the little kid down. The little kid looks up at Burt. Then up at me. At least the little kid's not gonna get killed now. Maybe I am, but the kid's not. I see dry blood on Burt's nostril. I stop in front of him. His buddies close in a circle around us. 'Stop it!' I scream and aim a punch right at the dried blood on his nose.

"The punch lands. I throw myself on the big brute, hitting

him and getting slammed. I kick him, hit him, scratch him. For a second he gets me down and climbs on top of me, when the little kid jumps on his head. He gets distracted and I squirm away. Burt's swingin' at me. I keep trying to get away, but his buddies close in tighter. Finally I dive at his legs, thinkin' I can knock him down. He falls, but before I can get away he grabs hold of me again. He smashes me in the face. He cocks his arm to finish me off when the little kid throws sand in his eyes. He screams and grabs his eyes. I push him off me and jump to my feet. The little kid's clingin' to me. Burt's moaning and holding his eyes. I look at his buddies. 'Who's next?' I ask.

"Nobody says anything. Finally I turn and walk away. The guys take off. The little kid's still holding fast to me.

"That was the first time I beat somebody up, Jonas. If you can call it that. After that I grew like a weed. Now guys want to see if they're as tough as me. I've had to fight a few times. A guy as big as me people like to challenge. But I don't like to fight that much, so, whenever I can, I challenge 'em to a contest, not a fight. I tell 'em if they win the contest, I'll fight 'em. I tell 'em I'll fight if they can throw a rock further than I can into the lake. I always go first and pick a rock so big they can't lift it. And I tell 'em they have to throw one the same size into the lake." He laughed a big belly laugh.

Then he stopped laughing. "But there are people in this world who need to be beat up. People like Burt."

35.

Jonas carried the bucket of clams he had dug for Sally. It was his fourth day of showing kindnesses to her. He had asked her what he could do for her, and she said, "Nothing," and turned away. So he had to think up kindnesses. He dug the clams and then went to supper at Daniel's. He spent the evening listening to Daniel tell stories.

He was lying in his hammock looking at the stars when he suddenly remembered the clams. He had set them along the trail to Daniel's. Now he searched for them in the dark. There was no wind, so the mosquitoes were eating him alive. Finally he found them, and he hurried along the trail toward Sally's, waving his hand around his head to ward off the bugs.

He tripped in the darkness. "Damn it!" he yelled as he fell. He lay on the ground, a sharp pain in his shin from having hit something on the ground. And he was horrified that he had sworn. He hadn't sworn since he decided to be a Christian at age ten.

He laid his head on the ground. Let the mosquitoes eat me alive, he thought. What's the matter with me? Why should I be lying on the ground, appalled that I swore, when Sally's daddy didn't act guilty at all? Instead of feeling guilty, he winked at Sally. Every time Jonas thought of him winking at her, his fists clenched automatically. What's the matter with me? He had almost cursed earlier in the day when he dropped his side of the net and a load of fish slid onto the deck. Brawn swore instead.

Jonas got up on his hands and knees and began to search for the bucket. He had thrown it when he started to fall. The mosquitoes chewed on his back and neck. He found the bucket. There weren't any clams left in it. He crawled on his hands and knees, searching for the clams by touch. He clamped his mouth shut to keep from swearing again. When he had finally located a dozen out of the original two and half dozen, he gave up searching for more.

Jonas felt anything but kind when he set the bucket of clams on Sally's porch and slunk off through the mosquitoes.

36.

Theresa came down to Daniel's boat one evening. Jonas was lying in his hammock when she came on board. He sat up, swinging his feet onto the deck.

"Have you ever wanted anything a whole lot, Jonas?" she asked.

Jonas wanted Sally a whole lot, but he didn't want to talk with Theresa about it. "You mean some *thing*?" he asked.

"No, have you ever wanted something to happen so much that you can see in your mind exactly what it would be like?"

"Sure," he said. "The first time I saw this island in a dream. When I was sure God was sending me here, over and over again I pictured the island in my mind. The first time I stepped off the dock onto the island I almost felt as if I'd been here before."

"Then maybe you'll understand," she said. He nodded his head, hoping he would, afraid he wouldn't. "I've never told anyone this," she continued, turning away from him to look at the shore. She didn't say anything.

"Is this a confession?" he asked, trying to help her out.

"No, no, I haven't done anything wrong. It's just I want to do something that isn't usual."

"I'm doing something unusual," Jonas said. "I'm only twenty years old and I came to this island to preach."

"You are unusual," she said. "But nice," she added. He thought she blushed. Maybe it was just the sun which was getting low in the west. She was leaning against the gunwale, small and pretty.

"I want to have my own tug," she said.

"You want to own a fishing tug?"

"Yes, I want to be the captain. I want to know this lake. I want to ride out storms on this lake. I want to know the fishing grounds." As she talked she whirled from the gunwale and flung out her arms as if balancing on a beam, covering the entire lake with her sweeping gesture. "I want to ride the waves." Then she relaxed and tapped the floor with her foot. "I want a tug as good as the *Edna*. It seems like such a grand idea." She turned her palms upwards as if to receive a gift. "I'd love it. I'd love it." Then she let her hands drop. "But whoever heard of a woman owning a tug?"

"There was a woman in the Bible who was a general."

"There was?" Her eyes widened.

"Yes, her name was Deborah. She was an Israelite. There was an Israelite man general who was too scared to go into battle, so she led the troops."

"I am not scared. I love the lake. I could do it. I know I could if I just had the chance."

"You'll need money."

"Yes. How will I get the money?"

"Pray."

"Pray?"

"Yes, unless God builds the boat, you will captain in vain."

"How do you know God so well?" she asked, her hands on her hips.

"I don't know him well enough," said Jonas, ruefully. "But I talk to him. He talks to me. I read the Bible."

"I'd like to know him like you do."

"Talk to him."

"How do you talk to him? Do you pretend you're talking to someone in the air?"

"You know how to talk to a friend, right? Let's talk to him right now."

"Right now?"

"Sure."

"Okay, but you start."

So Jonas started, and then she said some things. Afterwards she said, "What did you say about God building the boat?"

"Unless God builds the boat, you captain in vain."

"Do you really mean God can build me a boat?" she asked wistfully.

"Certainly. He will use people. Starting with me." He went over to the wooden box that he kept his belongings in. He took out twenty-five silver dollars. He still had some left over in the box. He started to hand the twenty-five dollars to her.

"I can't accept that kind of money," she said, backing away.

"There are two conditions if you accept the money," he said.

"What are they?" she said suspiciously.

"One is that you don't tell anybody, and, two, that you follow my lead."

"Do what?"

"Give secretly to someone in need."

She stood eyeing the money and scuffing her foot on the deck.

"You just prayed about a tug. This is an answer to prayer."

"I don't know," she said. She seemed to be relenting.

"This is only the beginning of what a tug will cost."

"You're sure now?" she said, reaching out her hand.

"You agree to the conditions?"

"Yes."

Only then did he hand her the coins. When she left the boat, she went skipping along the shore.

Wistfully he watched her. Maybe she's the one he ought to be thinking about ... but, no ... it was Sally that he wanted. He had come back for Sally. Sooner or later she had to see that he had come back for her. It was a week since he had come back, and still she wouldn't talk to him. If Philena was right, Sally wouldn't have him back because she didn't trust him, and she didn't trust him because of what her daddy did. Her daddy. Her daddy had stolen Sally from him. Jonas was going to have to steal her back.

37.

At dawn one morning in the third week of June, Jonas walked the path that led across the island to the cluster of cabins called the East Side. That's where Sally's family lived. He wanted to have a look at her daddy. He wanted to see someone who had raped his daughter. He didn't tell Sally or anyone else what he was going to do. Sally wouldn't have anything to do with her daddy since she left home. Sally still wasn't talking to Jonas.

The people of the East Side fished the east and north sides of the lake. The westerners, like Daniel, fished the west side and south side of the lake.

In the faint light he searched the docks for a tug named *Tamarack*. The fourth tug he found was called *Tamar*. *Tamar*? Who would name their tug *Tamar*, the woman in the Old Testament who had been raped by her brother? He was peering at the tug when a man walked down the dock carrying gear.

Without thinking Jonas said, "Who would name their tug *Tamar*?"

"*Tamar*?" the man said stepping past Jonas and hoisting the gear over the gunwale.

"*Tamar*," Jonas repeated, pointing to the name on the hull.

"Oh, it's supposed to be *Tamarack*. One of my boys was painting it this spring, and he got into a fight with his brother and never got the job done. By the way," he said, sticking out his hand, "my name is Arnold Bjornson."

Sally's father. Jonas stood for a moment as it sunk in. He took the hand. "I'm Jonas Anderson."

"You kind of surprised me," Arnold said. "I'm not used to seeing tourists this early in the morning, but welcome to the island anyway. You'll find it's a pretty place. Now if you'll excuse me, I have to finish getting the gear ready." He turned away.

"I'm not a tourist. I'm the new preacher over at Little Oslo."

Arnold turned back. He had thinning, graying hair, a narrow, weathered face, and was short and compact. "Ah," he said, "you are Sally's new boyfriend. Pleased to meet you." He sounded pleased.

Meeting this man who seemed so pleasant jarred Jonas. He said the first thing that came to mind. "I know what you did to her." Jonas got tears in his eyes. He felt like a fool. He wiped the tears on the back of his sleeve.

Arnold took a step toward him, a puzzled look on his face.

"What? I didn't catch that."

"I know what you did to her."

"I don't know what you're talking about," he said quietly.

Jonas stared uncertainly at him. "You know what you did to her."

"What has she been telling you that I did to her?" His voice was still soft, but it had an edge to it.

"You ... she ... " Jonas stammered. What had he gotten himself into? He glanced around. He saw a couple of other fishermen carrying gear to tugs at other docks.

"I think you should tell me what she's been saying about me." Jonas looked back at Arnold, trying to read his face. Arnold nodded, encouraging him to speak.

"You forced yourself on her," Jonas said.

Arnold stiffened. He seemed to grow as he pushed himself up on his toes. "She's telling lies to you. Damn lies, that little bitch." His eyes were suddenly small and hard like bullets.

"You're the one who's lying." Jonas thought about Jesus calling the Pharisees names: hypocrites, snakes, brood of vipers. He wanted to scream at the man: Lying hypocrite! You're lower than a snake! You have snake spit on your lips! But he was a preacher. He was supposed to be master of his tongue.

Arnold leaned forward on his toes, his fists clenching. Jonas thought he was going to get hit. Then Arnold dropped back on his heels and loosened his hands. "Sorry about my language, preacher. I have to remember you're her boyfriend. Of course you're going to believe her. But, hey, do I look like the kinda guy who would mess with his daughter? That's disgusting even to think about. Where in the world did she come up with such an idea?"

"You're Samantha's father."

Arnold just shook his head sadly. "That's disgusting. She's covering up for being fast with her boyfriend. I always told her: *be sure your sins will find you out*. Her sins found her out."

Jonas knew he should leave right then and he started to. He brushed past Arnold on the dock. But he couldn't leave. He spun around. "Now I know why Sally has never looked at you again. You're evil."

Arnold gave him a bemused look. "She sure has you wrapped around her finger."

"She doesn't have me wrapped around her finger."

Arnold grinned. "Maybe she does; maybe she doesn't." Arnold stopped grinning. "But I can tell you one thing for sure—that girl's lying to you."

Jonas shook his head fiercely.

Arnold held up his hand to keep Jonas from interrupting him. "But her lying is understandable. It's understandable, and once you understand, you won't be so hard on her. You see, women want it as much as men. Maybe more even. But they don't like to admit it. They keep it a big secret and act like it's only us men who want it. But it's true; women want it. I don't blame her for getting pregnant. She wanted it just like all the other women since Eve. God made women to want it bad. But it's hard for women to admit it. So when they get in trouble, they tend to lie a little. But don't be too hard on her for lying. It's just the way women are." He winked at Jonas. Jonas hit him as hard as he could in the eye that had winked.

"Uffda," Jonas said, looking at his fist, shocked at how it hurt, not quite believing he had hit a man. He looked up at Arnold who was touching his eye with his hand. There was blood coming from a cut above his eye.

"You little turd!" he growled, moving toward Jonas. Jonas decided to kick him in the crotch next.

Somebody grabbed Jonas from behind and held him. "What the hell's goin' on, Daddy?" said whoever was holding him. Jonas tried to wriggle away. He couldn't.

"Some guy lookin' for a beating, Eugene," her daddy said as he smashed his fist into Jonas' face.

He drew back his fist to swing again, but Jonas spoke first. "He raped Sally," he said. Maybe whoever was holding him would let go now. He didn't.

"Lies! He's lying, Eugene!" muttered Arnold. Again his fist smashed into Jonas' face. Again. Jonas thought he would pass out.

"Hey, Daddy, give me a turn," said the one holding him. Arnold held Jonas, twisting one of his arms behind his back so hard Jonas thought it was coming out of its socket. He saw a fist coming toward his stomach. It knocked the wind out of him. He bent over, holding his stomach, gagging, gasping for breath. The last thing he remembered was the man stepping back, a foot flashing upward toward his groin, and pain exploding like a tree hit by lightning.

When he came to, he was being dragged off the dock onto the beach. The hands dropped him. He curled up and drifted to sleep. He woke, his face a mass of pain. Slowly he remembered that he had been beaten. He didn't dare move for fear he would be hit again. But there was no sound except the lapping of the lake against the shore. When he looked, he could only open one eye. All the tugs were gone. When he tried to stand, a shock went through his ribs. His loins ached fiercely. Slowly he made it to his feet and began stumbling back along the trail the way he had come that morning.

38.

When Jonas staggered back to Little Oslo, the first person he met was Samantha, playing outside Sally's cabin. She took one look at him and started to cry.

"I look that bad, huh?" muttered Jonas as Samantha ran into the cabin. He kept on walking. All he could think about was getting to Philena's house where he could lie down. Daniel's tug would be out on the lake. He needed some place to lie down.

"Jonas!" called Sally. He stopped and slowly turned toward

her. "What happened to you!" she cried running toward him.

"I got hurt," said Jonas. He turned once more toward Philena's. He wanted to lie down.

"What happened?" she said, tugging at his arm.

"I just want to lie down."

"Come in and lie down." Jonas allowed her to lead him into the cabin and to her bed. After he painfully lowered himself to the mattress she said, "I'll get you a cold cloth for the swelling." She went to pump water. He fell asleep.

The cold cloths on his face wakened him. He pushed them away. "It will help the swelling," she said, gently putting them back. He was too tired to think. He fell back to sleep. Sometimes he was dimly aware of the changing of the cloths. One time he heard a man's voice. Another time a lamp was lit.

Then he awoke to the sound and smell of eggs frying. His head still hurt, but he didn't fall back to sleep. He opened his eyes. Only one opened; the other was still swollen shut. He was facing the wall with bright sunshine streaming in from the east window above him. He turned to face the room. Daniel sat on a chair beside the bed eating sunny-side up eggs. Sally brought Daniel a roll with strawberry jelly on it.

"You're awake," she said to Jonas.

"Yes."

"Good," said Daniel. "You had us worried. How do you feel then?"

"My head and side hurt and I can't open my one eye, but I'm alive."

"Can I make you some eggs?" asked Sally.

Jonas nodded. Sally went to make the eggs.

"Ya, who beat on you?" asked Daniel, an edge on his voice.

Jonas was silent. "Who beat you then?" Daniel asked again. Still Jonas was silent.

"Did you get hit so hard you can't remember?"

"I remember."

"Tell me then. We got to make this right, you know. I should radio the sheriff."

Jonas was still silent.

"So you don't want to say," said Daniel. He took a bite of an egg. "Ya, Jonas, whoever did this to you could've killed you. The island can't have this kind of thing happening."

Jonas shook his head.

"Were you getting vengeance then?" When Jonas still didn't respond, Daniel went back to eating his eggs.

Sally brought Jonas eggs and a roll with jelly on it. "Start with this," she said. "If you want more, I'll make you more." Jonas sat up and ate.

Daniel finished his eggs. "Ya, I do not think it is good to order a man to do something that he is not ready to do. But, uffda, Jonas, you do tempt me. Nay doggone. We got to make this right, you know." Jonas had never had Daniel angry at him. But still he was silent. Daniel stood up. "Ya, there are fish out there waiting for me. Jonas, when you are ready to talk, I'll still have my ears." He left.

"Jonas, who hurt you?" asked Sally, sitting on the bed.

"Your daddy and your brother."

Her eyes grew big. "What?"

He repeated himself.

"You've never met my daddy and my brother," she said, her eyes flashing.

"I asked around and found out that your daddy lives on the East Side. You told me his tug is called *Tamarack*. So I went to see him."

"Why?" she demanded.

"I wanted to see him. I wanted to see what a man who would rape his daughter looks like." He shook his head, his eyes down.

"I ended up hitting him. I didn't go there to fight him."

"You have no right having anything to do with my family," she stormed. "No right. I don't want anything to do with him. I hate him."

Jonas stared at the floor through his one good eye. He seemed to cause nothing but misery for Sally.

"I want to know everything. Tell me everything that

happened," she said. She sat down on the end of the bed.

"I thought you didn't want anything to do with your daddy," he said, closing his eye.

"I don't. But now that you went and got into a fight with him, I have to know everything."

"Are you sure?"

"I am sure. I don't want to have anything to do with him. I don't. I don't. I don't. I want to forget he exists. I want to forget him completely. But now I can't forget him because you dredged him up. Don't you see? I can't stand him. But now that you've dredged him up, I have to know all about it." Jonas opened his eye and looked puzzled. "Don't try to understand," she said. "Just tell me what happened."

"I went to see him. I didn't have any plan. I just wanted to see him. When I got there I found his tug, only now it looks like the name is *Tamar* because your brothers got in a fight while they were painting it and they never finished."

"How'd you find that out?"

"I was standing on the dock staring at the name when your daddy came carrying gear. He told me."

"When did I tell you that his tug was named the *Tamarack*?" she interrupted him.

"When you told me about him attacking you. You said that he and your brothers came home on the *Tamarack* from fishing."

"I don't remember but go on."

"We talked a little bit, and then it popped out of my mouth that I knew what he had done to you. First he acted mad when I told him, and I thought he was gonna hit me, but then he started talking instead. He said you were lying to cover up for wanting it from that boy. He said I shouldn't be mad at you because that's just the way women are. I can't remember all he said, but at some point he winked at me. When he winked at me, this volcano erupted in me. I went berserk. I hit him right in the eye that winked at me."

"You hit him first?" she asked, amazed.

"Yup. At first I didn't want to believe that I hit him. But

my hand hurt. When I hit him he acted surprised. He stood there like he didn't know what to do next. I was gonna kick him in the crotch if he came at me."

"Jonas, you were going to kick him in the crotch?" she asked, incredulously.

"Yes."

She started to laugh. She laughed and laughed so hard that the bed jiggled and Jonas' ribs hurt. "Jonas, I can't believe you'd do that." She laughed some more. She slid over next to Jonas and hugged him.

"Ouch!"

"Sorry," she said, easing up, but still laughing. "You hit him in the eye?" Jonas nodded. "And you were gonna kick him in the crotch?" Another nod. She laughed and kissed Jonas on the head. "Notice, I didn't kiss you where it hurts." She kissed his head again. She laughed some more.

Then she began to cry. "I hate him but I love him. I'm so glad you hit him in the eye," she said fiercely, "but I'm sad, too." Her voice dropped. Then raising it she cried, "He's my daddy!" Jonas painfully eased his arm around her shoulder. She shook it off.

"He *was* my daddy. But not anymore." She stopped crying, wiping her tears on the blanket. "What happened next?"

"Your brother Eugene grabbed me from behind. Your daddy got a mean look in his eye and hit me over and over. Then your daddy held me while your brother hit me. When your daddy let go of me, I fell on the dock. Your daddy kicked me when I was down. The next thing I remember is being dragged across the sand. I fell back to sleep. When I got awake all the tugs were gone. When I had the strength, I got up and walked back here."

"You shouldn't have had anything to do with my daddy. He's a bad man. I never told anyone before what he did to me, because I thought if I told and he found out, he'd kill me. Now *you* went and told him. I'll never be safe."

"I guess I messed up again," Jonas said. She nodded. "I will sleep here and keep you safe," Jonas offered.

She looked at him with a sad smile on her face. "Jonas, I wasn't going to have anything to do with you after you left me. Now look what you've done."

"What do you mean?"

"I means it's going to be hard to send you away now that my daddy beat you up."

"Don't send me away. I'll protect you."

"Jonas, you can't protect me."

"I can, too."

"Jonas, nobody can protect me from my daddy." Jonas was silent. "Nobody can protect me from what he did to me. Nobody."

"God can protect you."

"Then why the hell didn't he protect me the first time?"

"I don't know," said Jonas, flinching at her language.

"And why the hell didn't he protect you?"

"Maybe because I swung first," said Jonas with a crooked grin that hurt. Then he added, "Please don't swear."

"Jonas, I'll say 'hell' if I want to. Don't sit there and act so holy. Good grief, you may be a preacher, but you just got in a fight with my daddy."

"You're right. I'm not much of a preacher. You can say 'hell' around me." For the first time he felt a deep shudder within himself: he had attacked a man.

"Jonas, don't be too hard on yourself. You're a preacher and a human being." She patted him on the knee. "But, Jonas, I need to be alone now."

"I'll sleep outside. Close."

"Jonas, I appreciate the offer. But no. Can't you see that I can have you in my life only when I choose you? I can't have you in my life because my daddy beat you up. Or because you make wild promises to protect me. I can have you in my life when I am ready. I was ready and you left me. I was ready and I told you the most horrible secret of my life and you left me. Now I am not ready to have you back. Some day . . . maybe. But not now. Now you have to leave."

Jonas stood up. He felt weak, but he left.

39.

While Jonas was recovering at Philena's, Brawn and Hank came to talk to him. Theresa poured strong coffee for the four of them. They all sat around the table drinking.

Brawn got right to the point. "We want to take care of the scum who beat the snot out of you. Whoever did this to you is askin' for it." Hank nodded in agreement.

"I don't want more trouble," Jonas said.

"No trouble at all," Hank said. Hank was a thin man of about thirty-five who was completely bald. He was a member of Daniel's crew and had been courting Philena for some time. "You just tell us who used your face for a rug, and we'll take care of 'em."

"I got into trouble in the first place by being vengeful. No more vengeance," said Jonas, feeling tired.

"From the looks of it," said Brawn, "you got into trouble tryin' to do the job yourself. You needed help. We'll help," he said, smacking a huge fist into his palm.

Jonas kept putting them off.

Finally Hank said to Brawn, "Maybe taking a few punches has turned this lad into a clam without a shell. Maybe he's decided to let people walk on him."

"Let's lay off a few days," said Brawn. "Give him a few days to heal. Then he can join us. That'd be best. He oughta be able to get in a few licks with us."

After they left Jonas wrote a letter to his family and church asking them to keep praying that he'd love the people of the island. He assured them this was his deepest need.

40.

Late the next Saturday afternoon, when Daniel had the day's catch stored, he suggested that he and Jonas go for a walk. They left Little Oslo and walked north in silence along the shore. There was a brisk wind and the sound of waves pounding the shore. Six days had passed since the beating, and the last of the bruises had disappeared from Jonas' face. Even his ribs had healed.

"Well then, how are things with you and Sally?" Daniel said when they were a quarter of a mile down the beach.

"Not so good. She doesn't want to see me for awhile."

"Jonas, you've been doing a lot of growing up since you came to this island."

"I have?"

"Ya." They walked on in silence.

"Why do you say that?"

"I've been keeping an eye on you." Daniel stooped and picked up a piece of driftwood from the sand. He turned it over a couple of times and handed it to Jonas. "Run your hands over this."

Jonas touched it. It was a smooth piece of wood about three inches in diameter and eight inches long with a knobby head. "Take it with you," Daniel said as he started to walk again. "That's what the lake does to wood. Polishes it. See the grain. The lake brings out the grain in wood, too. I can see life working on you like the lake worked on that piece of wood." Abruptly he said, "I've been thinking about who beat you up. You need some help dealing with that."

"I promised not to tell."

"I know you did, but I made no such promise. The person who raped Sally is the person who beat you up."

Jonas gasped. "You know about Sally's daddy? Sally is sure no one knows. How do you know?"

"Ya, sometimes I just know things. Sally wouldn't tell who raped her when she moved in with Alice and me. You knew she lived with us when she had her baby?" Jonas nodded. "And here she was, only sixteen years old. She said it wasn't her boyfriend. 'A stranger,' she said. I didn't believe her. It had to have been someone from the island. Sally told no one, but I knew sooner or later she'd tell you. You are so young and innocent. You call forth confessions from people, Jonas. Then when you showed up with your face beat in and refused to say who had done it, I knew it was someone with power. Ya, only family has the power to make us keep secrets that destroy us. You don't have a family here. Sally does."

"I promised not to tell."

"I haven't told anyone and I won't. Of course, there's much speculation as to who did it, including that it was Sally's brothers because they don't like you messing around with Sally. You and Sally may one day tell, but not me."

"What should I do?"

"First, tell me what you did."

"Daniel, please don't make matters worse. *I* made them worse. Sally is so angry at me, she won't have anything to do with me. I don't want to make matters worse. Please don't make things worse."

Daniel touched Jonas on the arm. Jonas stood with his head bowed. "I don't want to make matters worse," Jonas repeated.

"I know you don't," said Daniel. "I can't promise that things won't get worse, but you have a better chance of not making things worse if you're not walking alone. You would've been better off talking to someone before getting in a fight with Sally's daddy."

"I have God."

"Yes, you have God. And God told you to go fight Sally's daddy, right?"

"Not exactly."

"What do you mean, 'not exactly'?"

"God didn't tell me to fight her daddy. He hasn't said anything about her daddy."

"Have you asked him what to do about her daddy?"

"No."

"I didn't think so."

"I'm afraid to be too sure about what God tells me anymore. I sinned so bad when I said God had called me to another island and he hadn't."

"Ya, it's good to be a little scared to announce God's

thoughts."

"Why?"

"As you so ably showed us all," Daniel said with a chuckle, "it's easy to put the wrong words in God's mouth. It is good that you're afraid of speaking for God. It is also good for you to learn that God, as a general rule, works through people. Who do you suppose told me who beat you up?"

"God?"

"I believe so. But I didn't know for sure until you told me. I'm not offering to be God in your life, Jonas, but I am offering to help you hear him more clearly. Right now you're out on the lake like that piece of driftwood once was. I'm not going to rescue you. But I'll watch and listen for Jesus with you."

"I like that," said Jonas. For a moment he had an urge to throw himself in Daniel's arms and cry: "Save me!" Instead he took a deep breath and sighed.

"I went to see Sally's daddy. I didn't plan to fight him. I just wanted to see him. I wanted to see what someone looks like who would do something so terrible. But when I got there and saw him, I walked up to him and told him I knew what he had done to his daughter. I don't know why I did that. I got angry at him working on his boat, his life going on as if nothing had happened. Sally keeping it a secret from everybody. I just wanted him to know I knew.

"At first he was mad at me. But pretty soon he was explaining why Sally lied to me because she didn't want to admit that she wanted it. He said that's the way women are. Then he winked at me, and I remembered Sally telling me that he winked at her the next day when her mother was accusing her of spending the night with her boyfriend. When he winked, I blew up. I hit him in the eye. I was surprised how my hand hurt. He was surprised that I hit him, and I don't think he knew what to do. I'm ashamed to say this, Daniel, but I was gonna kick him in his crotch next. I was so angry at what he did to Sally. I've never hit anybody in

my life . . . well, not an adult. I used to fight with my younger
brothers . . . but I have never gotten into a fight with anyone
outside my family.

"Then one of Sally's brothers came up behind me and held
me so I couldn't move, and her daddy started hitting me. Then
her daddy held me and her brother hit me. Then I fell on the
ground and her daddy . . . " For the first time since the
beating, Jonas began to cry. Daniel put a hand on his shoulder.
"He kicked me in the crotch and I don't remember any more."
Jonas sobbed. He rubbed the piece of driftwood as he cried. It
was smooth, solid, and knobby.

"I'm glad you hit Sally's daddy," said Daniel.

"What?"

"Ya, that's what I said. I'm glad you hit her daddy." He
paused as if thinking. "Yes, Jonas," he squeezed his shoulder
and let go, "I must confess that rage jumps up in me, too, at
what Sally's daddy did. I have a hankering to take a swing at
him. All I'd have to do is pass along the word to a few other
men, and they'd be glad to go over there and step on that
low-down snail. I could go for some vengeance. What
happened to Sally was horrible." He started to walk rapidly.
Jonas followed.

"But my own urge for vengeance isn't the reason I'm glad
you hit him. I'm glad you did it because then you were like
Peter taking a swing at Jesus' attackers when they came to
arrest him." He stopped by a boulder, turned, and faced
Jonas. "But as angry as I am, I know that they that live by
the fist die by the fist. You remember what Jesus did when
Peter sliced off the ear of one of those cockroaches coming to
arrest him?"

"He touched the man's ear and healed it."

"Yes, we have to remember that," said Daniel.

"What do you mean?"

"In the long run, Jesus had healing in mind, not busting
people's faces."

41.

Jonas brought Jackson a bucket of clams and some fish. Jackson had been drinking. He wasn't drunk, but he wasn't exactly tied to the dock either. He was morose and didn't respond to Jonas' attempts at conversation. Jonas fixed the fish and clams, and they ate silently together.

After the meal Jackson took a short pull on the bottle. Jonas asked about his garden.

"What garden?" he asked sullenly.

"The garden of Eden," said Jonas, irritated with Jackson.

"Huh?" he grunted.

"The garden that you and I planted," answered Jonas, glad that Jackson hadn't picked up on his smart comment. "How is it?"

"I haven't looked at it lately."

"Let's look at it." He stood up and grabbed the back of Jackson's chair, wheeling it toward the door. Jackson reached back and yanked at Jonas' arm. The chair whipped around, forcing Jonas to one knee. "Do not ever take a man where he is not ready to go," he hissed. Jonas bowed his head, his eyes blurred with restrained anger. He thought about making a fast move of his own and knocking Jackson over, chair and all. But, Jesus, he had already punched one man. He wasn't going to start another fight. He had just been trying to shake Jackson out of his bad mood. He thought working in the garden would be good.

He sighed, relaxed, and waited for Jackson to let go. His eyes cleared. He noticed that one of the bolts to Jackson's back wheel was coming loose. He'd have to tighten it.

Jackson let go. Jonas got up and went over to the cupboard where Jackson kept his tools.

"What the hell are you doing?" demanded Jackson.

"The bolt on your back wheel is coming loose," said Jonas, pulling out a small wrench and motioning with it. Jonas tightened the nut, put the wrench back, and headed for the door.

"Where the hell are you going?"

Jonas stopped and looked at Jackson. "To the lake, I guess."

"I thought you wanted to do some gardening."

"I didn't think you . . . "

"I'm ready now."

Jonas had to do some thinking if he was ready. He still had an inkling to overturn Jackson's chair and spill him on the floor. "Okay," he said, finally.

Even the weeds weren't doing particularly well in Jackson's garden. The moss hadn't done the trick. So, they started to clear out what weeds there were.

"Why don't you stop drinking, Jackson?" It was a question Jonas had wanted to ask for some time.

"Why should I?"

"*Wine is a mocker and strong drink is raging. Be not drunk with wine but be filled with the Spirit.*"

"I like my spirits in a bottle. As long as I have a bottle I have spirits." He looked at the bottle on the chair a few feet away. "The Spirit you're talking about isn't available like my spirits."

"The Holy Ghost is always with us."

"Was he with you when I had you on your knee in there? It appears the raging spirits in a bottle are stronger than your Spirit."

"He was with me."

"How?"

"You tell me."

"Watch your prideful tongue, son."

"You know, don't you?"

"Know what?"

"You know about the Holy Ghost."

Jackson pulled himself along the ground to the next clump of weeds.

"I know about the Holy Ghost."

"Why don't you give yourself to him instead of the bottle?"

"Remember, I was once an Episcopal priest."

"Yes."

"Remember how I told you after I went back to that burned-down school I decided to be good. I tried. I went to seminary. But in the end, I went back to drinking. It was like a race between the spirits and the Spirit. After seminary they sent me to minister to the Indians in Minnesota. They sent me to minister to the Indians that the Great White Father corralled on godforsaken patches of land called reservations. The Indians drank firewater and so did I. After awhile I stopped trying to fool anyone that I was a priest.

"I started back east and, when I got to the shore of this lake, I started painting. I couldn't support myself as a priest, so I took up painting. In the summers I'd come to this island and prowl it and paint it. Then four winters ago I fell down drunk. When they found me they had to take me to Milwaukee, and the doc cut off both my legs to save my life from gangrene. I knew the bottle had won the race of the spirits then." He stopped and looked longingly at the bottle on the seat of his chair at the end of the garden. "Those spirits are powerful."

"The Holy Ghost is more powerful."

"You can look at me and still say that?"

"Yes."

"You can look at yourself and say that?"

"What do you mean?"

"I hear the gossip of the island. I know what goes on."

"What?"

"Recently you were beat severely. Currently Sally is ignoring you."

"I am weak but the Holy Ghost is strong."

"If the Holy Ghost is so strong, why doesn't he help you? Why didn't he help the Indians?"

"He is helping me."

"You could have fooled me."

Jonas was crouching, pulling on a deep-rooted weed with both hands. Straining against the weed he said, "Jesus went through weakness in his life, too. From the moment he hit the Garden of Gethsemane until he was dead, he was weak, but he was being helped. An angel helped him in the garden. And it was okay for him to be weak. For awhile. If he wouldn't have been weak, he wouldn't have showed how powerful God was." The weed let loose and Jonas went back on his butt. He looked over at Jackson who had stopped weeding. Their eyes met.

"Do you really believe your weakness will show how powerful God is?"

"Yes."

"Do you always believe that, Jonas? You never have any doubts?"

"I have doubts," Jonas admitted. Jackson didn't say anything. "I had bad doubts after I survived the storm. I thought God had told me to go to another island. After he washed me back on this island I realized I must have made up the call to another island. If I put words in God's mouth once, maybe I have before. Maybe I will again. How can I know if it's me talking or God? Then I went and threw a punch at a man. I started a fight. Sometimes I wonder how long God will put up with someone like me. Yes, I have doubts. Big doubts." Jonas still sat on his haunches holding the clump of weeds. He tossed them aside and went back to weeding. He wished he had more faith.

"It's funny," said Jackson. "When I heard that you'd been washed overboard miles out in the lake and swept back to this island, I was almost persuaded to believe in the power of God again."

"You were?" said Jonas, stopping weeding.

"Yes," said Jackson. "That lake has taken many men. I've never heard of another man the lake not only gave up, but delivered fifteen miles back to this island. That seemed like a story out of the Bible. It made me think that maybe if God could overcome the lake, maybe he could overcome the bottle." He looked back at his chair. Jonas followed his eyes. They looked at the bottle on the seat.

"But who knows," Jackson said.

That night Jonas wrote a letter to his family and church asking that they pray that God use his weaknesses to love the people of Norsk Island.

42.

The last Sunday in June, Jonas sat in front of the people of his church to confess for the second time. Daniel and his wife, Alice, Philena, Hank, Theresa, and Brawn were there. This time Sally was there, too. Jonas had fought the idea of confessing. He had a hard time not cheering every time he remembered hitting Sally's daddy. He also had a hard time not feeling deep shame every time he remembered.

"As all of you know, I got into a fight. I was angry and I punched a man, and then I took a beating. Part of me is glad I threw the first punch. I can't tell you why I fought because it involves others, but I can tell you I felt justified." Jonas was careful not to look at Sally. "The person I got into a fight with had done something very wrong. I was angry, and so I swung at him. Ever since then, I've tried to convince myself I was right, since he had done something so wrong. But Jesus keeps washing away my excuses with wave after wave of scripture.

"*Dearly beloved, avenge not yourselves, but rather give place unto wrath: for it is written, Vengeance is mine: I will repay, saith the Lord. Therefore, if your enemy hunger, feed him; if he is thirsty, give him drink: for in so doing thou shalt heap coals of fire on his head. Be not overcome of evil, but overcome evil with good. Romans 12:19-21.*

"I tried to take vengeance on a man. I did not try to overcome evil with good, but with my fists."

Jonas sat in silence for a long time. He was confused. When he confessed to the church that he had run away, he cried the whole time. Now he didn't shed a tear.

"I can't think of anything more to say. I was wrong. I need to be forgiven by God and by you."

"Jonas," said Philena, "this is much bigger than you. You can't carry all the guilt." She was sitting next to Hank who had come to worship. Daniel nodded in agreement.

"What do you mean?" asked Jonas.

"I don't know," she said. "It's like a storm has swept through the island and brought ruin. You came to help. Instead, you have a round with one man about his ruined house, and then you act as if the devastation of the island is your fault."

Jonas was puzzled.

"Jonas," said Daniel, "something is wrong with your confession. It's like you took a pebble from a beach that has boulders on it and threw it into the lake. Then you ask us to tell you that the beach is clean."

"I want to be clean," said Jonas. "That's why I confessed. I want to be clean."

"Now I understand," said Daniel. "At least it's beginning to make sense." Then he stopped.

"What makes sense?" asked Jonas.

"Tell me more about wanting to be clean."

This is no way to be a preacher, Jonas thought. Everyone's eyes were on him. What did I mean about wanting to be clean? "I feel defiled because I took vengeance when I should have been letting God take vengeance. I want to be clean and pure. I want to be white as snow."

"Were you feeling defiled before you got into the fight?" Daniel asked.

The question stopped Jonas short. Of course not, he was going to say. I wasn't defiled until I sinned. But something stopped him. "I think maybe I was," he said.

"That's what I thought," said Daniel. "You were trying to clean up your life by fighting this man."

"But that doesn't make any sense," protested Jonas.

"Perhaps this man has sinned against you. Perhaps he has defiled *you*. Perhaps to be clean you need to forgive more than you need to seek forgiveness."

"I just want to be clean."

"And innocent," added Philena.

"Let's lay hands on Jonas and pray for him. He is walking though deep waters," said Daniel. Brawn and Hank hung back, but the others gathered around him and prayed. When

Sally laid her hand on his shoulder, it was the first time she touched him since she asked him to leave her cabin after the beating. The only thing later that Jonas remembered from the prayer was Daniel saying, "Lord, take Jonas into the lake as many times as you need to clean him up." He wondered what that meant.

43.

Jonas walked north along the shore. It was the first Sunday of July, the first Sunday after his second confession. They had sung several songs, then Jonas told the story of Jesus' arrest and healing the high priest's servant's ear. Jonas went on to talk about Jesus teaching us to love our enemies.

Alice was deaf. Daniel had developed a method for talking to her through motions and touch. Alice read lips, but sometimes she had a hard time understanding. At those times Jonas stopped talking long enough for Daniel to use his hands to tell Alice what had been said. Jonas liked watching the way Daniel's hands flowed in so many directions when he talked to Alice with them.

After worship everyone went home. Jonas ate lunch at Daniel and Alice's and then went for a walk. For the first time since the storm he approached the place where the undertow deposited him after the storm.

He picked his way up the steep slope to the top of the bluff, the highest point on the island, and watched the lake. The waves crashed against the rocks below. He traced the path of the undertow, wondering what forms beneath the surface caused the tow.

Looking back along the shore, he saw a woman leave Little Oslo and begin to walk in his direction. He glanced back across the water. Even from this height he couldn't see the mainland. The woman was closer now. He could see that it was Philena. When she reached the bluff she climbed through the boulders up the slope. The lake was calm and blue. Philena stood beside him, catching her breath, watching the lake with him.

"This is where you washed ashore, right?" she asked when her breath was even.

"Yes. You can see where the undertow gathers strength right there, then curves in and bounces off the shore. That's where I surfaced."

"I'm glad God brought you back to the island."

"You are?" Jonas looked at her for the first time since she reached the top of the bluff. Tears formed in the corners of his eyes. He looked back at the lake and sighed. Even though she had told him that before, he was glad to hear it again.

"Yes. You spoke of loving our enemies this morning. I never heard that before. You spoke like an old man even though you're only twenty."

"What do you mean?"

"You spoke with wisdom. The island needs your wisdom. All too often the East Side people and the Little Oslo people act like enemies. But I came out to talk to you about Sally. She needs you."

"Needs me?" Again Jonas looked at her. "She doesn't act like she needs me."

She turned directly toward Jonas. "She needs you." Philena's eyes were a pale blue. *She needs you,* those eyes said.

She needs me. He breathed deeply, sighed, and turned back to the lake. She needs me. I know I need her, but she needs me, too. He tried on the thought like a new pair of boots from his mother.

"How do you know she needs me?" Jonas asked, half afraid she would take the words back.

"I haven't talked to her but I know. Twice lately I've seen her watching you. One morning she was watching you while you were sleeping on Daniel's boat. Another time she watched from the trees when you were coming back from fishing. When the boat docked and you stepped off the boat, she left for her cabin. I could tell by the look on her face."

"Why doesn't she say she needs me?"

"She will. In time. But in the meantime there is something you should know. Everyone on the island knows who beat you up. Everyone. It was Arnold and his son from the East Side. And everyone knows you took the first swing. Folks besides Arnold and his boy from the East Side say they saw you take the first swing. Nobody knows why. But there are lots of ideas floating around about why. Maybe he wouldn't give you permission to marry Sally. Or maybe her daddy did her wrong and you went after him. Or maybe you got Sally pregnant and, when you told Arnold, he insulted you and Sally, so you took a swing at him. There are lots of possibilities folks are mulling over."

"What do you think happened?" Jonas said, his voice barely above a whisper.

"I think Sally's daddy did her wrong and real bad. It's always been a mystery about who got Sally pregnant. Nobody believed it was a stranger. And her boyfriend at the time swore it wasn't him. I know the boy and I believed him. It was so hush-hush I thought it was her brother. It never occurred to me that it might be her daddy. But after you took a swing at him, it came to me. I haven't said a word to anyone else, but, if *I* thought it, someone else will. There are some Little Oslo people who would like an excuse to beat Arnold senseless. He has a way of raising hackles. Religious and always mouthing off."

"I promised Sally I wouldn't tell."

"You don't have to tell me anything, Jonas."

"Maybe I should leave the island. I keep causing so much trouble."

"Jonas, you talked about loving your enemies this morning. You said loving your enemies is hard. It is hard." She pointed to the rocks below and said, "It's as hard as coming from the lake into those rocks. Most men who came at those rocks from the direction you did died. Most men who love their enemies die. Jesus did." Jonas looked down at the water and the rocks. Even in a calm lake the waves whispered and slid ominously among the rocks.

"There are enemies on this island," she continued. "There were enemies on this island long before you arrived. Jonas, you came through those rocks, not on a calm day like today, but during a storm. You came through and lived. You came through those rocks and told us to love our enemies. Don't leave."

They watched the water circulating through the rocks for a long time.

"What should I do?" asked Jonas.

"Love Sally. She's going to need you. And love your enemies and the enemies of your enemies." She put her hand on Jonas' back as she finished. They stood there watching the water slip around and over the rocks. He felt the warmth of her hand. He wished that she would put her arm around him and hold him like his mother.

She took away her hand and they walked back to the west side.

44.

It was the darkest part of the night just before dawn with the *Edna* chugging out to the fishing grounds to pull in the gill nets and pick the fish. Brawn, Hank, and Jonas stood waiting to reach the nets.

"Jonas, I found out who treated your face like a dance floor," Hank said out of the darkness.

"Good," came Brawn's voice. "I haven't forgotten that somebody's due one."

Jonas was silent. Suddenly the night air turned clammy.

"It was Sally's father and brother," Hank said.

"I thought it had to be some scrub fisherman from the East Side," said Brawn.

"How'd you find out?" asked Jonas, struggling to keep a quaver out of his voice.

"I was digging some salt at the salt lick the other day. An

old fellow there from the East Side was wondering why you picked a fight with Arnold. I asked what made him think you picked the fight. I acted like I knew who was fighting, even though I don't believe you started it, Jonas. He told me he saw you take the first swing. He was on the boat right next to Arnold's when he heard yelling and looked over and saw you take a swing at Arnold. I told him I didn't know what you and Arnold had to fight about."

"I promised Sally I wouldn't tell."

"Speaking of Sally," said Brawn. "I haven't seen the two of you together lately. Something happen between you?"

Jonas gripped the net line in the darkness. He thought about the unsuspecting fish caught in the gill net. Even though it was dark he could imagine their mouths moving silently when the net plucked them out of the water. Even fish get taken where they don't want to go.

Brawn's chuckle spilled out of the darkness. "Maybe she didn't like you trying to whip her old man."

Silence returned like a net settling at the right depth.

Brawn snorted. "Maybe she's unhappy that you didn't finish the job. She's had nothin' to do with her old man since she moved to Little Oslo."

"Brawn, take it easy," said Hank. "Don't take offense, Jonas; he's just kidding about Sally. That's your business."

"But I wasn't kidding about helping you take care of Arnold and his boy," said Brawn. "I offered when you came back with your busted face. I still mean to help you."

"I remember," said Jonas, "but I don't want to hurt them."

"If you didn't want to hurt him, how come you took a swing in the first place?"

"I did want to hurt him then. I wanted to hurt him and I wanted to hurt him bad," said Jonas.

"So you were outnumbered the first time. Me and Hank and some others will help even the number. Then you can hurt him bad like you wanted to in the first place."

"But I don't want to hurt him now."

"You just said you wanted to hurt him bad. You sound to

me like you still wanna hurt him. I don't know what your
reason was, but it seems to me you got even more reason to
wanna hurt him bad now," suggested Brawn.

Daniel cut back on the throttle and began to angle the tug
next to the buoys that marked the gill nets.

"I have a good reason," said Jonas quietly. "Good reason to
want to hurt Arnold. But since I hit him the first time, I saw
a place in the Bible where Jesus told his followers to love their
enemies. I follow Jesus. Arnold is my enemy. I will love him,
not hurt him."

"How are you going to love him?" asked Hank, his voice as
quiet as Jonas'.

"I don't know."

"I know," said Brawn. "We'll hit him a few times. When he's
on the ground begging for mercy, then you can love him."

"No," said Jonas. "I don't know how to love an enemy like
Arnold, but it can't be to beat him up like he beat me up. I
didn't love him when I hit him, and he didn't love me when
he hit me. That's not love."

"What are you going to do then?" asked Brawn.

"I'm going to pray."

Brawn snorted. "Sorry, preacher," he said.

45.

Jonas huddled on a makeshift bench under a canvas canopy
he had rigged on Daniel's boat. He was wrapped in a wool
blanket Sally had made, watching the steady rain wash across
the deck. The boat rose and fell and occasionally bumped
against the dock.

Jonas opened the blanket and looked at the book again. *Ye
have heard that it hath been said, "Ye shall love your neighbor
and hate your enemy."* He slipped his finger between the
pages to keep his place as he shut the book and pulled the
blanket around him.

The deck was slick with rain. For an instant he saw a picture of Sally's father slipping on the deck, hitting his head, blood running onto the deck, the rain washing it away. Jonas blinked to erase the picture from his mind. He opened the blanket and the book and read again, *But I say unto you, Love your enemies, bless them that curse you, do good to them that hate you, and pray for them that despitefully use you, and persecute you.*

Jonas stared out from under the canopy through the rain at the gray marble sky. He looked at the place on the deck where, in his mind, Arnold had gashed his head. He imagined covering Arnold with his blanket and bandaging his head. His blood was on his hands as he bandaged.

Back to the book. *That ye may be children of your father which is in heaven ... Abba! Abba!* I want to be your son! he prayed. He imagined holding out his hand and letting the rain wash off the blood. He looked down at the book. *... for he maketh his sun to rise on the evil and the good, and sendeth rain on the just and the unjust.*

He peered through the rain but he couldn't see Sally's cabin. She was a just woman. Last night she came out on the porch and thanked him for the fish he was delivering to her. It was the first time she had spoken to him since he left her cabin after her daddy's beating. Every day he had delivered fish or clams to her porch.

Rain covered the island. He looked at the drops making tiny leaps on the deck. In the same way the rain was making tiny leaps on the roof that sheltered Sally's daddy and brother.

For if ye love them which love you, what reward have ye?

Do not even the publicans do the same? Jonas wondered if publicans were as bad as a daddy who raped his daughter.

Brawn liked Jonas. After all, he had offered to whip Sally's daddy for him. Many times since the offer Jonas had seen Sally's daddy in his mind, cringing in fear before the huge redhead. Jonas restrained a smile each time. It was easy to love Brawn.

And if ye salute your brethren only, what do ye more than

others? Do not even the publicans do so? Jonas wondered if no one waved to a publican. Did only another publican wave to a publican? What did publicans do that was so bad? Everyone must have known at the time.

Hardly anyone knew what Sally's daddy had done. Jonas brought fish and clams to Sally because he loved her. She had loved him. He wanted her to love him again. Should he put a bucket of clams on her daddy's porch? It was easier to think of her daddy cowering before Brawn.

He looked back at the place on the deck where he had imagined her daddy falling. The blood made him think of Peter slicing the high priest's servant's ear. He wondered if, for a moment, Jesus thought it would be easier to let it bleed. But he had reached out, stopped the blood, and healed the ear by touch.

Be ye therefore perfect, even as your Father which is in heaven is perfect.

Jonas closed the book and pulled the blanket close around him. He couldn't see how it was possible to be perfect. He looked at the drops making tiny leaps on the deck.

46.

Theresa got a tug. It had a bad case of dry rot. She was going to have to replace a lot of it, one board at a time, but she had a tug. It was a tug that had sat in dry dock down the beach for a couple of years. The owner abandoned it when he had a new tug built. Theresa bought it, and one afternoon Jonas began helping her pry off the dry rotted boards.

"I wish my daddy was here," said Theresa as they carried a board to the scrap pile.

"Do you wish he was here to help you?" asked Jonas.

"Yeah, but that's not the main reason. Sometimes when Daniel is nice to me I miss my daddy so much."

"What do you miss about him?" They began prying on the

next board.

"I miss his smell. When I was a little girl I used to love his smell when he came home from fishing. He smelled like a man and a fish." Her voice saddened, "I miss him patting me on the shoulder like Daniel just did. When I became part of my daddy's crew and we would be coming across the lake heading toward home, he would stand with one hand on the helm and one hand on my shoulder. We didn't talk. We just cut through the waves toward home. And," she brightened, "I miss him smiling at me. I never knew how important my daddy was until he wasn't."

She stopped prying on the board and looked out at the lake. "I love this lake, but this lake will never take the place of my daddy. Jonas, I still want to know a story from the Bible that tells me how a girl can love a lake that stole her daddy."

"God is as fierce as this lake," Jonas said, sensing something stirring within him. "He didn't take your daddy, but he expects you to love him even though he didn't save your daddy for you."

"Is there a story?"

"There is," said Jonas, seeing the story for the first time. "Jesus had a mother. She got to be with Jesus all his life. When she gave birth to him she wrapped him in a blanket and smiled at him a lot." He smiled, remembering his mother cooing to his youngest brother. "She stood in awe when the wise men brought gifts to her son, the baby they said was a king. Later she shook her finger at him when he was twelve and stayed in Jerusalem to dazzle the teachers of the law with all he knew." He remembered a scolding he got for staying at the pond on their farm too long when he was building his first raft. "And she was proud of her boy when he turned the water into wine for her. She got to travel with him part of the time when he was healing and teaching and the crowds were in awe."

Jonas sighed as he looked out at the calm lake. "But God is fierce. His mama was there when they killed him too. She was there when *Abba* allowed evil men to have their way with him."

"Who's *Abba*?"

"It's a word for 'father' in Aramaic, the language Jesus spoke. Our preacher back home said it was like saying 'Daddy' in Aramaic. In the Garden of Gethsemane Jesus said, '*Abba, father, can't you let this cup pass from me? But not my will but yours.*' Jesus called God '*Abba.*'"

"I like that," she said. "*Abba*. Daddy."

"It was *Abba*'s will that Jesus allow himself to be killed. And his mama saw him killed. She was so close to him on the cross that he could talk to her. On the cross he said to her, '*Behold, your son,*' and nodded in the direction of his disciple, John. To John he said, '*Behold, your mother,*' and nodded in the direction of his mother. John took care of her from then on."

"What does that have to do with the lake stealing my daddy?"

"God is as fiercely wonderful as this lake," Jonas said, his arm sweeping across the lake. "His mama stood by the cross while this fierce storm swept across the lake and stole her boy. A storm allowed by God. Just like the storm that swirled across this lake and cast your daddy into the deep. Theresa, the lake did not go away when that storm stole your daddy. *Abba* is even more wonderful than this lake. *Abba* was still there after Jesus was buried, still there after the storm."

"I think I understand. In a storm, good and evil get all mixed up."

"Yes," said Jonas, "but when the storm passes, the good still stands as wonderful and powerful as this lake. The storm passed and Jesus rose from the dead. He and *Abba* are still there."

"What happened to his mama?"

"She never got to be with her son like she did before the storm. She must have seen him after he rose from the dead, but then he went to heaven."

"So it's never the same after a storm?"

"It is never the same after a storm," said Jonas, "but the lake is still there."

"There are new things after a storm, too," said Theresa. She pointed to the place high on the hull where the name of the boat was painted: *Joanna*. It was named after the mother of the captain who owned it. "I am going to rename this boat *Abba*."

47.

One afternoon in the second week of July, after they finished loading the boxes of fish onto the *Lillian*, Jonas asked Daniel if he could talk to him. Daniel invited him to supper. After supper they sat outside the cabin on a bench and talked. There was a stiff breeze that kept the mosquitoes at bay.

"Daniel, I have been here over two months," said Jonas. "It hasn't been like I thought it was going to be. It's true I am a preacher and hired man here just like God called me to be. But so many things have gone wrong. I thought I was going to marry Sally. But then she told me about her daddy. And then I put words in God's mouth and ran away. God sent me back, but Sally would have nothing to do with me. I tried to win her back by being nice to her. I tried to do something kind every day. Brought her fish and clams. But then I got into that fight with her daddy. Now everyone on the island knows who beat me up. Pretty soon they'll figure out why I started the fight with him. When they do, I'm afraid they'll run him off the island. Sally hates her daddy, but I have this feeling she won't like it if he gets run off the island. I'm afraid she'll hate me more. I don't know what to do. God didn't send me to this island to cause trouble, but I sure have caused a lot of it."

Daniel stood up from the bench, took a cloth off the railing that was waving in the wind, and folded it up. He held the cloth as he sat down on the bench again.

"Jonas," said Daniel gruffly, "the trouble was here before you came, but I don't suppose knowing that will help you much. What has God been saying to you then?"

"Love your enemies," Jonas said miserably.

"Why do you sound so miserable?"

"I don't want to love Sally's daddy, and, if I do, Sally will hate me even more."

"Ah!" snorted Daniel, "now the truth comes out."

"What do you mean?"

"You think that to love your enemies will separate you from your friends."

"I guess I do. Brawn and Hank want to get some guys together and go beat up Arnold and his boy. I don't want them to, but I'm afraid if I don't join them, they'll have nothing to do with me. And Sally . . . she hates her daddy. But if I did something kind to him, she'd hate me."

"Jonas," said Daniel sharply as he stood up and faced him, "you speak the truth and you deceive yourself at the same time. The truth is that to love your enemies you must risk losing your friends. As humans, there is nothing more that we despise than a Judas. To love your enemies puts you at risk with friends who have the same enemy. They may see you as a traitor."

"But I am not a traitor," protested Jonas, looking up at Daniel.

"Jonas, you are very afraid that you are."

Jonas blinked. "But I am not," he said. "I am not. I just want to do what Jesus says."

"I know you are not a traitor," said Daniel, sitting down beside Jonas. "Jesus knows you are not a traitor," he continued. Then he paused. "There is one thing I cannot do for you, Jonas, and there is one thing I can do for you. I cannot love your enemies for you. Loving your enemies is like dragging something mysterious and smelly out of the dark. You learn something about yourself when you love your enemies. You also learn something about your friends. Jesus will have his hand in the dark dragging with you. Do you hear me?" Jonas nodded.

"Now," said Daniel, standing up again, "come with me for the one thing I can do." Jonas followed him as he strode along the trail and headed alongside the row of cabins. Jonas caught up with him just as he was knocking on Sally's door. They stood there, Jonas behind Daniel, waiting for her to answer. Jonas didn't dare ask Daniel what he was up to.

Sally answered the door. "Hello, Daniel," she said, surprise and welcome in her voice. "Come in." Daniel walked in and Jonas saw her look of surprise when she saw him.

"May I have a word with you, Sally?" asked Daniel gruffly. It was more a command than a question.

"Yes, I guess so," she said.

Daniel took off his hat and held it in his hand. Jonas hastened to do the same. "Young lady," Daniel said, gesturing at Jonas, "this young man is in love with you and exceedingly miserable about not spending time with you. I thought you ought to know that then. In fact, I think the two of you have some talking to do." Jonas was embarrassed. He looked down at the floor. "Of course," said Daniel, "providing you are ready, Sally."

Sally was silent for a long time, looking from Daniel to Jonas and back again. Jonas noticed two flies scrambling over a bread crumb on the floor.

"Hi, Daniel. Hi, Jonas," called a small voice from above them. They all looked up. Samantha waved at them as she peeked through the railing of the loft.

"Samantha, beddie-bye time," Sally said.

"Goodnight, Samantha," said Daniel.

"Goodnight," echoed Jonas.

"Bye-bye," she said as she waved and then disappeared back to her bed.

"While you're making up your mind, Sally," said Daniel, "I have something to say to Jonas. Jonas?" He motioned with his head for Jonas to follow him as he walked out the door.

Once the door closed behind them, Daniel said, "Remember the old captain I told you about whose son took over the boat and couldn't find the fish?" Jonas nodded. "Eventually the son learned the lake. Funny thing is, he learned the lake with the help of his enemy. There was another captain his age who was a great fisherman. He delighted in outdoing the old fisherman's son. The old fisherman's son hated it. They'd come back from fishing at the same time, and the old fisherman's son would be done unloading his fish in less than five minutes. The other fisherman would take up to half an hour, he had so many fish. He would taunt the old fisherman's son and invite him to help him with the unloading.

"The old fisherman's son complained to the old fisherman about the braggart. One day the old fisherman told his son to put the boat in dry dock and sign on as a crew member with the braggart captain.

"The old fisherman's son was appalled.

"'You did not learn the lake from me,' pointed out the old fisherman. 'Perhaps you can learn it from him.'

"And so, after much grumbling, that's what the old fisherman's son did. He put his boat in dry dock, bit his tongue, and signed on with his enemy. He was miserable the whole time he worked for this man who delighted in calling him the 'would-be-captain.' But he kept all his senses alert to the lake. He watched, listened, smelled, touched, and even tasted the lake every day that they fished, and he learned the lake from his enemy. Eventually he went back to his own boat, and this time he was a much better captain and fisherman."

"What are you saying?" asked Jonas.

"What can you learn from the story?"

"Are you saying I should learn from Sally's daddy?" asked Jonas. He was appalled by the idea.

"I am saying that even our enemies can give us good gifts if we are ready for them. We better go back in now." He opened Sally's door. Jonas was still shaking his head, trying to puzzle out Daniel's story when they entered.

"Have you made up your mind?" asked Daniel.

"Yes, I will talk to Jonas," she said in a small voice. For a moment Jonas saw a little girl in Sally.

"You won't be needing me any more," said Daniel, as gruff as ever. He left.

48.

"So," Sally said, facing Jonas after Daniel shut the door behind himself, "you didn't dare to come here yourself so you got Daniel to bring you." Jonas thought he detected a hint of a smile as she stood with her hands on her hips. But he wasn't sure.

"I didn't even know we were coming here," he protested.

"Did he blindfold you and lead you here by the ear?"

"No, he told me to follow him. But I didn't know where he was headed to until he was almost here. He didn't tell me what he was going to say to you. I didn't know." He held his palms out face up. She continued to stand with her hands on her hips, staring at him with dark green eyes. "Should I leave?" he asked.

She laughed and dropped her hands to her sides. "No, Jonas, don't leave. I just had to give you a hard time. Sit down." She motioned to the table. "I want to know about this misery Daniel was talking about."

Jonas sat down and she put the coffee pot on the coal-fired cook stove. After she sat facing Jonas across the table he said, "I love you and I want to be with you. Also, I am miserable because I'm afraid I'm a traitor if I love my enemy."

"What are you talking about?"

"Your daddy."

"I wondered if you were talking about him when you preached about loving enemies."

"I was thinking about him. He is my first real enemy."

"What do you think about doing when you think of loving him?"

"I haven't even thought about what to do. I've been too afraid I will hurt you to think that far."

"You must have thought of something."

"The only thing that's crossed my mind is to bring him fish or clams like I've been bringing you."

The coffee pot gurgled. Sally poured coffee and set the cups on the table. The coffee steamed in the cool evening air.

"I've missed you," she said to Jonas.

"You have?" She nodded. Jonas pushed his coffee back and bumped the table as he stood up. Coffee sloshed out. "I'll wipe that up later," he said. He walked around the table and stood by Sally. She looked up at him, her green eyes dark and wide in the lantern light. She had the look of a little girl who wants to know, "What are you going to do with me now?"

Jonas reached out for her hand. She gave it to him. He helped her up. She clung to him, her hair against his cheek.

"Sally, I love you and I don't want to hurt you."

"It's going to hurt to love me."

It doesn't hurt now, thought Jonas, as he held her and breathed deeply of the cool evening air.

49.

A week later as Daniel's tug left the dock for the fishing grounds, Philena and Hank announced that they planned to get married.

"Congratulations!" yelled Daniel from the wheelhouse.

"Hank is gonna get hitched!" yelled Brawn from the stern.

"Hank has got himself a mermaid!" called Jonas, entering the jesting. Hank and Philena laughed as they stood holding hands. Jonas noticed that Theresa didn't smile. Later when Daniel assigned them to clean fish together, he asked her about it.

"I feel strange," she said. "I've seen how much they like each other and my mom is happy, but Hank is not my dad. I haven't said anything to them because I don't want to spoil it for them." Even as she talked her eyes followed her mom at work, plucking fish out of the gill net. "My dad was big and strong like Brawn. He had a big, booming voice. Hank is tall, but he's slender and quiet."

"Hank will never replace your dad," said Jonas. "Philena

has told me about Gresig. He sounds like a wonderful father. Your mom really loved him. There will never be another like him."

"How can she marry again then?"

"I don't know. Maybe she doesn't like to be alone." They worked in silence then. Jonas was much quicker at cleaning fish now, but he doubted that he would ever be as fast as Philena or Theresa.

"Do you ever think of getting married?" asked Jonas.

"Yes, I do, but then I wonder if I will. I plan to be a captain of a boat. That means if I married a fisherman, I would be his captain. I don't know if that would work."

"Maybe he won't be a fisherman, or maybe he'll be captain of his own boat."

"What's happening with you and Sally?" she asked, changing the subject.

"We had a long talk last night."

"Do you think you'll get married?" There was something shy in her voice that made Jonas look at her, but she didn't look at him.

"I hope so," he said. "I don't know, but I hope so."

Daniel called Jonas to the helm. "You'll be doing your first wedding, right?"

Jonas looked up. "You mean marrying Philena and Hank?"

"Yes, I usually do the honors on the island, but now that you're the preacher, I expect you'll do the marrying and burying."

"Yes," said Jonas. "Our preacher back home gave me a book that tells you how to marry a couple."

"I usually talk to the couple before I marry 'em, just to make sure they both know what they're getting into."

"I've never done that before."

"Your preacher do that back home, or did he marry anybody who wanted to get married?"

"I think he married anybody who wanted to get married. Of course, at the wedding he always asked if there was anyone who had a reason that the marriage shouldn't happen."

"Ya, I figure it's best to talk to the couple ahead of time. No surprises at the wedding that way."

Jonas wasn't too keen on talking to someone about marriage, not being married himself. There were all kinds of things he wasn't too clear on about marriage.

Daniel sensed his hesitancy. "Hank and Philena will be a good couple for you to practice on. Tell 'em you want to talk to them before the wedding, and go over to Philena's some night for supper when Hank is there. It'll be easy."

50.

The next Sunday, the first in August, was very hot. The lake and sky were hazy, azure mirrors of one another. That afternoon Jonas borrowed a skiff from Daniel, and Sally asked Philena to look after Samantha. Jonas rowed himself and Sally about half a mile out into the lake beyond Rock Point. Jonas had never seen the lake so still.

"I'm going for a swim," said Sally, kicking off her sandals. She dove into the lake. "Oh, this is cool," she exclaimed when she surfaced.

"I'll join you," said Jonas, standing up in the boat.

"No. One of us should stay in the boat," she said. She flipped on her back and began to float. Her dress billowed out. She closed her eyes. Jonas was hot. He leaned over the gunwale and splashed water on his face to wash off the sweat. He watched Sally as she floated, her arms out, an occasional kick keeping her head above water. As she breathed in, her bosom rose out of the water; when she breathed out, the lake covered it. For the first time Jonas thought of Sally without clothes on. He looked away, embarrassed at the thought. But if they married . . . when they married, he would see her. He looked at Sally. Her bosom still rose and fell. He looked back at the island. It was a hazy green in a blue world.

He looked at Sally. Her blonde hair fanned out in the water.

Her dress had floated up, revealing her knees. He looked at her shape, outlined by her wet, clinging dress. He swallowed.

"What are you looking at?" called Sally, looking up at him.

Jonas felt his face redden. "I was looking at you," he said.

She turned and swam a few quick strokes to the boat. Holding on to the side she said, "What did you say? My ears were under the water; I couldn't hear you."

"I was looking at you."

"And what did you see?"

"I saw a beautiful woman. A woman I want to marry."

"And that caused you to turn so red?"

"I . . . I . . . was looking at you."

"And I am embarrassing?"

"No."

"What did you see when you were looking at me?"

"Well, uh, well, your body."

"My body! I have a dress on."

"Your dress came up and I saw your knee."

"My knee. Is that all you saw?"

"I saw your top, too."

"My top," she yelled. "My dress didn't go up that far, did it?"

"No!" said Jonas, horrified. "I mean this top," he motioned toward his chest.

"I don't like you looking there."

He was feeling very hot. "I want to swim now."

Sally swam to the back of the boat and Jonas helped her in, but when she was in the boat she hugged Jonas, burying her face in his neck. The water from her dress cooled him. "Do you like to look at me?" she asked in a muffled voice.

"Yes, you are as beautiful as this day."

"When I saw you looking at my chest, I suddenly remembered my daddy looking at me that same way."

"I'm sorry. I shouldn't have been looking."

"I want you to look at me, Jonas. I just don't want to be reminded of my daddy." She sat up and looked out across the lake. "Mostly it was fun to be with my daddy when I was little.

He played with me. But then it was always bad, too. One day when I was thirteen or fourteen, I had a sliver in my finger. I asked Daddy to get it out. He started working on it, and I wasn't paying any attention. At some point I noticed that he had stopped moving the needle. I looked at him and he was staring right at ... at me." She motioned toward her bosom. "He looked up at me and he had this look on his face. I pulled my hand away from him. Now I think that if I hadn't, he would have touched me." She shook her head in disbelief. "He looked all ready to touch me. After that I wished I never had a chest."

"You never told your mom?"

She clucked her tongue. "You just don't tell my mom things like that. No telling what she'd say. She'd probably blame me for having evil thoughts." Side by side they stared at the hazy lake. She turned to Jonas. "You know what I want?" she said with a small smile.

"What?"

"I want to say, 'Look at me, Jonas!' She flung one hand out and up and the other down and out. She arched her back and tilted her head up so that her bosom rose and drew his eyes. She held the pose for an instant and then crossed her arms, bent over, protecting her chest.

"I would like that, too," said Jonas, "but you better not do that again until we're married."

Sally burst into laughter. Jonas looked at her, puzzled. "You sound so serious," she giggled.

"I am serious."

"I know you are, and that's what's so funny and wonderful about you."

"The more I look at you, the more I want you."

"What's wrong with that?"

"I can't want you too much until we're married."

She sighed deeply and then sat down beside him. "Jonas, what does the Bible have to say about love? I know it says we are to love our enemies, but what does it say about love between a man and a woman? Daddy was always quoting,

'*Wives submit to your husbands,*' but is that all it says?"

"No, it says much more. You know the story of the Garden of Eden, right?"

"No, I can't remember Daddy telling us anything about the Garden of Eden."

"You've never heard that story?" Jonas asked in amazement.

She shook her head. Jonas reached for his Bible which he always carried with him. He opened to Genesis and began to read. She scooted next to him so that they were touching as he read. He had no sooner read the second verse than Sally leaned over the edge of the boat, scooped up a handful of lake water, and poured it on his head. Shocked, he held out the Bible to keep it from getting wet. Sally laughed. "Why did you do that?" he sputtered.

"*And the Spirit of God moved upon the face of the waters,*" she intoned with a deepened voice, quoting what he had just read. In the same tone she continued, "I suddenly had the urge to move the waters upon your face." She laughed again.

"Do you want to hear this?"

"Yes, I'll be a good girl now." She slid next to him again. He resumed reading. He expected to be interrupted at any moment, but every time he glanced up at her she was listening intently. He made it all the way to verse 26. "So God imagined us," she said. "When I sew I imagine what the design and colors and feel of the cloth will be when I'm finished."

Jonas looked at what he had just read: *And God said, "Let us make man in our own image; after our likeness: and let them have dominion over the fish of the sea . . . ."* "Yes," he said, "he imagined us and imagined us to be in his image . . . to be like him."

"What does it mean to be like him?"

"It means to be like the king of creation. Kings have dominion over their kingdom."

"My daddy acted like the king of the roost in our home."

"God is a good king. Your daddy is bad."

"If God is king, why would he let Daddy be so bad?"

"I don't know. God lets us choose whether we want to be good or bad. I guess that's what the Fall is about."

"What's the Fall?"

"We'll get to that part."   He kept reading. He liked the warmth of her next to him, even if her dress was wet. He was well into the next chapter when she snorted, "*It is not good that man should be alone*. What about women?"

"I'm sure God doesn't think it's good for a woman to be alone either," he said, turning and looking directly into her eyes with a hint of a smile.

She raised her eyebrows, "You don't, huh?"

"No, I don't," he said, and he leaned over and kissed her. "Besides, when God said, '*It is not good that man should be alone*,' woman hadn't been created yet."

"I thought you already read that he created them in his image, male and female."

Jonas looked at the Bible. "I guess I did. But I haven't gotten to the part where it tells about how woman was created. It tells that in a few verses."

"But it already said he created them male and female on the sixth day."

Jonas looked again. "It does, doesn't it?"

"Yes, it does. Why does it say they were created male and female on the sixth day and say that man was created first in chapter two."

"I don't know."

"Keep reading. I want to hear about how women were created."

Jonas resumed reading. As he did so, he kept puzzling why it would say two different things about how women were created. Sally poked him in the ribs. "So we were made out of one of these in the second story. Now I know how come my daddy always referred to Mom as his rib."

"Your daddy seemed to talk about the Bible a lot, yet you never heard about the Garden of Eden. I don't understand."

"Daddy read the Bible in our family, but he wouldn't let anyone else read it. Not even Mom. She remembered lots from the Bible when she was a kid, and so she'd argue with Daddy about the Bible. He wouldn't let her or us read it because he said we wouldn't understand it."

"You've never read the Bible?"

"No, I don't have a Bible."

"Here, read mine." He thrust the Bible toward her. She took it shyly. "Start reading here," he said, pointing to verse 19. After she started reading he realized that he had already read those verses, but he let her read.

She stopped reading. "God is funny," she said. "He says that it is not good for man to be alone, so he makes animals and brings them to Adam, but they aren't what Adam is looking for." Jonas didn't respond. He thought her comment was sacrilegious, but he had to admit that was the way it sounded.

Then she said, "Say, this is what you read to me the first day we met, when I asked you what the Bible had to say about married love. *Therefore shall a man leave his father and mother, and shall cleave unto his wife: and they shall be one flesh.* I sure did give you a hard time that first day, didn't I?"

"You sure did. I had never had anyone talk to me like you."

"I still can't believe I told you that first day about being forced. I'm mouthy, but I even surprised myself when I said that."

"For a moment when you first said it, I thought maybe you were just saying it to give me a hard time. Trying to shock the young preacher. But then I realized you were serious."

"I *was* trying to shock you that day, but I got carried away and said things I didn't mean to say. But you gave me a hard time too. When you said, '*Eloi, Eloi, lama sabachthani*?' and told me it meant 'My God, my God, why have you forsaken me?' it was like slipping those words right into my heart. It was like I opened a crack in my heart a quarter of an inch by telling you I was forced, and you slipped those words in, and I knew I would never be the same. I have never been able to close up all the way since then."

"I'm glad you opened your heart to those words."

She continued reading, "*And they were both naked, the man*

and his wife, and were not ashamed. I don't want to read anymore," she said, closing the book and setting it on the seat behind them. She swung her feet around so that she sat beside him but facing him. She looked into his eyes. Jonas wondered why she wanted to stop reading. Was she embarrassed about what she had just read?

But as they continued to gaze at each other, he forgot his question. He sensed she was waiting. He opened his arms and she came to him. Their lips met. Gently at first, but then searchingly. They parted and looked at each other. Then they kissed again. He marveled at the tenderness and desire in her lips. It was better than a drink from the artesian well after working up a sweat hauling hay on the hottest day of the summer. They parted, but held each other's eyes. Her green eyes looked as wide as the lake to Jonas. They took another drink; this time he explored her back, neck, and head with his hand as they kissed. He pressed her against himself. For a long time they alternated between kissing and looking at each other. Maybe an hour. Maybe two hours. Jonas lost track of time. They kept shifting to new positions to kiss, because no position on the skiff bench was comfortable for long.

She was half lying across his lap with her head nestled in the crook of his arm when she looked up at him and said, "I love you, Jonas." Jonas remembered the first time she had said those words—the night she told Jonas who had raped her. She hadn't said them since. "Let's stay here forever," she added.

"Sally, I love you." He looked around at the placid lake, the distant island, and back at Sally. "The Garden of Eden must have been like this moment."

She chuckled, "We still have our clothes on."

"We could . . . " his voice trailed off.

"Jonas!" she exclaimed.

"I was only teasing. I meant that the Garden of Eden must have been as peaceful and good as this moment."

"I know," she said. She reached up and touched his face.

"Today," said Jonas with a smile at her and a movement

that rocked the boat, "the Spirit of God moved upon the face of the waters."

51.

When they came back with the skiff, Samantha met them at the dock. They went to the cabin and Sally started fixing supper. Jonas helped mainly because he was still glowing from their time on the skiff and he wanted to be close to her, but Samantha kept tugging at his hand. She wanted to show him something. Finally he gave her his index finger. She led him out of Sally's cabin, down the path past the other cabins. She left the path and led him into a grove of pines south of Little Oslo. The ground was a spongy floor of needles.

"Look," she said, pointing up. Jonas looked. There, about twelve feet off the ground, large, black wasps flew in and out of a nest. The nest had grown to a foot in diameter. "I found them when me and Joel were playing in the woods. He said we should run away because those big bees would sting us and kill us. Will they kill us?" They stood side by side looking up at the nest, watching the wasps enter and leave.

"I don't think so."

"I don't think so either. Know how I know?"

"How?"

"They are my friends."

"How did they become your friends?"

"They don't sting me."

"Do you come here often?"

"Every day."

"What do you do?"

"I sing to the bees." In her small voice she sang: "Jesus loves the little bees, red and yellow, black and white, they are precious in his sight, Jesus loves the little bees of the world." She stopped singing and said sadly, "I've tried to follow the bees to see where they fly to, but they fly too fast. Jonas, can you run after them to see where they go? I want to know."

"I don't think I can run fast enough either."

"I want to know where they go," she said with a hint of a pout.

"Where do you think they go?"

"They fly up in the air . . . so maybe . . . heaven?"

"What do you think they do in heaven?"

"Jesus takes care of everything, so maybe Jesus is giving them paper."

"Paper?"

"For their house," she said pointing up at the nest.

"I think Jesus made them so they can eat leaves and make leaves into paper to make their nest," Jonas said.

"Oh," she sounded disappointed.

"Do you wish they flew to heaven?"

"Yes."

"Why?"

"They could ask Jesus."

"Ask Jesus what?"

"What I want to know."

"What do you want to know?"

"Why all other kids have daddies but not me."

"I will be your daddy."

"But other kids are borned with daddies."

Jonas knelt beside her, looking at her small innocent face, the large eyes, soft cheeks, the mouth that was shaped like Sally's. "You wish you were borned with a daddy?" She nodded. "Everybody is borned with a daddy," he said. "You can't be born without a daddy."

"I don't have a daddy."

"Everyone has a daddy, but sometimes daddies leave and those kids never sees their daddies. But they still have daddies."

"I have a daddy?" Her eyes brightened. "A real daddy?" He nodded. She jumped up and down. "I have a daddy! I have a daddy!" She danced out of the grove.

Jonas looked up at the bees. He too wished they flew to

heaven. He wished he could send a note: How are you going to take away the sting of who her daddy is? Instead he went out of the grove and followed a little girl flying home on the news that she had a daddy.

By the time he reached Sally's cabin, Samantha was back outside again. She stood silently, looking crushed, tears seeping out of her eyes. "What happened?" asked Jonas, crouching beside her.

"Mommy doesn't want to hear about my daddy. She made me go back outside."

"Why did she do that?"

"I don't know."

Jonas was angry. He stepped into the cabin. "Sally," he said sharply, "what's going on with you and Samantha?"

Before he could continue, Sally interrupted him. "Jonas, I want you to meet my mother." Stunned, Jonas halted in mid-step. He followed Sally's motion. There at the table sat a slender woman, her gray hair tied in a bun. She wore a faded blue dress gathered at the waist with a belt. "This is Ethyl," said Sally. "Mom, this is Jonas."

52.

"Young man, I am glad to meet you," Sally's mother said. Jonas stood there, looking first at her, then at Sally.

"I'm glad to meet you," he said, still standing by the door. "Come in and have a seat," Sally said. "My mom said she wants to meet you." Jonas looked at Sally, trying to read her face. How did she expect him to act around her mother? She looked strained, but she motioned him toward a bench at the table where her mother sat. "I'll make some coffee for you, Jonas, and coffee for you, Mom," Sally said.

Jonas eased himself onto the bench at the end of the table, at a right angle to the bench that Ethyl sat on. He glanced at Sally at the counter. Her back was to him. He looked at Ethyl.

She was looking at him in frank appraisal. He felt like a yearling at a sale barn in front of a buyer. "Sally seems to have a special interest in you, so I wanted to meet you," she said. "You're smaller than I thought, but your red hair makes up for your size. Redheads have spunk, and Sally needs a man with spunk. She has a lot of spunk, so she needs a man with more."

"Sally," she said, looking at Sally who was putting the coffee pot on the stove, "he does have spunk, doesn't he?"

"Yes, Mom," she said, not bothering to turn around.

"Good. He needs spunk to keep you in line."

"He doesn't keep me in line."

"See what I mean," her mother said, looking at Jonas. "She disagrees with me all the time. If she does the same with you, you're going to have nothing but trouble." Jonas thought it was time to say something but she continued, "She wasn't always so contrary. Oh, she was always strong-willed, but she and I got along. I have a strong will of my own, so I could keep her in line when she was younger. But then when she got to be fourteen or fifteen, she thought she could do what she wanted. She got herself a boyfriend, and even though her daddy told her to stop seeing him, she went ahead anyway. I don't know how her daddy knew about that boy, but I agreed with him because I knew the boy didn't have enough spunk. Sally led him around by the ear . . . "

"Mom!" interrupted Sally. She was still at the stove, but she had turned around and was facing her mother with her hands on her hips.

"It's true," said Ethyl to Jonas. "She had him waiting on her hand and foot. One day they had been up at the bluffs at the north end of the island and she forgot her sandals there. She told me they'd been wading in the waves. Anyway, it was just about dark when they got home and I saw she didn't have her sandals. She made him go back to get her sandals, in the dark. He went, meek as a lamb."

"You wouldn't let me go get them," Sally said.

"You wanted to go with him, after dark, after spending all

afternoon with him. I know what happens at times like that and you do too, Sally."

Sally stared at her mother but didn't say anything.

"See, she does have spunk, doesn't she?" Ethyl said, addressing Jonas. "Spunk is good. I have it myself. But a spunky woman needs a spunkier man."

Jonas tried to think of something spunky to say. Sally brought cups of coffee for the three of them. She sat down opposite her mother. After taking a sip of the coffee Ethyl said, "This coffee isn't strong enough." She pushed the cup toward Sally.

Sally pushed the cup back, "Fix it the way you like it."

"I will," she said and went to the kitchen, poured the coffee back into the pot, and added grounds.

"Say something to her," Sally whispered fiercely to Jonas. Her back was to her mom in the kitchen.

"What am I supposed to say?" he mouthed back.

"Anything. Get her off my back," she whispered.

"Alice says that Sally is a great help with the resort," said Jonas to Ethyl who was still standing in the kitchen. Sally rolled her eyes. Apparently that wasn't what she had in mind.

"Sally always was a good worker," her mom said. "It runs in the family for us women. My mother was the buyer for Daddy's store in Chicago. She bought everything the store sold. If Daddy would have been the buyer, they would have gone broke in no time flat. She was teaching me to be a buyer when I met Sally's daddy at the fish market. Boy, was that a mistake. Meeting that man. Inept men seem to run in our family too. I thought he was such a great fisherman. He always shipped so many. He didn't tell me he was shipping for another crew that caught twice as much as him. But the women in our family never give up. I've never given up on him.

"Sally taught herself to sew when she was just a little girl. She could always make such pretty clothes. I never had the luxury of anything pretty around the house until Sally came along. Her daddy spoiled her by bringing back pretty cloth when he went to Milwaukee. He'd bring her pretty stuff, but never me. That's just like him," she sighed. She poured a little coffee in her cup and tasted it. "Still needs more time," she said. She sat down at the table again.

"I'm beginning to doubt you do have any spunk," she said to Jonas. "You've hardly said a word. Tell me about yourself."

"I'm twenty and I've been on the island for about three months. I came here to be a preacher," he was speaking rapidly for fear that she would interrupt him. "I support myself by being a hired hand. Sometimes I work on a fishing crew when they need an extra hand; other times I do carpentry. Whatever needs to be done."

"What about your growing up?"

"I grew up on a farm northwest of Milwaukee. I have seven younger brothers and sisters. I gave my heart to the Lord when I was ten."

"What kind of farmer was your daddy?"

"We milked cows and grew hay and grain."

"No, I mean was he a *good* farmer? Did he support his family?"

"Oh, yes, he did. We weren't rich, but we ate good and always had money to buy shoes."

Her mother got up and went to check the coffee again. Sally was shaking her head. "What am I supposed to say?" mouthed Jonas. Sally threw up her hands. "What?" mouthed Jonas.

"It doesn't matter," Sally mouthed back.

"That's better," Ethyl said after she had seated herself again and taken a sip of the steaming coffee. "Sally says you are spunky. What makes you spunky?"

"Jesus," he said.

Ethyl shook her head and turned to Sally. "Religious men are trouble. Your daddy is always spouting the Bible like he's the Lord himself. Every religious man I know hides behind the Bible because he's too weak to stand on his own two feet."

"Jonas is different," protested Sally. "He's not like Daddy at all."

"Show me," Ethyl said to Jonas.

Jonas looked at her, and for the first time since he had walked through the door and met her, he smiled. He got up and walked to the kitchen counter and got his Bible from where he had set it earlier. He paged through it and then read, *"Then certain of the scribes and Pharisees answered saying, 'Master, we would see a sign from thee.' But he answered and said unto them, 'An evil and adulterous generation seeketh after a sign; and there shall be no sign given it, but the sign of the prophet Jonas: For as Jonas was three days and three nights in the whale's belly; so shall the Son of man be three days and three nights in the heart of the earth.'* Matthew 12:38-40." He closed the book.

Ethyl snorted, "That doesn't show me anything."

"That's right," said Jonas, "I'm not showing you anything."

"What were you trying to prove? That you can read?"

"The scribes and Pharisees asked Jesus to show them a sign to prove himself. He refused."

"But it said something about Jonas," she said, wrinkling her brow suspiciously.

"Jonas spent three days and nights in the belly of the whale when he tried to run away from God."

"Your name is Jonas, too. Are you trying to be high and mighty or just confuse me? Say right out what you mean."

"I mean that the scribes and Pharisees were not going to get a sign they wanted."

"But that doesn't show me that you're not hiding behind the Bible like my no-good husband. It sounds to me like you are, reading me strange things about somebody named Jonas."

"That's right. You don't know whether I am hiding behind the Bible like your husband. And you won't until you see me go through a hard time. Strength isn't in words. It's in action in the worst of situations."

"It seems to me you had a chance to show your strength when you took a swing at my husband. Instead you got yourself beat up good."

"I swung at your husband out of foolishness and weakness. Your husband and son showed great weakness when they beat me up. You will have to wait to see whether I'm strong like Jesus or weak like the men in your family."

There was silence. Sally looked from Jonas to Ethyl. Their eyes were locked. Just then the door squeaked as it was slowly pushed open. Ethyl turned and looked and so did Sally and Jonas. A tear-stained Samantha stood in the doorway. "Do I still have to stay outside?" she asked sadly.

"Oh, child, come here," said Ethyl, holding out her arms. Samantha started toward her. "You were so sharp with the child when she came home," Ethyl said to Sally.

Sally jumped up and intercepted Samantha. "Baby, I'm sorry I made you sad," she said kissing Samantha's head. "Let me make it up to you." She carried her out, closing the door behind her. "What about supper?" Jonas said, but it was too late. He stared at the closed door.

53.

Slowly he turned back to Ethyl. He still had half a cup of coffee. He gulped it down. He must be on his way. He tried to think of something polite to say. It was late Sunday so he couldn't excuse himself to go work. And he was supposed to eat supper. Maybe he didn't need a reason. Maybe he could just say, excuse me, and leave.

"That daughter of mine. I walk all the way over here to visit her, and she just leaves. At least I have you to talk to." Jonas stared at the coffee grounds in the bottom of his cup. "You need more coffee," she said as she took his cup and refilled his along with hers.

"This is most fortunate," she said. "I have a chance to talk to you alone. I thought I was going to have to ask this of Sally, and, contrary as she is toward me, I really didn't expect an answer. But I need one, so I'm going to ask you."

Jonas inhaled deeply and blew out through his lips. She waved her hand at him. "Don't act exasperated with me," she said. "You haven't even heard what I have to ask you." Jonas never used sugar, but now he stirred some into his coffee. He prayed as he watched the sugar dissolve: please, God, help me with this woman.

Ethyl leaned across the table and lowered her voice. "My no-good husband hasn't told me why he beat you up. I want to know why."

Jonas leaned so far back on his bench that he lost his balance. He fell over backwards, throwing his coffee cup to keep from scalding himself. As he scrambled back on his feet, Ethyl began to laugh. "I'm sorry, but you looked so funny. I'm glad you didn't scald yourself. Here, let me get a cloth and wipe up the mess." By the time Jonas set the cup back on the table and had the bench upright, she had found a cloth. She began to wipe the floor vigorously. "There," she said, hanging the cloth back in the cupboard where she had found it. She sat back down. "Sit down," she motioned to Jonas. "Oh," she said, standing up again, "I should get you some more coffee."

Jonas shook his head as he watched her pour another cup. God, what was he supposed to tell this woman? Please, Sally, come back in here.

"There," Ethyl said, setting the cup in front of him. "Be more careful this time. Now tell me what you and Arnold were fighting about. Don't worry about me getting mad at you for fighting with my no-good husband. I know you probably had a perfectly good reason."

Jonas shook his head. "Your husband should tell you."

"That no-good husband of mine," she exclaimed. "Why, I didn't even know about the fight for almost two weeks. He kept it from me. He and my son, conspiring against me. I don't even know what's happening in my own family. I found out because my son was showing off to his girlfriend, flexing his muscles, lifting her off the ground, not letting her go. It started out as play, but then he hurt her, and she got mad and called him a brute. He tried to grab her, but she got away. I was about to put a stop to their nonsense when she told him that he better not touch her, or she'd scream bloody murder about why him and his daddy beat up that boy.

"My boy looked at me and I looked at him. I could tell she had said something that stopped him cold. In fact, both of them cooled off when she said that. 'What's this about?' I asked. Neither one of them would tell. When my no-good husband came home, he wouldn't tell either. So I started asking around, and I soon found out they had beat up Sally's new boyfriend. Nobody seemed to know why. Of course, I'm sure everybody thinks something juicy's going on, but I want to know the truth. Have you got Sally pregnant?"

Jonas blanched. "No," he said in disbelief. "She's not pregnant. I didn't . . . ." He stood up and began backing toward the door. "Look, ma'am. Sally is not pregnant. I want to marry her, but she is not pregnant. That wasn't the reason at all for the fight. I can't tell you more. Sally or your husband have to tell you. Not me."

"Come back here," she said. Jonas stopped backing toward the door, but he did not return to the table. "Did he say bad things about Sally?" She studied her coffee cup, her brow furrowed like she was trying to fit the pieces of a broken cup back together. "Arnold always treated Sally like she was a princess when she was growing up. Then when she got pregnant with Samantha, he turned sour on her. He's had nothing to do with her since. Maybe that no-good husband of mine said bad things about her." She lifted her eyes and looked at Jonas. "Were you defending her honor?"

Jonas was sorely tempted to respond, but he shook his head. "Sally or your husband have to tell you."

"But it was you that got into the fight!" she said.

"It has more to do with your husband and Sally than me."

"Now that's interesting," she said, sounding pleased.

Oh, no what did I say, he thought. "You'll have to ask your husband or Sally," he repeated.

"So you *were* defending her honor," she said, triumphantly. "I knew it. That no-good husband of mine was talking bad about his own daughter."

"It was nice meeting you," he said as he backed to the door. This time she didn't stop him until he had actually opened the door.

"Oh, one more thing," she said, hurrying over to him. He waited warily. "I'm sorry you got beat up for defending my daughter's honor." She touched his cheek. He backed onto the porch. "That was very sweet of you," she said. "Now find Sally and tell her I want to see that grandchild of mine."

Jonas shut the door and heaved a huge sigh of relief.

54.

Jonas fried a trout on the small stove in the fish house and sat on the dock to eat his supper. Bread, fish, and the first tomatoes from Jackson's garden. Jackson had insisted that he share his "first fruits" with him. The tomatoes were small but tasty. He kept glancing up the beach, watching for when Ethyl left Sally's cabin. Ethyl wanted time alone with Sally, so Jonas volunteered to fix his own supper. As he munched he remembered kissing Sally earlier that afternoon. It seemed an age ago that they had been alone on the lake for three hours. With the coming of evening the breeze off the lake was picking up. The earlier haze was now forming clouds that raced along, threatening to become thunderclouds. Jonas wondered if he should go tell Ethyl to start for home if she didn't want to get rained on. He quickly shook off that thought. He didn't want to deal with her again.

He'd rather remember the time on the lake. He had never dreamed kissing could be so good. Or could last so long. Sally's lips felt so good. In fact, her whole body felt good, he thought dreamily. At least the parts he had touched with his hand—her back and neck and hair and arms. And the parts he had kissed—her lips and cheeks and neck and hair.

He was so caught up that he almost missed Ethyl's leaving.

In fact, he would have if the wind hadn't carried a child's voice to him. He looked up to see Sally and Samantha waving to Ethyl, who was waving a final farewell from partway up the path to the East Side.

Jonas quickly washed his plate and fork and frying pan in the lake and hurried to Sally's. Sally was getting Samantha ready for bed. "Tell me a Bible story for bedtime," called Samantha when she saw him. When she was ready for bed she climbed into his lap and said, "Tell me about baby Jesus." She never tired of hearing about Jesus wrapped in swaddling clothes in the manger with angels singing to shepherds, wise men visiting, cows mooing, sheep baaing, and Mary and Joseph admiring him.

Sally had coffee ready for them when Jonas finished the story and had sent Samantha up to the loft. Jonas could sense the tension in Sally as soon as he sat down. "My mother drives me nuts," she said vehemently. "When I still lived at home I used to think of her as The Tongue. No wonder she and Daddy fight all the time. She cuts him down and everybody else. I don't know how Eugene and Floyd can stand to still live with her. She bosses them around something terrible. I see her three, four times a year when she walks over here. That's more than I can stand. She doesn't ask me to come and visit her because she knows I won't."

"I was sure surprised to come in the door and find her here," Jonas said.

"I never know when she's going to come. She just shows up. Poor Samantha. Mom had just come in and sat down when Samantha comes barging in with the news that she has a daddy. I could've died. So I grabbed her and told her to go out and play. I never did get it straight why she announced she has a daddy. She kept talking about the bees and you."

Jonas explained his and Samantha's conversation in the pine grove by the wasps' nest. "When I told her that everyone had a daddy, even if their daddy isn't around, she got so excited. She wants a daddy like other kids."

"Well, I've decided she's at least going to have a mom who

can say she's sorry to her. I heard Philena and Theresa get into a fuss the other day when I was over there. Philena said some pretty mean things to Theresa and, after while, she stamped out. Philena and I kept on talking, but pretty soon Philena announced she needed to say she was sorry to Theresa. She went and did it. That's something new in a family for me. I decided right then and there that I was going to try that with Samantha. This afternoon was my first chance, after I had told her to get lost. She said she was sorry, too. I told her she didn't need to be sorry, just forgive. So she said, 'Forgive you, Mama.'" Sally smiled, remembering the moment.

Sally's smile faded. "My mom is so hard to put up with. But I couldn't stand it when you weren't giving in to her. I was sure she'd say something really mean to you. So I just had to get out of there. I hope you didn't mind."

"No, I think I minded less than you." He grinned.

"I couldn't believe how you wouldn't give in to her. She says she likes spunk in a man, but she can't stand spunk in anyone except herself. She can really dice up people with her tongue."

"It was the Lord that helped me. I didn't know what to say to her when she was questioning me, but then all of a sudden I knew."

"Jonas, you are so loveable. So innocent and strong at the same time." She squeezed his hand. Then her face clouded, "She didn't say anything that cut real deep did she?" Jonas shook his head no. "So what did the two of you talk about when I was out with Samantha?"

"She wanted to know why I got in a fight with your daddy."

"You didn't tell her, did you?"

"No, no."

"You better not."

"I told her that she should ask Arnold. Or you."

"She was too cheerful at supper. I wondered what had happened."

"She . . . she thinks she knows the reason for the fight," stammered Jonas.

"I thought you didn't tell her."

"I didn't."

"Well, what *did* you tell her?"

"She asked if I had gotten you pregnant and I said no."

"She asked you that!" Sally widened her eyes and laughed.

"What's so funny about that?"

"Asking you, a preacher, if you got me pregnant? I would've loved to see the look on your face."

"I was shocked," admitted Jonas.

"Only my mother would have the nerve. Okay, you told her you hadn't got me pregnant. What else did you tell her?"

"Then she asked me if I was defending your honor. I just kept telling her she had to ask Arnold."

Sally's face darkened. "What did she mean, 'defending my honor'?"

"I think," said Jonas, trying to remember, "she said that maybe her no-good husband had said something bad about you, and so I was defending you against what he said. I just repeated that she needed to talk to Arnold. But she latched onto the idea that I was defending your honor. I was afraid to correct her. She might've gotten more out of me. Besides, in a way, I *was* defending your honor."

Thunder rumbled in the west. It was nearly dark. Jonas saw a flash of lightning far out on the lake. A question had been forming in his mind ever since his conversation with Ethyl. He wondered if he dare ask it. He decided to test the waters. "You never told your mother who raped you?"

"I told no one until I told you. No one."

"Your mother kept calling Arnold her no-good husband." He paused, searching for words. Sally looked at him; he could sense the tension growing in her. "She was hard to talk to," he continued. "She talks so much it's hard to get a word in." He was still searching. "She's such a strong woman that she might kill Arnold if she knew what he did."

"What are you trying to say?" Her voice was tense.

"I wondered if you ever thought of telling your mother what happened?"

"So she would kill him? Is that what you're thinking?" she demanded.

"No, no. It's just that I know you can't count on your daddy because he raped you, but a girl oughta be able to count on at least one of her parents."

"Count on them for what?" The question was almost a snarl.

After a moment's hesitation he said, "To protect you."

"I can't count on either of my parents. You're dreaming if you think my mother would've believed me then or would believe me now. She would always stand up for Daddy."

"She kept calling him her no-good husband. Maybe she knows what he's like."

"She calls him her no-good husband, but nobody else better speak a bad word against him. One time when I was thirteen or fourteen and he and I were starting to get into arguments, I complained to Mom and called him my no-good daddy. She slapped my face and told me to respect him." Tears formed in her eyes. "She always took his side!" She broke into sobs. Jonas moved over and held her. She cried and cried into the front of his shoulder.

When her sobs finally stopped, Jonas said, "I am so sorry. Someone should've taken your side."

"There was no one," she said. Fresh tears. Jonas could feel his shirt getting wet.

"Now there is someone," he murmured.

"You?" came her muffled question.

"Me a little, but God a lot."

"What can he do?"

"He saw what your daddy did to you, and I don't know what he will do, but we will find out."

She lifted her head from his shoulder and looked at him with lake-green eyes. He kissed the tear stains beneath each of her eyes.

55.

Jonas filled the spoon with the last of the peas on his plate. On the way to his mouth one rolled off the spoon, skidded off the plate onto the table, and headed for the floor. Without thinking he made a grab for it with his left hand. As he did so, the rest of the peas on the spoon went flying across the table, some bounding onto Hank's and Philena's plates, others skipping onto the floor. Red-faced, he looked down. He opened his left hand and looked at the errant pea he had saved from the floor. He looked up. Philena was laughing behind her hand. Hank speared one of Jonas' peas that had landed on his plate and ate it. Jonas used his fork to stab the few peas that had landed on the table. When he leaned over to begin capturing those that were on the floor, Philena said, "You can just leave them. I'll sweep them up after supper."

"You want to talk to us about our getting married," Hank offered.

"Yes," said Jonas, eager for everyone to think about something other than peas.

"What do you want to say to us?" asked Philena, dropping her hand from her face.

Jonas didn't know exactly what to say so he concentrated on Genesis. For ten minutes he talked about God and male and female and leaving and cleaving and being one. Hank's and Philena's eyes wandered from the table to the floor to the wall with an occasional peek at each other. He hoped they didn't ask any questions.

"What's cleaving?" Hank asked when he was done.

"Being close and loving," said Jonas.

"And what does being one flesh mean?" asked Philena, a smile at the corner of her mouth.

"Sexual intercourse," he said.

Her smiled disappeared and her eyes widened. Hank shifted in his chair, leaned over, picked up a pea, and placed it on the table. Jonas had a sinking feeling. He had read those words in a book on married love that his preacher back home had given him. But this was the first time he had actually said them. Maybe you weren't supposed to say them out loud. He had to say something. Hank and Philena stared at their plates as if they had never seen them before and might be tested on what they looked like. "It is important in marriage," he said.

"We love each other," Philena said.

"Yes," Hank said.

"That's very important," said Jonas. Again there was an awkward silence.

"Is there anything we need to know for the wedding?" asked Hank.

Relieved, Jonas grabbed his book with the wedding ceremony in it.

"That doesn't sound too hard," Hank said when Jonas finished.

Jonas pushed his chair back from the table. "Well, thank you for supper," he said.

"Is that all?" asked Philena. She sounded disappointed.

"I'm new at this," Jonas said.

"Think of a question to ask us," said Philena, "while I get us some more coffee." Jonas pulled his chair back to the table and tried to think of a question.

He took a sip of coffee as she sat down. "Philena, why do you want to marry Hank?" he said.

Philena looked shyly at Hank and smiled. "I always thought Hank was too quiet for me to marry," she said. "Gresig was a huge man with a big, boisterous voice. He liked to talk. Hank is small and quiet. Too quiet for me, I thought. But then one day on the way home from fishing, he and I were standing by the prow, the breeze blowing in our faces. I was doing the talking, which is the way it always is with Hank. I can't even remember what I was talking about. I was just babbling. I didn't even know if Hank was listening. Then he touched my arm. It took me by surprise. I turned to him. He was pointing toward the island shoreline we were approaching. I looked, and there was a heron flapping laboriously above the water along the shore. A heron highlighted by the setting sun. I watched the bird, and then I turned back to Hank. 'He works so hard to fly,' was all he said. I looked back and saw the bird disappear around the bend of the island. Then we docked and put stuff away and I went home. All I could think about was, 'He works so hard to fly.'

"That night I went to bed, but I couldn't get to sleep. I felt like crying every time I thought of those words. At first I didn't know why, but it made me think of Gresig. That didn't make sense. Gresig was big, but he moved so easily. Then it struck me. The heron was flying all alone. He was working so hard to fly, and he was all alone. I cried for Gresig a long time that night. I have worked so hard to fly alone since he died. I hadn't cried like that about Gresig for, I don't know how long, it must be three years. I finally cried myself to sleep."

An embarrassed smile broke out on her face. She looked at Hank. He nodded at her. "The next morning when I woke up, the first thing I thought of was Hank's hand on my arm. I could remember as clearly as if he had just touched me a moment ago. Then I thought of those words, 'He works so hard to fly.' This time I wasn't sad. This time I wanted to know the man who could speak so beautifully. From then on I began to listen to Hank. I still like to listen to him." She laughed and put her hand on his arm. "I still don't hear a lot, but I do like what I hear, and I like not flying by myself."

"Hank," Jonas said, "why do you want to marry Philena?"

"I didn't figure I was ever going to get married," Hank began. "Not that I was against it. I just didn't know how to go about it. No woman ever paid much attention to me either. At least not that I noticed. Not being a talker I didn't know what to say around women. Philena was different. I was thinking about her long before she ever took notice of me." He grinned. "But I never knew how to get her attention. It never dawned on me that pointing out a bird would do the trick. I didn't know about the bird thing for a long time. All I knew is that she started asking questions, and pretty soon I was talking to her." He took a long, slow drink of coffee.

He grinned, "I liked that. Then one day she invited me for supper. That scared me good. It was one thing talking to her on the boat. She said Theresa wasn't going to be there. I said I'd come. I almost chickened out and didn't go at all. At the last minute I did go, but then I stood in the yard, too scared to knock."

"I kept waiting for him," said Philena. "Finally I looked out the window and saw him pacing in the yard. I knew he was scared, but I expected he would knock any time. But he didn't knock and he didn't knock. I took a peek again. He looked so scared I thought he was going to bolt. I looked around for something handy. First thing, I saw a dishpan of water. I grabbed it, opened the door, and flung the water out without even looking. I was lucky. It hit him right in the face. Of course, I acted horrified. I ran out and grabbed him by the hand and apologized over and over again for not looking when I threw the water. Then I led him into the house and dried him off with a towel." Philena was laughing.

"At first I was shocked," Hank said, "but then she apologized, and she treated me so good, drying me off and all, that I forgot about being scared. After that it seemed easy to be with her, even at her house. Pretty soon it seemed natural to think of getting married. Even after she told me why she threw the water. I figured I might never've went in that house if she hadn't thrown that water."

56.

After Sally finished putting Samantha to bed, she wanted to know all about Jonas' meal with Hank and Philena. They laughed together about Philena tossing dish water on Hank.

"So you know that if I ever throw dish water on you, it's because I want you," laughed Jonas.

"When are they getting married?" Sally asked soberly.

"The last weekend in August."

"When is their engagement party?"

"Next Saturday night." Jonas frowned, "By the way, what happens at an engagement party?"

Sally didn't reply. He glanced at her, wondering if she had heard. She was staring away from him, a tightness in the corner of her eyes. He had a sinking feeling. "What is it?" he asked.

"I can't go to the party."

"Why not?"

"Daddy will be there."

"He will?"

"Yes, when there is an engagement party, everyone on the island goes. Everyone. Daddy will be there dancing up a storm. I can't ever go to an engagement party."

"So," he shrugged his shoulders, "don't go."

"Jonas, you don't understand. I'm not thinking about Philena's and Hank's party. I'm thinking about our engagement party."

"Ours?" he said.

"Yes, ours," she said.

Jonas took some time to sort out what she might be talking about. "You want to announce our engagement?" he ventured.

"Yes."

"But you can't go to our engagement party because your daddy will be there." She nodded. "So that's why you agreed to get married earlier, but you weren't ready to announce our engagement?" She nodded. "I have never gone to an engagement party since he forced himself on me. I'm the only one on the island who doesn't go. Everybody gave up trying to get me to go because I always refused."

"Do we have to have an engagement party?"

"I want an engagement party. I wouldn't feel married without one. Everyone here has an engagement party."

"I'll tell your daddy he can't come to ours."

"Sure," she said, disbelieving. "I'm sure he's going to stay away. The only way he would stay away is if he couldn't walk, and then he'd probably take a skiff and have my brothers carry him to the dance."

"I could break his leg," he offered with a grin.

"It's not funny," she said. "Look what happened last time you tried something funny."

Jonas got up and began to pace. "There's got to be some way," he said. "I could tell Brawn and Hank to keep him away."

"And what reason would you give them for why they're to keep him away?"

"I'm thinking."

"No, Jonas, no. You told me you weren't going to cause any more trouble. If you try to keep him away by threatening him, there will be trouble. He will get all the men from the East Side on his side. With all the drinking, there are already enough fights at engagement parties. It won't work."

"I want to marry you," he said emphatically.

"And I want to marry you."

"Isn't there something we can do?"

"Pray?"

"I don't want to pray. I want to get married."

"What did you say?"

"Oh, I didn't mean that. I'm just frustrated. Your daddy is driving me nuts. He's this monster controlling our lives. We can't do anything without worrying about him."

"I don't like it when you get angry at me."

"I'm not angry at you. I'm angry at your daddy."

"But it's me you are almost shouting at, not Daddy."

Jonas forced himself to sit down. He held his hands behind his head, looked at the ceiling, closed his eyes. "I don't know what to do," he said.

"Jonas . . . " She paused until he looked at her. "Jonas, be gentle with me." Her green eyes were wide and dark in the lantern light. She was half turned away from him, as if she might be about to escape. He let his hands slide slowly from his head to his sides, her eyes still holding his. She glanced away for a moment and then back to him. She shook her head slightly. "I don't need you to figure it all out tonight. I just need you to be gentle with me."

"I still wish . . . " he began but stopped when a tear formed in her eye.

"Not tonight," she said. "You're too wound up. Talk to Daniel. He will help. Tonight I just need you to be gentle with me."

"Okay." He breathed in deeply and slowly let his breath out. Her eyes were so large they seemed to surround him. He thought of the pond at home just after sunset. The air was still full of pale light, but the pond was dark. In the summers he used to come home at dusk, head for that dark, inviting pond, and dive in, letting it wash away the grime of the field and ease his aching muscles.

"Do you know what I mean—be gentle with me?"

"Not exactly."

"I don't know what I mean either. It's just that when you were pacing up and down I had a feeling you might hurt me."

"You look tense, too," he said softly, as if speaking to a sparrow on the edge of a bird feeder that might take flight at any moment.

"I am. I can't talk about Daddy without feeling like he could come in that door at any moment." They both looked at the door.

"I used to come home from working in the field. I would be all tense and tired. I would go for a swim in the pond. It cleaned me off and soothed all my aching muscles."

She shook her head. "I can't swim when I'm scared of my daddy."

He felt a momentary surge of anger at this man who could instill such fear even after four years. But, he reminded himself, her daddy is not here. She is, and she wants me to be gentle with her. Her head was down. He leaned across the table and gently stroked her hair. "How can I be gentle with you tonight?" he asked. She kept her head down. He gently stroked her hair again.

She lifted her head. There was a hint of a smile and defiance in her eyes. "You could wash and braid my hair."

He raised his eyebrows. "You want me to wash and braid your hair?"

"Only if you will be gentle."

"I'll be gentle," he promised. She was silent, frowning slightly. "You really want me to wash your hair?"

She was silent. Then she said, "Yes," firmly, as if she had just made up her mind.

"I don't want to do anything that will upset you. First you ask me to, and then you act like you don't want me to, and then you want me to. It's hard to know."

"Let's not talk about it. Just do it. Put the teakettle on and heat up some water."

Jonas put on the kettle and stood shifting from one foot to the other, checking the water as it heated up. Then he got the basin, poured in half the water from the kettle and added cold water until it was the right temperature. He set the basin on the table. Following Sally's instructions, he found the shampoo, brush, band, and towel. Sally watched him with an embarrassed smile. It was the first time he had seen her embarrassed. He didn't speak.

She knelt on the bench and put her head in the basin. He cupped the water and wet all her blonde hair. She lifted her head up slightly, the water running into the basin. He poured shampoo into his hand and rubbed it into her hair until it was lathered. "Rinse time," he said. She put her head back into the basin and he sloshed water on it, rinsing most of the shampoo out. She lifted her head up. "I'll have to get fresh rinse water," he said.

As he smoothed the water out of her hair, he remembered smoothing the water out of the wool of a lamb that he washed after it had been chased through a mud puddle by their dog. "This will catch the drips while I get fresh rinse water," he said as he moved the basin and put the towel on the table. Quickly he threw the soapy water out behind the cabin. Then he poured the rest of the teakettle water into the basin and added cold water. Sally still knelt with her hair dripping over the towel. He moved the towel and she put her head back into the basin. "This feels so good," she said. Jonas splashed water on her hair.

"It's rinsed," he said. She lifted her head up and he dried her hair with a towel. He wanted to kiss her hair and put his face into the damp tangle. Something stopped him. Instead he brushed her hair over and over again until it shone. "Do you braid your hair into three strands?" She nodded. He divided her hair and began to braid, the motions familiar from the times he had braided rope on the farm. When he was finished, he fastened it with a band.

Sally went over and looked at herself in the mirror. Jonas stood behind her. Their eyes met in the mirror. She sighed very deeply. "You were gentle with me, Jonas."

57.

The next day Jonas helped Daniel and his crew boil some gill nets to clean off the slime. The nets needed cleaning every so often to keep them from rotting. They built fires under huge pots and eased the nets into them. After each net had been boiled, they hung it up to dry.

When they had hung the last net, Daniel set the crew to cleaning and repairing the tug. Jonas asked if he could be assigned a job so he could talk with Daniel. Daniel said he could help him peel some tamaracks for spiles.

"What's on your mind?" asked Daniel as they walked to the pile of tamaracks.

"Sally and I want to get married."

"That's great," Daniel said gruffly, looking at him with a grin. "You didn't waste much time once you started talking to each other again." Jonas nodded but he didn't grin back. "Haul these sawhorses out and set them up on the beach. We'll lean the tamaracks up against them to do the peeling. I'll get us the knives." Jonas carried the two sawhorses out and set them up, digging out the sand on the high side so they were level.

"You don't seem very enthused for a man who just announced he's getting married then," Daniel said when he arrived with the knives.

"There's a problem," said Jonas. "You know that Sally never comes to an engagement party, right?" Daniel nodded. "The reason she never comes is because of her daddy. She can't stand being around him."

"That is a problem," Daniel said. They both grabbed one end of a tamarack and dragged it off the pile and onto the sawhorse. They leaned a second tamarack on the other sawhorse. They straddled the tamaracks and with broad knives began to peel the bark off.

"I suppose you could get married without having an engagement party then," Daniel said. "Of course, her daddy would expect to come to the wedding. But you could always go to the mainland and find a justice of the peace and come back and tell us you're married."

"Elope?" The word came out louder than he meant it to. He looked around. No one seemed to have noticed.

"It was just an idea."

Jonas shook his head. "Sally wants an engagement party. She says she wouldn't feel married without an engagement party."

"How do you think you ought to handle this problem, Jonas?"

"I don't know what to think. She hasn't seen her daddy in four years, but it's like he has a rope around her neck and she's scared to death any moment he'll pull it. I want to get that rope off, but I don't know how."

"Jonas, she is going to have to take that rope off her neck herself. You can't. You start messing around with the rope on her neck and she's going to think you're pulling on it. You'll have a fierce fight on your hands."

"How will she ever do it herself if she hasn't in the last four years?"

"She won't do it by herself. She'll have help." Daniel stopped peeling, took his cap off, wiped his brow on his sleeve, and replaced his cap. "The first speech Jesus ever gave he quoted Isaiah saying he had come to set the captives free."

"I don't think I have enough faith to simply pray Sally free. He's really got his hooks in her."

"You aren't going to be able to simply pray her free," said Daniel, resuming the peeling.

"I thought maybe I could help by praying," said Jonas, tossing aside a peeling.

"Ya, you will, but more by praying for yourself."

"What do you mean?"

"Give me a hand turning this log over so I can get the bark on the underside." They turned the log over. "Ya, what do I mean? How can I put this?" He tossed a peeling on the growing pile of stripped bark. "Now we use motors, but when I was starting out we used sails. One of the first things you learn about sailing is sailing into the wind by tacking. You can't go into the wind directly. You have to tack."

Jonas kept peeling strip after strip, but he was listening to every word. "There has been a strong wind blowing against you and Sally," Daniel said, "that started even before the two of you got together."

"What do you mean?"

"When Sally's daddy did what he did, he taught her to the marrow of her bones that no man can ever be trusted. That's a mighty strong wind blowing against the two of you. If you try to go directly into that wind, Jonas, you are never gonna make it. The two of you might as well head back to shore and forget fishing together. But if you tack into that wind, you can use that same wind to get where you want to be together."

Daniel peeled two more long strips before he continued. "Ya, now what does that have to do with praying for yourself? This is the way it is. You are young and you grew up on a farm and you did carpentry where you learned to saw in a straight line, the shortest distance between two points. When you are sailing into the wind, the shortest distance is not a straight line. But your greatest temptation is to head straight into the wind. That's what you did when you got in a fight with Arnold. And you got blown right back up onto the shore as far as Sally was concerned. She didn't think she could trust you as the captain of her tug, and she was right. You tried sailing directly into the wind. Pray to learn to tack."

They fell into silence. It was true. He wanted to sail right into the wind. He wanted to directly have an engagement party and get married. But how could he tack toward marriage with Sally? They both wanted to get married. Why didn't they just elope? But no, Jonas had a feeling that was heading into a wind. He wished he could do something about the wind. "I wish I could change the direction of the wind," he said.

Daniel stopped his peeling and gave Jonas a sad smile. "If wishes were fishes ... no sailor has ever changed the wind."

"What can I do then? I don't know how to tack against her daddy's wind."

"You don't tack *against* the wind; you tack *with* the wind."

"I don't know how to tack with her daddy's wind. I never know when a gust is coming. We seem to be sailing along fine, and then something about what her daddy did hits. I never know when it's going to happen."

"Jonas, sailing with Sally is sailing with tricky winds. Is it worth it?"

Jonas pulled a peel free of the tamarack. He swallowed. "Are you saying it's not worth it?"

"No, I'm just asking."

"Oh, it's worth it. I love her."

They went back to peeling. "Jonas, your best bet is to assume that when you are with Sally, you always need to be tacking with the wind her daddy stirred up."

"I know how tacking works with sailing, but I don't know how it works with Sally and me."

"A sailor develops a feel for the wind and the slightest change in wind direction, especially when he's tacking, so he can adjust the sails. You need to develop that same feeling for Sally. Sometimes she wants to be close and sometimes she doesn't, right?" Jonas nodded. "Sometimes she likes being touched and sometimes not, right?" Again Jonas nodded. "You have to sense the wind and tack with the wind."

Jonas remembered washing Sally's hair. It had seemed like a strange thing to do; he sort of enjoyed it, but it didn't seem like the way a man and a woman were supposed to be together. He couldn't imagine his dad ever washing his mother's hair. He decided to tell Daniel about it. Daniel listened to him intently.

When he finished Daniel said, "Jonas, that was good tacking. A great bit of sailing."

"It was?"

"Ya, that is exactly what I mean by tacking. Both you and Sally were tacking on that one. Great feel for the wind."

Jonas smiled. Already he was enjoying the memory of the hair-washing much more. But he still had a feeling he didn't quite understand. "Could you say exactly how we were tacking?" he asked.

"There is a strong wind from her daddy's betrayal that keeps her from trusting you. Yet if the two of you are really going to be one, both of you have to move in the direction of trusting each other. She wants to be close to you. She wants you to be gentle with her. She asks you to wash her hair. You gently wash her hair. That is tacking. That was great sailing, Jonas."

One of the crew called Daniel who went to check some work on the tug, but Jonas kept peeling, Daniel's praise ringing in his mind again and again.

58.

As Jonas swung Samantha up onto his shoulders, she squealed with delight. "Let's go for a stroll along the shore while your mama's fixing supper," he said.

"Don't be too long," Sally called after them as Jonas bent his knees to make sure Samantha didn't hit her head when they passed through the door.

"Let's go talk to the sea gulls," urged Samantha. Jonas

walked north along the shore until they came to a series of boulders that studded the shore and extended into the lake. They were sprinkled with gulls. "Ah! Ah!" screamed Samantha in a greeting to the gulls. Jonas brushed clean a flat rock and sat down, putting Samantha on his lap. "You talk to them now," said Samantha.

"Ah! Ah!" cried Jonas.

"Ah! Ah!" echoed Samantha.

"Ah! Ah!"

"Ah! Ah!"

The gulls paid no heed to them. Jonas began to laugh. "Samantha, I don't think they understand us."

"If we had wings they would understand us."

"How so?"

"Then we could fly up in the air and talk in their ears. Then they would hear us."

"Why don't you talk in my ear."

"Ah! Ah!" she screamed in his ear.

He leaned backwards and almost fell off the rock. He had to grab Samantha to keep her from falling. She laughed. "You heard me," she said.

"Yes, I heard you," he said ruefully. "I wanted you to talk like a girl in my ear, not scream like a gull."

"Okay," she said, moving toward his ear.

He leaned away. "Now you promise to talk like a girl, right?" She nodded. He leaned forward. For the longest time her mouth was next to his ear. He waited. He moved back and said, "Can't this girl think of anything to say?"

"I want to scream like a gull."

"But that will hurt my ear. Say like a girl what the gull wants to say." He leaned forward.

She put her mouth next to his ear. "I want to poop on your head," she said. She broke into laughter.

Jonas pulled away. "Samantha, that's not nice to say."

"But that's what the gull wanted to say."

"Humph. Why did the gull want to say that?"

"Because he pooped on Grandpa's head and now he wants

to poop on your head."

Jonas frowned. "Samantha, did a gull really poop on Grandpa?"

She nodded. "Grandma said so."

"She told you?"

"She told Mama. I heard."

"Let's talk about something else."

"Okay. You talk like a girl to me." She leaned her ear to him. "Ah! Ah!" he squeaked faintly into her ear.

"Talk like a girl, not a gull," she cried.

"I tricked you," he said. "I'll talk nice now." He leaned over to her ear. "If I were a sea gull I would catch fish for you. If I were a sea gull I would carry you across the lake and fly you to my dad's farm. If I were a sea gull I would show you where I grew up. I would show you to my mom and dad and brothers and sisters. I would tell them that you are my little girl."

"More! More!" she cried.

"If I were a sea gull I would clean up the lake for you. If I were a sea gull I would fly you to the moon. If I were a sea gull I would . . . " Suddenly he choked up. He wanted to say, If I were a sea gull I would fly you and your mama away from the other side of this island forever . . . away from Arnold . . . away from the bad . . . I would fly you away.

She nudged him. "More! More!"

"If I were a sea gull I would fly you home for supper right now. It's time for us to be home."

"I want more," she said, her lower lip dropping into a pout. "I want to fly more."

"We'll fly more on the way home." He lifted her up onto his shoulders and headed for the cabin.

"If I were a sea gull I would fly you to my dad's farm, and you and I would play hide-and-go-seek. I would count to fifty and you would hide. Then, wherever you hid, I would find you and give you a kiss."

"More! More!" she cried like a sea gull perched on his shoulder.

"If I were a sea gull . . . "

59.

After supper Jonas went to visit Jackson. He heard the sounds of a fiddle playing as he approached Jackson's cabin. Jackson didn't answer his knock so Jonas went in. Jackson glanced at Jonas but kept on playing. Smiling, Jonas shuffled his feet a few times trying to keep up with the fiddle, but he soon gave up. When Jackson finished the song he set his fiddle on his knee and said, "Son, you dance like a man who is up to his knees in cow dung. You never learned how to do a proper jig?"

"No, I've never been to a dance. I don't believe in dancing."

"You do not believe in dancing?" he said incredulously. "Do you know what I miss most about being legless?"

"No."

"Dancing. God created us to dance. Don't you remember that when King David started feeling great, he not only danced, but danced so wildly that his loins showed?"

"No," said Jonas, appalled at the thought.

"Go read your Bible, preacher. You will find that I tell the truth. Not only did he dance that wild, but his wife, Michal, got upset that he had let all the maidens see the family jewels. David did not take too kindly to Michal's criticism of his dancing, so he never gave her the pleasure of him again. Moral of the story: watch out when you criticize dancing."

"I'll look that up," he said, stiffly.

"Why do you not believe in dancing?"

"It leads to adultery and fornication," Jonas said reluctantly.

"That is not what Jesus taught. He taught that adultery begins with the eyes," Jackson crowed. "Perhaps you are going to take his advice and pluck out your eyes lest they lead you to fornication."

Jonas didn't say anything.

"When you do not dance, you are cutting off the legs God gave you for dancing."

Still Jonas didn't answer. He did not want to waver. Better

to be silent.

"Listen," said Jackson. Then he put his fiddle under his chin and played a hauntingly beautiful "Amazing Grace."

They were silent when he finished.

"That song could almost make an old sinner like me believe," Jackson said. Then he rolled over to the table and drank from the wine jug. "I will stop trying to convince you about dancing, son." He wiped his lips. "Except for one more argument," he added with a grin. "One would think God's grace would make it possible for you, Jonas, to be free to dance without falling into bed with the nearest woman you're not married to. But enough of dancing. No, one more thing." Throwing up his hands, he said, "Dance for me, Jonas. I have no legs but you do. My mind is on dancing because Hank stopped by tonight and told me about their engagement party coming up. I am preparing to fiddle. Daniel will be playing his accordion and Brawn will be thumping the tub. The best times on this island are engagement parties and wedding dances. I feel so good those nights I hardly need a drink. Of course, there are those who have too much before the night is over. And there is the obligatory fight or two. But it's a good time. You can come without dancing. Old Lady Bills' fast dancing days have been over for a long time, but she still has a good time."

"I don't know if I will come or not. Sally never goes to them. I might stay home with her."

"That girl reminds me of an Indian on a reservation."

"What do you mean?" Jonas asked warily.

"You know I was a missionary on an Indian reservation in Minnesota. What a farce! Imagine me, a missionary. Well, the Indians act just like her. The only difference is she doesn't drink every day yet." He took another pull from his jug. "Well, the Indians in this country were raped, too. This land used to be their land," he said swinging the jug in a wide arc. "Then we came along and raped them and killed them, just like we killed the buffalo and herded them onto tiny reservations. They don't have any tribal life left to speak of. They don't have any leaders because we've killed them all. They don't have land to hunt and fish on like they used to because we have the land. All they know how to do is depend on the BIA for life. Plus they drink, make babies, and kill each other. But we goddamn whites make sure they don't have any other life. Pardon my language. Don't get me talking about Indians or I'll have to imbibe until I'm unconscious." He took another drink. "Well, what did you come here for?"

"You said that Sally reminds you of the Indians. I don't understand."

"Oh, yes. I remember her after her baby was born. She was pale as a ghost. I knew she'd been raped. The only time she came out of her cabin was when she worked for Alice. Philena visited her; otherwise she was by herself all the time. She had a baby and wasn't married. Indians are getting pregnant all the time without being married. You can't be treated like dirt, which is the way we treated the Indians, and have a family life. Sally's family shipped her over here the way we shipped the Indians off to reservations. You get hooked up with her and you'll end up like a paleface married to a squaw living on a reservation."

"No," protested Jonas. "It's not going to be that way."

"How is it going to be?"

"She is a new creature in Christ. It won't be that way."

"What are you going to do about her family? Her family treated her like the whites treated the Indians. The Indians are no longer a part of this land—they're exiles in their own land. The Indians can't fight the whites and Sally can't fight her family. Are *you* going to fight her family? I hear you already tried and failed."

"We won't fight her family."

"See, you're going to be a white man marrying a squaw and living on a reservation. You may as well become accustomed to it and stay home from Hank and Philena's party."

Jonas took a deep breath. "We won't fight her family directly, but we will indirectly." He hurried on. "Daniel has taught me some things about sailing. You can't go directly into the wind, but you can go that direction by tacking. We're going to tack with Sally's family."

"And, how, exactly, do you plan to do that?"

Jonas thought back to his conversation with Daniel. "We're going to start by building trust between the two of us. When her family made her the outcast, they broke trust with her. If Sally and I are going to fight against that broken trust, we're going to have to do it by learning to trust each other. With Jesus' help we're going to do just that."

"My, you are a confident young man," said Jackson. But then he sat looking thoughtfully at Jonas. Finally he said, "I am impressed."

"I got my ideas about how to handle this from Daniel."

"They are good ideas." Again he lapsed into silence. He scratched his jaw. "I am thinking back to my days on the Indian reservation. I think when we raped them and murdered so many and robbed them of their land, we not only destroyed their trust in us, but we destroyed their trust in each other." He dropped his hand and stared unseeingly where his legs had once been. "I'm thinking of one old man in particular on the reservation. He lived before the days of the reservation. I used to talk to him and he would tell me about the old ways. He told me so many stories, but he always ended them by saying, 'But none of our ways saved us from the white man.' I went and got drunk every time after I talked with him. But I always went back to hear more, because the old ways seemed such good ways. And then he would say, 'But none of our ways saved us from the white man,' and I would go get drunk again." He lifted his head and looked at Jonas, "But you think you have ways that can save you from her family?" It came out half-question, half-statement.

"I have mostly thought about how to build trust with Sally."

Jackson shook his head. "The Indians can't ignore us whites. We are the conquerors. Indians can't do anything without looking over their shoulders at us. That's why they drink so much. Who cares what others think when you drink? The Indians couldn't go back to their old ways because we took the land. And when we took their land, we took their old ways. The Indians tried to fight for awhile. It was useless. I didn't know what the Indians should do. So I got drunk with them until the church sent me away. This island is my reservation. It's Sally's reservation too."

He wagged his finger at Jonas. "If you marry her, you will be moving onto the reservation." He paused, stared at the jug but did not drink. "I did not know what the Indians should do. I could not tell them the Gospel. A man comes to me because his daughter was raped by a white farmer. I am to tell him about Jesus, the God of the man who just raped his daughter? I got drunk instead. The Indians understood that."

"God is not the God of rapists," protested Jonas.

"Try telling that to the Indians."

"Rapists go to hell."

"Try telling that to the Indians. Try telling them that all the white men who stole their land are going to hell. This island was stolen from the Indians. You're living on stolen property. Would you tell the Indians you're going to hell for living on their stolen property?"

"I didn't steal this land."

"Oh, and if you did go to the Indians and tell them that rapists and thieves go to hell, and told the truth that whites stole all the land, what do you think would happen? Some white would put a bullet in you. Indians can't speak the truth, and neither can any white man."

"I don't know any Indians," Jonas said.

"Jonas, you are driving me to drink, coming over here and talking to me about all this misery." Jackson took another drink. "It's true that you don't know any Indians, but you do know Sally's family. You still haven't told me how you're going to handle them."

"Sally and I will ignore them."

"Humph. I told you the Indians can't ignore the whites. The whites have too much power. Sally's family has the power to make life miserable for her, and they aren't gonna stop just because you move onto the reservation. I moved onto the reservation and tried to help the Indians. I couldn't stop the whites from walking on the Indians like they were cigarette butts."

"Sally's family isn't walking on Sally. Her mother came to visit her just the other day."

"Do not fool yourself. Everybody knows Arnold treated her like dirt when she became pregnant. He made her life miserable until she moved over here. From what I hear, her brothers didn't treat her any better. Arnold quieted down as long as she was a good Indian and stayed on her reservation over here. But now you come along, and you get into a fight with Arnold. That is not being a good Indian, Jonas. From what I hear, Arnold is getting stirred up. Stay on the reservation. Forget the engagement party. It's probably a good idea you do not believe in dancing."

"What have you heard about Arnold getting upset?" asked Jonas. He could feel his palms were damp and cold.

"He's been bragging that he 'cleaned your clock good.' He refers to you as 'the snot-nosed preacher.' He says that if you cause any more trouble, he'll run you off the island."

Jonas sat in stunned silence. It was the first time anyone had reported to him what Arnold was saying after the fight. He swallowed. "What do you think I should do?" he asked.

"About what?"

"About Arnold?"

He shook his head. "I didn't know what the Indians should do. I certainly do not know what you ought to do." He leaned back in his chair and looked at Jonas. "You could do what I do and the Indians do." He wagged the bottle.

"No, thanks," Jonas said.

"What will you do then?"

Jonas shrugged his shoulders. "I will pray and do what God tells me to do."

Jackson shook his head slowly. "You really believe that." It was as much a statement as a question.

Suddenly Jonas felt better. "Yes, I really believe," he said.

"Keep believing. Now let me be alone." Jackson swung his chair around, turning his back to Jonas.

60.

The next evening when Jonas came to Sally's for supper, she greeted him with a big hug and a kiss. Then she pushed him back. Still holding him with both hands she said, "Jonas, I've made up my mind. I'm going to the engagement party next week. I am so happy. I feel so free." She twirled around and glided back to Jonas.

"Can I go, too?" asked Samantha.

"You certainly can," she said, glancing at Samantha. She kissed Jonas again, and then looked at him. Jonas tried to smile. "What is that sick smile on your face supposed to mean?" she asked.

"What about your daddy?"

"What about him?"

"Don't you think there might be trouble?" he said uncertainly. "I mean. . .why. . .after all these years, why do you want to see him?"

"I don't want to see him. It's just that I want to go to the party. I'll just ignore him."

"What made you change your mind?"

"I just changed it. Can't I just change my mind?"

"You seemed so sure you never wanted to see him again . . ." his voice trailed off.

"Something did happen to change my mind," she said defiantly. Jonas waited. "I'll tell you after supper," she said, glancing at Samantha. During supper Samantha told about following the bees from Hank's hive to the flowers and back again. Jonas and Sally listened and avoided each other's eyes.

After Samantha was in bed they sat at the table with coffee. "Hank and Brawn visited me last night after you went to Jackson's," Sally said. "They told me that Daddy's been saying he's going to chase you off the island if you cause any more problems. They also said they want you and me to come to the engagement party, and they don't want any trouble. Tonight they're going to talk to Daddy. They're going to tell him that he can come to the party, but only if he doesn't cause any problems. They are going to make him promise. Do you realize how happy that makes me, Jonas? I have always felt like Daddy could do with me whatever he wants. But now he can't. Brawn is bigger than Daddy. And Brawn said he'll watch Daddy like a hawk to make sure he doesn't cause any trouble that night. I've never had anybody to protect me before. I am so happy." Her eyes were dancing. "I haven't danced for years."

Jonas noticed that the room was beginning to fill with shadows as the sun set. He got up and lit the lantern.

"Why are you acting like such a cold fish?" she asked. "You should be happy. You'll get to dance with me."

"I don't believe in dancing."

"You don't believe in dancing?" she said, startled.

"In our church back home, we didn't believe in dancing because it leads to immorality."

She clicked her tongue and shook her head, "Jonas, Jonas, Jonas. Dancing is so much fun. I grew up dancing, and it never led to anything but fun. Jonas, Jonas, you need to smile. I am in such a good mood. I am not going to let you steal it away by not dancing." She leaped up and tugged at Jonas' hand. "Dance with me," she said. He didn't move. She tugged harder. Reluctantly he stood to his feet. She began trying to dance with him, but he was immobile. The voice of every preacher whom he had ever heard preach on temptation rolled over him like the surf of the lake. He shook his head. He would not give in.

She stopped tugging at him. She took his hand and lifted it, kissing the back of his hand. Her quietness caught his attention. "You are afraid to dance," she said.

He nodded. "I don't want to sin. I'm afraid we'll get carried away, that we'll sin."

"Jonas, you have been the perfect gentleman with me. Almost too perfect," she said, arching her eyebrows. Jonas could feel his face turn red. "I am not worried about you getting carried away."

"Maybe I could go but not dance."

"Jonas, do you still want to marry me?"

"Sure."

She touched his cheek. "I wasn't going to let myself be sad, but now I'm getting sad," she said. "I remember as a little girl, going to all the dances on the island. Mom and Daddy never danced because Mom refused to dance. But I remember how Daniel, when he was dancing with Alice, always ended by leaning her backwards, her weight on his arm, and she would look up into his eyes and they would laugh. I wanted to grow up and have a man hold me like that at a dance."

"But I don't know how to dance."

"I could teach you."

"But what would people think, a preacher dancing?"

"Daniel has been the nearest thing to a preacher on this island, and he plays at the dances. People would think it strange if you didn't dance."

"Let me think about it. I'll tell you tomorrow." He drank the coffee. He began to picture a fight breaking out at the dance. A fight between him and Arnold. No, he shook his head, he would not let it happen. Once was enough. But if he did not fight, others would. Maybe he should leave the island. He shook his head. He did not want to leave. There was sure to be drinking, and if there was drinking, there would be a fight. He remembered the boys his age in high school, reveling in the fights that regularly broke out at the dances. A few beers always brought on the fights. He shook his head.

"What are you sitting there thinking about so morosely?" asked Sally.

"I'm afraid there's going to be a fight at the dance."

"Are you planning to fight Daddy again?"

"No, but when there's drinking, there's bound to be fighting. I won't fight him, but Brawn will or Hank will."

"Where's your faith, Jonas?" she asked, standing up. Her smile took the bite out of her words. "Come, Samantha is asleep. Let's go for a walk."

Jonas followed her out the door and along the beach. He forced himself to stop thinking about the dance. The western sky was pale over the lake, while the east was dark above the trees of the island. Any moment the stars would appear. He wanted to look at the stars. The air was still. They walked in silence, their hands linked, listening to the waves gently confiding in the shore. He saw Daniel coming down the path toward the lake. "There's Daniel," he said.

"Hi, Daniel," Sally called. "The lake's as still as a pail of water sitting on a porch tonight."

"Ya, it is a still one."

Suddenly Jonas had an idea—talk to Daniel about the dance. Before he could say anything, Sally said, "Daniel, tell Jonas it's okay for a preacher to dance."

Daniel was about to walk by them, but he stopped. "Are you wanting him to dance with you at the engagement dance then?" he asked.

"Yes, and he has this foolish notion that it's sinful to dance. I told him you play at the dances, so it can't be wrong."

"And what do you say?" he looked at Jonas.

"I was taught that dancing was wrong because it leads to immorality."

"Okay, that is what you were taught. Is that what you believe?"

"Yes," he said, hesitantly.

"Then don't do any dancing."

"But I want him to dance with me," said Sally.

Daniel lifted his cap and scratched his head. "Ya," he said, "Jonas, what do you think of that?"

Jonas shrugged. "I don't know what to think. I've always thought dancing was sinful." He laughed nervously, "Probably fun, but sinful. Sally just told me how you and Alice dance. She told me about how when she was a little girl, she wanted to grow up and have a husband who looked at her with love when she danced with him. When I think about that, I want to be the one. . . It's just hard for me to think that dancing is okay."

"Sally," said Daniel, "you have a man whose heart is in the right place. You have trusted Jonas here with a lot. You can trust him with your heart's desire for a dancing man then."

"What is that supposed to mean?"

Daniel grinned. "What it means, young woman, is that you have made your case, and now is the time to let him decide what he's gonna do."

"You're just taking his side."

"Ya, it would appear so, but—don't tell him—really I'm taking your side." He gave her a grin.

"I think I'm being buffaloed," she said, but she was smiling.

Daniel wagged his hand, passed them, and went on walking down the beach. "Wait," said Jonas. "There's something else I want to talk to you about." Daniel paused. Jonas caught up with him, glanced hastily at Sally, then plunged ahead. "Sally is coming to the engagement party. So is her daddy. Hank and Brawn went over to her daddy tonight to warn him not to make any trouble. But I'm afraid there will be trouble anyway."

Daniel looked from one to the other. "I had not heard of this," he said soberly. He looked at Sally. "I am very glad that you're coming to the dance. It is a great act of faith."

"Or foolishness," said Jonas. "Her daddy has been saying he will drive me off the island."

"If you cause any more trouble," interrupted Sally, "and you promised not to. You promised."

"I won't fight him, but no matter what your daddy promises when he is sober, it'll be different after he's drinking. Hank and Brawn will probably be drinking. There will be a fight and I'm afraid. You might get hurt, Sally."

"Jonas, you weave wisdom and foolishness together like baling wire and twine and completely forget about Sally. You should not forget about Sally."

"What do you mean?" he protested. "I'm not forgetting about her. She'll be hurt if her daddy starts acting up."

"Nay, Jonas, your woman wants to get in the lake with you,

and you are fussing about the temperature of the lake."

"I don't understand."

"Sally is going to the dance because of you, not because of Hank and Brawn."

"I am?" "She is?" said Sally and Jonas together. They looked at each other and laughed. Then they looked at Daniel.

He stroked his beard. "Ya," he said, "I have been keeping an eye on you, Sally, ever since you came to live with us. Other than helping out Alice, you've spent most of the time hibernating in your cabin. Now that Jonas is courting you, you are out and about. The two of you went out on the lake last Sunday. Even when Jonas is gone you are out of the cabin more. So it doesn't surprise me that you want to come to the dance. Jonas, here, has made the world a safer place for you."

"I just don't like what might happen at the dance," Jonas said. "I don't want to fight her daddy again, but I want her safe. Can't you see?"

"Maybe I should stay home," said Sally.

"Jonas, you can't stop a fight from breaking out at the dance. So what can you do?"

"What can I do? I don't know."

"I will tell you what you can do. When you were back on the farm and a day looked like rain, you didn't keep the cows in the barn all day just in case. You let them graze and kept the barn door open, and when the storm came, the cows went in the barn then, right?"

"Right."

"You can't stop the storm, but you can keep the barn door open. You and Sally go to the dance and frolic in the pasture. If it starts to rain, head for the barn. Now, if you don't mind, I am out for my evening walk by the lake."

They watched him walk down the shore. Jonas turned to Sally. She grinned at him through the dim light. "Want to frolic in the pasture?"

Reluctantly Jonas gave in. He smiled weakly. "Yes, I want to frolic with you."

61.

The morning sky was hazy and promised a sweltering day as Jonas sat on the bluff above the lake. It was early in the morning on the second Sunday in August, and he still didn't know what he was going to preach on. He paged listlessly through his Bible; the words were hazy like the sky. Old Testament or New Testament. The gospels or Paul's letters. The prophets or the psalms. Nothing beckoned.

He looked out at the shimmering and distant lake. He was sitting in the shade of a boulder, back from the edge of the bluff so he couldn't see the shore. He could hear the faint swish and slosh of the lake among the boulders and rocks at the foot of the bluff. He stood up, clutched his Bible, walked to the edge, and peered down at the water tumbling its way between the rocks. He shivered, thinking of coming through those same rocks during the storm.

He followed the current south to the whirling pool where he had beached. He remembered his desperate praying during the storm. He smiled. He certainly did not deserve to survive that storm, and yet he had. Why had God saved him?

He went down the back of the bluff, worked his way over and around the boulders down the south slope, until he came to the tiny beach beside the pool. The water lapped at his feet. He studied the surface of the pool, trying to read the treacherous currents. Why had God saved him? To be chased off the island by Sally's father? That didn't make sense.

He waded a couple of steps into the pool, feeling ahead with his toe, knowing that he might step into a drop-off. Was going to the dance with Sally going to be his fall again?

He left the pool and placed his Bible on a rock. He didn't want it getting wet if he slipped. Again he waded into the pool. He could feel the pull of the current. An undertow had dragged him toward land and into the pool during the storm, so the undertow must go out as well. He wondered if it left by the same path on which it came in, or if it swirled around and then slipped out through another passage to rejoin the lake.

He had a sudden longing for home. Maybe it would be best if he were kicked off the island. He could go home. He remembered his farewell conversation with his mother. After his dream of the island beckoning him, he had told his parents about God's calling him to the island. He told them at Sunday dinner following church. As he had expected, his mother cried. His father's dark eyes furrowed, but he nodded. His younger brothers and sisters had fallen silent. Finally his father spoke, "Jonas, you are sure this dream was from God?"

"Yes, especially now that I know there is such an island."

"Then you are right to go."

Eventually his mother dried her tears and said, "Jonas, I knew you would leave some day, but it's not easy." She smiled through her tears.

The following Sunday, the night before Jonas was to leave, after the rest of the kids were in bed, she told Jonas she wanted to have a farewell talk with him. They had sat on the porch swing looking over the farm. Jonas sat at the far end of the swing, quite sure he did not need a farewell talk. "I have three things to tell you. Three things for you to take with you. Your daddy knows bigger words than I do, but I do get said what I got to say. There are things I wish were different. Jonas, you were the oldest. You had to work the hardest." She waved her hand at the farm. "You made this farm, not as much as your father, but you made this farm. You've been working on it since you started feeding the pigs when you were six." There was a catch in her voice but she continued, "The other kids will miss you. You have been a good older brother. But now that you are going, I wonder if Dad and I have given you what you need. We tried the best we could."

Jonas nodded.

"Time will tell," she said. "I feel like we could have done more. All this week I have been asking Jesus what more I can do for you. Your clothes are all ready and I have thought of three things to tell you. They ain't fancy things, but they are true. The first is the hardest." She began to cry. Jonas waited, having a hard time sitting still so as not to jiggle the swing. She took a hanky out of her apron pocket and wiped her eyes. "You can't ever come back, but what you want is always ahead of you," she said, and buried her face in her handkerchief.

What? thought Jonas. Never come back? He felt a sudden gloom. He began to move back and forth. Never come back?

"Stop jiggling, Jonas."

He stopped. "Did you say I can never come back?"

"Oh, Jonas," she said, "you can visit, but you can never come back and be our little boy again." She patted him on the knee. She asks Jesus what more she can do for me, he thought, and then she tells me I can't come home? I don't want to come home. I'm leaving.

As if reading his mind she said, "This may not make sense to you now, Jonas, but someday it might. Sooner or later, all of us want to go back. I remember the first time you wished you could go back. It was when I weaned you."

Jonas felt his face redden. His mother never talked about these kinds of things.

"I started carrying James," she said, "only four months after you were born. I had to dry up before James was born. He was gonna need milk. I stopped about a month before he was born. You would've been just about a year old. You cried and cried. But I had to chase you away. There was no way to go back. James was about to be born. I wanted to hold you so bad, but for a day or two I couldn't even hold you on my lap. I felt so bad for you. That was when Jesus told me that what you wanted is ahead of you. I took some comfort in that."

She seemed to be done with that one. Jonas breathed a sigh of relief. Only two more to go.

"Now this one is the happy one," she said. "Jonas, you have always been a serious boy. Your daddy and I have been serious, too, but we have always laughed together in bed after all you kids are in bed."

Jonas nodded. He had heard them laughing and always wondered what was so funny.

"Your daddy makes me laugh. When he has given up all his

working for the day and he comes to bed, he can laugh about life. He makes jokes about the biggest problems of life, and we laugh. He says the silliest things. When we were first married, I thought he was bad to make fun of sad things. But he said to me, 'Don't you think Jesus and God laughed over raising him from the dead? They played a great trick on the Evil One. There isn't a sadder and funnier story.'

"So when you get done working very hard all day and you have nothing to show for yourself but more work to do tomorrow, try laughing like Daddy and me.

"The last one." She paused for a long time. "Let's swing," she said. They pushed off and the swing went back and forth. "The last one," she said. "You have been shy about girls but that won't last." She laughed. "That won't last." She was looking sideways at him, but he looked straight ahead. "Jonas, a good wife can make or break a man. I have asked Jesus what to tell you about a wife. There seems to be not much for me to say. The best I can come up with is that I feel in my bones you will choose right. Your daddy has been good to me. You've learned from him. You know how to work, and you've had to take care of the other kids. You will know how to take care of a wife. I think you will choose right."

She stopped the swing. "Now I will stop making your face turn red. I have done my best." She had gone into the cabin.

In all the time he had known Sally, he had never thought about that conversation with Mama. He smiled. He liked to remember his mama's voice, "I think you will choose right."

Suddenly the sandbar he had been standing on gave way, and he pitched forward into the water. An undertow pulled him under. He flailed to the surface for a moment and saw that he was being drawn toward the rocks on the far side of the pool. He dove under the water and began a desperate attempt to swim against the current. One of his feet kicked against a rock. He twisted frantically to grab the rock to keep from being swept away. First with one hand and then the other he caught hold of the rock. He was still under the water. He needed to get free of the undertow. He felt around with his feet for something solid to kick off from. He found another rock, then eased himself into a crouch with his feet against the rock. If he pushed off, he might push himself directly into a boulder. But he had to do something.

He launched himself up and toward the side of the current. As he did, his hand brushed a rock and he used it to add to his thrust. Suddenly he was free of the current. His head popped out of the water and he gasped for breath. Just as suddenly another undertow grabbed him and propelled him back to the sand. Gasping for breath he crawled onto the beach. He turned and looked back at the pool. It looked calm on the surface. "You can't ever come back, but what you want is always ahead of you," he heard his mother say.

When he stopped he dried his hand on a bush and then leafed through his Bible where it lay on the rock. He remembered a psalm about being weaned. He searched. There it was. *Lord, my heart is not haughty, nor mine eyes lofty: neither do I exercise myself in great matters, or in things too high for me. Surely I have behaved and quieted myself, as a child that is weaned of his mother: my soul is even as a weaned child. Let Israel hope in the Lord from henceforth and for ever.* Psalm 131.

He would preach a sermon that you can't ever go back, but what you want is ahead of you.

62.

Jonas went to Sally's cabin the third Saturday night in August to walk her to Philena and Hank's engagement party. He reached for her arm to escort her. He dropped it as if it shocked him. "You've been drinking," he stammered.

"So?" she said, putting her hands on her hips. "I had a beer."

"Why?"

"I'll tell you why," she said. "Because this isn't easy for me.

I thought a beer would help and it has. I'm ready to go." She held out her elbow for Jonas.

"I didn't know you kept beer here." It was the only thing he could think to say.

"I got it from Jackson. Now let's go."

Jonas stood there, shaking his head. He was going to marry someone who drank?

"You can't drink beer."

"I can and I just did," she said, shaking her elbow at him to get him to take it.

"I thought you understood that you can't be a Christian and drink."

"Jonas, please don't preach to me. If I don't go pretty soon, I won't, and I have to go. Now are you coming or not?"

Jonas bowed his head. He felt sick. She smelled like beer. He thought of his Uncle Stan throwing up while playing third base during a family softball game. Jonas, who was nine and the runner on third, kept his foot on the base for fear of being tagged out, even though he was worried his uncle was going to puke on him. He hadn't, but it was close. Uncle Stan was his dad's youngest brother. An older cousin told him that his dad had almost gotten into a fight with Uncle Stan the first time he brought beer to Grandma and Grandpa's Sunday picnic. All Jonas knew was that his uncle always brought beer. Even during Prohibition. His Grandma and Grandpa acted as if he was drinking Kool-Aid like everyone else at the picnic. The longer the picnic went on, the louder his uncle got, and the more he stumbled during the softball games.

That was the only time he remembered his uncle throwing up. Jonas' Dad used a shovel to cover the vomit with sand. His cousins always joked about Uncle Stan's drinking and tried to get him to give them beer. As soon as they were sixteen or seventeen, his cousins found someone to sell them home brew. Jonas was the only one who refused. When he smelled beer, he always remembered the sharp smell of Uncle Stan's vomit at his feet.

"Are you going with me or not?" Sally repeated.

Jonas shook his head, searching for words.

"Well, if that's the way you're going to be," she said, "Samantha, let's go." Without looking back, Sally pulled Samantha with her toward the door. Samantha looked back.

Jonas tried to speak. He hadn't meant for them to leave without him. Still no words came. Sally shut the door.

Jonas felt a surge of anger. "I'm not going until I know why I'm going," he yelled at the closed door.

"God, why should I go?" He threw up his hands. "Should I go?"

The door opened. Samantha stood in the door. "I want you to go with us," she said in a small voice. He couldn't see Sally, but she held Samantha's hand in the open doorway.

"I'm not going until I know why I'm going," he said.

Sally stuck her head in the door. "And I'm not a good enough reason?" She shut the door hard.

Jonas, who was standing next to the table, hit it with his fist. "What am I to do? I don't want to fight. I don't want to dance. I don't want to drink. I don't want to sin. I don't want to be around sinners. What am I to do?"

You don't want to be around people who sin?

"That's right," he responded out loud. "I don't want to fight, I don't want to dance, I don't want to drink, and I don't want to be around people who do."

You don't want to be around people who sin?

"You heard me."

And what was I called?

"What are you talking about?"

And what was I called?

I don't know.

I was called a glutton and a winebibber.

"So?"

I was called that because I was around gluttons and winebibbers.

Jonas slumped down on the bench beside the table. "I don't want to be around gluttons either," he said, half-heartedly.

Do you want to be around me?

"I want to be around you."

You will find me at the dance.

"At the dance. I will find you at the dance?" He shook his head. He threw up his hands in surrender. "At the dance. Okay, I will go to the dance. I will look for you there, and if you are not there I will leave." He opened the door and banged it shut with his elbow. It hurt. Rubbing his elbow, he walked down the beach toward the sounds of the squeeze box, fiddle, and tub bass. Through the pine trees he could see a sliver of a moon just beginning to rise in the east.

63.

"You came!" shouted Samantha as she broke away from a herd of children and leaped into his arms.

"Yes." He looked at Sally standing on the other side of the dance area. About a dozen people were dancing, including Sally's daddy. A couple dozen people stood around the dancers. The musicians stood on a makeshift platform. Jackson's chair had been lifted up onto the platform. He sat in it playing fiddle. Daniel played the button accordion, while Brawn stood with his foot on the bottom of an upside-down tub that had been turned into a bass drum. A string stretched tight from the bottom of the tub to the top of a pole. Brawn held the pole with his left hand and plucked the string with the other. Lanterns hung on poles above the platform and on the sides of the dance area.

Jonas lifted Samantha onto his shoulders, and Sally's mother, Ethyl, sidled up to them.

"Look at that no-good husband of mine," her mother said. "He's already dancing. By the time the night is over he'll have danced with every woman in the place except me."

"Why doesn't he dance with you?" asked Jonas.

"I don't dance," she said archly.

"What is your reason?" Samantha shouted in Jonas' ear.

Jonas moved his head away from her mouth, his ear ringing. "Don't yell in my ear."

"What is your reason for coming?" she said, lowering her voice.

"I came to be with Jesus."

"He's here, isn't he?" she squealed.

Jonas shook his head. "If you yell again, I will have to set you down."

"Jesus is here," said Samantha. "He's everywhere." She squirmed. "I want to get down now," she said. Jonas set her down. She circled the dancers, climbed onto the stage, sat down, and looked up at Daniel as he squeezed the accordion. Daniel winked at her.

"I'm glad Sally decided to stop being unsociable and came to a dance finally," Ethyl said. "When she stopped coming, everyone talked about her."

Jonas did not want to talk about Sally. "Ethyl, I have never danced before. Would you be so kind as to give me instructions?"

Ethyl's mouth moved a couple of times like a fish on land with no sound coming out. "Young man," she said, finding her voice, "I will not be made a fool of. I am too clumsy to dance."

"I thought it would be nice to learn with someone who's not an accomplished dancer. Everyone else seems to know what they're doing. If I'm going to make a fool of myself, I'd just as soon not be alone." He smiled at her.

"Well, it will just have to be someone else."

"Perhaps you could explain the dances. You must be an expert from all these years of watching."

"You are a persistent young man. But I am helpless at explaining things like dances. Just watch, and then do what the rest are doing. Look at that no-good husband of mine. He just chose the youngest dancer here. He probably thinks he's going to teach her," Ethyl snorted. Rachel, Brawn's sister who had just turned sixteen, was Arnold's new partner. Ethyl babbled on while they watched.

After the tune, Daniel announced a break. Jonas watched

Daniel make his way through the crowd toward him. "Excuse us, Ethyl," Daniel said and took him by the arm and led him away from the crowd into the darkness. "Jonas, why are you not with Sally then?"

"She's been drinking."

"Beer?"

"Yes."

"All the more reason to be with her," he said urgently.

"I don't even know if I want to marry her now. I can't marry someone who drinks."

"Nay doggone, Jonas. Have I not taught you a thing about being a captain? What did I tell you not two weeks ago about tacking with the wind? What did I tell you?"

"You said that you can't go directly into a wind, so you tack with the wind."

Daniel spoke rapidly, his Norwegian accent stronger than ever. "Ya, you did hear then. There is a terrific storm brewing right now. This is no time for you to be off pouting by yourself. This is the time to be the captain of your ship. Ya, you get over by Sally and you stay with her through this whole thing. When there's a storm, a boat needs a captain more than ever. Now go." He gave Jonas a gentle push.

Jonas took a step toward the crowd, then turned back to Daniel. "What storm is brewing?" he asked.

"For pity's sake, Jonas, this is the first time Sally has laid eyes on Arnold for four years then. The first time Arnold has had to face her in four years. This is good." He pronounced it "goot." He reached out to Jonas, pulled him to him, put his arm around him. "See," he pointed to the group milling by the dance area. "See." Sally was sitting on the stage talking to Jackson. Jackson handed Sally his bottle and Sally took a pull on it. Jonas looked down. "Ya, don't look down, Jonas. I want you to look at that woman of yours while I talk to you. A captain doesn't hide in his cabin just because he doesn't like the look of the weather." Jonas looked up. Sally handed the bottle back and brushed a strand of hair out of her eyes as she talked with Jackson. "See that woman, Jonas? She is sitting there right this moment because of you."

"I'm not making her drink," protested Jonas, moving away.

Daniel let his arm drop. "Nay doggone, Jonas, I am not talking about her drinking. I am talking about her being at the dance. She is here because of you. She has been hiding in a hole for four years. Now she comes out because of you. She's got somebody to stand by her and so she comes out. Any moment now she is going back to that hole if you don't get up there and stand by her. I don't know when she'll come out again if that happens." He stepped next to Jonas and put his arm around him, giving him a squeeze. "You are a good man, Jonas. Ya, don't forget it." Jonas didn't move away. In the silence he let Daniel's words sink in.

He shook his head. "Daniel, I don't know how to handle someone who is drunk." Daniel was silent. "But I guess I can try."

"Ya," said Daniel, "what is that song you have us sing? "We've come this far by faith." With his accent it came out, *"We've come this far by* fate."

Jonas stood looking at Sally sitting on the stage talking to Jackson. He had told Jackson he would tack with trust. But how could he do that when Sally had broken his trust by beginning to drink? He realized Daniel was waiting for a response. "I'll be there in a minute," Jonas said. Daniel gave his arm a squeeze and went back to the dance.

Jonas leaned up against a pine in the darkness and then slid slowly to the ground. He wiped his brow. How could he tack, how could he build trust, when she was so untrustworthy? His fists curled and he hit the ground with the back of his hand.

Do you do well to be angry?

"Yes, I do well to be angry," he said aloud and immediately hoped no one heard him.

"Jonas!" Samantha was standing between him and the dance, calling him.

"I'm here."

"Jonas!"

"I'm here," he said louder.

She found him in the dark and crawled into his lap. "I was wanting you," she said.

He stared at the people milling around the dance area.

Do you do well to hurt this little one?

He grunted in surprise.

Samantha stirred. "What's the matter?"

He didn't say anything.

"I don't like Mama to be funny," she said.

"What?" he said.

"She's talking funny and scary."

"Loud, you mean?"

"Ya." She turned and snuggled closer to him. He held her, feeling her small heartbeat against his chest. Suddenly she stood up and tugged at his hand. "I want you with Mama."

She trusts you'll love her mother no matter what.

He wiped his eyes on the back of his hand and stood up. "Okay, Samantha, lead me to your mama."

64.

After Samantha led Jonas to Sally, she ran off to play with the other kids who were chasing each other in and out of the crowd. When Jonas sat down next to Sally, she pulled her feet up on the platform, turned her back to him, and faced Jackson. "Jackson, I could use another pull on your baby bottle," she said loudly, tossing her head and laughing. Jackson looked at Jonas over her shoulder. Jonas shook his head.

"I think you've had enough, Sally," Jackson said.

"Hey," she said. "You owe me. I keep you warm at night with a blanket I made with my own hands. And you won't give me another nip? Jackson, just one more. I won't drink it all. Just one more," she said, sounding as if she were a mother coaxing a child to take one more bite of oatmeal. Jackson didn't look at Jonas as he handed her the bottle.

She swung her feet onto the ground, took a long drink, and looked at Jonas defiantly. Her eyes had the unsettled, green look of the lake before a storm. She set the bottle on her lap and wiped her mouth. Then she held out the bottle to Jonas. "Jonas, you oughtta try this. You'd smile more. Coochicoo," she said, pretending to tickle Jonas under the chin with her free hand.

"No thanks," he said.

"Oh, Jonas, you are such a grouch."

She spun her feet around, facing Jackson, and handed him the bottle. Daniel and Brawn came back to the platform, getting ready to play again. Sally got to her feet and stared at Jonas. "Are you going to be mean all night, or are you going to dance with me?"

Jonas stood up. "I'm going to dance with you."

"Well, well, the preacher is going to dance. Aren't you afraid," she said loudly, lifting her eyebrows, "you'll be fornicating with me by the time the night is over?"

Jonas felt his face flush a deep red. His eyes blurred. As they cleared he kept them on her, not daring to look to see who all had heard her. In the stillness he was sure every eye was on them.

"Ya, Brawn wants to do a little dancing, but Jackson and me will play a peppy little tune named the 'Evergreen Waltz,'" called Daniel from the platform, and the band started to play.

People around them began to move again. Jonas continued to stare at Sally. She laughed nervously. "Well, that's what you're so worried about, isn't it?" she said. Her laugh almost sounded like a sob to Jonas. He remembered the first night she had come on the boat and he heard her crying in the darkness. Out of the corner of his eye he saw Samantha standing still, watching them.

"Sally," he said, "you can say mean things, but unless you tell me to leave, I'm going to stay by your side tonight."

She stared at him for a moment, her eyes furrowing into a frown. She shook her head, "Let's dance then." They stood up and he put his right hand on her waist and slipped his other into hers. This much he knew from having studied the other dancers. He looked at the other dancers, hoping for a sign about what to do next. Brawn, gliding by with Theresa, gave him a wink. "You've got to do more than stand by me," Sally said with a laugh and a shake of her body to get his attention. "You've got to lead me."

He looked at her. "I don't know what to do next," he confessed.

"It's a three-step," she said.

Jonas started to his left. Sally glided with him. One, two, three. He stopped. She stumbled over his foot. He quickly reached out a hand and kept her from falling. She started to giggle. She looked at him. He could feel his face turning red. She laughed. "I took three steps," he said.

"Three steps," she giggled. Soon she was laughing so hard she began to double over, and Jonas practically had to hold her up. He started to smile.

She looked at him, still laughing. He began to get the giggles. "There's more than three steps?" he asked, shaking with laughter.

"Three steps," she said and went into another spasm of laughter. She laughed so hard tears formed in her eyes. In a moment, when he seemed to have control of his laughter, he bent to kiss the tears from her cheek. She jerked with laughter and her cheek banged into his nose. With a sudden picture of how ludicrous he must have looked, he clutched his nose and went into another round of laughing.

He was weak with laughter and she was leaning on him. Laughing, wiping his eyes, half holding her to keep her from falling, half to keep himself from falling, he set out for the edge of the platform. Like pool balls they careened off other dancers, eventually collapsing on the platform.

Daniel and Jackson were well into another waltz by the time they both stopped laughing. He had his arm around Sally when she turned and snuggled up close to him, burying her face in his neck as if she were hiding. There was something childlike in her at that moment. He held her very tight. Instinctively he searched the dancers, looking for her daddy. Arnold was dancing a slow waltz with Rachel, Brawn's sister. As Arnold turned, Jonas could see him staring over Rachel's shoulder into the darkness. Jonas followed his eyes but saw nothing.

Jonas glanced down at Sally. Her blonde hair lay tangled on her shoulders. He closed his eyes and squeezed her tight. He caught a whiff of beer on her breath. He turned his face away. Oh, Sally, he thought, am I going to marry someone who drinks? Then in that instant he remembered: *Surely I have behaved and quieted myself, as a child that is weaned of his mother: my soul is even as a weaned child.* She had quieted herself. He kissed her hair again and held her tight. He closed his eyes. He knew that above the lamps the stars shone. He also knew that if Jesus were there that night, he would hold Sally like a weaned child. He let himself feel her hair on his cheek, her breath in his neck, her bosom on his chest, her arms around his chest. Her weight on his left arm as he held her, left hand clasping her lower back, his right arm across her back and holding her shoulder, the chill of the night and the incredible warmth of her.

A couple of songs later Jonas blinked his eyes open. Again he searched for Arnold. Arnold was dancing with an East Sider that Jonas didn't know. It was a fast song, and the men and women were flying in the tight little area on the beach. Jonas marveled that they didn't bump into each other. Out of the corner of his eye he saw Samantha start walking towards them. He turned just as Brawn swung Theresa too close to Samantha. Theresa's heel tripped Samantha. Jonas wanted to jump up, but he was holding Sally. In that moment, Arnold leaped to the fallen Samantha. He knelt over her. Jonas could see the look of concern on Arnold's face. Arnold touched her shoulder. Jonas could see him ask, "Are you okay?"

"Sally," Jonas said, "Samantha was just knocked down." Sally sat up, blinking rapidly. When she saw Samantha she let out a high-pitched cry like a wounded rabbit. She raced to

Samantha, Jonas trailing her. Arnold was helping Samantha to her feet. "Get your hands off her," Sally screamed, pulling Samantha away.

"Quit acting like a bitch," he muttered, stepping back.

"Did he hurt you?" Sally asked, leaning over Samantha. "Did he hurt you?" she repeated. Samantha shook her head. Sally, apparently not catching the shake of the head, shook Samantha. "Did he hurt you?" Samantha began to cry.

Sally put her arms around Samantha and glared at her daddy. "Now look what you've done," she screamed. "Don't you ever touch her again. If you do, I'll kill you. Don't ever touch her, ever." Arnold was backing away from his furious daughter.

Jonas picked up Samantha, put her head on his shoulder, and patted her back.

"What did you do to her?" demanded Sally.

Arnold couldn't back up anymore because Brawn had planted himself behind him. "I didn't do nothin' to her," Arnold said, his eyes darting from face to face in the crowd that was gathering around him and Sally. "She fell," he said. "She got knocked over. I was just helping her up."

Sally glanced at Brawn towering behind Arnold. Brawn nodded at her. Emboldened she said, "You knocked her down."

"No," protested Arnold.

"Who did then?"

Arnold shrugged his shoulders. "How am I supposed to know?" Brawn put his hand on Arnold's shoulder. Arnold shook it off. "Keep your mud hooks off me," he said and spun around. He took a step backwards when he saw who was behind him. Brawn gave a nod toward Sally. "Lady asked a question. Answer it."

Arnold slowly turned halfway back toward Sally, his head swiveling between Sally and Brawn. Finally he settled on looking at the ground. "I don't know who it was," he muttered. "Somebody swung close to her and she fell, so I thought they knocked her down."

"I saw who it was," said Jonas. He saw Arnold's head snap

up. Jonas turned to Sally, "I saw what happened. Samantha was coming toward us, and she wasn't looking where she was going. Brawn swung Theresa by, and Theresa's heel caught Samantha's foot and Samantha fell. Arnold saw her fall and helped her up." Sally looked at Jonas in disbelief. "Ask her," said Jonas, nodding to Samantha.

"What happened, Samantha?"

"I was coming to you, Mama. I fell. That man helped me up." She pointed to Arnold.

Arnold snorted. "So, Sally, you're back to your old ways of lying again."

Jonas felt a surge of rage. Barely aware of setting Samantha down, he took two steps and faced Arnold. "The truth will win out, Arnold. . ." he said, pushing his finger into Arnold's chest. Arnold swatted it away. ". . .and when it does you will lose."

Arnold laughed, but his eyes didn't laugh. "Are you looking for a good lickin' again? Once wasn't enough?"

Brawn grabbed Arnold by the collar and lifted him off the ground. "Now's your chance, Jonas," he said. "Hit him." Arnold kicked futilely at Brawn, but Brawn ignored him. "Hit him," he repeated.

"Get your hands off him, you big lummox," shouted a voice that Jonas didn't recognize.

"Yeah, you big lummox," cried Ethyl.

"Wait, wait," said Jonas, suddenly fearful that a brawl was about to break out. "Set him down, Brawn. I just want to say one more thing to him. Set him down." Everyone at the dance had crowded around Jonas and Arnold.

Brawn reluctantly set him down. "Stay put," Brawn ordered. "Listen to what the preacher has to say."

"Arnold, I told the truth just now about you and Samantha. Hide from the truth, and you're a prisoner. Tell the truth and you're free."

Now that he figured he wasn't going to get hit, Arnold could smirk again. "Fancy words, preacher, fancy words. The truth is, the last time you mouthed off to me, I knocked you out cold. And I can do it again, too."

"The truth is," said Jonas, "the last time I took matters into my own hands. Next time I'll let truth have its way with you." Jonas spun on his heels, picked up Samantha, took Sally by the arm, and walked away. The crowd parted for them.

65.

Jonas sat on the far side of the platform catching his breath. He felt hot, as if he had fought Arnold, and not merely with words. The band was playing again and the crowd was back to dancing. Jonas looked at Sally, anxious to see what she was thinking. Sally, holding Samantha, shook her head as if disapproving, but she also smiled wanly. "So you're being the hero, protecting me again, huh?" She didn't seem to be entirely displeased.

"Who was that man?" asked Samantha.

Jonas and Sally looked at her, then at each other. Jonas waited. "That man is your grandpa."

"How come I never get to play with my grandpa like other kids?"

Sally looked at Jonas as if to say, you take over.

"Your grandpa is also Sally's daddy, and they have not been getting along, so they haven't talked to each other since before you were born."

Samantha looked up at Sally with large solemn eyes in the lamplight. "Did he say mean things to you?"

Tears formed in Sally's eyes. She looked away.

"Yes, he did mean things to Sally," said Jonas. He paused. "Maybe someday he'll say he's sorry," he said. Sally gave him a look of disgust. "But maybe not," he added.

"He helped me up when I fell," said Samantha.

"Yes, he did," said Jonas.

"He said mean things to you too, Jonas."

"Yes, he doesn't like me too much."

"Does he like me?"

Jonas felt like crying. He reached over and took Samantha in his arms. "Samantha, you are full of good questions tonight. I don't know whether he likes you or not. I do know that God likes you and Sally likes you and I like you and Daniel likes you and lots of people like you." He kissed her on the head.

Samantha seemed to have run out of questions. Sally leaned over and kissed Samantha and wiped her tears on Jonas' shoulder. Jonas slid closer to Sally and put his arm around her. Samantha wiggled around until she was between them. Sally and Jonas each put an arm around her. Together they listened to the music and watched the dancers. Arnold was not dancing. Sally leaned her head on Jonas' shoulder above Samantha. Samantha wiggled upwards into Sally's lap and put her head between their heads. She kissed Sally.

Jonas laughed. "I think this little girl wants to be in the center of our love."

"I think she wants to be in the center of my attention," said Sally.

"You're probably right," said Jonas.

"I like you, Jonas, but I love Mama," Samantha said.

"That's okay," he said. "You had your mama long before you had me."

"And I have you both," laughed Sally.

"But me first," said Samantha.

"I definitely had you first," she said.

Samantha sighed. Within a couple of minutes she fell asleep.

66.

Jonas and Sally put Samantha to bed and left Ethyl in the cabin to look after her. When they walked out the door, Sally was very quiet. A few steps away from the door she stopped.

"Jonas, I feel terrible. I'm not in the mood to dance at all."

"What's the matter?"

"You should have hit me for what I said to you in front of all those people."

"I'd rather forgive you."

Sally looked down at the ground, scuffing a tree root exposed by the path to the pale starlight.

"I don't deserve it."

Jonas nodded. The wind whispered in the pines. "I didn't deserve you after I ran away from you and then got into a fight with your daddy. I didn't deserve you forgiving me."

"First your face turned red, and then you turned white after I mouthed off."

"I felt sick," he said.

"And now I feel sick." Jonas nodded and she scuffed the root some more. Without looking up she said, "Can you forgive me?"

"I think I can."

"That's a lot," she said looking up at him. Her eyes were shadows in the starlight, but she was looking at him. He wished he could see her eyes.

"I forgive you," he said.

She squeezed his arm very hard. "I feel like dancing."

They walked hand in hand back toward the dance. Sally pulled Jonas to a stop. "Did you hear something?" she asked.

Jonas, who had been replaying his run-in with Arnold, shook his head. Then he realized that she might not have seen him do that. "No," he said aloud.

"Sally," came the voice again, half-whispered, half-called, from a stand of pines between a couple of the tourist cabins.

Sally tightened her grip on Jonas' hand and stepped closer to him. They both peered toward the pines. The sliver of a moon was now well above the trees. Jonas couldn't make anyone out in the shadows of the pines. "Who's there?" demanded Sally. Jonas jumped at the sound of her voice.

"It's Floyd," came back the voice. "I gotta talk to you. Come over here."

"What do you want?" called Sally.

"Who's Floyd?" asked Jonas.

"I don't want Daddy to see me with you, Sally. Just come here," said the voice. Sally stood hesitating, still holding Jonas' hand.

"Who's Floyd?"

"My brother. Not the one who hit you; the younger one."

"Sally, this is for your own good," said the voice.

"Let's talk to him," said Jonas.

He took a step forward, but Sally held him back. "What if somebody's with him?" she said. They both stood listening, trying to decide if there was more than one person in the grove. Other than an occasional snatch of music from the dance and wind in the pines, they couldn't hear anything. In the stillness, Jonas caught a faint whiff of beer. He was glad she seemed to be sobering up.

"Are you alone?" Jonas called.

"Yes," said the voice, "but not for long."

"Let's go," said Jonas. This time Sally followed. They stepped into the pine grove, peering through the darkness.

A figure stepped from behind a tree up the slope on the east side of the grove. "Over here," he called. They approached. Sally's hand felt damp and cold in Jonas' hand.

"What do you want, Floyd?" demanded Sally. Her voice sounded more confident to Jonas than her hand did.

"Daddy sent me to look for your boyfriend," he said. "He wants to beat him up again."

Jonas felt a sudden pain in his ribs, remembering the last beating. He touched his eye, the one he couldn't see out of for days after the fight. He shivered and looked back toward the beach. "Are they coming right now?" he asked.

"No, I followed you when you took the little girl home. I'm supposed to run back and tell Daddy and Eugene where you went. I haven't told them yet. I wanted to talk to Sally first. But if I don't get back there soon, Daddy will send Eugene."

"Talk," she said.

"I gotta know. . ." Suddenly his voice began to slow, ". . .if it's true. . ." He stopped. Sally squeezed Jonas' hand so hard he almost yelled.

"If what's true?" Her voice was hard.

"You know. . ." Again his voice trailed off.

"No, I don't know."

"I mean what he said about Daddy." They could make out he was gesturing at Jonas.

"Why do you want to know?" asked Sally.

"Well, I mean. . .you know, if he did that . . .well, that's pretty bad." He stopped. "I mean, it's our family," he said emphatically, as if that made everything clear. Sally was silent.

"Eugene told me about the fight," he continued. "He and Dad were bragging about it afterwards. But later Eugene, when we were alone, told me what he said." Again he gestured at Jonas. "You know . . . he said . . . uh . . . Daddy . . . well, if it's true, it's terrible."

"If I tell you it's true, what are you going to do? Why are you so interested in my life? I haven't seen you in over four years."

"I thought you didn't want to have anything to do with us," Floyd protested. "Daddy said you thought you were too good for us. But now when I hear this . . . I just want to know."

"Floyd, it's true, damned true," she said. Her hand squeezed Jonas' so hard that he squeezed back in self-defense. He could see Floyd shaking his head in the darkness.

"When did it happen?" Floyd's voice sounded small.

"Nine months before Samantha was born," she said.

"You mean Daddy's . . . ?" his voice rising in disbelief.

"Yes, that's exactly what I mean."

"Are you sure . . . I mean . . ."

"Do I have to spell it out for you, Floyd? I was a virgin. Daddy's the only one who ever fucked me."

"Sally . . . " Floyd half cried in protest.

"You asked."

"I know, I know . . . but it sounds awful."

"It is awful," said Jonas, who feared that Sally wasn't as sober as he had hoped. He had never heard her say that word.

"Neither one of you knows how awful," Sally said. They stood in the grove in an uncertain silence, the wind breathing through the pines and the music in the distance. Sally's hand began to relax in Jonas'.

"So now you're going to tell Daddy where Jonas is so he and Eugene can beat him up?" Sally said flippantly.

"No," protested Floyd.

"Well, what are you gonna do?"

"I guess I'll tell 'em that I lost him in the dark."

"My name is Jonas," said Jonas, tired of being referred to as "him."

"Jonas," said Floyd.

"And you, Jonas," Sally said, bumping against him playfully, "here's another chance for you to be my hero."

"Sure," said Jonas, his voiced layered with doubt.

"Don't be such a sourpuss," she said. "I'm serious. Here's your chance to be my hero."

"I don't want to be a hero."

"I need a hero."

"Exactly what do you mean by that?"

"Well, I better get going," said Floyd. He left.

"I am a damsel in distress. Rescue me." She threw herself on him, and he stumbled but managed to keep from being knocked over and to keep from dropping her. Her head rested on his shoulder.

"Sally, please be serious."

"'Sally, please be serious,'" she said through her nose into his ear. He winced. Then she sighed and said in a normal voice, "Jonas, I am serious. I don't want to go back to that stupid dance. And I sure don't want you getting beat up again. I hate my daddy. All I can think of is how I want another drink. I hate myself for drinking. I hate myself for saying awful things to you. I'm a mess. The day is a mess. I need a hero, someone who knows what to do. Someone to save me," she said dramatically.

"I forgave you."

She sighed and leaned against him. "You did, didn't you."

She paused and sighed again, "But I still need a hero."

"Jesus is the only hero."

She lifted her head from his shoulder and looked around. "I haven't seen him around tonight," she said wistfully.

"It's funny you should say that," he said. "When I was being so stubborn about not coming to the dance tonight, he said that I would find him at the dance."

"Hey," she said, "that's right. I'm not the only one who was being awful tonight. You were, too. You were a brat when you wouldn't come with me earlier tonight." She laid her head back down on his shoulder and murmured, "So have you seen him at the dance yet?"

"I can't say I have. But the night's not over. Let's go back to the dance."

"You want to, even though Daddy wants to beat you up?"

"Sally, you went tonight, even though he did worse to you."

"Yes, but I had to drink three beers to get enough courage."

"I don't need any beer," Jonas said hastily.

"I wasn't suggesting that." She leaned her head against him again and asked, "If we go back, will you dance with me again?"

"If you still want me to."

"I like the sound of your heartbeat," she said. Jonas squeezed her and stood feeling the wind on his face and the weight and warmth of her head on his chest. "Jonas," she murmured, "you have a lot of learning to do, but I'll teach you to dance. But are you sure it's a good idea to go back?"

"I have a feeling that tonight's a good night for sailing into the wind," he said.

She nodded her head against him.

"Okay," he said, "let's go." He began to gently separate himself from her.

"Wait," she said, clinging to him. "What are we going to do about my daddy?"

"Daniel tells me that I have to tack when I'm in a strong wind. So I guess I will tack."

"What's that supposed to mean?"

"With tacking. . ."

"I know what tacking is. Just tell me what tacking has to do with Daddy."

"I don't think we should fight him. That would be going directly into the wind. I think we should go back to the party but ignore him. Just pay attention to each other. That's how we'll sail into the wind." He kissed her on the lips.

"We could," she said, talking through the kiss, "pay attention to each other without going to the dance." She kissed him, a long kiss. When her hand, slowly inching down his chest, passed his navel, he jumped apart from her.

"Oh, Jonas, don't be such a stick-in-the-mud. I was only teasing. I'll go back with you to the dance," she said, reaching for his hand. "But how are we going to keep Daddy from beating you up before we get there?"

Jonas wished she wouldn't have dropped her hand so low. He had been enjoying that kiss. He tried to think. "Let's see, we can't swim because we'd arrive soaking wet. Let's go inland and walk along the ridge to circle around the dance from the west. They won't be expecting that."

67.

Jonas led Sally west through the trees along the ridge. They each swatted mosquitoes with one hand and kept track of each other in the dark with the other hand. He strained for sounds of Arnold or Eugene. All he could hear were frogs and insects. He was surprised at how loud the night noises were. Maybe night was always this loud, but he hadn't noticed until he was trying to hear.

Suddenly they heard the sharp crack of a tree branch breaking ahead of them, and someone, not twenty feet away, shouted, "Damn it!" Sally grabbed Jonas and clung to him. They stood very still, holding their breaths, straining to hear. They could hear nothing more through the din of the night.

Jonas was about to suggest they move off the path.

"Damn it," moaned a voice, "damn it."

"It's Daddy," Sally whispered in Jonas' ear.

"Damn it, that hurts," Arnold moaned again and again. Then he fell silent.

Jonas and Sally stood next to each other in the darkness, the sounds of frogs and insects screaming in their ears. Jonas hunched his shoulders to move his shirt up and down and chase the mosquitoes off his back. "We better get outa here," he whispered in Sally's ear.

"Get outa here?" she whispered. "He's hurt. He needs help."

"We can send somebody to help him," Jonas whispered.

"Eugene!" Arnold called weakly. His call seemed to be swallowed up by the sound of the night creatures. "Eugene, I can't get up," he called again.

"We better get off the ridge," whispered Jonas. "Eugene might be coming up the ridge, too." Sally let him lead her a few feet off the ridge back towards the beach. Then he paused to listen for Eugene and to rub his back against a pine to scratch the mosquito itches.

"He needs our help," Sally whispered, but she made no move toward Arnold. How can she think of helping him? wondered Jonas. He shook that thought off. He wished he had thought of it. It would be the right thing to do.

"Floyd," Arnold called, then went back to muttering about it hurting. Again he yelled softly, "Floyd! Eugene, somebody come here."

"He needs help," Sally said, and began moving back toward the trail, pulling Jonas after her. "Daddy?" she called softly when they were back on the ridge. There was no answer. They moved a few feet, threading their way through the scrub pines. "Daddy?" she tried again. Again no answer. "Daddy," she said sharply, "you better speak up or we may step on you."

"Sally?" came Arnold's voice from a pine a few feet ahead and to the left.

"Yes, it's me. What happened?"

"I tripped and wrenched my knee. Man, does that sucker hurt. I can't stand up."

Sally kept inching toward his voice. "I want to make sure we don't step on you," she said.

"If you've got that boyfriend with you, don't come any closer," he said, hardness returning to his voice.

"Daddy, you need help."

"Hey, I need help, but I don't need his kinda help. I don't need nobody kickin' me when I'm down."

"I'm not gonna kick you," said Jonas. He restrained a smile at the picture of kicking Arnold.

"Sally, send your boyfriend to get Floyd and Eugene."

"I'm not leaving Sally with you," Jonas said.

Jonas saw a small pine shake, and Arnold let out a fresh cry of pain. "If I could get up, I'd coldcock you, boy."

"I'll go get Eugene and Floyd," said Sally.

"Don't leave me, Sally," pleaded Arnold. "I need you. Don't leave me alone." Jonas flinched. Something in Arnold's voice sent a flash of fear through him. Jonas moved quickly forward, trying to pass Sally who had been on ahead. He wanted to be between Arnold and her.

"What are you doing?" she asked, irritably.

"I want to check out his injury," he said, holding her arm, trying to move by on the narrow space between trees.

She shook her arm impatiently. "Don't," she said, reaching for him as he slipped by. Her arm jolted him in midstep and he lost his balance, tried to catch it, and tripped on something. He flung out a hand to break his fall and hit Arnold's head. His hand glanced off Arnold, his shoulder hit the man, and he slid off him, landing face-first in grass and gravelly dirt.

Arnold let out a whoop. "You son of a bitch." Something struck Jonas in the back. Automatically he sucked in and choked on grass and pine needles. Coughing, he was hit again. Realizing Arnold was clobbering him with a fist, he rolled away until the hitting stopped. Coughing, gasping, he tried to catch his breath.

Sally crouched, touching his leg, "Are you okay?"

Jonas couldn't speak. He needed to lie still and cough it out.

"Are you okay?" said a worried Sally, tugging at his leg.

"The son of a bitch hit me while I was down," complained Arnold.

"Oh, shut up, Daddy," Sally said. Jonas kept coughing.

"What's going on here?" boomed Brawn from above them.

"Where have you been?" demanded Sally. "You said you were gonna stick to Daddy like a hawk."

"Lost him," pronounced Brawn. "Lost the scrawny bugger in the dark. Had to drop my tub right in the middle of a song. Slippery sucker. Found him though." Brawn paused. "What're you guys on the ground for?"

"Jonas tripped," Sally said.

Jonas managed to stop coughing long enough to spit out most of the rest of the turf that had stuck in his front teeth. He sat up and coughed again. Sally patted his back.

"Why's he coughing?"

"I don't know."

"I got a mouthful of grass and stuff when I fell," Jonas finally got out. "Then Arnold whacked me in the back and I sucked in and choked on it." He ran his tongue over his teeth and spit again.

"Where is he?" asked Brawn.

Jonas looked around. He could hear Arnold dragging himself away. Jonas crawled after him and grabbed his boot. "Here he is," he said. Arnold let out a surprised yelp of pain. Jonas let go. "He keeps hurting me when I'm down," said Arnold.

Jonas spit out the last pine needle and stood up.

"You won't let them hurt me, will you, Sally?" Arnold whimpered.

"Daddy, what am I gonna do with you?" Sally asked.

"You decide, Sally; we'll do it," said Brawn.

"I need a doctor," Arnold said.

"Daddy, you were mean to me," Sally said in a small voice.

"Don't start on that," pleaded Arnold. "Can't you see I'm down. My knee . . . I can't defend myself."

"I couldn't defend myself either," Sally said sadly.

"Don't need to defend yourself against the rat now," said Brawn.

"I slept out in the woods by myself that night," Sally said.

"Sally," pleaded Arnold.

"You hurt me and left me." Her voice broke.

"Let me take care of his other knee and we'll leave him for the night," said Brawn.

"Don't do that, Brawn," Sally, started to cry, "I was so alone when he hurt me and left me alone." Even though he couldn't see her clearly, Jonas knew that tears were streaming down her face.

"Sally, don't," pleaded Arnold. Don't what? Jonas wondered. He tried to make sense of the words.

"When I came home I had to lie to everybody," sobbed Sally. Jonas put an arm around Sally's shoulder. She did not draw close to him. Arnold didn't say anything. Jonas let his arm drop to his side, but he stood as close to her as possible without touching her.

Finally her sobbing stopped. "Daddy, I lied for you," she said through sniffles. "I lied for you but I couldn't see you anymore. I couldn't see you. All these years and I couldn't see you."

Arnold didn't say anything.

"Rat, say something," said Brawn.

"Maybe you should leave me here," Arnold said.

"What do you mean?" asked Sally.

"You want to hurt me so much, so just leave me here."

"I don't want to hurt you," Sally said.

"You keep talking," said Arnold, "when I need a doctor."

"Daddy, don't you care?"

"About what?" he asked, sullenly.

"About *me*," Sally said, her voice rising.

"I'm lying here in dire pain and you start bringing up the past. I need a doctor."

Jonas wanted Sally to stop. Anything she said, Arnold was going to hurt her more. "Sally," he said, "should we carry him back to the dance? Eugene or somebody can get his boat and take him to a doctor."

"Daddy," she said, "why did you do it? I just want to know why?"

"I don't know what you're talking about," Arnold muttered. His words were almost lost in the cacophony of the night creatures.

"Daddy, all I want to know is *why*?" she insisted in a small voice. Arnold was silent. "I was never mean to you, was I, Daddy?" Her question hovered in the air like a firefly.

"Nah," he said, a sudden bitterness in his voice, "you were a good girl."

"What was wrong with being a good girl?" asked Sally, her voice still small.

"Shit! I don't know," he said angrily. "I need to get to a doctor. The mosquitoes out here are eating me alive and I can't move. For crying out loud, Sally."

"I was a good girl," Sally said sadly. "It was bad to be a good girl."

"No," Jonas said, "it's not bad to be a good girl."

"It was to Daddy," she said. Jonas didn't know what to say and Arnold was silent.

"Mosquitoes are getting to me, too," said Brawn.

"The mosquitoes can eat us all alive," said Sally fiercely. Jonas and the others waited for her to go on. "I have one more question," she said, lowering her voice. "Daddy?" She paused for so long that Jonas wondered if that was the whole question. "Daddy, I might never get to talk with you like this again."

"What does that mean?" muttered Arnold.

"So I have to ask you," continued Sally, sounding smaller and smaller. "Do you hate me, Daddy?" Jonas suddenly pictured Sally as a five-year-old girl in a nightgown, standing in the living room doorway, blinking in the light, asking a question of her father who's sitting with a group of adults who've been laughing and talking. The question silences everyone. Don't send her back to bed, Jonas implored silently.

"Sally, you always did say the craziest things," Arnold said.

Jonas reached out for Sally. This time she came to him, burying her face in his neck. She started to cry again. This time she made no sound, only shook silently in his arms, her tears dampening his neck.

"Well, are you gonna figure out a way to get me outa here or not?" said Arnold. "If you're not gonna, at least go find Eugene and Floyd and tell them where I'm at." Jonas knew something had happened between Arnold and Sally. He didn't know what, but he could tell Arnold was suddenly feeling sure of himself.

"Sally, what do you want us to do with the rat?" asked Brawn. "Drown him or haul him out of here?"

Sally lifted her head. She put her mouth to Jonas' ear. "I *had* to know," she whispered. "Now I know I can ask what I have to ask and say what I have to say." She squeezed him very tight and then whispered again, "Now I know." She kissed him on the ear, sending goose bumps all the way down his leg.

Pushing away from Jonas she announced in a clear voice, "Daddy, I didn't like spending the night by myself in the woods when I was hurt bad. Carry him out."

68.

The dance came to a halt when Brawn, Jonas, and Sally arrived carrying Arnold. Brawn had picked him up under the shoulders and Jonas and Sally each had a leg. Sally had started out with the bad leg, but she wasn't strong enough to hold it steady. Arnold moaned or yelped every time his leg moved the wrong way, so they switched and Jonas took the bad leg. Jonas could hold it better, but not well enough to stop all of Arnold's yelps. Once they were off the ridge and onto the lakeshore it went better. Jonas kept wondering what Sally meant when she said, "Now I know." They had seen Floyd

coming down the beach from the north. But Floyd had
suddenly turned and run back north without a word. Arnold
hadn't seen his son.

"Your head is bleeding," said Sally as soon as they entered
the lantern light. For the second time that evening the
dancers crowded around them. They carefully set Arnold
down on the ground. Sweat and blood mixed in streaks from
his hairline down the right side of his face.

"That's where your boyfriend hit me," said Arnold.

"What happened?" asked Daniel, arriving from the stage.

"I need water and a bandage," said Sally, who was kneeling
beside Arnold, looking at the cut.

Daniel looked around, spotted Theresa, nodded at her, and
said, "Get what you need off the *Edna*." Looking at Jonas he
asked, "What happened?"

"He tripped on the ridge. Sally and I found him." Jonas
stopped. He was sure that Daniel was wondering what he and
Sally and Arnold were doing on the ridge.

"And did I hear him say you hit him?"

Jonas bit his lip. "I know it sounds stupid, but I tripped
when I was going to help him and fell on him."

"It looks like just a scratch, Daddy," Sally said. Jonas
winced. Arnold didn't deserve to be called Daddy.

Daniel crouched and began asking Arnold about his knee
injury. The crowd started murmuring as conversations
resumed. Jonas stared at Sally who was touching Arnold's
head, tracing the outline of the scratch. He wanted to look
away but he couldn't. Theresa arrived with a small bucket, a
rag, and bandages. Daniel sent Alice home to get a long
bandage to wrap Arnold's leg. Sally began to wash Arnold's
face. She not only washed where it was bloody, but the sweat
from his whole face. Jonas watched and bit his lip so hard he
tasted blood.

Do you see me?

A startled Jonas said, "No." He was quite sure he had
answered aloud. He was relieved when no one stared at him.

Do you see me?

No.

I am washing Arnold's face.

Tears blurred Jonas' eyes. He turned and walked away from the small knot of people. He walked back to the docks and out the far end of one, leaned against the post, and cried. Finally he said, "Is that what you are like?"

I am.

Jonas kept trying to stop crying. He should be back with Sally, but every time he turned to go he thought, "I didn't know what you were like," and cried some more. Finally he lay down on the dock, scooped up water, and washed his face.

As Jonas returned he saw Ethyl striding down the beach with Floyd behind her. Eugene was coming from another direction. A few of the dancers were scattering when Jonas and Ethyl arrived at the same time. Sally had just finished bandaging Arnold's face.

"What are you doing?" barked Ethyl. Both Arnold and Sally looked up at the sound of her voice. Neither of them said anything. Ethyl stood with hands on hips, breathing heavily, glaring at them. Jonas was not sure whom she was addressing.

"Sally, what are you doing to him?"

"Bandaging a cut on his head." She turned back to finish taping the bandage.

"Get away from him," Ethyl said, taking a step toward her. Sally ignored her, taking her time with the taping. Ethyl glared at Daniel and the others in the circle. "What have they done to you, Arnold?" she asked.

"I tripped and hurt my knee really bad," said Arnold. "Then he hit me when I was down." Arnold pointed at Jonas.

"It was an accident," said Sally. "Daddy was hurt and calling for help in the dark. Jonas and I went to help him, and I bumped Jonas who fell on Daddy."

"I'll take over from here," Ethyl said. "Get out of the way."

"Mama," Sally said in protest, and she didn't move away from Arnold.

Ethyl got down on her knees and began looking at the bandage. "You did it all wrong," she said and ripped off the bandage. Arnold let out a yelp of pain. "Give me that tape." Sally, still holding the tape, didn't move. Ethyl reached across Arnold and grabbed the tape.

"Jonas can handle this," said Daniel. Jonas' head snapped up and he gaped at Daniel. "Jonas can handle this, so we'll start the dance again," Daniel said, looking at the people who were still watching. Daniel caught Jonas' eye, "You can handle it." He moved away, as did all of the others except Floyd, Eugene, Sally, Ethyl, and Arnold. Brawn hovered in the background, refusing to return to playing the bass tub. He was going to watch Arnold like a hawk even if he was down.

Alice arrived with a roll of bandages to wrap Arnold's knee. Ethyl was busy bandaging Arnold's head again. Alice handed Sally the roll. Daniel and Jackson began playing, and the dance started again. Suddenly Sally stood up. "You left Samantha alone," she said staring at her mother. Ethyl didn't look up. Sally looked around frantically. Her eyes settled on Brawn. "Brawn, will you go stay with Samantha? If she wakes up, I won't be able to hear her down here."

"Don't need me here?" he said.

"*Somebody* needs to be with Samantha." Brawn disappeared into the darkness.

"I need a doctor for my knee," said Arnold.

"It's that bad, huh?" said Ethyl, reaching for his leg.

"Don't!" yelped Arnold.

"I didn't even touch it."

"Well, don't touch it. It kills me every time I have to move it."

Ethyl looked up at Floyd and Eugene. "Don't just stand there," she said. "You have to walk home and get the skiff. We have to take him to the mainland to see a doctor." They left.

Arnold lay with his eyes closed while Ethyl finished bandaging his head. Sally stood by his head with the roll of bandages for his knee in her hands. She was watching her mother. When Ethyl finished with his head she looked at Sally, "Give me that." Wordlessly, Sally handed the roll to her mother.

Ethyl held the rolled-up bandage on the inside of his knee with one hand and slid her other hand under his knee.

"Damn it, Ethyl!" he exploded, his eyes flying open. She jerked her hand out. "You're hurting me," he said.

"How do you expect me to wrap your knee if you screech like a baby? You don't want to get it hurt worse, do you?"

"Can't you do it without hurting me?"

"I'll help," said Sally, crouching down beside Arnold's knees.

"You haven't had anything to do with him for four years and now you're going to help?" Ethyl snarled, staring at her daughter.

"Mama," said Sally.

Jonas thought he saw a glint of a tear in the corner of Sally's eye. He knelt by Arnold's feet. "I can lift the lower part of his leg, Sally can lift his knee, and you can wrap it," he said.

"What's going on here?" asked Ethyl.

"We'll help," Jonas said.

"Arnold, what's going on here? Do you want them to help?"

"They helped carry me here after I fell."

"I thought you said he hit you after you were down."

"He did hit me," Arnold said, closing his eyes again. "He said it was an accident, and he helped carry me out. Let them help. I just don't want it to hurt."

"Why are you staring at me that way?" Ethyl asked, looking at Sally.

"Mama, you just don't understand," Sally said, shaking her head.

"No, I don't understand. What are you crying about?"

"You always thought you took care of me, so you'd never believe that you didn't."

"What are you talking about?"

"I'm talking about Daddy hurting me."

"He didn't hurt you. If he hurt you, why are you so eager to take care of him?"

"She's being good to him even if he doesn't deserve it," said Jonas.

"Stay out of this," said Ethyl. "You haven't answered my question, Sally."

"Mama, you act like nothing hurts you. Well, I know what it's like to be hurt. Mama, I couldn't tell you. You would have just been mad at me."

"Stop crying," Ethyl demanded.

"She's your daughter," said Jonas.

"I told you to stay out of this. When you," she said, looking hard at Sally, "say such terrible things about him—and I've heard what you're saying—why are you trying to be nice to him now?" Her voice was rising. "Why couldn't you have thought of being nice before you started telling lies? Everyone on the island is hearing your lies, Sally. Are you feeling guilty for your lies? Lies!" She was almost shouting. Through her tears Sally looked right back at her mother.

Sally shook her head, "Not lies, Mama."

Ethyl waved her hand over top of Arnold. "He's here, Sally, he's here. Say your lies to his face. Not behind his back. Say them to his face. Say them."

Arnold lay with his eyes closed. "Ethyl," he said, "I need a doctor."

"You need to hear the lies your daughter's telling about you."

"I've heard them," he said.

"To your face?" demanded Ethyl.

Arnold didn't respond.

"At least you can have the decency to tell them to his face."

"Not lies, Mama."

"If it's the truth, say it. If it's not the truth admit you've lied. Admit it."

Sally dropped her head, shaking it, her shoulder shuddering as she cried. Jonas didn't know what to do. "Ma'am," he said, "is this a good idea?"

She turned on him. "Are you afraid of the truth?"

"No . . ." he started to say.

"Yes, you are," she said. "I know preachers. His father was a preacher. They can't stand the truth either. They always want things nice. Well, it's not nice to marry someone who's a liar, preacher. It's not nice. You better face it. Not only that, she was drinking tonight. I could smell it on her as soon as I got here. And that's the truth, preacher."

Sally lifted her head. Through tears she said, "Mama, you didn't take care of me."

"You not only accuse him," Ethyl sputtered, "but me as well. And you want them to help, Arnold?"

"Mama, I know you tried," she said in a quiet voice.

"What are you talking about?" Ethyl's question was nearly a wail.

"Mama, I remember what you used to sing to me at night when I was scared." She started to sing a lullaby in a little girl's voice, "*It's a scary, scary world but your Mama sings you love tonight. It's a scary, scary world but your Mama sings you smiles tonight. It's a scary, scary world but your Mama sings you safe tonight.* Remember, Mama, you sang that to me at bedtime when I was little." Another burst of tears began to stream down her face. "I know it's a scary, scary world, Mama, but you couldn't always keep me safe. All I ask, Mama, is for you to say you couldn't keep me safe."

Her mother was silent. For a moment Jonas was hopeful. "Of course, I remember singing you that song." She was silent again. "I know somebody hurt you. I mean I never did quite believe your story. I couldn't keep you safe from that, but I can't believe you would make up such a terrible thing about your daddy. Goodness knows, I know he's no good, but he would never do that. You'd think if you were going to lie, you'd make up something believable."

"Mama," Sally said, shaking her head, "I know you don't believe me and you probably never will, but Daddy knows I'm telling the truth."

"The only reason I can think of for you sticking to your lies is you want to marry this preacher. It doesn't make sense."

"The truth, Mama."

"If you really believe it is the truth, I want to hear it from you. I want you to say it to my face and to your daddy's face."

Sally bowed her head. Jonas pleaded, "Don't."

"Don't what?" snapped Ethyl.

"Don't make her say it."

"Don't make her lie to my face? Don't make her accuse her daddy to his face instead of behind his back? Is that what you mean?"

Jonas looked at Arnold. His eyes were closed. Sweat had formed on his face again. He looked away. "What he did was so shameful," Jonas said. His throat was tight.

"The lies that she has been telling are shameful," said Ethyl triumphantly.

"Mama," Sally said, lifting her head, "I will tell you."

"Your lies you mean?"

"One evening Daddy and Floyd and Eugene came back from fishing. I was swimming. . ."

"For crying out loud, Ethyl," said Arnold, struggling to sit up, "leave the girl alone. Wrap my knee. It needs to be done before the boys get back here with the skiff. I wanta be ready. This knee is killing me."

Sally looked directly at Ethyl. "Do you want to hear the whole thing, Mama?"

Ethyl dropped her eyes. Jonas saw her face flash with rage for a moment. She looked at Arnold. "We'll wrap your leg," she said. He lay back down and closed his eyes. Jonas and Sally held his bad leg while Ethyl wrapped it. To Jonas she seemed unnecessarily rough as she wrapped it. Arnold grimaced several times, but he didn't yelp once.

69.

For a moment when they began to dance, Sally leaned against Jonas and he almost stumbled from her weight. Then she straightened. It was a slow dance and she coached him through it. About halfway through, to his amazement, he caught on, and he led her through the rest of the dance. When the song finished, Sally guided him to the side of the dance area opposite her parents. "Jonas, I love you," she said, as they stood hand in hand, watching the other dancers. "I'm so glad you were with me tonight. I am so glad you *are* with me." She pulled him close and kissed him.

"I didn't do very much," he said.

"You didn't need to do very much. You just needed to be with me. And you were." She looked at the dancers. "I can't believe it," she continued, "I got to say so much tonight." She turned back to Jonas. "I said it!" she said passionately. As Daniel and Jackson began to play a lively waltz, she pushed him toward the dance area. "Now I want you to dance me fast," she said.

Jonas glanced up at Daniel on the stage. Daniel nodded and winked. Jonas turned to Sally with a light feeling. He suddenly knew they would dance her dream dance. He knew he could do it. He stumbled three times in the first song. But when the next fast waltz came along, they were as nimble as water skipping over rocks in a fast running creek. On the corners her blonde hair lifted off her shoulders. Her laughter was like a thousand fireflies. When they stopped to catch their breaths after the song, they clung to each other and he smiled until it hurt.

They danced again and again. With the slow dances they moved like cattails in a gentle breeze; with the lively songs they were as quick as swallows swooping at sunset.

When the dance ended, they sat on the edge of the platform. Jonas suggested they go spell off Brawn who was looking after Samantha, but Sally said she needed to stay until she saw her daddy off. Daniel took down all the lanterns except the one above where Jonas and Sally sat and the one on the pole above Ethyl and Arnold, who were thirty feet away waiting for the skiff. Jonas was tired and began to doze, only to wake when his head fell almost to his knees. He would straighten up, lean against Sally, only to start his slow descent again.

Finally the skiff arrived. Eugene, Floyd, and Jonas carried Arnold on board. Everyone was tired; few words were said.

Sally and Jonas stood on the dock until the boat slid into the darkness.

Jonas was ready to walk Sally home, but she stood silently at the end of the dock, staring into the darkness. Jonas stood with her. Finally she said, "He's really gone. I can hardly believe it. Ever since I moved I have slept with a knife by my bed. A fish knife. I was never going to let him hurt me again. Never."

They stood in silence. "Did you think of your knife tonight when you were so close to him?"

"You know, that's funny, but I didn't. I never thought of that knife until now."

"You were so close to him, carrying his leg, bandaging his head. I couldn't quite believe you were doing that."

"I couldn't either."

"How could you do it?"

"He was all alone in the woods just like I was. I didn't want him to go through what I did." Jonas was silent. She continued, "Many times I've thought of hurting him. I have a little whetstone and I keep that fish knife sharp. Many times as I've sharpened that knife I've thought of cutting him. Especially since I've known you. Sometimes when I'm sharpening it, I see myself stabbing him." Her voice dropped to a whisper, "Sometimes I see myself cutting it off." Jonas felt her shudder next to him.

"Especially since you knew me?" asked Jonas.

"Yes," she quietly. "Before I met you I had this cold dark spot in me, and I wouldn't feel anything or think anything when I sharpened the blade. But then you came to the island talking about Jesus. Even before I met you I asked Philena what you preached about. I can't remember what she said, but as she talked I could feel myself getting all stirred up inside. I'd go back to my cabin and cry and do all kinds of crazy things. I'd take a blanket at night and go out into the woods behind the cabin. I didn't want other people to hear me, so I'd cover my face with that blanket and scream. That all happened in the week before I met you.

"One night I began stabbing a rotten log in the woods, pretending it was Daddy. I'd lean it up against another tree and stab it like it was Daddy standing up. Sometimes I'd stab it on the ground like it was Daddy lying down. One time I stabbed it all the way through the log on the ground and broke the blade on a rock underneath. I had to buy a new one. All this happened after you came to the island."

"It must have been the Holy Ghost," said Jonas.

"I thought I was going crazy," said Sally. They were silent. Jonas sensed she had more to say. "I was scared of you when you came to the island," she continued. "That's why I never came to hear you preach. But I kept seeing you around the island. I thought you were cute. That scared me more.

"I never told you this, but the night before I met you was the first time I ever got drunk. I wanted to go see you preach the next day, but I was too scared. I couldn't stop thinking about you. I thought drinking might help. I bought a jug of wine from Jackson and started drinking." She giggled. "That helped me stop thinking about you. First, all I could think of was peeing. I had to pee so bad. Then all I could think about was how was I going to make it to the outhouse. I was so wobbly. I finally made it to the outhouse, and then I got sick. I had to decide whether to pee first or throw up first. I don't even remember which I did first! Pee, I think. I was so sick. And it was all your fault, Jonas." She gave him a playful push.

"I definitely think it was the Holy Ghost," laughed Jonas.

"So you can imagine my shock the next day when I wake up with this terrible headache, finally drag myself out of bed, only to find you taking care of Samantha." She chuckled, "I don't think I was too nice to you that day."

"Not that first time," said Jonas, "but you've been making up for it since then." Then he added, a little puzzled, "The first time we met you acted like you'd never seen me before," said Jonas.

"I probably did act that way. I certainly wasn't going to tell you that I couldn't stop thinking about you. I know I was mean when I came out and found Samantha with you. Before you, I never trusted her around any man. I tried to make up for it by making you soup for supper that night."

"So that's why you were so ornery when we first met, and a little later you're making clam soup for me."

"Yes," she said, "I was scared of you, but I sure had my eyes on you, too. I thought you were so cute." She kissed him. He didn't mind the faint taste and smell of beer. It was fading. "I still do," she added. They stood on the dock and kissed for a long time.

Sally broke the kiss. "Just think," she said, "I don't have to sleep with a knife tonight." Her laughter skipped over the lake.

Sally waited for him while he put out the two remaining lanterns and stored them in the shed. He walked her home.

70.

"You want me to wait for you?" asked a yawning Brawn as he paused at the door to Sally's cabin. "I'm going right past the tug."

"No," said Jonas, "I'll be here a bit."

Brawn left. He had been asleep, head resting in the crook of his arm on the table, when they arrived home. Jonas sat down on the bench, his back to the table. Sally was checking Samantha.

"She's fine," said Sally, returning and sitting close to Jonas. Jonas put his arm around her. They kissed, but it was awkward on the bench. Sally swung her feet up on the bench, her back to him, and lay her head in his lap, her eyes dark and shining like emeralds in the lamplight. He leaned over her and whispered, "You are beautiful." They began kissing. Soon he was cradling her head and shoulders with one arm as they kissed, gently caressing her legs with the other.

She struggled to sit up. "This bench is not very comfortable," she said. Jonas glanced around the room.

Nothing looked very comfortable. "Let's lie down," she said. Jonas followed her into her room. The single bed was narrow, and when they lay down, Jonas worried about falling off. Soon Sally shifted on top of him and he stopped worrying about falling off. While they kissed, Jonas ran his hands over her back and legs. They murmured about love as they moved and squeezed each other in the darkness. Jonas touched more and more skin. She kissed his neck hard and goose bumps raced down his back and leg. He tugged at her dress. More skin. He wanted to be close to her. As close as possible. Their tongues touched and tussled. Jonas unzipped her dress and rubbed all over her back. He tried to undo the clasp, but it wouldn't come apart. He kinked and squeezed the straps, and still the hooks clung to each other. He traced the outline of the clasp with his fingertip to find out how it worked. He tried again. Still no luck. Gradually he realized that Sally had become very still. He dropped the clasp and lay with a sinking feeling. What had gotten into him? He should leave right now.

Sally lifted herself up on her elbows and he moved to kiss her. She turned from his mouth but gently kissed his cheeks, chin, and eyes. Then she kissed him on the mouth, a light kiss, and said, "Jonas, I am ready."

"I am, too," he said quickly. Then she lay her head on his shoulder and was very still. Jonas waited.

"This is so comfortable," she said, dreamily. "I could sleep all night like this."

Jonas gave a little jiggle. "I'm not ready to sleep yet."

"Oh, but this is so nice. Don't go yet."

"I wasn't planning to leave," Jonas said hastily.

"What were you planning to do?"

"I thought you said you were ready."

"I am." But she made no move.

Finally Jonas said, "I can't do it alone."

She lifted her head quickly, "Exactly what do you have in mind?"

"I thought you said you were ready to . . . you know . . . and so I thought you'd take . . . off."

"Ready to what?"

Jonas had a feeling he had misunderstood something. Still, she was waiting for an answer. Several phrases went through his mind. Finally he said, "Sleep together."

"You thought I said I was ready to sleep together like in *sleep together*?" Jonas nodded.

Suddenly she started to laugh. "What's so funny?" asked Jonas.

"You are my preacher boy. You are." She laughed some more. "Just because I danced with you tonight doesn't mean I want to sleep with you as in *sleep with you*." She laughed more. Jonas didn't know whether to laugh or be grumpy. She was making fun of him.

"What did you mean when you said you were ready?"

"Marriage, redhead, marriage."

"I thought you meant you were ready to sleep with me."

"Are you telling me that you want to sleep with me as in *sleep* with me? Because if you do, I may just oblige. You are rather desirable right now." This time she jiggled.

Jonas swallowed. Suddenly he pictured himself making this confession to his congregation. "I think I better go home," he said.

"Ah, shucks," she giggled, "you lead me this far and you want to go home?"

"Yes, I better go." He zipped her dress back up. Maybe they had gone so far he was going to have to confess this. He felt bad, until suddenly a thought winked in the darkness like a lightning bug. "You really do want to marry me?"

"That's what I was trying to tell you."

"Tomorrow we can talk to Daniel about marrying us."

"I want to get married in two weeks."

Jonas was surprised. "Why so quick?"

"I don't think I can keep you waiting any longer," she giggled, giving her hips a wiggle.

Maybe they didn't need to wait two weeks for the first time, thought Jonas. He quickly shook that idea off.

"Are you trying to squirm out from under me?" asked Sally.

"It's awful hard to think pure thoughts in this position," Jonas said. Sally burst out laughing, then moved off him. They lay side by side.

"Is this better?"

"A little," he said. "It would even be better if I stood up." But he didn't move. "Two weeks might not work," he said. "Hank and Philena are getting married next week. We have to have an engagement dance at least a week ahead of the wedding, I would think. We can't have the dance on the same day as Hank and Philena's wedding. How about three weeks?"

"Two weeks," she said. "Daddy hurt his knee. I want to get married when he can't come. I don't know how long he's going to be laid up, but I want to get married soon."

"Who will give you away?"

"Certainly not Daddy."

"I agree," Jonas said, emphatically.

"I'd have Daniel give me away, but he's going to marry us. Maybe Daniel could do both."

Jonas listened to the wind in the pines beside the cabin. "I will have to make us a bed," said Jonas.

"Can't get your mind off beds, can you?" chuckled Sally. She turned toward him and they kissed.

"I'm sorry, Sally," Jonas said quietly. "I got carried away tonight. I may be a preacher, but I didn't act very good tonight."

"You are a man," Sally said, touching his lips in the darkness, "as well as a preacher. Otherwise I wouldn't be marrying you."

"I could have hurt you tonight," he said.

"What do you mean?"

"Both of us would be sad if we had slept together tonight. I wanted to so bad. You would have been hurt. I didn't want to stop."

"I was a little amazed myself." She laughed. "A good thing you got caught on my strap." She sighed. "Up until then I liked everything you were doing. I liked it a lot."

"You did?"

"Yes, I didn't want it to stop either. But then when you were pulling on my strap I got scared. I don't like to be scared."

"I don't ever want to scare you, Sally."

"You will scare me, Jonas. You can't help it. I've spent a long time being scared. It's not going to stop just because we get married. All I ask is that if I get scared, you stop and wait for me."

"I will stop," Jonas said, fervently.

"Jonas," her voice sounded far away even though she was close, "when we do it, I want it to be like this. Like tonight."

"That's okay with me," Jonas said, wondering exactly what she meant.

"Daddy was over me." She shuddered. "I can't stand thinking about that."

"I think you can do it lots of different ways," said Jonas, trying to remember conversations he overheard at school.

She turned and kissed him. "Let's not do anything, but I want you to hold me again." She stretched out on him and lay her head on his shoulder. "I feel so comfortable like this." They were silent. Jonas heard the wind in the pines. "Are you thinking impure thoughts?" she asked.

"I'm trying not to," he said.

"Just hold me."

He held her. Gradually he relaxed. He timed his breathing so that when she breathed in, he exhaled; she exhaled, he breathed in. He thought about being on a teeter-totter, up, down, up, down, breathe in, breathe out, breathe in, breathe out.

Something startled him awake. He realized the first birds were beginning to sing before dawn. Sally woke too. "We fell asleep," he said.

"We did, didn't we," she moved sleepily off him.

"I better go," Jonas said, getting out of bed. He kissed her and left, hurrying back to the boat, hoping that since it was Sunday morning and after a dance he wouldn't meet anyone. He didn't. He swung into his hammock and fell back to sleep.

71.

Sally wakened an hour later, full of energy. She went over to Daniel's and invited him and Alice for lunch, set the table for five, and prepared a fish batter. Samantha was excited about having guests. She chattered happily away, following Sally everywhere as she worked. They went to the fish tank and got fish, cleaned, and filleted them. She washed potatoes and put them in the oven so they would be done when church was done. And she was the first one to the beach for church that morning.

After church Jonas said, "We have to go see my folks. We can't get married until they meet you."

"I invited Daniel and Alice for dinner," she said. "I want us to talk with Daniel right away." She began to hurry toward the cabin.

Jonas followed her. "You did hear me about my parents?" he asked.

"Yes, I heard," she said. At the cabin she put Jonas to work dipping the fish in the batter and frying them, while she tested the potatoes and finished setting the table and straightening up the cabin.

"That is okay with you, going to meet my folks?" Jonas asked.

"If we have time. There are so many things to do in two weeks. I have to make a dress."

"This is important to me," Jonas said.

"Why is it important to you?" she asked, pausing at the table with the butter dish poised in her hand.

"I just think it's important," he said.

"What's so important it can't wait till after dinner?" Daniel called through the screen door in his gruff Scandinavian accent. "Ya," he continued inside, "you might as well learn you make better decisions on a full stomach." He patted his stomach.

Jonas and Sally finished preparing the meal in silence.

Samantha took Alice by the hand and led her outside to show her a pretty butterfly. Samantha chatted away to Alice and Alice enjoyed her, although she couldn't hear a word Samantha said. Daniel sat on a chair next to the wall, leaned back, and seemed to fall asleep.

During the meal Daniel effortlessly translated the conversation to Alice with motions of his hands and fingers. Samantha was the center of attention. Daniel told her stories about the lake and fishing. When the stories were scary, her eyes grew like saucers, and when they were funny, her freckles danced as she laughed. When the meal was over, Daniel pushed back his bench, patted his stomach, and complimented Sally on her cooking. Then he made a signal to Alice and she left with Samantha.

"So," Daniel said, pulling his bench around to face Jonas and Sally, "you tell me you want to talk and you invite me for a fine meal. I like that. Eat and talk," he said patting his stomach again. "What do the two of you want to talk with me about then?"

"We want to get married," said Jonas. He sat on a bench with a corner of the table between him and Sally.

Daniel chuckled, "Now why do you suppose I am not surprised to hear that then?" He chuckled some more. "Ya, that sounds like a good idea to me."

"We want you to marry us, and we want to get married two weeks from yesterday," said Sally.

"Two weeks from yesterday," said Daniel, thoughtfully. "You're in a big hurry then."

"Yes," said Jonas. He didn't want Daniel to think the quick wedding was only Sally's idea.

"Ya, well," said Daniel, "the Bible does say there is a season." He looked from one to the other. Jonas thought he ought to say something more, but he didn't know what to say. He wasn't sure Daniel would approve a quick wedding because Arnold had hurt his knee. "So," continued Daniel, looking at Sally, "what is it that you like about two weeks from yesterday?"

"Well," she said with a flip of her shoulders, "Daddy hurt his knee real bad last night, and I think he'll be laid up for at least two weeks, so I thought it would be a great time to get married."

"I see," said Daniel. He nodded. "And you think it's a good time to get married too, Jonas?" Then he added, almost as an afterthought, "When Arnold's laid up?"

"We've been talking about getting married for quite awhile," said Jonas, aware that it might not seem that long to Daniel. "Now seems like a good time," he went on lamely. "As long as we have time to go visit my folks first," he said. "I think it's important that my folks meet Sally."

Daniel nodded some more. He turned to Sally. "You must have a good reason to want your father to miss the wedding then?"

"I do," she said. She threw up her hands. "I might as well say it because you know already. Everyone on the island seems to know. It was my father who forced himself on me, and I don't want him anywhere near when I get married."

"You are a woman of great courage," said Daniel.

"I still don't want Daddy anywhere near the wedding."

"Uffda," grunted Daniel, his Norwegian accent becoming even thicker. "By talking about your courage, I wasn't saying you need your daddy at your wedding. Nay, your courage is in telling the truth." He turned to Jonas, "You have a woman of courage."

"Do you think it's okay to get married now so Arnold can't be there?" asked Jonas.

"What do you think?" Daniel asked calmly.

"Uh," Jonas said, trying to figure out what he thought, "I do want to get married to Sally. Last night when we talked it seemed like a good idea, but this morning it seems a little funny. I mean Arnold hurts his knee so we quick get married. . ."

"You do understand why I don't want him at the wedding?" Sally asked, her eyes flashing.

"Oh, yes," said Jonas. "I don't want him there either."

"Well then," said Sally, as if that settled it.

"What are you worried about, Jonas?" asked Daniel.

"I don't know," said Jonas, shaking his head, puzzled.

"You said you want your folks to meet Sally," said Daniel. "That makes sense to me."

"It does?" said Jonas, suddenly relieved that something made sense.

"Ya, families are important."

"I wish I knew why two weeks from yesterday makes me nervous," said Jonas. "You seem so relaxed," he said to Sally.

"Well, Jonas, if one of you wasn't a little nervous, I'd have to be nervous for you," said Daniel.

Jonas and Sally stared at Daniel.

"Somebody has to be nervous. Look," he said, "when there's clouds and we go out fishing, I get a little nervous. I got to be careful. Any fool can get in a boat and head out on the lake and get himself and his crew in trouble before he knows it. Going to see your folks before you get married is being careful."

"That's fine," said Sally, nodding her head. "If we have time."

"You don't sound so convinced then?" said Daniel with a gentle smile.

"Look at my family," she replied.

"Jonas has," chuckled Daniel. "He's taken a good look. Now it's your turn to look at his."

"Why do I want to look at his family?"

"Well, you are going to be living with them from the minute you say 'I do.'" Sally looked doubtful. "I don't mean," he added, "that you will live in the same house. But you are marrying into his family and he is marrying into yours."

"Marrying into my family?" she spluttered.

"He sure is," said Daniel. "The two of you are either going to be at war or at peace with your families. One or the other. It ain't gonna be easy then." He sat back and laughed. "Not too many men get in a fistfight with their future father-in-law the first time they meet."

Sally and Jonas stared at him. "You are too young to know how funny that is," Daniel said, still smiling. "Ya, some things in life are so sad that you have to laugh a little about them. But the two of you are doing well with Sally's family. I noticed last night. You both did a good job of peace in a bad situation. You'll have to do more of that." Jonas remembered him and Sally carrying that bad leg. He shivered.

"So," Daniel concluded, "Sally, you should meet Jonas' family and make peace with them, too. Not that Jonas' family is exactly like your family, but," he shrugged his shoulders, "you'll still spend your life at war or peace with them. You might as well start off right. Parents have a way of getting owly when one of their offspring gets married and they didn't even know it was in the works."

"My family knows that I'm going to marry Sally," Jonas said. "I've written to them."

"I hope your family isn't like mine," she said.

Jonas was silent. He hoped Sally got along with his mom. They both had a way with words.

"One other thing I know about families," said Daniel. "Families are made up of stories. The two of you will be adding to the stories of your families. Now's a good time for a couple of stories. I want to hear a story from each of your families. Jonas, your turn first. Think of Sally, and tell me a story from your family that reminds you of her. And Sally, you do the same thing with Jonas and your family."

"A story," Sally said, her inflection letting it be known that she thought this was a crazy idea.

"Either something that happened when you were growing up or a story you heard."

"I can't think of any," she said.

"How about you, Jonas? Maybe if you tell one, Sally will think of one."

Jonas gazed at Sally, thinking. "When I first met you," he said, "you had this sad look on your face. That reminds me of my grandma. One Sunday when we were playing softball at my grandma's, I was thirsty, so I decided to go to the house and get a drink from the pump. As I was walking to the house I saw Grandma standing inside the screen door watching the game. She looked so sad. About the time I got to the porch, Grandpa came up behind her and put his arms around her. He said something to her. I didn't hear what, but she broke into this happy smile." Jonas sighed. "I'll always remember that smile. I think I saw Grandpa do that other times, too—make Grandma smile. I like to make you smile, Sally. It's like everything is going to be okay."

Jonas was finished.

"The only story I can think of," said Sally, "is a silly one. But you asked. It's about a redheaded woodpecker." Jonas must have looked surprised because Sally snapped, "I never made faces at your story so don't make faces at mine."

"I'll be good," said Jonas. He smiled at her and winked.

She stared at him a moment. Then her face softened and she continued, "You have red hair. That's what reminded me of the woodpecker. I was sad when we moved to this island. I had to leave all my friends. My first friend on the island was a redheaded woodpecker. My daddy hated it. Sunday was the only day Daddy slept late. And it seemed like every Sunday that woodpecker would peck real hard on a hollow tree outside our house. Rat-a-tat-tat. He probably did it every morning, but we only paid attention on Sundays when Daddy was trying to sleep.

"I loved to watch that woodpecker. When he flew, he swooped. I would try to follow him through the woods. I always lost him, sooner or later, but I loved to follow him. One day I was following him, and I lost him like usual. When I lost him, I would go back home. But on this day I was sad, because Mom and Daddy had been having a fight the night before. They said a lot of mean things to each other. I decided to climb a tree and look around. Nearby there was a pine tree with nice branches for climbing. Partway up this tree, I suddenly heard a rat-a-tat-tat above me. I slowly looked up, and there, only ten feet above me, was my redheaded woodpecker. I was so thrilled to see him. I watched him for what must have been five minutes. Then he flew away.

It's the closest I ever got. I saw him lots after that, but I never got that close to him again. I climbed that tree many times, but he never came back to the tree when I was there. My happy feeling stayed with me that morning even after he flew away. I skipped all the way home that day."

She paused, her face soft, her eyes bright. Jonas and Daniel were silent. Her face darkened. "You didn't like my story."

"Oh, I did. That was a very good story," Daniel said.

"What was good about it?" she asked doubtfully.

"It's a story of a holy moment for a little girl who needed someone to be close to," Daniel said slowly.

Sally sighed. Then she laughed. "I do like being close to my redhead." She scooted close to Jonas.

Daniel chuckled, "Ya, and he's a little more cooperative than your redheaded woodpecker."

"Rat-a-tat-tat," said Jonas.

"My little redheaded woodpecker," chuckled Sally. She reached out and tickled Jonas' ribs.

"Ya," said Daniel, "you have lots of good stories to tell each other."

Jonas and Sally smiled at each other.

"Well, then, let's plan the wedding," Daniel said.

"You do think it's okay to get married quick to keep Arnold away?" asked Jonas.

"Jonas," said Daniel. "I don't know all the reasons why this worries you so much." He scratched his head. "Do you have doubts about marrying Sally?"

"No, I don't think so. I heard God say that we should get married, and that was when we barely knew each other. Now I know her more, and God hasn't told me any different." He turned to Sally, "And I sure do want to marry you."

"You know that Arnold doesn't approve of you marrying his daughter. What about your family? Are they going to approve?"

Jonas thought for a moment before he answered. "I think they will."

"They know your interest in her?"

"Yes. I have written them. But I still want them to meet Sally."

"I see," said Daniel. "I have a hunch you want more from them than to simply lay eyes on your woman."

"I think so," said Jonas slowly.

"Ya, it would be good for the two of you to go see your family before the wedding. You need to find out."

"What if there's not time before the wedding?" said Sally.

"I'll let the two of you work that out. Now let's plan your wedding."

When they finished going over the wedding ceremony Daniel said, "We need to think about how we fit your engagement party and wedding with Philena and Hank's wedding. They get married this coming Saturday. Usually the engagement party is at least a week before the wedding. That won't work for you because of Hank and Philena's wedding. Ya, tell you what. There's no law that says you have to have an engagement party. Let's have the wedding the day you want it and have a wedding dance that night instead of an engagement dance. How does that sound?"

"Do we have to have a wedding dance?" Jonas asked. He was wondering how he would ever explain a wedding dance to his parents.

"Ya, celebrations are good. Getting married is something the whole island celebrates. We got to dance, you know."

"I like the idea," said Sally, smiling. "I'll get to dance with my husband." She squeezed Jonas' leg.

Jonas slipped his hand into hers but was silent. Finally he blurted out, "I don't want to spend our whole wedding night at a wedding dance."

Sally laughed. "I'm going to keep you at the dance until the last person goes home."

Jonas allowed a smile. "That's what I'm afraid of."

"Ya, well," said Daniel, a smile at the corner of his eyes, "the sun'll set many times for you, Jonas." Jonas waited for him to say more but he simply went on, "So does a wedding in the late afternoon and a wedding dance sound good then?"

"Yes," said Sally, all smiles.

Jonas nodded. "Okay."

"One more thing," said Daniel. "Some night before the wedding, I want the two of you to come for supper so I can talk to you about married love."

Sally and Jonas looked at each other and nodded to Daniel.

72.

Jonas woke at dawn, certain that he and Sally were going to visit his parents before the wedding. To the gentle rocking of the tug and the sloshing of the water along the shore, he wrote a letter to his parents. He told them about the wedding and that he was coming soon to introduce his bride-to-be. He smiled as he wrote. "Bride-to-be," he repeated softly looking out at the lake. The words tasted like cold, fresh milk after working up a sweat in the barn. He left the letter with Alice to go out on the *Lillian* the next day.

"Bride-to-be," he said, smiling to himself, as he walked the shore toward Sally's cabin.

"We can go to your parents," Sally said gaily as he walked in the door.

"Wonderful," he said and gave her a hug. In the coolness of the morning she felt warm. "We have to make sure that we are back by Saturday so I can marry Hank and Philena."

Samantha, who had just awakened and come down from her loft, ran to Jonas and jumped. He caught her. "Good morning, sunshine," he said and gave her a kiss on the cheek.

"We can buy the material for my dress in Milwaukee on the way to see your parents," Sally continued. "They will just have to put up with me sewing my dress while we're there. I need to start sewing on it as soon as possible. Your mom will let me use her sewing machine, won't she?"

"I'm sure she will. And we can buy the rings in Milwaukee, too."

"I've written the invitation," she said, picking it up from the table and handing it to him. "If you like it you can take it over to Jackson and have him letter them. We will need twenty-five." Jonas glanced at the invitation. He noticed with a pang that it came from him and Sally and not their parents. "Is it okay with you?" she asked.

"You are right," he said with a sigh, "in having it come from you and me. My parents might be disappointed, but we have to leave your daddy out. They'll just have to understand." Samantha was squirming so he set her down.

"You don't seem to be too happy," Sally said.

He looked her up and down, then raised his eyebrow. "All I have to do to be happy," he said, "is to look at my bride-to-be." He grinned.

"You're sure?" she said, pointing at the invitation.

He looked her up and down slowly. He looked in her eyes. "I am delighted," he said, pausing, rasing his eyebrow, "to join you in inviting folks to see you and me become one. Uh, I mean, exchange our vows." He laughed as she turned a slight pink. "Only you and I will witness our becoming one."

She turned sideways and struck a provocative pose. "I am glad," she said in a husky voice, "you weren't planning to become one on the beach. But, Jonas," she said, drawing out his name, "I don't know if I can wait. Come to me now." She fluttered her hand by her hip.

This time Jonas could feel *his* face turning red. Samantha eyed them with a puzzled look. Sally moved her shoulder drawing his eyes. "Well," she said, "what are you waiting for, my redheaded woodpecker?" Then she laughed.

"Wow," said Jonas, stepping to her with open arms, "you are attractive."

"Well, I should hope so," she said. Samantha began tugging at her mama. After a moment Sally gently pushed him away. "But if we are going to see your folks, I have lots to do. So do you. Can you take this invitation over to Jackson and ask him to letter twenty-five of them?"

"Is he good at it?"

"Oh, yes. He has a quill and does beautiful lettering."

"I have time," he said. "Daniel doesn't need me until later this morning." As he walked out the door she gave his rump a squeeze. He spun around. But she quickly closed the door to a crack and, giggling, peeked through it.

Jonas pushed playfully against the door. "Woman, you want me? Here I come."

"Now, now, Jonas," she said still giggling, "you must take Jackson the invitations."

"You sure do make it hard to leave," he grumbled happily. He blew her a kiss. "I'll be back," he said.

"Rat-a-tat-tat," she said.

73.

"Come in, come in," said Jackson, irritation in his voice. "Oh, it's you," he muttered when Jonas stepped in the door. Jackson sat in his chair with wheels, eating a bowl of oatmeal.

"Who were you expecting?" asked Jonas.

"I finished my last jug last night and I thought you were Brawn. He's bringing me more." He continued eating in silence.

Jonas thought it best to say as little as possible. He laid the invitation on the table next to Jackson. Jackson glanced at it. "So you're getting married," he said. He finished his bowl in silence. Jackson held up his hand. It was shaking. "I need a steady hand. You better go find Brawn and tell him I need my wake-up medicine." Jonas stood silently. He didn't like the idea of going to get alcohol for Jackson. "Come back when you have the medicine," Jackson said.

Jonas shrugged his shoulders and left. Outside Brawn came up the path carrying two jugs and whistling cheerfully.

"Morning," Brawn said with a nod. Jonas held the door for him.

"About time," Jackson growled. "Give me one of those." He

took a long drink. He wiped his lips on the back of his hand. "Now I can act civilized."

Brawn set the other jug on the table. "So long," he said with a wave. As he closed the door he started whistling again.

"A man of few words," said Jackson, nodding in the direction of the door. He picked up the invitation and waved it. "Now how many of these do you want?"

"Twenty-five."

He studied the invitation. "I see you aren't wasting any time. Not that it's any of my business, but what's the hurry?"

Jonas hesitated. If he told the truth he could just imagine Jackson's comments. But it was the truth, so he told him.

For the first time that morning Jackson smiled. It was a sad smile. He shook his head. "Your life is getting small, Jonas. Remember me telling you about the old man on the Indian reservation who would say, 'But none of our ways saved us from the white man.' He told me their hunting grounds got smaller and smaller. When they were put on reservations, that was the last in a long series of attempts by the good Indian people to make themselves small enough for the white people. Oh, sometimes they fought back. But mostly they made themselves smaller and smaller. You know, if you go across America, you'll find cities from Manhattan in New York to Tacoma in Washington with names that come from the Indians who lived in the region. Indians covered this continent. Now they live in a few, small, scattered reservations.

"Jonas," he shook his head, "setting the wedding date while her daddy is laid up. You are getting smaller. Very soon you'll be a midget."

Jonas sat silently. He felt a calmness inside. He thought about the pond back home at sunset; sometimes when it was calm he would slip into it very quietly, trying not to break the stillness. For once he did not feel the need to counter Jackson. "You are right," he said, "I am getting smaller." He smiled at Jackson.

"And that doesn't bother you?"

"Yesterday I had this feeling that I should go see my parents

before we get married. Sally wasn't too keen on the idea. This
morning when I woke up, I knew we were going to go. I just
knew. When I talked with Sally, she had decided we should go.
Ever since then I have had this feeling that getting married
is right. Even getting married in less than two weeks so that
Sally doesn't have to have her daddy at the wedding. I am at
peace."

Jackson pursed his lips and blew through them. "Indians
can never be at peace," he said. "I saw you and Sally carrying
her daddy the other night. He was helpless, but he won't stay
that way. White people never do. If you and Sally get strong,
he will cut you down. Jonas, I lived on a reservation. I
know."

Jonas sat down on a stool facing Jackson. "Jackson," he said
with a smile, "can't you say an encouraging word? I am
getting married. You should celebrate with me. You should be
happy. We are even going to have a wedding dance. I'd like
you to play at it."

Jackson shook his head. "Young and foolish."

Jonas chuckled. "Old and gloomy."

"I performed the ceremony for a few Indian couples in my
time. Jonas, it was always so sad." Jonas thought he was
about to cry. Jackson shook his head. "You just don't know
what it is like on a reservation."

Jonas felt Jackson's sadness weigh on him. "Jackson, I have
been called to this island," he said slowly, talking even though
he did not know where his words were going to take him. He
looked out Jackson's window. He saw a redheaded
woodpecker light on a tree trunk. He heard the rat-a-tat-tat.
Slowly he pulled his gaze from the bird. He smiled at Jackson
who stared at him quizzically. "Marrying Sally is right." He
glanced out the window. The woodpecker was still there. "You
left the reservation, Jackson. I have come to this island to
stay." He steered his gaze from the window and looked at
Jackson. "Maybe you should have married an Indian woman.
I think that would have been better than marrying the
bottle." He glanced back at the bird which left the tree in a

looping flight, framed by the window until it veered left. He stared through the window, wondering if the woodpecker would return.

"You have a quick tongue, Jonas. I hand that to you." He waved the invitation. "When do you need these by?"

Jonas turned back to him. "Thank you, Jackson. You just helped me say something very important. I have come to this island to stay. It may be small, but I am here to stay. That's why I'm getting married. I am here to stay."

"I'm glad you think so. Now when do you need these?"

"How soon can you get them done?"

"I can get them all done in two and a half days."

"We are going to need at least five for my relatives. The earliest we'll need them will be tomorrow."

"I'll have those done later today."

Jonas started to leave. "Jonas," Jackson called when Jonas was at the door. Jonas turned. "Welcome to the island," Jackson said. Jonas nodded his acceptance and waved good-bye.

"Wait," Jackson said, "I have one more question. Are you sure?"

"Since God has called me here, this island is my home and these are my people."

"Even people like Arnold?" Jonas hesitated, holding the open door. "This island is Arnold's home, too."

"Arnold is one of my people, too," said Jonas.

Jackson stared at him, shaking his head. "I'll get these done," he said, waving the invitation.

Outside on the path Jonas looked for the redheaded woodpecker, but he didn't see it.

74.

Jonas walked back towards Sally's cabin, keeping an eye out for the woodpecker. He was so busy looking up that he almost stepped on Samantha.

"What are you looking at?" she asked.

"I was looking for a redheaded woodpecker."

"I was looking for you," she said. "And I found you."

"That you did," he said, scooping her up in his arms. "Why were you looking for me?"

"I want to tell you a secret," she said, her green eyes flashing a deeper green in the pines.

"I love secrets."

"I get to meet your daddy and mama."

"You do?"

"Mama said."

"Well, then I guess you will."

"And I am going to tell them a secret," she said, throwing her head back and laughing.

Shifting his voice into a bass he asked, "And what secret are you going to tell them?"

"That you are my pretend daddy."

"So I am your pretend daddy?" She nodded. "And what is a pretend daddy?"

"A pretend daddy is a . . ." She paused as if she were trying to come up with an answer. ". . . woodpecker," she said, throwing her head back again in laughter.

"Now you are being silly. What is a pretend daddy?"

She looked down and spoke in a small voice, "A made-up daddy. My pretend daddy. He was always nice to me. Mama didn't like him, but I did. He was my pretend daddy and he was nice to me."

"Sally didn't like your pretend daddy?"

"He always said good-night to me real nice. One time I told Mama and she got mad. She said no daddy said good-night to me. I didn't tell her anymore. But my pretend daddy still said good-night to me."

"And now I am your pretend daddy?"

"Yes," she said, planting a kiss on his cheek. "My other pretend daddy said good-bye." She hid her face in his neck.

He waited for her to say more. She was quiet. "Were you

sad when your other pretend daddy said good-bye?"

She nodded her head, still hiding in his neck. He held her, gently swaying on the path, the breeze whispering in the pines. "Did you say good-bye to him?"

"I hid under the covers," she said in his neck. "I didn't want to say good-bye."

"What happened then?"

"I peeked and he was still waving good-bye. I hid again. Then I peeked again. He was still there." She giggled in his neck. "He wanted me to say good-bye. I didn't want to."

"What happened?"

"I fell asleep. The next night he still wanted me to say good-bye. And the next night, too. Lots of nights. He wasn't a very nice pretend daddy anymore. Last night I waved good-bye to him." She sounded sad.

"What happened then?"

"He went away and I cried under the covers." He was pretty sure he could feel tears on his neck.

"That was very sad," he said patting her back. She nodded her head in his neck. "I'm glad you told me. It's nice to be close when you're sad." He rocked her gently, swaying to the rhythm of the pine bows moving in the breeze. He glanced around for the woodpecker, but he didn't see it. "How did I get to be your pretend daddy?"

"You are real and pretend," she said, lifting her face from his neck. He kissed the tears on her cheeks.

"Real and pretend?"

"Real like real and good like my pretend daddy."

"That's perfectly clear," he said, with a chuckle. "I'm glad to be your pretend daddy."

"You are my real pretend daddy."

"Okay, I will be your real pretend daddy." He continued on the path toward the cabin. "And you can tell my parents that I am your real pretend daddy, and I will tell them that you are my real pretend girl." Samantha giggled and Jonas smiled.

75.

That night Sally was somber when she finished putting Samantha to bed. Jonas had made tea and they sat at the table and drank it.

"We've got to decide when we are going to my folks and when to have supper with Daniel so that he can talk to us about married love." When Jonas said "married love" it made his lips pucker like a tart apple.

"Whenever," Sally said listlessly.

"You don't seem very enthused."

"Oh, it's not that."

"What is it then? You were having so much fun working on wedding plans today, and now all of a sudden you act like a flat tire."

"It's the invitations," she said.

"The invitations?"

She nodded as if she had answered his question. He scratched his head. "What about the invitations?"

"How are we going to get them over to the East Side?"

"I'll take them," volunteered Jonas.

"You'll take them?"

"Do you want to take them?"

"No."

"But you don't want me to take them over?"

"The last time you went over there you got in a fight with Daddy and Eugene. Daddy is laid up but Eugene isn't. I don't want you to get in another fight."

"We can ask somebody else to take them," he suggested. She frowned. "You don't like that idea either?" he asked.

"You don't understand. I should take them over."

Jonas leaned back so far on his bench that he almost fell over. "You're right, I don't understand."

"I should," she said. "It's my wedding, and I ought to invite my people."

"They're my people, too."

"Your people?" she said wrinkling her nose.

"Yup," he said. "Today I realized that all the people on this island are my people."

It was her turn to lean back on her bench. She clasped her hands behind her head and stared at him. "They're your people and my people," he insisted.

She laughed. "I'm not arguing with you, Jonas. I'm just trying to figure out what you're talking about."

Jonas leaned forward. "Did you know that Jackson used to be a priest on an Indian reservation in Minnesota?" She nodded. Jonas straightened up, suddenly realizing that what he had started to say was going to make Jackson look bad and probably get Sally mad.

"What about Jackson and the Indian reservation?"

"Jackson left the reservation because he was drinking all the time. He says he drank because the whites destroyed the Indians' way of life, and they were never going to let the Indians have a way of life. The Indians were powerless to do anything. . ." His voice trailed off.

"What does that have to do with my people being your people?"

"Jackson thinks your family has treated you like the whites treated the Indians."

"What?"

Jonas plowed ahead. "He says that when you moved over here, it was like you getting put on a reservation. He says that when I marry you, I'm going to be on the same reservation."

"That's nonsense," she said. "You don't believe that, do you?"

"I told him that when I marry you, this whole island is going to be my home and all the people are going to be my people."

She giggled. "You told him that?"

"Sure. What's so funny about that?"

"I like it, because then the whole island will be my home, too." But then her face darkened.

"What?"

"I'm still scared to take the invitations to the East Side."

"Let's do it together."

She dropped her head, bit her lip, and looked up at him. "Together?" she said doubtfully.

"Sure."

She slowly took a drink of tea. "Together?" she said a little less doubtfully.

"In twelve days we're going to be doing lots of things together. Living together. Sleeping together. Eating breakfast together every morning. Surely we could deliver the wedding invitations to the East Side together." Suddenly he moved forward and said with mock seriousness, "And even I don't think that's going too far before the wedding."

"Okay," she giggled, "we'll do it together. It'll be worth it just to see the shock on my mother's face when we knock on the door. Only we have to do it tonight so I don't get cold feet."

"Tonight!" said a startled Jonas.

"Oh, definitely tonight." This time Jonas caught her mock solemnity.

"I can think of better things to do tonight."

"Like what?" she asked in her most innocent voice.

He slid around the corner of the table from his bench to hers, bumping the leg of the table and sloshing tea out of their cups. "Kissing," he whispered in her ear.

She whispered in his ear, "I thought you wanted to fornicate."

Jonas jerked back. "Don't say that."

Sally slid her hand under his shirt. "I really want you tonight," she cooed. Jonas still held back. She laughed, pulling her hand back. "Jonas, you are so fun to tease. But I'll stop now. Come kiss me." Jonas kissed her lightly on the lips. She held the kiss. He put his arms around her and they kissed more. She swung her feet up on the bench and lay back in his arms. He held her and they kissed for a long time. They paused for a moment. "When we are at your folks, can we go swimming in the pond on your farm?" she murmured.

"Sure," he said as he moved back toward her lips.

"Let's take the invitations to the East Side tomorrow

afternoon as soon as I have all the cabins cleaned, come back for supper with Daniel and Alice, and then on Wednesday go see your folks."

"Sure," he said as he moved back toward her lips. This time she kissed him.

76.

The next afternoon Jonas and Sally set out for the East Side. They left Samantha with Alice. When they got to the East Side it was nearly four o'clock and most of the tugs were back from the day's fishing. Sally led them past several cabins. She knocked at a door. She held Jonas' hand tightly as they waited. "Come in!" yelled Ethyl.

"I don't want to go in," Sally whispered. She knocked again.

"Come in!" yelled Ethyl. Sally knocked again.

They heard a chair scrape and then the door jerked open. "For crying out loud . . ." her voice trailed off. Her eyes opened wide and her mouth opened and closed soundlessly.

"Here's an invitation to our wedding, Mom," Sally said and thrust it into her hand.

"Who is it?" bellowed Arnold from the cabin.

Ethyl stared at them. "We wanted to give you one first," Sally said. "We'll deliver the rest now," she said backing away from the door.

"Who is it?" bellowed Arnold again.

Floyd appeared behind Ethyl in the doorway.

"A wedding invitation?" Ethyl said, finding her voice.

"You're getting married?" asked Floyd. Sally kept inching backwards, tugging at Jonas.

"Who's getting married?" bellowed Arnold.

Ethyl looked down at the invitation. A chair scraped in the cabin and then Arnold hobbled into view. He was using crutches and his leg was wrapped in elastic bandages. "They're getting married," Ethyl said, holding the invitation out to him.

Arnold looked through the door and then at the invitation. "Let me see that thing," he said, hooking one of his crutches in his arm pit and grabbing the invitation. He, Ethyl, and Floyd crowded together and read the invitation.

"Hey, that's too soon. Wedding dance afterwards and I won't be able to dance with the bride," Arnold said.

"You're pregnant, right?" pressed Ethyl.

"Maybe my foot will be better by then," said Arnold. "The father always gets to dance with the bride. Now that you're getting less snotty, maybe you'll dance with your old man again, right?"

"Let's go," said Sally, pulling at Jonas.

"Sally is not pregnant," said Jonas. He turned and followed Sally.

Behind them Floyd said, "At least you could act decent to Sally. She's getting married, for God's sake."

"She didn't even stick around to talk," said Ethyl.

"Don't get too big for your britches, Floyd," Arnold said in a hard voice. "Just because I'm on crutches doesn't mean you can lip off to me."

Sally pulled Jonas around the side of another cabin—a side with no windows—and clung to him. She was shaking.

"You did it," Jonas whispered. They had walked from Little Oslo to the East Side in silence. At any moment Jonas had expected her to turn back. "You did it."

"He makes me so mad," she hissed between clenched teeth. "He wants to dance with me. What are we going to do if he comes to the wedding? He could come on crutches."

"I don't know," said Jonas. He wanted to say, "We'll get married anyway," but he held his tongue.

"What will we do? I don't want him anywhere near me when we get married."

"God will make a way."

"That's easy for you to say."

Jonas sighed, "I suppose it is."

"And Mom makes me mad, too. Asking if I'm pregnant! She always thinks bad of me."

"How about that look on her face when she opened the door!"

Sally laughed. "She looked like a fish out of water, her mouth opening and closing and no sound coming out." She fell silent, shaking her head. Finally she said, "Are you sure you want to marry into my family? They are such . . ." She swore.

"Floyd stuck up for you."

"Yes, he did, didn't he." She paused. "He's the youngest and always did mouth off." She wasn't trembling as much now.

"Yes, I do want to marry into your family."

"You do?"

"Yes."

She moved apart from him so that she could see his face. "Why?"

"First, I love you. Second, I kind of like your mom, even if she has a big mouth. Third, I hate what your daddy did to you but . . ." He stopped and looked out over the lake. It was a deep blue in the afternoon sun. "Something Grandpa used to say makes sense to me now. He'd say, 'If God got rid of all the bad people, that'd be all of us. God puts up with us as long as we live, hoping we'll let him change us for the better.'" He turned back to Sally. "I can put up with your daddy, Sally." Suddenly he found tears in his eyes.

"Why are you crying?"

"I don't know." He wiped them on the back of his sleeve.

"It's okay. I just wondered . . ."

"I guess I really want you, Sally. I'll put up with your daddy so I can have you."

"You sound like you're afraid you'll lose me."

"I do?"

"Yes."

"Maybe I am afraid I'll lose you. You know, you say, 'What are we going to do if he comes to the wedding?' and I get scared. I don't want to lose you." More tears came.

She reached up and touched his wet face with her finger.

"You do love me, don't you?" He nodded, looking at her through his tears. "Jonas, I said I will marry you and I will. I don't want Daddy at the wedding, but I will marry you. Daddy has screwed up my life so much. Couldn't I have my wedding without him screwing it up? Is that too much to ask? That's all I ask, Jonas. That's all I ask." Now she looked like she might cry. Jonas dried his tears.

He pulled her to him. "I am so glad you want to marry me. Very glad." He squeezed her tightly and then moved back. "I don't want your daddy to screw up our wedding either."

A couple of screen doors slammed and they heard the voices of children. "We better deliver the rest of these invitations," she said.

After they delivered the invitations to each of the other cabins, a couple of boys asked Jonas to play catch with an old softball. Sally stood at the end of the trail back to Little Oslo and waited while he tossed the ball back and forth.

"Pop up," yelled Jonas and threw the ball high in the air. The two kids bumped into each other, fell over and missed the ball. "Call for it next time," he said as he popped another.

Ten minutes later Sally said, "We better get going. Alice and Daniel are expecting us for supper." Jonas said good-bye to the boys and walked arm in arm with Sally along the trail. "You seemed to be having fun," she said.

"It is fun. I used to play catch with my younger brothers a lot."

"Do you want to have boys?"

"Sure. Do you?"

"I don't know. Having kids seems scary."

"You already have Samantha."

"She's not scary, but if we have a baby, it might be a boy." She wrinkled her nose. "My brothers were brats. I had to take care of them."

"I hope you change your mind. I think kids are wonderful, even boys."

"And who knows what kind of fiends they might grow up to be."

"They might grow up like me. I'm not a fiend." He gave her a squeeze.

"How do I know?" she said, jostling him with her hip.

"I have been a perfect gentleman."

"Thank God!" she said, grabbing him and kissing him passionately on the lips. She pushed her hips against him. Jonas returned her kiss a little less enthusiastically.

When they parted and began walking again he said, "Sally, I don't understand you. One minute you act wild, and the next moment you act scared to death of me."

"That's me," she said. "One minute I think you're a man and all men are disgusting, and the next minute I want to tear your clothes off and climb all over you."

"Uffda," said Jonas.

"Do you still want to marry me?"

"Definitely." They walked in silence. "But I think we ought to talk to Daniel about this."

"Talk to Daniel?" she squealed.

"He said he wants to talk to us about married love."

"He can talk all he wants about married love, but I'm not saying a word. And you better not say anything to him about me either."

"I'm more worried about you being disgusted."

"You better not say anything to him about that."

"What can I say?"

"Nothing. Just listen. Let Daniel do the talking."

"You seem to have made up your mind," said Jonas, grinning at her determination.

"I have."

77.

Daniel took a careful sip of coffee and smiled at Jonas and Sally who sat on a couch facing him. "Ya, married love. When I said that I wanted to talk with you about married love, I am sure you were curious and maybe even a little scared of what I might have to say. It's such a mystery. Like an unexplored sea. We want to know all about it, but we don't want to fall overboard and drown."

He took another drink of coffee. Jonas and Sally were crowded next to each other. Jonas took her hand. Daniel took another sip.

"You sure neither one of you wants any coffee?" They shook their heads. He set his cup on the table near his rocking chair. "I am going to tell you two stories; one for you, Sally, and one for you, Jonas. These will not be embarrassing stories, but I hope they will be guides for you. The first story is for you, Sally. A story from the old country.

"Once long ago there was a young woman who went out in the forest. She had grown up in a farming village that was full of bad blood. The people in that village fought each other almost as much as their enemies outside the village. When she was old enough to get married, she refused to marry the man whom her parents had chosen. 'He has bad blood,' she said. Her father said, 'Obey your father or you must go away.' She went away in the forest.

"She was a very skilled woman. In the forest she quickly learned to hunt and trap. She built her own cabin. And she sewed her own clothes from animal skins. The only thing she did not do was bake bread.

"Word spread through the forest about this skillful woman.

"One day an old man came to visit her. 'The chief in my village has sent me to ask you to marry his son.'

"Now the young woman knew the son of the chief. She traveled all over the forest as she hunted, and she knew that the son was a great hunter and was always straightforward and gentle with those he hunted with. 'Must I give up hunting?' she asked.

"'No,' said the old man. 'He would be honored to hunt with you. He only has one request—that you bake him bread.'

"'I have never baked bread,' said the young woman.

"'Perhaps you could learn,' said the old man.

"'Perhaps,' said the young woman. 'Is that his only request?'"

"'Yes,' the old man said."

"She had admired the chief's son from a distance for many months, and he came from a village with good blood. 'I will marry him,' she said."

Daniel took a drink of coffee. Setting down the cup he continued, "So plans were made for a great wedding. The announcements were sent out and the old man made many trips between the young woman in the forest and the chief and his son to plan the wedding. Each time the old man finished with the business of planning this great event he would ask, 'Have you baked any bread yet?' Always the young woman would reply, 'Not yet, but I will.'"

"Finally it was the week of the wedding, and the old man had made the final plans with the young woman. As he prepared to leave he asked, 'Have you baked any bread yet?'"

"'Not yet, but I will.'"

"The old man said, 'You are a very skillful woman and worthy of the chief's son. What is it about bread-making?'"

"'I saw my mother make bread. She hated making bread. When I went into the forest I realized I did not ever have to put my hands in dough.'"

"The old man looked at her thoughtfully. 'Perhaps there is another reason, too.'"

"'Perhaps.' She smiled for the old man was wise. The old man waited. 'The village,' she said, 'that sells the best flour for making bread is the village I left.'"

"'I know," said the old man."

"'If you get me the flour, I will bake the bread the chief's son wants,' she bargained."

"'If you buy the flour today, I will go with you,' bargained the old man."

"So the young woman and the old man returned to her village for the first time since she had left. The people of her village stared at her, for they had heard of the great wedding that was being planned. She walked through their stares to the mill and bought the finest flour. Afterwards the old man returned to his village, and she returned to the forest and made very good bread.

"After the wedding the chief's son was true to his word and welcomed the young woman on his hunting journeys. She was true to her word about making bread.

"She discovered she delighted in kneading bread dough and in the aroma of fresh baking bread.

"Often when they returned after a hunt or after she had baked bread, she would knead his shoulders and back, and it was like the smell of fresh baked bread to her."

Daniel's cup of coffee had cooled. He drank the rest of it and then refilled it.

78.

"Now a story for you, Jonas. This is a lake story. When I was a young man and had not yet moved away from home, we lived on Green Bay. My grandparents were very old and walking was hard for them, especially for Grandma who had arthritis bad. Every so often I would row them several miles in a skiff to visit Grandpa's brother who lived up the shore. One day as I was rowing, they fell to telling their love story. They talked Norwegian. Grandpa began.

"'Once when I was young and courting my good lady, I took her out sailing. I was showing off, taking her far out on the sea. She protested, but I sailed out further and further. Suddenly I noticed clouds building in the west and realized we needed to get back to shore. I tried to act calm as I turned back toward shore, but soon the wind was pushing us further out. I tried tacking, but the wind was too strong and the waves too high. I needed to get the sail down and the storm anchor out. And I needed help fast. I ordered her about, and, between the two of us, we got the sail down and the storm anchor out. I thought the boat would go down at any moment. We fought the waves and the wind for what seemed like hours before the storm passed. We were worn out and soaked to the bone when the storm stopped and we saw the shore. I lifted the sail. I looked at my lady and knew, rightfully so, that she was furious. As we sailed toward the shore, her silence was like a reef. Common sense would have me sail around the reef, but I was a young man in love and I guess I had uncommon sense.'

"Grandma snorted when he said that.

"'As we were nearing the dock,' continued Grandpa, 'I said to her, "I want to take you out for a sail again tomorrow."'

"Grandma couldn't hold her tongue anymore. 'I did not say a thing to him,' she remembered. 'I couldn't believe his gall. I stepped onto the dock and left without a word.'

"'When she took off, I wondered if I should have kept my mouth shut,' chuckled Grandpa, 'but again I thought maybe I had spoken just right. Time would tell.'

"'The next morning, much to my relief,' continued Grandma, 'there was a big storm. There was no way to go out on the lake. But then, wouldn't you know, late in the afternoon the storm cleared up and the sea calmed. I was in a fix. Finally I decided to go out on the sea with this brash young man again, but I would teach him a lesson. I went to his house and told him that I was not going sailing with him, but, if he wanted, he could go out on the sea with me. Your grandpa was so in love that, of course, he agreed. Once we were in the boat, I rowed us out about a hundred feet from shore and then threw the oars overboard.'

"'I thought she had lost her senses,' said Grandpa.

"'He did,' said Grandma, 'but I knew exactly what I was doing.'

"'I stood up to dive overboard to get the oars,' said Grandpa, 'and she told me to sit down.'

"'Such a look on his face,' laughed Grandma, her eyes twinkling through her wrinkles.

"'I sat down,' Grandpa said. 'The boat was drifting further into the lake. I decided to count silently to a hundred, and, if we were still drifting, I was going after the oars no matter what she said.'

"Grandma went on, "'I'll get this one," I said, pointing to one of the oars, "and you get that one," I said, pointing to the other one. Then *I* dove.'

"'I didn't know her too well,' said Grandpa. 'At that point I didn't even know if she could swim, so I waited to make sure that she wasn't going to drown.'

"'You found out that I could swim.'

"'Like a fish, my lady. I found out that you are an excellent swimmer.'

"'I got back to the boat with my oar first.'

"'Like I said, she is a good swimmer. But still I was very angry. Especially when she said, "Do you want to go out further?"'

"'He wouldn't answer me for the longest time. He was being stubborn,' said Grandma.

"'Finally I asked, "Why did you throw the oars into the lake? We're lucky the sea didn't take us out any faster. You could've killed us both." All she said was, "Do you want to go out further?" Finally I muttered, "Further." While she was rowing, she turned the boat and exclaimed about the beautiful sunset. I stewed in silence.'

"'Sulked, you mean, dear. He missed a beautiful sunset. I let him help row back to shore when the stars came out. When we were a few feet from the dock I stopped the boat and said, "Let's make a couple of promises."'

"'Oh boy, I thought,' Grandpa said, 'what now?'

"'It was very simple,' said Grandma. 'I offered to promise never to throw his oars overboard, and I wanted him to promise never to take me where I was not ready to go.'

"'I saw the wisdom of those promises,' said Grandpa with a twinkle. 'I have only taken her as far as she wants to go, and we have gone a long way.'

"'And I,' said the old lady, 'have taken good care of his oars, and we have gone a long way.'

"Their hands touched. 'I think those were our true wedding

vows,' said Grandpa.

"Uffda," Daniel said, "this coffee is cold. Well, the stories have been told and the morning is coming early."

Daniel walked with Jonas and Sally to the harbor. The stars shimmered above the waves. "Ya, you are going to need a honeymoon spot then. I think I can help you out there. I have a brother who has a resort up by the Dells. Labor Day is coming up right shortly and business drops off. Tell you what. I'll write him a letter and send it on the *Lillian* tomorrow. To pay for a few days' stay, the two of you could probably give him a hand for a day or two at the end of your honeymoon. He'll have work to do to get ready for winter. I'll give him a good word about you."

Daniel said good-night to them. Honeymoon spot. Jonas thought that sounded like the promised land. Jonas was about to find out what it was like to be in a place that flowed with milk and honey. He smiled.

79.

The train steamed out of Milwaukee and headed northwest. Jonas bounced Samantha on his knee while Sally cradled the material for her wedding dress on her lap. Samantha stood up on Jonas' lap and reached for a cord hanging from the ceiling. "Don't touch that!" Sally yelled. Jonas pulled her back onto his lap again. "If you pull that, you'll stop the whole train," explained Sally.

Samantha's eyes grew large. "The whole train?"   She stared up at the cord.

"Yes, the whole train."

"How long 'til we get there?"

"About half an hour," Jonas said.

"Then can I stop the whole train?"

"When we get there, the whole train will stop without any help from you."

"Oh," she sounded disappointed.

"The cord is there to be pulled only when there's an emergency."

"What's a 'mergcy?"

"When something bad is happening like a fire. The engineer stops the train at each town, but if something bad is happening that the engineer can't see, anyone can stop the train by pulling that cord. Each car has a cord like this one."

Samantha stood up again. "I'll watch for a 'mergcy."

Sally caught Jonas' eye. "Are you still feeling like pulling the cord on the wedding?"

Jonas looked at her warily. "Did I say I was thinking of pulling the cord!"

"You said you were nervous and wanted to see your parents. Now that I bought the material for the dress, I sure hope you don't change your mind!"

Jonas laughed. "Is the wedding dress the only reason you hope I don't change my mind?"

"That did sound a little funny, didn't it?"

"I am on the wedding train and I am a little nervous, but I think I'll stop being nervous after we see my folks."

Sally frowned. "What do you expect to happen?"

"I expect we'll get their blessing on our wedding."

"And if we don't?"

"I haven't thought about that. I think we will get their blessing."

"That sounds pretty iffy to me."

"I can't explain it," he said.

"What can't you explain?"

He scratched his head. Samantha, who was standing on his lap began to help him, vigorously scratching his scalp. He shook his head. "That's enough, Samantha. I was nervous that you wouldn't want to see my parents, but I'm not nervous about them giving us their blessing. They will. I told you what my mom said before I left—that she thought I would pick a good wife." He smiled broadly. "I've picked a very good wife."

"I hope you're right about your folks," she said. "I don't like having my life decided by people I haven't even met."

They were silent.

"I gotta pee," Samantha announced.

Jonas held the wedding dress material while Sally took her to the rest room. He looked in the sack and ran his fingers across the edge of the white material. He looked at the lace she had bought for the veil. He wondered what the world looked like through a veil. He was about to check when Sally came back with Samantha. Sally took back the material.

"When we get back home," she said, "I want to visit my family."

Jonas stared at her.

"I've been thinking about my story, the one that Daniel told from the old country. Remember how the bride had to return to her village to get the flour?"

Jonas nodded.

"You say you want a blessing from your folks. Well, I need something from my folks, too. I don't know if I will get it. I don't even know what it is, but I am going back. And I want you to go with me. And Daniel. Maybe Brawn, too."

"I don't know what to say," Jonas said finally.

"You don't have to say anything. You just have to be with me."

"What are you going to say?"

"I don't know, but I'll think of something."

80.

"This is a surprise," Jonas' mother said, standing on the porch of the white, two-story farm house, wiping her hands on her red-checkered apron. "Jake, go out to the field and tell Dad that Jonas has brought company."

Jonas and Sally stood close together in the yard. Samantha was hiding her face in Sally's shoulder. The three of them were the center of a loose circle of Jonas' younger brothers and sisters, all seven of them, five boys and two girls, who were staring shyly. Jake, his sixteen-year-old brother who was now a good two inches taller than Jonas, broke away from the circle to bring the news to their dad. Jonas introduced each of them to Sally, who solemnly shook their hands. All their names started with J. Samantha refused to come out of hiding.

"How am I supposed to remember so many names?" Sally asked with a grin, looking from one to the other. They smiled shyly at her.

Jonas gazed at his mother. He couldn't remember having noticed what she looked like before. She was tall, about an inch shorter than Jonas, who was the same height as his dad. She was slender, wore a pale blue dress under her apron, and had short fingernails because she chewed them regularly. Her hair, which she wore in a bun, seemed more gray than when he had left.

His mother blushed under his stare. "Come in and sit down," she said, turning away from them. "I'm just peeling potatoes for supper. I can peel a few more. We have fresh potatoes from the garden."

Jonas and Sally followed her into the house and sat close together on the couch, Samantha still hiding in Sally's neck. Joel, Jonas' youngest brother who was Samantha's age and the only other redhead in the family, shyly came in holding out a bird's nest. "I found this in the tree by the barn," he offered. Jonas took the nest and admired it. Within minutes, all of his brothers and sisters except Jake were crowded around with treasures for him to admire. A drawing of a horse, a homemade milking stool, a turtle, a new pair of shoes, bird feathers, and dolls. Samantha came out of hiding and took the doll offered to her by one of his sisters.

"I should help your mother with supper," Sally said and moved to the kitchen.

Soon Jonas was on the floor wrestling with three brothers and one sister. Another sister played dolls with Samantha on the couch. For a moment when he was on his back, he saw

Samantha staring at him, looking as if she was going to cry. He gave her a wink and a smile. "It's okay, Samantha. I'm not getting hurt. This is fun." Joel tackled his head and he lost sight of Samantha. He could capture three, but never all four. The fourth would jump on his back, and soon one or two of the others would wriggle free. Then he'd let them take him down, make an escape, and begin capturing and taking them down again. They laughed, grunted, and challenged each other over and over.

"Jonas, welcome home," his dad said. Jonas sat up. The three oldest scrambled off him.

"Hi, Dad," Jonas said. Joel tackled Jonas' head again. Jonas pulled him off, held the struggling little boy at arm's length, and stood up. Samantha quickly jumped off the couch and hid behind Jonas. His father held out his hand. Jonas shook it. He picked up Samantha to introduce her to his father, but she hid her face in Jonas' neck and refused to look at his dad. Jonas laughed. "Dad, this shy little girl is Samantha. Samantha, this man is my dad." Samantha still refused to look. "That's okay, Samantha. You can hide as long as you need to." Jonas moved to the kitchen and introduced Sally. They all stood in silence.

Dad looked like he always did except when he dressed for church. He had on a faded red cap to protect his bald spot from the sun. He wore a faded blue shirt that had big wet spots under his arms and stuck to his sweaty back. He had on faded blue overalls, complete with dirt spots, and scuffed, brown work shoes. His hands were big with thick fingers from hard work.

"The cows need milking. Do you still have the touch, Jonas?" Dad asked.

Jonas rubbed his hands together. "I bet I do." He passed Samantha to Sally.

In the barn Jake already had the dozen Holsteins in their stanchions. Jonas sat on the milk stool, bucket between his knees, and squeezed a teat. He sighed when he heard the metallic ring of the stream of milk hitting the bottom of the pail. This was home. He quickly regained the rhythm of squeezing one teat, then the other. Soon the bottom of the pail was covered with milk. He closed his eyes, leaned his head against the cow, and listened to the whisper of each stream into the milk in the bucket. He finished the first teats and switched to the other two. The bucket grew heavy between his knees. He thought he might have to empty the bucket before he finished the cow, but there was an inch to spare.

He took the bucket out to the milk room and poured it into a milk can standing next to the cream separator. He went back and milked three more cows. He smiled when he finished the last cow. "Hey, Dad, I haven't lost the touch."

"You haven't," said his dad as he stood up from the last cow. While Jake let the cows out of the stanchions and chased them out of the barn, Jonas and his dad went to the milk room to separate the cream. His dad poured the milk into the large metal bowl that topped the separator. Jonas turned the crank, and the cream streamed out one spout into a cream can while the milk streamed out another spout.

As Jonas cranked his dad said, "So this is the woman you are going to marry."

"Yes."

"In your letters you wrote that she had a child." Dad poured milk into the separator bowl. "But you never did say about the child's father. You don't have to say a thing, Jonas, if you don't want to. I know that life is full of mysteries. And certainly there is forgiveness. But it is natural to wonder why she did not marry the baby's father."

Jonas kept cranking. What should he say? What would Sally want? The cream can was full, so Jonas stopped cranking. They waited while the stream slowed and stopped, and then his father moved the full one aside and replaced it with an empty one. Jonas started cranking again.

His dad was pouring another milk can in the separator bowl when Jonas said, "She was raped by her father." His dad stared at him, still pouring. The bowl filled with milk and slopped over the edge. "Dad," Jonas said, nodding towards the separator bowl.

His dad slowed down his pouring to let the separator bowl empty some. Then he poured the rest of the can in and set it down. "You did say 'her father.'"

Jonas nodded.

His father went for a rag. He returned, added more milk to the separator bowl from another can, then knelt and began wiping up the spilled milk. When he stood up he said, "That must have been pretty tough on her." Jonas was surprised to see tears in his dad's eyes. His dad wiped his face on the back of his sleeve.

They finished the separating, washed the separator and milk cans, and then carried the cream cans to the well house. On the way to the well house his dad said, "You know your grandma had the same trouble with your great-grandpa. Your mother's side. It's tough business, but God does see us through these things."

They set the cans in the artesian well tank. The flowing water would keep them cool until the creamery truck picked them up in the morning.

81.

"When do we get to play hide-and-go-seek in the barn?" Samantha asked pulling on Jonas' hand.

Jonas, who had just stood up from the table after supper, looked down at her. "So you remember that promise of mine?" She nodded. Jonas looked around and saw the eager eyes of his brothers and sisters. Hide-and-go-seek was one of their favorite games. "How about right now?"

There was a sudden chorus, "Not it! Not it! Not it!"

"Not it," said Jonas.

"Out of the house with this racket," said their mother.

"You were the last to say 'Not it,'" said Joel to Jonas.

"You're it."

"The barn door will be base," said Jake.

"But you have to touch it from the outside," said Janey, the oldest girl.

"And no fair guarding base," said Joel.

"Samantha and I will be it," said Jonas, scooping up Samantha and balancing her on his hip. "We'll count to a hundred inside the house and then open the door and yell 'Ready or not.'" His brothers and sisters streamed out the door.

"I'll help with the dishes," Sally said.

"But you wanted to work on your wedding dress. Go ahead. I can handle the dishes," said Jonas' mother.

Sally hesitated. "I'll help clear the table and then start on the dress."

As Jonas counted to a hundred he watched Sally and his mother. Sally moved easily around his mother, carrying the dishes from the table to the kitchen. His mother dipped hot water out of the reservoir on the cook stove for washing dishes.

When he reached one hundred he lifted up Samantha, told her to close her eyes, stepped outside, closed the door, and yelled without looking, "Ready or not here we come!"

"Ready or not here we come," yelled Samantha. They opened their eyes.

He scanned the red, arched-roofed barn with the haystacks on one side and the woodshed on the other. "I don't see anyone, Samantha, but let's go find them."

As they crossed the yard to the barn she yelled, "Ready or not here we come."

"Shhh," he said. "We have to find them and tag them before they touch the front barn door."

"Where are they hiding?"

"That's for us to find out." He lowered his voice as he approached the front of the barn. "Now we have to be very quiet so that we can see them before they see us. We'll try to stay between where they're hiding and the front door." He began to whisper, "Samantha, you are going to be my secret weapon in this game. You'll help me, right?" Her eyes were wide. She nodded. He walked to the corner of the barn by the haystacks. "I'm going to have you stand right by this corner. Right here." He pointed to the side of the barn. "I want you to peek around the corner," he whispered, "and if you see anyone coming from that side of the barn, yell, 'Daddy!' real loud. Then I'll quick run and tag the person before they get to the front door. While you're peeking, I'm going to be sneaking around the haystacks to see if I can catch somebody hiding in the stacks." Jonas had a broad grin. He was excited. "Got that?"

She nodded. "Yell 'Daddy!' real loud."

"You got it, Samantha." He set her down. He started toward the stacks, then stopped and looked back. She was watching him. "Peek around the corner," he mouthed, motioning with his hand. She looked puzzled. He returned. "Remember," he whispered, "you're supposed to peek around the corner." To show her, he peeked around the corner. Janey came around the opposite corner, her pigtails flying as she dashed for the door. "Whoa!" he yelled, and raced to cut her off.

She beat him to the door, touched it, and yelled, "Safe!"

"Shucks, Janey," he said, "you beat me." She flashed him a smile and began to chase their collie, Lady, who was barking excitedly. Jonas returned to the corner, stationed Samantha, and began stealthily checking the haystacks. He glanced to see if Samantha was peeking around the corner like she was supposed to. She was. He started around the stack.

"Daddy!" came her small voice.

He left the stack, raced past Samantha and around the corner of the barn at full speed. He slowed. No one was in sight. He stopped and turned to Samantha. "What happened to the person you saw?"

"I didn't see nobody." She looked scared.

"Why did you yell 'Daddy!'?"

"I couldn't see you."

"And you got scared?" She nodded. He picked her up. "I guess my bright idea isn't going to work. Let's go look for people together. When we spot somebody, I'll set you down and run, and you run after me. Okay?" She nodded again.

It didn't work. Samantha would talk and give their position away, or she would start crying when he set her down to chase somebody. Time after time his brothers and sisters beat him to base. Jake was the only one he hadn't found. He knew Jake's plan: find such a good place to hide that he would be the last one found. Usually someone else would be tagged trying to get to base. Or the person who was It would give up searching for him.

Jonas talked Samantha into playing with Janey so he was free for the hunt. He had covered the haystacks and woodshed well enough to know he wasn't there. That had to mean he was somewhere in the barn. He slipped through the front door of the barn and let his eyes adjust to the dim light of the cream room. He scouted the room. No Jake. He stepped into the long alley at the center of the barn. On one side of the alley stood the empty stanchions; in the front of the stanchions the concrete was beveled into a trough for feeding hay and grain; the other side of the alley held a closed-in grain room, a water tank, and three calf pens. There were calves in two of the pens; the other was empty. He glanced up and down the barn. "Hey, Jake," he yelled, "you better have a great hiding place because you're the last one." No movement or sound gave Jake away. The calves stared at him through the boards.

He checked around the water tank. No Jake. He checked the grain room. No Jake. He checked the calf pens. No Jake. He checked the hay in the trough. No Jake. He was now at the far end of the barn. He looked back to see if he had missed a hiding spot. None. He climbed the ladder to the haymow and pushed up the trap door. He climbed into the mow and was about to drop the door when he heard a splash. He wondered if a cat had fallen into the tank. He quickly laid down on the floor and stuck his head through the open trap door. A sopping wet Jake slipped through the door of the cream room. "Whoa!" yelled Jonas. He swung back down through the trap door and dropped to the floor. Jake was safely ahead of him. Jonas tore into the cream room, but by the time he got there Jake was nowhere in sight. Jonas grabbed the door, yanked it open, and fell over Jake who was sitting on the ground just outside the door.

Jonas scrambled off the moaning, wet Jake. "Did I hurt you?" he asked Jake.

"Daddy!" Samantha was crying. Janey came up carrying her. "Daddy," Samantha said through her tears.

Jonas stood up and took Samantha. "What's the matter?" he said.

"You didn't come when I said 'Daddy!'" Jonas held her tight.

"When you went in the barn she got scared," explained Janey. "I tried to keep her happy so you could find Jake."

"Thanks a lot," said Jake, who was sitting on the ground rubbing his ankle.

"You wanted your daddy, didn't you?" Jonas squeezed Samantha in a big hug. He glanced up to see Janey sticking out her tongue at Jake. Jake, still sitting on the ground, laughed and reached for Janey's leg, but she danced out of the way.

"What happened?" Jonas asked again.

"I twisted my ankle coming through the cream room," said Jake. "I heard you yell just as I was turning the corner. I pushed off on it funny." He wiggled it. "It doesn't hurt too bad."

"You were hiding in the cow tank?" Jonas asked in amazement.

"Ya," Jake grinned.

"How'd you breathe?"

"When I heard you coming, I slid under the water and breathed through a piece of pipe."

Jonas shook his head. "Samantha, your uncle Jake is the best hider there is." Jake leaned back on his hands, his elbows extended, and looked at Jonas. Jonas couldn't read his look. "What?" he asked.

"Nothing."

"Nothing? You're thinking something."

"Hey, I don't have to say everything I think, do I?"

"No, you don't. I was just curious."

"It's a little strange having you come home a dad."

"It is a little strange, isn't it?"

"I'm not strange," said Samantha, looking at Jake. "You're strange."

"Now that's no way to talk to your uncle," said Jonas. Samantha turned her back to Jake. Jonas looked at Jake and shrugged his shoulders. "Sorry," he said.

"He swims in his clothes," said Samantha.

Jake laughed. "I am a little strange."

"Come to think of it," said Jonas, "she's right. It was a little strange to hide in the cow tank with all your clothes on."

"But it worked, didn't it," said Jake, who prided himself on thinking up new ideas. He had spent most of his twelfth year working on a perpetual motion machine.

"Ya, it worked," granted Jonas, giving him a playful shove on the shoulder. "Now you better see if your ankle works." Jake stood up and tested the ankle gingerly.

"It works," he said, but he had a limp as he and Jonas walked toward the house.

82.

"You have a good seamstress," Jonas' mother told him from the kitchen when he walked in carrying Samantha following the hide-and-go-seek game.

"Sally, you mean?" he replied. Sally was at the table leaning over cloth with patterns pinned to it. She was cutting with a scissors. His mother came and stood next to him. "She already has most of the pattern cut out, and it isn't an easy pattern either," she said.

Sally picked up Samantha and brought her back to Jonas. "Could you get Samantha ready for bed, Jonas? I'll put her down after she's all ready. I want to keep sewing." Jonas nodded.

"We played hide-and-go-seek, Mama," Samantha said.

"Did you have fun?" Sally asked distractedly as she handed her back to Jonas.

"I got to yell 'Daddy!' real loud."

"Good. Now you spend a little more time with Daddy. Mama's going to keep sewing on her wedding dress." She returned to the table.

"She likes sewing," Jonas said to his mother.

"She's good." She paused. "I think she could teach me a thing or two about sewing."

With new eyes Jonas looked at Sally hunched over the sewing machine. He knew she sewed, but he never knew that she was extra good at it.

"Daddy!" Samantha suddenly yelled.

"Shh. I'm right here, Samantha. I'm not deaf."

"I just like to yell 'Daddy!'" She yelled it again.

Jonas was embarrassed. "Don't yell in the house," he said.

"I have a daddy I don't know and a daddy I do know," she said.

He and his mother looked at her. "The daddy you do know is going to get you ready for bed," Jonas said, avoiding looking at his mother.

"The girls will sleep on the floor in the front room," said his mother, "so Sally and Samantha can have their room upstairs."

Jonas washed Samantha, helped her into her pink, flannel nightgown, told her the story of Daniel and the lions' den, and then brought her to Sally. Sally took her upstairs to put her to bed.

As soon as Sally disappeared upstairs his mother said, "Jonas, it's a beautiful night. Let's swing on the porch a few minutes." Jonas knew what that meant.

"The mosquitoes will eat us alive," he said. He wasn't sure he wanted to hear what she wanted to talk about. Most likely she wanted to talk about Sally.

"The wind is picking up," she said. Jonas followed her out. The sun had set and the wind had picked up. There was a large pine tree in the front yard. It sighed and creaked in the wind.

"I'm so glad you brought Sally home and her darling little girl," she said after they sat down on the bench swing. Jonas nodded. "Samantha is such a cute little girl."

"Yes, she is," Jonas said stiffly.

"Remember the last time we swung together?" she asked.

"Yes, just before I left home."

"Do you remember what we talked about?"

"Yes, you told me things to help me in life." He wondered where this line of questioning was going.

"I remember it very well," she said. "I was so sad. You were leaving home, and I wanted to give you some wisdom to take with you. Do you remember what I said?"

"You said that what I want in life is ahead of me. And you talked about how Dad makes you laugh in bed. You said I should learn how to laugh more. And . . ." he paused. She had said that he would choose a good wife. Did she still think so? He remembered the mixture of pride and embarrassment he felt when she talked about him choosing a wife. He had looked forward to choosing a wife, but it had seemed a long way off. Now he had chosen.

His mother laughed. "Are you having a hard time remembering?"

"You told me that I would choose well when I chose a wife." His voice was a little louder than he meant it to be.

"You remember," she said, pleased. "You have chosen well."

"I have?"

"I like her. She has spunk."

"What do you mean?"

"You have to have spunk to make your way in life as early as she did. She was on her own when she was only sixteen or seventeen. She practically runs that resort since the woman in charge is deaf and can't talk to the customers. That takes spunk."

Jonas was amazed at how much his mother had learned about Sally. Then he smiled at her. *You have chosen well.* He didn't know why he knew he must visit his parents before his wedding. Now he knew. *You have chosen well.* He needed to hear those words.

Then her face tightened. She looked away. Jonas waited uneasily. "Dad told me how it happened." Jonas watched the branches of the pine bob in the wind. He did not want to listen.

"Men can be so mean. Women just have to watch out for mean men." She sighed, "But even when you watch out, you can't always stop a mean man. Let's swing." They pushed off together, lifted their feet, and began to swing.

"Jonas, don't ever be mean to her."

"I won't," he said, aghast.

"It won't be easy not to, you know. She'll expect you to be mean like her dad. When she acts like you're being mean, it'll be hard not to be."

"I won't be mean to her."

"I hope not."

"I won't," still watching the swaying branches.

"My grandpa was mean. He used to beat his wife and kids. My mother, your grandma, she suffered like Sally. She used to tell me to stay away from mean men. She said once a man turns mean, there's not much you can do. Some women think they can change a man, but about all you can do with a mean man is stay away from him. You can't change him. Your grandma married a man with a soft heart. Grandma always said it took her about ten years before she believed Grandpa wasn't going to hurt her. I married a man with a soft heart, too. Your dad has never lifted a hand against me. He's a good man. Jonas, every day I pray that my boys won't get a mean streak."

Jonas turned. In the dim light from the window he could see tears in her eyes.

83.

Jonas floated on his back in the pond. After Lake Michigan, it felt like bath water. The water covered his ears and the world was perfectly silent and the sky was deep and filled with stars. He breathed in and his chest rose in the water, breathed out and the water covered his chest, breathed in and rose in the water. He floated, named the families of stars, and thought about what his mother had said about his grandma and great-grandpa.

Someone squeezed his foot. Startled, he reared up, his head went under and he came up choking. Sally's laughter rang out. He paddled while he coughed and caught his breath. "You scared me," he said.

"I wanted to surprise you."

"You certainly did that."

They paddled water, looking at each other in the starlight. "This pond is hot," she said.

He nodded. "Compared to Lake Michigan." He motioned with his hand and floated to her. They kissed, their lips brushing. He touched her side and slid his hand down. Her dress was floating. He pulled her close. They pressed their lips together, seeking each other. Their heads went under. They parted and rose to the surface, laughing.

"You're with me in the water."

"Yes. I was tired of sewing and was lonesome for you. The mosquitoes were bad coming down here."

"There's a dock in the middle of the pond. We can hang onto that." They paddled to the dock, held on, and embraced with their other arms. They kissed. She fit her lips to his, and Jonas could feel his longing rise in him. When they paused for a breath she asked, "What were you doing out here all by yourself?"

"I was thinking." He sighed. His longing was slipping away. "About?"

"I heard from both Mom and Dad today that my

great-grandpa messed with my grandma."

"He did?"

Jonas nodded.

"So I'm not the only one in the world."

"I guess not."

"What else did they say?"

"My mom talked about how mean men can be and how she prays every day that her boys won't have a mean streak."

"I like your mother. She has spunk."

"What did she say to you?"

"She talked nice to you about my sewing."

"What makes you think she has spunk?"

"She told me right out not to let my daddy ruin my life."

"She did?"

"Yes. Your dad must have told her right after you told him because, while we were clearing the table, she said she knew what had happened with my daddy. She said he belonged in jail for what he had done."

"She did?"

"Yes. She's the first person who said that to me."

"Jail?"

"Yes, jail."

"I never even thought of him going to jail."

"Well, he should."

"I know he should. What else did she say?"

"You'll like this. She said I was marrying a good man. She thinks you have a soft heart and that's just the kind of man I need. One with a soft heart."

"She said that?"

"Yes." She leaned toward him and kissed him hard.

"Let's go up on the dock," he said. "I think the wind will keep the mosquitoes away." She climbed onto the dock, the water running off her dress, splashing in his face as he waited his turn. On the dock he lay beside her and they kissed. He held her and kissed her for what seemed like hours. Sometimes they sat up. Sometimes they laid side by side.

84.

Jonas got up at 5:30 on Saturday morning to help with the milking. He found he missed the familiar motions that he and Jake and his dad had gone through for years. He was nine when he started milking, and, except for two times when he was sick, he had milked every morning and night since, until the previous spring. Putting feed in each of the troughs, calling the cows, closing the stanchions, washing the teats, milking, letting the cows out, separating the cream, putting the cream in the well house, the cheerful whistling of his father as they worked. It all came back to him with a freshness that entranced him.

As they left the well house his father said, "Last night you were talking about building a bed next week. There are some nails left over from when we built the barn. I can spare a few. Save yourself from buying them on your way back to the island."

Jonas followed him to the tool shed. His dad pulled out a box from the floor under a bench, put a couple of handfuls of tenpenny nails into a cigar box, and handed it to Jonas.

"That should do it," his dad said.

They needed to leave on the 7:30 train in order to catch the *Lillian* to get back in time for Hank and Philena's wedding. After breakfast the whole family gathered by the Model T in the front yard to say good-bye. His dad was giving them a ride to the train.

"You didn't forget anything now, did you, Jonas?" his mother asked.

"I double-checked the house," Sally said. "I didn't see anything."

"You're sure, Dad, you can't find somebody to do the milking so you could come to the wedding?" Jonas asked.

"He probably could find somebody, but things are a little tight right now," said his mother.

His dad nodded, a hint of regret in his eyes. "I'd send Mom, but we're starting to get a little bill at the store," he said.

Jonas nodded.

"Come and visit us again and as soon as you can," said his mother. She reached into her apron pocket and brought out an envelope. "Here's a wedding card," she said, handing it to Jonas. "There wasn't time to buy or make a present, but the next time you come, I'll have something. Wait a minute. I just thought of something." She hurried into the house. She came back with a folded white cloth. She handed it to Sally. "You put this up in your home. I embroidered it for a cousin who's getting married next month, but I'll get her something else." Sally unfolded the cloth and held it up. At the top of the cloth she had embroidered a house with a pine tree by it. Below the house she had embroidered a poem, and the tree and the house were enclosed in a border. She and Jonas read the poem, Jonas reading aloud:

God bless this house and where it stands,
Made here secure by rugged hands.
Bless thou the rooftree, beams, and floor,
And all that enter at the door.
God bless these fires burning bright,
And guide our homeward feet aright.

"It's beautiful," said Sally. She threw her arms around Jonas' mother and hugged her. They weren't that kind of family, so Jonas wondered what his mom would do, but she stood there and took it.

"Thank you so much," Sally said, letting her go.

"I'm so glad I thought of that," his mother said.

Everyone stood in the yard and waved as they drove away. On the way to town his dad told about his wedding day. Jonas had never heard him talk about it before.

"I was scared the day we got married. I remember doing chores that morning, and it suddenly struck me that, after today, I am supposed to support this woman. Up until then I hadn't thought about that. I guess I was all caught up in the fact that she was going to have me. She was part of a big family. There were two of us in my family, and my sister was fifteen years older and had been married as long as I could remember, so it really was just like I was the only one. My dad died when I was ten, and then the year before I got married, Mom died. That last year I lived with my sister and her husband, and they didn't have any kids. My brother-in-law was one of those real quiet types, and I never knew what he was thinking, so I always thought the worst. That year I met your mom and she came from a big family that was a lot of fun.

"I got to go on those picnics every Sunday afternoon in the summer, and everyone treated me good, so I hadn't really thought about the scary side of getting married. Until that morning in the barn. Then I got good and worried. I stewed about it the whole time I was helping my brother-in-law with the milking.

"We got married in November, and there had been an ice storm the night before. I was carrying the cream pail to the well house and really wasn't paying attention, and I slipped and fell and spilled half the day's cream. I was sure my brother-in-law was going to be mad. My mom had been a yeller, and she always yelled when I did things like that. My brother-in-law was carrying the other pail of cream. He looked down at me sprawled out on the ground next to the cream sliding over the ice and gets a little smile and says, 'Got some nerves today, huh?'"

Jonas' dad chuckled as he pulled into the train station and shut off the car. "That made me laugh. We got married that day, and things have gone about as good as can be expected. Now I have a whole tribe to support and I still get worried once in awhile. When I do I say to myself, 'Got some nerves today, huh?'" He laughed again.

While they waited for the train, his dad went over to the store across the street and came back with a small bag of Brach's peppermint candy for Samantha. When they heard the whistle blow, his dad shook hands with all three of them.

"I like your family," Sally said when they were on the train. There was the hint of tears in her eyes, as if it hurt a little to like his family.

85.

"By the authority invested in me by the state of Wisconsin and the church of Jesus Christ, I now pronounce you man and wife," read Jonas. He looked up at Hank. "You may now kiss the bride." Hank lifted her veil and they kissed, standing on the same platform that had been used at the engagement party. All the people of Little Oslo were at the wedding. I did it, thought Jonas. I married them. My first wedding.

There was a loud clap of thunder and a gust of wind caught Philena's veil. Hank grabbed the veil as it whipped over his head. Then the driving rain hit. People scattered like leaves as they dashed for cover. Jonas jumped off the platform, grabbed Samantha, and stumbled into a fish house followed by Sally. Several others took shelter in the fish house, too.

Jonas turned and looked out. Hank, arm around Philena, was guiding her through the rain up the trail toward her cabin.

He looked at the book still in his hand. It was soaked. He set it on a shelf and put his other arm around Sally, pulling her close to him. Samantha reached out and moved their heads together, and then leaned her head into theirs. She laughed. "A wet, three-headed monster," she said.

"Uffda, we got wet fast," Jonas said.

"I could see the storm coming across the lake behind you during the ceremony," said Sally. "I kept thinking, Jonas, hurry up. I couldn't stand it. I kept wanting to say, 'Wrap it up, Jonas.'"

"I didn't even notice it coming," said Jonas. "I was so busy getting them married."

"I noticed," Sally smiled wryly.

86.

Sally led the way on the path that wound across Norsk from Little Oslo to the East Side. Jonas followed her, and Daniel followed him. They were silent.

"Now the two of you just wait for me down by the docks," she said. "I want you around, but I have to do this myself."

It was after supper and the fishermen of the East Side were doing their shore work. Daniel laughed and joked with them about fishing, boats, and motors. They kept their distance from Arnold who was sitting on a stool, working on the engine for his boat. Jonas was silent, glancing in the direction Sally had gone.

Time passed. He and Daniel lent a hand to a man who was turning his skiff to patch it. Two men argued about the best design for a fishing boat. They disguised words as humor, but there was an edge to their voices.

Half an hour later, when the sun was ready to slide behind the trees, Sally returned. Her face had lost color even in the orange, evening sunlight.

"I didn't get them," she said and headed back up the trail.

The return home was silent as well. Sally went into Daniel and Alice's cabin to pick up Samantha. Daniel and Jonas stood on the porch. Jonas waited for some wisdom. Daniel shook his head. "Stay with her. Find out what happened. There's not much more I can say or you can do until she's ready to talk."

Jonas made coffee while Sally put Samantha to bed. Samantha fussed a lot. Jonas sat at the table, sipped coffee, and waited. He didn't even know what she had tried to get from her mother.

Finally Samantha was asleep. Sally sat at the table. Jonas handed her a cup of warm coffee. She cupped it in her hands as if she were trying to warm up. A tear formed in her right eye. Another in her left eye. Soon silent, steady streams flowed from her dark green eyes down her cheeks. Jonas slid over to her on the bench and put his arm around her. She set the cup down and started to sob. "What happened?" he asked. She didn't move closer. She hunched over and sobbed more. "What happened?" he asked again.

Jonas waited minutes, then what seemed like hours. He gave up asking. Sometimes she cried. Sometimes she grew still and stared at the lantern with a fierce stare that frightened Jonas. Sometimes she shook her head as if she were saying no. Sometimes he put his arm around her. Sometimes he leaned his elbows on the table, cupped his chin, and nodded off, only to wake to a new round of sobs.

It was in that half-awake, half-dream sleep that he began to think about his mother. He remembered his mother beside him, pointing out the stars from his new bedroom window and saying, "Stars are known by their families." He felt a darkness creep into him. *Stars are known by their families.* And then he remembered Daniel saying to Sally, "You are marrying into his family and he is marrying into yours." More darkness crept into him. *He is marrying into her family.* He would be known by her family.

He shook his head. It was right to marry into her family, wasn't it? This wedding was God's will, wasn't it? He was wide awake.

"I could just die," Sally said.

"What?"

She fell silent again. Finally she said. "I always thought I was wanted."

"You mean when you were born?" Jonas asked, puzzled.

She shook her head impatiently, "Just listen. My mother said she should have taken me to a doctor . . ." She started to cry again. " . . . to . . . " She sobbed louder. " . . . to take care of the problem." She dropped her head and sobbed. She raised her head. "She doesn't understand," she said fiercely. "She doesn't understand at all." She turned to Jonas, grabbing his arms with both her hands. "I need you to understand."

Jonas nodded and waited.

"She would have killed Samantha. She wished she had. She wishes she would have taken me to a doctor and had me fixed.

'You know, doctors can fix this kind of thing. You just have to know the right doctor,' she said.

"Jonas, no one can know what it was like. I am so glad I never told her until it was too late. I couldn't believe I was pregnant. I just thought I was getting fat. One day my mother said, 'You're pregnant, aren't you?' Jonas," she wailed, "I said, 'No, I can't be.' 'You certainly can be,' she said. 'You were raped, you said, so you can be pregnant.' Jonas," Sally whispered, "that's how I found out."

She sobbed. "And now Mom tells me she wishes she would have taken me to a doctor to get it taken care of."

Jonas shook his head. He wanted to go up to the loft and touch Samantha. "How did you get talking about that?" he asked.

She shook her head. "I asked for a set of pillows and pillowcases," Sally began to talk through her tears. "That's what I went there to ask for. She promised them to me when I was a little girl. She promised. She got them from her mother when she got married. They were supposed to be for guests, but she never used them. They were satin cases, embroidered and so pretty. One, pink embroidery, and the other, blue embroidery. She kept them in the same case as her china. I loved those pillows. I don't know why. I just did. I used to stare at them through the glass. I'd beg Mom to let me touch them. Once in awhile she'd open the door and let me touch them. I still remember the texture. Maybe that's why I love to sew. I've always liked the feel of good cloth.

"One day when I was seven or eight Mom got mad at Grandma, her mom. I don't know what it was about. Probably Daddy. Their fights always seemed to be about him. Oh, of course, now I remember what it was about. Grandma was visiting and she took the pillows out of the case for her and Grandpa to use. She didn't ask Mom. She just took them. Mom got mad and told Grandma she couldn't use those pillows because she was saving them for me when I got married. Grandma said that she had given them to her for guests, and she was a guest. But Mom insisted she was going to give them to me for my wedding, and she won. Grandma huffed and put them back in the cabinet. But now Mom won't give them to me. I wonder if she just said that to Grandma so that Grandma couldn't use them."

She turned her dark green eyes to Jonas. "I wanted them for our wedding night," she said sadly.

"Why won't she give them to you?"

"You, Jonas." She sighed.

"What did I do?"

"She won't give them to me because you are the cause for me 'making up this business about Daddy.'" She paused and a tear formed in her deep green eyes. She shook her head. Her pause became silence, a longer and longer silence.

The darkness began to creep back into Jonas. And this is the family I am going to be known by, he thought. He stared at the wick of the lamp. A sure, steady, flickering light driving back the darkness of the room. He needed something to drive back the darkness within him. Lord, he thought, this is the family I am going to be known by. He remembered a preacher telling about the ancient Greek who lit a lantern and wandered around looking for an honest man. What was his name? He couldn't remember. Suddenly Jonas wondered: if that old man put the lantern in my face, would he find an honest man? The darkness pushed harder. Could he be an honest man and be known by her family? Jonas desperately wanted to be an honest man.

"She doesn't understand," said Sally. "Jonas, do you realize that Samantha is as much Daddy's daughter as mine?"

Jonas stared at her. She stared back, her eyes narrowing.

"She is," she said.

Jonas nodded involuntarily.

"When I finally accepted that I was pregnant, I had to decide what to do. I didn't know that the 'problem could be fixed.' All I knew was that I was all alone. There was no one I could turn to. No one. I walked around in a daze. I don't think I said a word to anyone for weeks. My mother talked. I didn't. I couldn't eat. My mother forced me to eat. 'For the sake of the baby,' she said.

"I could hardly get up in the morning. I was like a shadow moving around the house— sewing, cooking, eating—silent as a shadow. I didn't know if it would ever be different. Except the baby kicked." She looked at Jonas, light in her green eyes. "One morning I was lying in bed, trying to force myself to get up, when I felt the baby kick." She laughed. "I laid there and laughed. I waited and I felt another kick. Somebody wanted me. I laughed some more. I laughed and laughed. Mom stuck her head in the room and asked me what was the matter. She looked like she thought I was going crazy. 'Nothing,' I said. I didn't want to tell her. I didn't want to share the secret with anyone. I had life in my tummy." She patted her stomach. "That morning as I lay in bed, I decided I was going to take care of the life in me. No one else was. I was.

"I got up, and within a week I had moved in with Alice and Daniel. I stayed with them over the winter on the mainland and promised to help with the resort starting in the spring after the baby was born.

"Spring came and I still hadn't had the baby. Alice and Daniel were going to leave me with some other people when they came to the island for the start of the fishing season, but I couldn't stand to be without them so I came along, even though we knew I might not get to the mainland and a hospital in time. Alice made me promise to wake her as soon as labor started. I woke her so many times that she finally told me not to wake her until I was really sure! When I was really sure, it happened too fast. There wasn't time. I barely had time to wake up Alice, who went and got Philena, and the two of them helped me. My baby was born, and I was no longer alone. I had life.

"Jonas," she said, looking at him with deep green eyes, "can you ever understand? I had life. I was as good as dead. I wanted to die. And then I had Samantha. No matter how she started out, she was life. Do you understand?"

Jonas nodded. "Samantha was new life and she was good," he said.

She held Jonas with her tear-filled eyes. "You understand. She was good, and I was not alone." She shook her head sadly. "So it rips me inside when Mom says she should have taken me to a doctor. I would have died. I would have had nothing to live for. Can you understand? I was so alone."

"I have never been so alone as you were," Jonas said, shaking his head. "No wonder those words fit so well for you, 'My God, my God, why have you forsaken me?'"

"Everyone had forsaken me. I was all alone until I felt the baby kick. Then I was not alone."

They sat in silence. The darkness began to creep back into Jonas. He looked at the flame in the kerosene lamp again. He wanted to be an honest man, but honesty contained so much darkness. He wanted a light honesty, not an honesty that stabbed him with darkness. He wanted to be honest about something she had said. What was it? He knew it was lurking in the shadows. He wanted to keep it there, but he wanted to be an honest man. What was it? Oh, yes. "Sally," he said, "something you said a little while ago stabbed me in the heart." She turned her face toward him. "You said," he continued, "that Samantha is as much your daddy's daughter as yours. That stabbed me in the heart." He began to cry.

"How do you think it makes me feel?"

Jonas could only nod mutely through his tears.

"Terrible," she said. "I was so glad she was a girl. I didn't want the baby to look like Daddy."

Jonas was horrified at the thought. "How could you stand it?" he whispered.

"Until that kick I couldn't." They were silent. Jonas stared at the flame in the lamp. "At that moment," she said, "I knew that life was good. All life. Even this life that had started out so bad. I couldn't have told you why. I just knew it. Now I know why. All life comes from God. Remember that sermon you did about the stars, about how God set them in the heavens and they show God exists?" Jonas nodded. "I saw a picture in my mind. A totally black sky and God lighting the stars one by one. Every star comes from God and so does every

baby. My life was like a black sky, and he lighted a life in me."
She sighed. "So in a way her life did not come from Daddy or
me. It came from God, and it was good."

They sat in silence. Jonas pictured the stars lit one at a time
in the black sky, pushing the darkness back. He thought,
honesty does push back the darkness. "You are an honest
woman," he said.

"What do you mean?"

"I admire your honesty. You let me think of Samantha as
your daddy's child. I could face it because you said it. I could
realize how horrified I am of the thought." His face bunched
in pain. "I want her to be my child. That's what I want. But
she will never be my child. Not in the way that I want her to
be. And then you show me how she is God's child. And then
I think, I will let her be who she is. Your child, your daddy's
child, God's child and . . ." His face relaxed and he laughed.
" . . . and a kid I love so much I could bust."

Her green eyes softened and she reached out and touched
his face. "I know you love her. And you know what else?"

He shook his head.

"I am not alone any more. First there was Samantha, then
there was Jesus, and now you."

He sighed, smiled, and said, "I want you, too."

"I just hope I can open myself to you as much as I have to
Samantha," she said as she reached for him.

87.

The day of their wedding, Jonas was up at dawn and went
with Daniel and his crew to pick the gill nets. Hank and
Philena were due back from their honeymoon on the *Lillian*
that day.

Jonas enjoyed the good-natured joshing about his wedding
day as he picked and packed the fish.

"Big day," said Brawn. "Of course, I wouldn't know about

these things."

"You will one of these days," said Daniel.

Theresa blushed.

"You'll have to come back from your honeymoon and tell us if it's worth it," Brawn said.

Theresa clicked her tongue and said, "Brawn."

"How we gonna know unless we ask?"

"I better ask someone who knows soon," said Jonas, "so I know what I'm getting into. Daniel, what was your honeymoon like?"

All ears turned to Daniel while their hands were busy with nets and fish. "I don't think Alice would like me telling tales on her then," he said.

"Tell some tales on yourself," Brawn said.

"It's kind of hard to tell them kind of tales just on yourself."

They all thought about that for awhile. Then Jonas laughed and said, "Well, Brawn wants to know if it's worth it?"

"Honeymoon or marriage?"

"Both," said Brawn.

"Let's see then." Daniel took his cap off and wiped his sweating brow with the back of his hand. "It's what you make of it."

"That's clear as mud," said Brawn.

"Ya, well, what is it you want to know then, Brawn?"

"I don't know," stammered Brawn.

That was the first time Jonas ever heard Brawn stammer.

"Ya, well, I think on the wedding day, what everybody wants to know is what's it gonna be like when you get to the bed part," said Daniel.

There was silence, each person looking at fish or net.

"Let me tell you a story about Ole and Lena. Ole was a bachelor, you know, for many years before he laid eyes on Lena. Then he laid eyes on her, and in no time at all they got married. When they come back from their honeymoon, all the other fishermen wanted to know what it was like. 'Uffda,' says Ole, 'it was like going out on the lake in the worst storm of the century. It was like trying to keep it steady in thirty-five foot waves. It was like getting caught in the breakers on a reef in the worst of storms . . . .' 'Uffda, Ole,' said another bachelor fisherman. 'Oh, it wasn't so bad,' said Ole." 'Me and the little lady went fishing and caught some of the biggest trout I ever laid eyes on.' Jonas laughed and then wondered why no one else did.

"Of course," Daniel continued, "when the honeymoon was done, all the women wanted to hear from Lena. 'Oh, my Ole, he's a good catch. But you wouldn't have known it at the start. We tossed and turned something fierce that first night, but nothing happened. Then the next day we went fishing. Uffda, put Ole in a boat and he sure is a fisherman,' laughed Lena. 'In the boat?' exclaimed one of the ladies. 'Ya, in the boat. Every day and pretty soon on the land, too. My Ole, he's like catching a big old trout.'" Daniel laughed.

After tonight, Jonas thought, I won't have to listen to stories, wondering what they're talking about. I'll know.

88.

Jonas spotted Ethyl and Arnold as soon as they pulled up at the dock in a skiff coming to the wedding. Arnold wasn't showing much of a limp as he headed up the dock. "My leg's fine. You can't keep a good man down, especially the father of the bride," he said as he shook hands with people. "I gotta give her away."

Jonas left before Ethyl and Arnold reached him. He knocked on Philena's door where Sally was getting dressed. Hank and Philena had returned on the *Lillian* earlier in the day. Philena answered the door. "Stay out, stay out," she said, holding the door so that only her head was visible. "You can't see the bride."

"I need to talk to her."

"I know you're a preacher and don't believe it's bad luck to see your bride before the wedding, but at least you could wait until she's without spot or wrinkle. I've just about got her ready."

"Her daddy just showed up and I want to talk to her."

"I heard that," Sally called from the interior.

Jonas took a step toward the door. Philena held up her hand through the crack in the doorway to stop him. "Stay out," she said, holding the door firmly. "I'm trying to tell you she doesn't have her dress on. We're making a last minute alteration."

"I'll stand behind the door and talk to him," Sally said. "You do the alteration. I'm so nervous I can't sew straight anyway."

"Okay," Philena said.

She closed the door and a moment later it opened widely. Jonas could see Philena hunched over the sewing machine with the dress flowing out from the machine. "So Daddy showed up?" came Sally's voice from behind the door.

"Yes, he says he has come to give the bride away."

There was silence. Jonas wished he could see her face. He stared at the faded wood grain of the door. "That's okay," she said.

"Okay?"

"Well, we can't very well get into a fight about it, can we?" she said sharply.

"I guess not."

"Listen, Jonas. My daddy might think he is giving me away. He might say the words, but he is not. I am giving myself to you. I just want you to remember that. No matter what happens, remember that."

"You will walk with him?"

"I will walk *by* him. Listen, Jonas. I am not going to let my daddy wreck our wedding. I will not. If you or I get into a fight with him it will wreck our wedding. I will walk by him to get to you. He will say his words, but then I will say my words to you and you will say your words to me. It is our words that count."

"Can you do it?" his eyes following a wood grain to the top of the door.

"Jonas, I can do it. Remember when I told you about the baby kicking. He tried to destroy me and God gave me new life. No matter what he tries today, you and I are starting a new life."

"You are right," said Jonas, staring at the faded wood grain of the door. "I love you."

"Jonas, when I walk by daddy I will be remembering the baby kicking."

"Next time it will be our baby kicking." Silence. Philena held the dress at arm's length, checking her work.

"Yes, next time it'll be our baby," he said, amazed at her sudden confidence when it came to her daddy. He hoped it lasted.

"Sally," called Philena, "it's ready for you to try on."

"Tell Daniel to include Daddy," Sally said. The door shut.

89.

When Jonas returned to the beach where the platform was set up for the wedding, he saw Arnold holding Samantha as he stood in a group of people talking to another fisherman. Jonas threaded his way through the group and held out his arms to Samantha. Arnold continued talking fishing, ignoring Jonas as he let Samantha move to him. Jonas turned to look for Daniel. "That's the man the bird pooped on," said Samantha.

Jonas glanced back to see if Arnold had heard. He was busy talking. "Yes, that's the man," Jonas said. He squeezed Samantha tight. Arnold sure had a lot of gall, picking up Samantha. He squeezed her again. "Are you all ready to be the flower girl?" Jonas asked as he worked his way through the crowd toward Daniel.

"All ready. Alice is holding the flowers. I know just what to do."

"You will walk to the front with Brawn's little brother."

"He's the ring bearer."

Jonas found Daniel. "Sally's daddy is here," he said with a tilt of his head in Arnold's direction.

"Ya," said Daniel.

"He wants to give her away. I talked with Sally, and she wants to go along with him. She doesn't want a fight."

Daniel raised his eyebrows. "And what do you think?"

"Is there gonna be a fight?" asked Samantha, her eyes big.

"No fight, Samantha. You can play. Stay on the beach. Just make sure you don't go in the woods and snag your dress or run and trip and get it dirty." He set her down. She wandered off slowly.

Jonas looked over at Arnold who was gesturing emphatically in his conversation with the same fisherman. What did he think? "I don't want to ruin our wedding either, but I hate to see him get his way. I hate to see him marching around here as if nothing happened. I hate it. Do you know that he was holding Samantha?"

Daniel nodded his head. "Ya, it's a tough one."

"Sally said she would walk by Arnold and would let him say his words, but it is *she* who is giving herself to me."

"And what do you think?"

"I don't know." He waited for Daniel to say something. Daniel stroked his beard and didn't say anything. "I can't think of anything other than just going through with it."

"Going through with what, the wedding?"

"No, letting him act like her father."

"Good, I hear a little fire in your gut. Keep going."

"He has no right to act like her father. No right."

"So what can we do about it on this day?"

"Nothing, I am afraid."

"Well, I do think Sally is doing something. Now you've got to do something."

"What do you mean?"

"It sounds to me like she has decided to be the true bride, even if her daddy is false."

"Yes," said Jonas excitedly. "She amazes me. She's such a good, honest woman."

"She will walk her own path even if her daddy is by her," Daniel said.

"But what can I do?" Jonas said. Daniel was silent. Jonas shook his head. "Her daddy never saw her as a daughter. Otherwise he would never have done what he did." He shook his head again. He took a deep breath. "I guess it's up to me to see her as a true bride."

"Ya, the path of the true groom."

"Do you think I can do it?"

"Well, I think that's what God has in mind."

90.

Jonas stood on the platform in his white shirt and black pants. Daniel stood beside him, Brawn behind him, Brawn's little brother behind him. Across from him Theresa stood, and behind her stood Samantha. They faced a series of rugs laid end to end to form an aisle that ran off the platform, down a plank ramp, and continued on for twenty-five feet. On each side of the aisle below the platform, people sat on benches made of planks laid on blocks of wood made of sawed-off sections of tree trunks. Jackson sat in his chair at the right end of the front row playing his fiddle. Arnold stood at the end of the aisle. Beyond Arnold the lake was shimmering in the early evening sun.

Then Jonas saw her. Sally was coming down the path to the south that led from Philena's cabin. Her white dress shimmered like the lake in the sun. Philena walked behind her, lifting the train of the dress to keep it out of the sand and grass. Jonas smiled. This is it, he thought.

Sally and Philena made their way to the foot of the aisle. Sally stepped onto the rug. Philena carefully set the train on the rug. Jackson ended the song he was playing, paused a moment while he arranged another set of song sheets on his stand, and then began to play the processional. Everyone stood up. Arnold stepped onto the rug and offered the crook of his elbow to Sally. She ignored his arm and took a step down the aisle. Jonas saw Arnold's lips move, and he knew he had said something to her. She ignored him and took another step. Arnold, rooted to the rug, looked up at the platform as if pleading for help. Jonas felt Daniel stir beside him. Sally took a third step, her train about to pass Arnold. Arnold took two quick steps, caught up, and shoved his elbow at her again. She ignored him and kept moving. Arnold scowled and dropped his arm to his side, and moved with her. She kept taking slow, stately steps, looking straight ahead. She is thinking, Jonas thought, about the baby kicking. His eyes felt wet. He blinked to clear them. She was coming up the ramp. She was coming to him.

Then she was beside him. She turned and took his hand. Jackson finished the song. "Who gives this woman to be married?" She squeezed Jonas' hand and whispered through the corner of her mouth, "Me."

"I do," muttered Arnold.

"Me," she whispered. Another squeeze of his hand.

"Dearly beloved, we are gathered here in the sight of God and man . . . " Daniel began. Jonas did not follow Daniel's words, only his voice. He knew that when it was his turn to speak, Daniel would tell them exactly what to say, just like the week before when he had read from the book and told Hank and Philena what to say. Sally was close to him. He could feel her warmth. Jonas thought about the first time he had felt her warmth. It had been down the beach a ways. He followed the rise and fall of Daniel's Norwegian accent, letting his voice keep his heart still as he waited for those moments when he would say, "I do." He thought about Arnold's elbow hanging in mid-air, only to collapse in frustration when Sally refused it. He bit the inside of his bottom lip to keep from smiling. She was leaving her father, coming to him. He thought of his own father coming in the door after the evening chores in the winter and saying, "Woman, only you can warm me up on a night like tonight." Jonas used to lie awake in his bed listening to the rise and fall of his parents' voices. He couldn't hear the words, but he could follow the warmth in their voices.

The first time Jonas said, "I do," it caught in his throat and came out like a croak. He felt his face turn crimson. He repeated clearly, "I do." Sally smiled at him through her veil. Each time she said, "I do," she spoke as clearly as a bell ringing along the lake.

"And now you may kiss the bride," Daniel said. Jonas lifted her veil. Her green eyes were wet and shimmering like the lake. Her lips were soft and welcoming. The next moment Jackson started the recessional and they were walking down the aisle. We're married, he thought. He grinned so hard he thought his face might break. And then they were at the end of the aisle. Philena met them and picked up Sally's train. They stepped aside until everyone had been ushered down the aisle. Then a couple of people moved the back benches, and Sally and Jonas, Ethyl and Arnold stood on the rugs, and people walked by congratulating them. Jonas kept grinning. When he wasn't grinning at the person congratulating them, he was grinning to himself: we are married.

91.

Jonas was stuffed. After the wedding Sally changed out of her dress while the women of the island set up tables overflowing with food. Then, after eating a feast of lefse, fresh trout, smoked herring, tomatoes from Jackson's garden only for the bride and groom, baked potatoes, and cake, he and Sally opened their gifts. They and several others carried the gifts back to her cabin. No, *their cabin*, Jonas corrected himself.

Jonas patted his stomach and watched as Philena helped Sally put the presents away. He decided to lend a hand and began to unpack the boxes. Sally wanted the house in order when they left for their honeymoon, and it wasn't that many presents, she had explained, before launching the project. Besides, it would take them a while to clean up after the meal and get ready for the dance, she had added.

After Philena left, Jonas pulled Sally into his arms. "We're alone and married," he said grinning.

"That we are," she said, "but I'm still not ready for the dance. I want to make sure I have everything packed for Samantha and for our honeymoon." She pulled away. Jonas was disappointed. She hesitated. "I don't want to have to worry about anything later," she said, flashing him a quick smile, "except my redheaded woodpecker."

"I like that," Jonas said, smiling. "I don't want you to have a thing on your mind later but us."

She went to the bedroom, carried out an old blue suitcase, set it on the table, opened it, and began checking through the clothes inside. There was a knock on the door. "See who that is, will you?" she said.

Jonas opened the door. Ethyl stood there holding two pillows. "I've got something for you and your wife. Here," she said and thrust one of the pillows into Jonas' hands. He stared down at it; a white, satin pillowcase with blue embroidery.

"Well, are you going to let me in, or do I have to stand here all day?"

Jonas stepped aside and she walked in. He closed the door. Sally stood beside the open suitcase, her hands on her hips. "I wanted to deliver these presents in person," Ethyl announced. She walked over to Sally, handed her a pillow, and said, "For my baby." Then she folded her arms, looked at Sally, and waited.

"I thought you said you weren't going to give them to me," said Sally in a small voice.

"I changed my mind. Oh, Sally, you looked so beautiful in that gown." She touched her eye.

She's crying? thought a disbelieving Jonas.

She shook her head. "I thought to myself, I just have to give these pillows to her."

Sally looked down at the pillow she was holding. She slid

her finger across the fabric and outlined a small embroidered flower. She raised her head, "How come you changed your mind?"

"I am not as mean as you think. It's just that you came barging in the other night, demanding those pillows."

"I wasn't demanding."

"You barged right in demanding those pillows and nobody demands anything of me." She smiled and snorted. "You make me so mad when you get on your high horse, Sally, and you have been on your high horse a lot lately."

"Thank you for the pillow," said Jonas, holding it out like a peace offering.

"You're welcome," said Ethyl with an emphatic nod of her head. "At least he's grateful."

Sally shook her head. "Oh, Mom," Sally said with a sigh.

"Don't, 'Oh, Mom,' me."

Sally shook her head and laughed the kind of laugh that made you think she wanted to cry. "What am I supposed to do with you, Mom?"

"Well, you could say 'thank you.'"

"I suppose I could." Sally ran her fingers across the pillow again. "You've given me something I've always wanted."

"Yes, I have. And you got married today." She rubbed her eye.

Sally hugged her pillow. "Thank you, Mom." Jonas ran his finger over the satin. He liked it. It was smoother than driftwood.

92.

Jonas stepped out of the cabin carrying the blue suitcase with Samantha's clothes for her stay with Alice and Daniel during the honeymoon. The first stars sprinkled the pale sky. He stood on the porch and inhaled the smell of the pines mingled with the smell of the lake. Sally stepped out beside him. "Ready?" he asked.

"Just a minute. Let's talk about tonight."

"Tonight?" Jonas' heart sank. What was there to talk about?

"I can't stand being around my daddy much longer."

"Oh," said Jonas, relieved. "Let's come back here early then."

"That's what I thought."

Jonas started to move. "Wait," she said, catching his arm. "I don't want to dance with Daddy tonight. I'll dance with anybody else, but not him." She pulled him close to her.

"As long as you dance with me."

She touched his cheek. "I am so glad you like to dance now." She put her head on his shoulder.

Jonas took a gulp of air and squeezed her. He let out the air and said, "I don't want anything bad to happen to you tonight. Not one thing."

She shivered and pressed closer. "Just make sure I don't have to dance with Daddy."

93.

"Well, folks, the bride and groom are here," said Daniel, "so Jackson will get us going with a great fiddle tune called 'Golden Slippers.' Jackson."

"I don't see your daddy," whispered Jonas as they started to dance.

Sally laughed a throaty chuckle. "You keep your eye out for Daddy; I'll keep an eye on you, handsome."

Jonas looked at her. He never knew when she was going to be afraid and when she wasn't. She was smiling, her green eyes dark and bright in the lantern light. "I think I'll forget about your daddy through this dance," he said.

"Me, too," she said.

They glided across the hard sand, weaving between other

couples. Jonas was so glad he had learned to dance. It was like floating on the music. Like floating together in the pond at his parents'. His lips tingled, remembering the night of kisses. Effortlessly the two of them moved and turned to the music, gliding, flying, turning, letting the music carry them. And then the tune was done.

Jonas and Sally laughed, holding each other, breathing, catching their breaths. They were at the edge of the platform. Jonas looked up at Jackson sitting in his chair. "Great fiddle-playing," he said. Jackson nodded.

"The father of the bride will now dance with his little girl."

Jonas whirled. Arnold had appeared on the other side of Sally. He was tugging at her arm.

"No, Daddy," she said pulling her arm back.

"Hey, I gave you away today; I get you back for one dance, don't I?"

Jonas could see he was trying to keep his voice light. "Tonight the bride chooses," Jonas said softly.

"You've had your turn," Arnold said with a smile that was pinched at the corners of his eye. "Now you'll be a good Christian and let her daddy, have his turn, right?"

Brawn appeared beside Arnold and tapped his arm. Arnold shrugged it off. "My turn, right?" he said in a little boy's voice. Brawn's hand spun Arnold around by his shoulder. For a moment Arnold stared up at Brawn, his eyes flashing like an arrow, but then he slowly lifted his hands with palms up. Brawn looked down, "Believe I heard the lady say, 'No, Daddy.'"

Arnold shrugged his shoulders in surrender and dropped his eyes. "She's my daughter but . . . whatever."

Just then Ethyl's shrill voice cut through, "Arnold, behave yourself. This is your daughter's wedding." Jonas turned to see her pushing her way through the crowd. He looked back at Arnold and almost took a step backward. Arnold's eyes were flaming arrows coming at him. He had never seen such hate. But instantly the fire left Arnold's eyes, and Jonas wondered if he had seen it. "I am the father of the bride,"

Arnold's voice had its forced lightness again. "I want what's best for everyone. I'll dance with the other ladies." He raised his voice, "And let's all have a good time for Sally and Jonas tonight." There were cries of agreement, and Jonas could feel the tension settle like a net released into the lake.

Sally was trembling when they sat together on a bench and watched the next dance. "I knew he would try to wreck it," she said. "He hates me. What did I ever do to deserve his hate? What did I ever do?"

Jonas put his arm around her. "You didn't do anything."

"I just couldn't dance with him. I could walk by him up the aisle, but I could not dance with him. I could not."

"You don't have to dance with him now."

"I know I don't, but he's got me scared to death. He's ruined it. My wedding night and I'm shaking like a leaf, I'm so scared." She held out her hand. It was shaking. She dropped it in his lap. "I hate him," she said. "I hate him. I hate him. I hate him. Oh, God, I didn't want him at my wedding. I didn't want him here. Why did he have to come? Why did God allow it? Why? What have I done to deserve this?"

"He scares me. When Ethyl told him to behave, I looked at him, and I saw pure evil in his eyes. If looks were bullets, I'd be dead. His eyes shot out at me. At least I think that's what I saw."

"Now you know what it's like. The last time I saw that look he forced himself on me."

They fell into a morose silence, but not for long. Ethyl came up. "Kids," she said, "don't let that pig ruin your night for you. He's just acting like a spoiled brat. I should take him home, give him a spanking, and put him to bed."

Jonas and Sally continued to stare up at her.

"You know he's just jealous. He doesn't want his little girl to grow up. Don't pay any attention to him. He'll get over it."

Jonas and Sally stared at her. Ethyl threw up her hands. "The two of you should be dancing. That's my opinion," she said, "but you do whatever you want." And she stalked off.

Jonas sat very still, wondering what Sally was thinking.

Sally started laughing. "My mother drives me nuts."

"So we're not supposed to pay any attention to him," Jonas said.

"To that pig. She called him a pig. Ignoring him is like ignoring a northeaster." She laughed again. "But she called him a pig. I like that."

Hank asked Sally to dance, and Alice came and put out her hand to Jonas. Jonas had never danced with anyone other than Sally, but he took Alice's hand. The music played. When the dance was done, Jonas bowed to Alice and they laughed together. Philena took Jonas' elbow next, and, as they danced, he saw Brawn swing Sally. As they flew by Jonas winked at her. He wasn't sure if she saw him, but the next time he swung into her sight, she winked back. As soon as the dance with Philena was done, another woman was at his elbow. At the same time, Old Lady Bills caught his eye, "I'll wait for a slow song," she said.

By the time Daniel called a break, Jonas had lost track of who all he had danced with. He and Sally sat on the backside of the stage, catching their breaths and drinking Kool-Aid.

When they had gotten revived Jonas said with a hopeful smile, "Should we go back to the cabin?"

"If we do, nothing will happen."

"What do you mean?"

"I mean I'm scared. I am not about to take my clothes off for anybody."

"Oh," said Jonas.

They sat in a dull silence. Jonas felt their wedding night slipping away like a boat that has hit a reef.

"We might as well stay and dance," he said forlornly.

"Oh, Jonas, you make me feel guilty."

"It's not your fault our wedding boat hit a reef before we got to bed."

"You're mad at me."

"No, I'm mad at your daddy."

She snorted. "Go beat him up then. Maybe you'll feel better."

Jonas thought about that. "I think I'd rather dance with you," he said seriously.

Sally laughed. "That I can do."

94.

After the break, Jonas and Sally each danced with several other people. Even some of the tourists. When they ended a dance near each other, Sally caught his eye. "I'm getting tired," she said.

They sat on a bench and watched the other dancers. Sally leaned against Jonas. He put his arm around her. Arnold swung his partner by in front of them. He was dancing with Rachel, Brawn's younger sister. They were laughing as they twirled by doing a polka. Sally looked away. Jonas gave her a squeeze.

When the song ended she said, "I want to dance with Daniel now. Could you ask him for me?"

Jonas looked at her. Even in the dim light of the lantern he could see the sadness in her eyes. "Yes," he said.

He made his way over to the stage. The band was just beginning another song so he waited by the edge of the stage, watching Jackson with his eyes closed playing the violin, Daniel swaying from side to side as he played his Hohner button accordion, and Brawn nodding his big head up and down as he tugged at the string on his bass tub. After the song Jonas walked to the front of the stage; Daniel leaned over to hear him. "Sally wants to dance with you once tonight," he said.

"You tell that girl I am honored. The next one we're playing is an accordion number, but the one after that Jackson can do a fiddle tune. Ya, my feet've been getting itchy. Tell her to get her feet ready to fly then."

Jonas sat down beside Sally. "He says to get your feet ready to fly after this song." Sally gave him a small smile.

The song ended and Daniel took off his accordion, set it down at the back of the stage, said a word to Jackson, and then hopped off the stage and made his way toward Sally and Jonas. They stood up. Sally waited for him with a tight smile. Daniel nodded to Jonas, took her hand, and guided her on to the dance area. She glanced back at Jonas. He winked and did a quick shuffle of his feet. She laughed and turned to Daniel.

"Folks," Jackson called out, "our illustrious accordionist wants the chance to make his feet fly, so here's Iver Johnstad's 'Hoppwaltz.' Hop to it Daniel." He put his bow to his fiddle, paused a moment, and then his fingers and bow flew. The high notes took off like a startled partridge, then settled into the rhythm of water skipping over rocks in the sunshine. Jonas tapped his foot to the music and watched Sally and Daniel. I'll never be able to dance that fast, he thought, but it sure looked like fun. Every time they turned a corner, Sally's hair flew. He found himself smiling. Sally was getting to fly. Maybe some day he could handle the fast fiddle tunes. He pictured Sally in his arms with her hair flying. He sighed. Maybe. Some day.

Then the tune was done. "Ya, Jackson, I'm good for one more then," called Daniel.

Jackson laughed. "Let's see if you can keep it up. 'Roger's Polka.'" He took a pull on his bottle, put it down, wiped his brow with the back of his hand, set his fiddle back to his shoulder, caught Jonas' eye, winked, hit one note, and then was off like a jackrabbit. Jonas laughed. There was something about Jackson's drama and the music that he loved. It made him want to fly, too. He looked at Sally and Daniel. Sweat glistened on Daniel's face. Jonas tapped his foot, then bobbed up and down to the music. He closed his eyes. Water and sunlight skipping over rocks. That's what it was like. His mother's laughter. A younger sister and brother giggling as they chased each other around the house. His father racing him to lunch at the house. His dad always beat him until he was sixteen. The first time he beat his dad they both stood bent over next to the house, gasping for breath, laughing. Then his dad reached over and squeezed his hand real hard.

His dad didn't say anything, but Jonas saw approval in his eyes. Jackson's fiddle was full of dash and approval.

When the song was finished, Jonas opened his eyes. Daniel and Sally were on the far side of the dance area. They stepped off. Daniel was talking to her. She stood beside him, looking down, listening. Jackson announced a break. The ladies brought out coffee and cookies and set them on a table. The dancers passed by the table, filling their cups and picking up the cookies. Jonas moved slowly toward the line, taking his time, waiting for Sally to join him. Daniel was still talking to her. Finally she lifted her eyes and looked at Daniel and laughed. She shyly stepped toward him, and he looked at her, then gave her shoulder a squeeze. As they parted, he patted her on the back. She walked over to Jonas and met him at the table. They poured coffee. She took a cookie and Jonas took two.

They sat down on a bench. "What was Daniel talking to you about?" he asked.

"It was so much fun dancing with him. He is such a good dancer. I felt light as a feather with him," she said. "And then he told me the silliest story." She shook her head. She dipped her cookie in her coffee and bit off the coffee-soaked part. "Such a silly story," she said laughing, sounding embarrassed.

"It sounds like you liked it."

"I did," she giggled, "and that's as silly as the story." She dipped her cookie and took another bite.

"Tell it to me," Jonas said, smiling through his uneasiness.

"It'll probably just be silly to you."

"Try me." What was this story that had cheered her up and embarrassed her?

She scooted close to him. "Promise you won't laugh."

"You're laughing," he said.

"You can laugh with me, but not at me."

"I'd never laugh at you." He squeezed her close to him. "I'll laugh my head off with you, but never at you."

"Lean close," she said, "I don't want anyone else to hear this." Jonas bent his neck and their heads touched. She giggled. "Don't laugh now," she said. "This is a little kid's story and I liked it, so don't laugh."

He gave her a quick, wet kiss on the back of her neck. "Ooo," she squealed. "Goose bumps."

He giggled and leaned his head back close to hers. "I'll kiss you and I'll give you goose bumps and I'll laugh with you, but I'll never laugh at you." This is crazy and fun, he thought.

"Once upon a time . . . that's how he started the story." Jonas nodded and then quickly kissed her neck again.

"Do you want to hear this story or not?" she said between clenched teeth with mock anger.

"I'll behave. Go ahead."

"Once upon a time there was a big bad wolf who lived in the big woods, and there was a little girl who got lost in the woods."

"Oh, sounds scary."

She pushed him with her shoulder to shush him. "The big bad wolf hid behind a tree, and when the little girl wandered into a clearing he jumped out, let out a fierce growl, and said, 'Me got you then!'"

"Nothing to laugh about yet," Jonas said. "Sounds scary though."

"I am trying to tell a story," she said, arching her eyebrows.

He lifted a hand, puckered his lips, and squeezed them with his fingers; then nodded for her to go ahead while he kept his mouth shut.

She snorted and continued, "'Me got you then,' said the big bad wolf.

"And the little girl said, 'My mother says that's very bad English. Now that you are in America, you have to learn how to talk like an American. You say, 'I have got you.'" Sally got lost in giggles. "Isn't that funny?"

"It depends on what happens next," Jonas said.

"It was so funny, Daniel trying to speak like the little girl without his accent."

Jonas laughed a little. "That would be funny."

"So the big bad wolf let out a terrific growl and said, 'I have got you then.'

"The little girl said, 'My mother says: "You don't end a sentence in America with *then*. You should say: 'I have got you, period.'"'" Sally giggled some more.

"So the big bad wolf let out a terrific growl and said, 'I have got you, period!'"

"The little girl said, 'My mother says: "You don't say, *period*; it is understood without saying that a sentence ends with a period."'" Sally laughed some more. "Daniel tried so hard to speak proper English when he was saying the little girl's part. It was so funny."

Jonas nodded.

"So the big bad wolf let out a terrific growl and said, 'I have got you without understanding.'" Sally shook with laughter.

"And the little girl said, 'I think your mother is calling you. She wants you to have some understanding.'

"So the big bad wolf stood in the clearing and was very confused.

"The little girl stamped her foot, 'Your mother is calling you.'"

Sally bent her neck and looked up at Jonas with very large eyes and said in a deep voice, "So the big bad wolf went home to his mother, who bonked him on the head for being so dumb." She twirled on the bench, then fell back with her head against Jonas' chest. He caught her and she looked up at him and burst out laughing, "Isn't that silly? I loved it." Jonas looked at her and laughed. The story was silly, but she was funnier. Her laughter had wings to it.

He looked at her and laughed some, soaring on her giggles. "It's a silly story and you are a silly girl." They couldn't stop giggling. Their giggles would die down, and then one of them would catch the other's eye and say with a deep voice, "And the big bad wolf went home to his mother who bonked him on the head for being so dumb." That would set them off again. They pushed against each other, laughing, holding each other for dear life.

95.

Daniel and Brawn climbed back on the stage. "Are you still tired, or do you want to dance with me?" said Jonas.

"This giggling has me ready," she said, standing up. They were the first two on the dance area.

"Jonas and Sally, here's a mazurka for you," Daniel called as he strapped on his accordion. "Anton Tomlen's 'Masurka,' a good old Norwegian couple dance for our newest couple."

The music caught Jonas immediately. The rhythm and sound caught him like the gentle eddy of a pool, and he and Sally glided across the sand. She felt light as a feather. He didn't have to think about what to do next. The music carried the two of them as they glided and turned and swayed. Suddenly the song reached for a series of high notes, and Jonas was lifted by sheer longing. He glanced at Sally to see if she felt it, too. Her eyes were closed. Then the song settled back into the gentle eddy of the pool. They turned, swayed and glided, as sure as a couple of trout deep in a pool. Jonas wanted those notes again. He found himself waiting, wanting the song to climb again. And then it did. Again he felt pure longing. He looked at Sally. This time her eyes were open. The lantern illuminated her face and her eyes were deep pools of longing. Jonas knew: she felt it too. The song returned to the gentle eddy. And their eyes never left each other's. They turned and moved like the wind in a pine. As the song ended with a breathy cry from the accordion, Jonas leaned Sally over backwards.

She laughed, "You remembered."

He nodded and straightened her upright. Then he took her hand, and they walked along the path to the cabin. As they moved away from the dance, they could hear the wind in the pines. They could smell the pines. They could feel the coolness coming off the lake.

In the cabin they stood in the darkness and she fit herself into his arms. He held her. He put his face into her hair and inhaled deeply. He moved to kiss her. She moved her face away.

"I want to see you," she whispered.

"I want you," he whispered, releasing her. He felt in the darkness for the lantern and matches. She waited by him. He struck a match, lit the lantern, put the chimney back on, and adjusted the wick.

He turned to her. Her eyes were large. Suddenly she giggled, "Why are we whispering?"

"I think," Jonas laughed, "because we are on holy ground."

"Holy ground?" she said glancing around.

"I look in your eyes and I know God is here," he said seriously.

"God is watching?" she half-grimaced, half-laughed as she glanced over her shoulder.

"This is our Garden of Eden," Jonas laughed, half-embarrassed. "Time to be naked and unashamed."

"Okay, Adam, you go first."

"Me first?"

"You just said this is our Garden of Eden."

"Okay," Jonas nodded his head, "me first." He started to unbutton his shirt.

"Wait, in the bedroom," she said, "the curtains are pulled in there." Jonas carried the lantern and they walked into the bedroom. She turned, "Let me, Adam." She unbuttoned his shirt and ran her hand across his chest as she looked into his eyes. He inhaled deeply. Then she slid the shirt over his shoulders and he exhaled. She set it on the dresser without taking her eyes off his. "Now your shoes and socks," she said. He sat down on the bed. She unlaced his shoes one by one and pulled them off. He inhaled deeply. Her face was framed by her blonde hair as she bent over his feet and pulled off each of his socks. He exhaled slowly and stood up. They held each other. He buried his face in her hair and breathed in as much of her as he could.

"My turn," he said.

"But you're not naked yet, Adam," she giggled.

"I'm a lot more naked than you are, Eve."

"Okay, my shoes and socks first," she said, pointing at her feet.

She sat on the double bed Jonas had made that week. He knelt by her feet and unlaced both her shoes. He pulled each of them off. Then he slipped off her white anklet and kissed her foot.

"Doesn't it smell?" she asked.

Jonas laughed, pulled the other sock off, and smothered that foot with kisses. Then he held it against his face. He shook his head.

"Rise up, Adam, you still have too many clothes on for the Garden of Eden."

He stood and she loosened his belt, unbuttoned his pants, and pushed them down. Quickly she pushed him lightly on the chest and he obligingly fell on the bed. She pulled his pants off his feet and said, "Put some covers on. I don't think Eve was as scared as me in the Garden of Eden."

Jonas pulled the covers over his waist. He groaned.

"What's the matter, Adam?"

He threw up his hands. "We're married," he said.

"Yes, we are, but that doesn't mean you own me."

"Who said anything about owning you?"

"Well, you act like you should be able to do whatever you want to do because you married me. I am not a cow."

Jonas laughed, a sad, try-to-laugh-at-a-bad situation laugh. He shook his head. "I know you're not a cow," he said, "and I'm not a bull."

"So don't act like it," she said.

"Mooooo," he said, in a low bellow.

"Stop that."

"What does the not-cow want the not-bull to do?" he asked.

"Unzip my dress."

He scrambled out of bed. "But keep the covers on," she said, covering her eyes. He wrapped part of the covers around him and tucked them in to keep them from falling off. She turned her back to him and he opened her zipper. "Close your eyes," she said.

He closed his eyes. He could hear the rustling of her dress. "Now you can open them," she said.

He opened his eyes. She wore a long nightgown. His eyes slid over to the dresser; a jumble of white underclothes lay next to her neatly folded dress. She dove onto the bed, tugging at the covers. Jonas let go, and with one quick pull the covers were on the bed and she disappeared beneath them.

Jonas stood staring at the bed. This is not what he thought his wedding night would be like. Should he take his underwear off? Adam never faced this problem, he thought ruefully. He kept his underwear on. "Sally, aren't you getting hot under there?"

Her head appeared. "The Garden of Eden was hot. How else could they stand it with their clothes off?" She ducked back under the covers.

Jonas shook his head. He looked at the still heap of covers. What should he do? Lie down on the bed and wait for her to come out? Chase her? He slipped out of his underwear and tossed them on his pile of clothes on the dresser. He looked at the lantern. Should he turn it out? No, he wanted light.

"Here, I come," he sang out and slid under the covers. She instantly turned to him, found his mouth with hers, and slipped on top of him. It all happened so fast.

"I don't know how . . ." he whispered.

"I'll help . . ." she breathed.

"Uffda," he grunted.

Sally became very still. Then she laughed. She rolled over and pulled the covers from their heads, fanned herself with her hand, and said, "It sure got hot fast in Eden."

"I'm sorry," he said.

She laughed again. "Oh, Jonas, it was just like Philena said it would be."

"What?" Jonas sat bolt upright.

She laughed again. "Calm down, Jonas. This is Eden. Philena said it's nothing to worry about if things happen fast on your wedding night."

"When were you talking to her?"

"I talk to her lots. I talked to her today, while she was helping me get dressed. Whew. It's hot in here." She pulled the covers down to her waist and fanned her face again.

One side of her nightgown was down over her shoulder. Sally laughed when she saw Jonas looking and straightened it. Jonas looked at her face. She laughed again. "You should have just seen your face. Your eyes were as big as saucers."

"I never saw such a wonderful sight."

She lay back down, so Jonas laid down, too. She sat up. "The pillows. We forgot to use Mom's pillows." She scrambled out of bed, opened a trunk, and pulled out the pillows. She threw one to Jonas who caught it. She put the other one on her side of the bed and patted it. "Nobody told me this was such a messy business," she said. She went and got a rag and wiped the bed. Then she rearranged the sheet and covers and plopped her head on the pillow beside Jonas.

She turned and faced Jonas who said to her, "So Philena said it's nothing to worry about?"

"Right. She said that people think they can climb into bed and know what to do and how to do it right off the bat, but it doesn't work that way."

"It sure doesn't," Jonas said.

She laughed. "You were really worried, weren't you?"

"Yes," he said.

She laughed again. "I wonder how it went for Adam and Eve the first time."

"I don't know," Jonas said.

"No, I guess you wouldn't." Jonas laughed.

They lay on their backs, heads on their pillows. He took her hand and they lay there. So this is what it's like to be married, Jonas thought. They lay quietly. He loved her laugh. Her laugh could lift him like a gust of wind could lift a seagull.

He turned toward her and she toward him. Her eyes were deep as green pools. He remembered the mazurka, dancing, waiting for the song to rise in sheer longing again. The first time had been like a May plunge into Lake Michigan. This time it was like the pond back home in July. The quiet sound of waves gently lapping at the shore. Testing the water with a toe. Wading. Diving under at the same time on the count of three. Splashing. Laughing. Teasing. Playing. Swimming. Floating.

Afterward they lay dreamily, Sally snuggled up to him, her head on his shoulder. So, Jonas thought, this is what it's like to be on your honeymoon. This is the land of milk and honey. The promised land . . .

Somebody banged on the door. They both lifted their heads. "Did you hear something?" Sally said.

"I thought I did," he said. They listened. Silence. "I thought somebody knocked."

"It better not be my brothers playing tricks."

They laid back and their heads sank in their satin pillows. Again somebody banged on the door.

Sally sat up. "Uffda, don't people know this is the Garden of Eden?"

96.

Jonas grabbed his pants, pulled them on, slipped his shirt on without buttoning it, grabbed the lantern, and walked to the door. He opened it.

"Jonas!" said Brawn. His voice sounded strangled and his chest was heaving up and down. "Jonas," he tried again, his face a blotchy red. For a moment Jonas thought he was drunk. "Jonas," his face crumpled, "Rachel . . . Arnold . . ." He sobbed and grabbed his face with his huge hand, as if to shove the sob back where it had come from, but sobs slipped through his fingers. He stared at Jonas with bewildered eyes over his hands.

Arnold dancing and laughing with Rachel darted into Jonas' brain. "Arnold?" he said.

Brawn nodded, his eyes imploring Jonas over his rough hand. Jonas reached out and held his elbow. Brawn dropped his hand, bowed his head, and cried freely. Jonas waited.

"What happened?" he said finally, full of dread.

Brawn lifted his head. "He . . ." and then he sobbed some more. He stared helplessly through his tears at Jonas. He hit the side of his own head with the heel of his hand as if that would bring him back to control.

"Did Arnold rape Rachel?"

Brawn's eyes bulged. He nodded, and then he grabbed his face with his hand and sobbed.

Sally came up behind Jonas, taking his other arm. "What happened?" she asked. Jonas glanced at her. She had put on her dress. Brawn dropped the hand from his face and stared at her, covered his face again, and cried some more.

"Arnold raped Rachel," Jonas said, looking at her. Her fingers dug into his arm. He barely felt the pain. Her face went white. He looked back at Brawn whose face was covered by his big, freckled hand.

"Who's with Rachel?" Sally asked.

Brawn lifted his head. Jonas dropped his arm. Brawn looked at her a moment through his tears, and then rubbed his eyes with his thumb and his fingers. "Mom and Philena," he said.

"She shouldn't be left alone," she said.

Jonas and Brawn stared at her.

"She shouldn't be left alone."

Brawn's eyes widened and he said, "He might come back?"

"No," she said. "It's just that she shouldn't be alone. I was all alone. She doesn't have to be alone."

"I came here because I want to get my hands on that son of a bitch," Brawn said.

"He's not here," Jonas said, but then he thought: what if he sneaked in and hid while he and Sally were . . . ? He turned and glanced around the room. What about the loft? He glanced up. It was too dark to see up there.

Sally had been following his eyes. She held his arm with both hands. Jonas turned back to Brawn. "What are you going to do when you find him?" he asked.

"Kill the son of a bitch," he said and let out another wrenching sob.

"Are you going to check the loft?" Sally asked.

"Yes," Jonas said. He turned, walked to the ladder, and began to climb, holding the ladder with one hand, the lantern with another. I am not looking for an honest man, Jonas thought, I am looking for a worm.

And will you let Brawn step on the worm?

Jonas almost missed a step. What should he do if Arnold was hiding in the loft? God, what should he do? His head was almost level with the loft floor. He turned and looked down. Brawn and Sally stood by the table looking up at him. He turned and resumed climbing. He stood on the ladder, his head and shoulders above the floor. He lifted the lantern. The light filled the small room. No Arnold. His eyes scanned the room again. The dresser. It was against a wall. The bed. It was made and flat. Samantha had taken her doll with her. He set the lantern on the floor and lowered his head so that the floor was eye-level. No one under the bed. The trunk. It was too small. Wasn't it? Jonas climbed into the loft and opened the trunk. It was half full of winter clothing.

"He's not here," he called and then climbed down the ladder.

"Got to find him," Brawn said. "Hank is rounding up people, too. Will you help, Jonas?"

Jonas looked at Sally. "I want to be with Rachel," she said.

"I'll help find him," Jonas said faintly, turning to Brawn.

"Bring a lantern," Brawn said. "Meet us at the platform."

97.

What Jonas remembered most about that night was feeling swept along in a storm. That and the mosquito bites.

A group of sweating, muttering men carrying lanterns milled about the platform. "What's the plan?" someone called.

Everyone seemed to look at Brawn. "Let's see," he said looking about the small crowd. Theresa, the only woman, stood next to him. His eyes settled on Floyd and Eugene. "You're family," he said. "Don't belong here." There was a murmur of agreement and Eugene hung his head. Floyd stared at Brawn, then turned on his heel. They walked away, Eugene looking at the ground, Floyd staring straight ahead.

"I'm family, too," Daniel said and walked after them.

"What?" barked Brawn.

Daniel turned. "Ya, this is sheriff's business. It's not good to take things like this into our own hands," he said. "I tried to get the sheriff on the radio, but it's broke. I'll fix it and get him over here. He's the law."

"Fix the radio," Brawn said tightly and turned from Daniel. Daniel walked away. Jonas stared after Daniel. Should he leave, too? Brawn looked at the men. His face was pale and hard in the moonlight. "All of us heard what Arnold did to Sally, and not one of us did a thing about it. That's why he was loose. I'm going to do something *now.*" His "now" rang out like a shot.

"Let's find the son of a bitch," someone said.

"Cut his balls off," someone said.

"String him up," said another voice.

"Find the son of a bitch and then we'll figure out what to do," Brawn said. "Search the dock areas first and then the cabins. Then the woods if need be."

"Find the son of a bitch!" became the rallying cry. "Find the son of a bitch!"

Jonas hesitated, looking at the darkness where Daniel had disappeared. Brawn grabbed his arm and said, "You know he needs to be found." Jonas remembered Brawn's yell just before the wave had swept him off the *Edna.* He went along. He needs to be found.

They searched fish houses, gear shacks, tugs, skiffs, docks, and cabins. It was when they fanned out and started searching through the woods that the doubts began to attack Jonas. The land of the mosquitoes. Cries of "Find the son of a bitch!" rose above the constant whine of the insects. Jonas swung his lantern and peered into the dark corners of tugs, skiffs, and sheds. They were looking for a dishonest man. Is this what he was supposed to be doing? What if they killed him when they found him? Jonas remembered the frozen look on Brawn's moonlit face.

At first Jonas tried to keep the mosquitoes off with his hand, holding a lantern in one hand, slapping and swatting with the other. As the night wore on, cries of "Find the son of a bitch!" died down, while the mosquitoes hummed in Jonas' ears.

Jonas wanted to be an honest man, not a hunter of the dishonest. He wanted to be an honest man, not a killer of the corrupt. What was he doing here?

He gave up trying to keep the mosquitoes off his body. His arm grew tired from holding the lantern aloft. He began to pray that they would not find Arnold. Even though he tried to keep the same distance from the lantern on his left and right, he found himself veering closer to one or the other. They worked their way over to the East Side, searched the buildings and vessels there, then spread out and headed north. And still Jonas couldn't pull himself away from the small cloud of locusts moving through the island's trees. His eyes grew tired from constantly peering through the tall grass, bushes, and pine trees. Always he feared he would see Arnold. He kept walking close to the pines, letting their branches scratch and soothe his mosquito bites. Sometimes he stopped a moment to rub his back against a tree like the cows did at home.

When they reached the north end of the island they congregated at a huge pine on a bluff overlooking the black lake. "Brawn, I have to say this," Jonas said, glancing up at the sweating giant. "I can't look any more. I can't be a part of hurting Arnold."

Brawn stared at him. "Nobody else," he said.

"We're never going to find him in the dark," someone muttered.

"He's got too much room," someone added.

"He probably looped around us and is home in bed," another voice offered.

They all looked at Brawn. His huge face was splotchy with mosquito bites and slick with sweat. He switched his lantern to his other hand and flexed the empty hand several times. Jonas imagined the big paw around Arnold's neck.

"Nobody else should get hurt, but you're right about not finding him tonight," Brawn finally murmured. "Tomorrow," he said emphatically. He turned without another word and started south through the woods, still holding his lantern aloft, his eyes sweeping from side to side. Theresa walked beside him.

Most of the men from Little Oslo had had enough of the mosquitoes. They kept as close as possible to the shore and its breeze which kept the mosquitoes at bay. Jonas followed them.

Back at Little Oslo he checked their cabin first. Sally wasn't there. He found her at Brawn's family's cabin. She sat at the table with Brawn's mother and Philena. When he entered they looked at him with bleak, drawn faces.

"You find him?" asked Philena.

He shook his head. "We'll look in the morning. How's Rachel?"

"She's sleeping," her mother said.

"Is Hank back?" Philena asked.

"He'll be here shortly. He's coming through the woods."

Philena turned to Brawn's mom. "Will you be okay?"

"I'll live," she said.

Philena stood up. "I'll come over in the morning."

Sally stood up, too. She didn't say anything. She just leaned over the table and touched her forehead to Brawn's mom's forehead. She held it there for a moment. For an instant, for the first time that night, Jonas felt tears well up in him.

Sally and Jonas got ready for bed without saying a word to each other. Jonas turned out the lantern and lay down beside her. "Hold me," she whispered. He held her. His mosquito bites itched something fierce. He tried not to think about the itching. He sensed she was crying. He lifted his finger to her cheek. It came away wet. He squeezed her. He held her and held her and held her. If only he could bear away her sadness. She turned, and her breathing became even and quiet.

Jonas lay in the darkness on his back. So this was my wedding night, Jonas thought, feeling like one big mosquito bite. Mosquitoes must be a part of the Fall, he thought, as he fell asleep. Moments later he woke with a start: how awful for Rachel. He thought he would be awake all night, but after awhile he went back to sleep.

98.

Jonas was in a half-waking state when God told him where to find Arnold. At least he was pretty sure God had told him. He'd have to check to make sure. He opened his eyes and rolled over to tell Sally. She wasn't there. He sniffed the air. No coffee or breakfast cooking.

He got up, dressed, and went out on the porch. Sally was sitting on a rock down by the lake, the golden light of the early morning accenting her hair. The air had the still, heavy feeling of a day when the temperature will doggedly rise, the air will slowly steam and churn until late afternoon when a sudden thunderstorm will charge angrily across the lake. After the thunderstorm the evening air would be fresh and clear. He looked out at the harbor; it was still as glass. Beyond the harbor the hazy light shimmered on tiny waves. He walked down to Sally.

"I don't want you to hunt down Daddy like a dog," she said.

"I agree," Jonas said. A seagull swooped down over the water. Jonas watched to see what it would pick up. Nothing, as far as he could tell. "I told Brawn last night that I wasn't going to help look for him anymore. They might kill him." Another seagull swooped down in the same spot. Something must be floating there.

"Your mom was right, though. He should go to jail."

Jonas stopped breathing. Jail? He hadn't thought that far.

That's what the sheriff would do. He let out his breath. His mind raced. If he had heard correctly about Arnold's hiding place, he would be sending him to jail. Or should he? Jail. He had never been to a jail. He had often walked past the jail in town when he was growing up. The low, brick building with the bars on the tiny windows had always given him a funny feeling. Bad people who had done bad things were hidden in there. He had always hurried past the jail. And now he should send somebody to jail? He blinked his eyes. A third seagull swooped down over the spot, and this one got hold of something. It flapped hard and lifted its catch out of the water, only to have it drop back. Some kind of fish. He turned to Sally. She was watching the gulls, too. "I guess he should go to jail," he said.

"I should have put him in jail the first time. It never would have happened to Rachel."

Jonas sucked in air.

"But I didn't know. I was all alone and I didn't know I could tell. I didn't know."

Jonas bit his lip. "I'm glad Rachel told."

"She might not have told either," she said, her eyes on the lake. "One of her younger brothers was using the outhouse and he heard her cry out. She screamed only once. Daddy slapped her face really hard, and she was so scared she didn't make any noise after that. Daddy had followed her after she left the dance. He caught up with her on the trail, said he was going to make a woman out of her, and started grabbing at her. That's when she screamed and he slapped her. He dragged her up in the woods and forced himself on her. Before he let her go, he told her to go home and go to sleep, because if she ever told anyone, he would be back and she'd wish she had never told. That's what she was going to do. Go home, go to sleep, never tell.

"But her poor little brother. He didn't dare leave the outhouse. Her scream really scared him. Finally he did come out, but he was scared to go back in the cabin. So he ran to his mom at the dance and told her something terrible had happened to Rachel. His mom was talking to Brawn when the boy ran up. When her mom got home, Rachel was in bed, shivering. She was so scared she hadn't even taken off her dress. Her dress was torn. She was bleeding." She continued to stare out into the lake. Jonas couldn't pull his eyes away from her drawn face.

"Poor Rachel," he said. The words sounded as empty as fish guts to him. "And poor you."

She dropped her head. Jonas could see the tears standing in her eyes. He put his hand on her shoulder. "Her mom held her," she said, lifting her streaming eyes to Jonas. "She held her." She lowered her head and leaned against Jonas. He held her while she shook and cried. He held her and stared blindly out at the water. Eventually he saw that three or four seagulls had landed in the harbor and were fighting over the dead fish. Others were circling and crying overhead.

Sally straightened up. Her cheeks were tearstained. "Her mother held her. I did what my daddy wanted. I lied to my mother and she never held me. And now when I did tell her, she doesn't even believe me.

"Last night," she continued, "while her mom sat there holding her, I sat and cried my eyes out. I could just feel how good it would be to have your mother hold you. And then this morning I had a dream. I dreamed that Mary Magdalene held me. It was a strange dream. I was at a lake and I was cleaning fish. It seemed like a ton of fish. I cleaned and cleaned and people kept bringing me more fish. I was so tired, but I was supposed to keep going until I was done. I thought I would never finish. It was then that Mary Magdalene came up to me. I didn't notice her until she put her hand on my shoulder. Next thing you know, my head was on her shoulder and I was crying and she was holding me. And she didn't even mind that I got her dirty with my hands. They were dirty from cleaning all those fish."

Jonas saw light in her green eyes. "That was a good dream," he said.

"You're sure?"

"I can see it in your eyes."

"I did like the feeling of it," she said, hugging herself.

"A dream that puts light in your eyes is a good dream. Besides, Mary Magdalene was a good friend of Jesus."

"I just read yesterday," she said, puzzling, "that Jesus wouldn't let her touch him after he rose from the dead. Why do you suppose that was?"

"I don't know," Jonas said.

They looked out at the harbor, thinking. The gulls were still fighting over the dead fish.

"I think I know where Arnold is," Jonas said.

She turned quickly. "Where?"

"I think Jackson is hiding him."

"Jackson? What makes you think so?"

"I think God told me when I woke this morning. It was a very clear thought."

"But you don't know for sure?"

"I didn't check yet."

"He does have to go to jail, you know."

He nodded. "Yes, and pretty soon Brawn is going to start looking for him again. We need to think of some way to get him off the island before Brawn finds him."

"He deserves to face Brawn," she said.

"I thought you didn't want him hunted down like a dog?"

"I do and I don't. You know what he did to me. Part of me would like to see Brawn get his hands on him, but part of me knows that wouldn't stop things. Then Brawn would have to pay. Daddy needs to pay by going to jail. Oh, I don't know," she said tossing her head, "we all pay. I am paying. Rachel is paying. Brawn is paying. We are all paying for him. But if he gets killed, then we will pay for murder. Oh, I'm sick of thinking about this," she said, standing up and turning. "I'll go make breakfast. You talk to Brawn." She pointed. Brawn was coming down the beach. She left.

Jonas turned and looked back at the cove. The seagulls were all turning and dipping overhead. They had finished with the dead fish.

"Letting everybody know that we're meeting at Daniel's dock in a half hour," Brawn said to his back. Jonas turned to Brawn. Brawn's eyes were red, his face beginning to bead sweat already.

"I think we ought to wait for the sheriff," Jonas said.

Brawn stood and rubbed his eyes. He didn't say anything, and Jonas began to wonder if he had heard him. He blinked at Jonas and said, "If we would have beat the shit out of him about Sally, this wouldn't have happened."

Jonas stepped back. He felt like he had been hit in the chest. Brawn stared at him and said, "I got regrets about that, you know."

Jonas nodded.

"Daniel tried to radio last night. Busted. Word'll get to the sheriff today or tomorrow. Sent word on today's boat." Brawn continued, his eyes hammering Jonas, "Meantime, I'm not sitting on my ass. No more regrets, preacher, about doing nothing."

Suddenly he slumped. "Jonas, I gotta do something," he pled.

"I understand wanting to do something."

Brawn toed the sand. Then he scuffed it with his heel.

"If you find him," Jonas said, "just hold him until the sheriff gets here. Don't do anything you'll regret later."

"Regret?" Brawn said, his head snapping up. He towered over Jonas. "He's the one who should have regrets. Regrets that he ever laid an eye on my sister."

Jonas held up his hand. "He can have plenty of regrets in jail," he said mildly.

"Jail?" Brawn barked. "Give him time and he'll be in a skiff and gone. We're going over to the East Side right now to see if he showed up last night. We're gonna keep looking. There are plenty of guys who are not gonna sit on their behinds and let him get away." He turned and strode off.

I'm not gonna sit on my behind either, Jonas thought, stinging at Brawn's words. Then he dropped his head. Calm down, calm down, he said to himself. He tried to wipe the heavy, humid air from his brow. Then he walked back to their cabin.

99.

Their first meal as a married couple was coffee and pancakes with syrup. Jonas ate six.

"I'm going to see if your daddy's at Jackson's," he said when the meal was done. "Do you want to go?"

She shook her head. "I don't think I could stand to see him."

He stood and helped clear the table.

"What about our honeymoon?" she asked, adding cold water to the hot water in the dishpan. She tested the water with a finger. "You didn't forget, did you?"

"No," he shook his head. "But I didn't think we should leave today."

She smiled wanly. "Do you think we'll ever get back to the Garden of Eden?"

He laughed, went over, and hugged her. "Take me back, take me back," he said. They held each other, her finger dampening his shirt. "We can take the *Lillian* tomorrow or the day after, if we have to wait that long," he said.

They parted and he walked to Jackson's cabin. Hazy, white clouds hung heavy over the island. He stood on Jackson's porch, ready to knock, when he heard men's voices inside. Jonas knocked. The voices went silent. A minute later Jonas knocked again.

"Come in," Jackson yelled on the other side of the door. He pulled the door open. "Patience," he snarled from his chair as Jonas entered. "What do you want?"

"Arnold," Jonas said.

Jackson peered out the door. "Are you running with the wolf pack like you were last night?" he demanded.

"What do you mean?" Jonas asked.

"You were part of that mob last night that was out for blood."

"It's just me."

"Where are the rest?"

"Heading over to the East Side. I told Brawn I couldn't be

a part of hurting Arnold."

"We've had a big change," Jackson said. "This island has suddenly become a reservation for Arnold. Now you get to be the white man, Jonas, and he gets to be the Indian. I was disappointed in you last night, Jonas. You went riding with the cowboys. I would have thought better of you."

"Is Arnold here or isn't he?" he said.

"And what do you plan on doing with your newfound power?" Jackson pushed.

"I can't stop Brawn and the others from trying to hunt him down, but I can try to keep him safe if I find him before the others."

"That's good news," Arnold said, stepping out from the bedroom. "I could use the help."

Jonas stared at Arnold. His graying hair was messed up, his eyes were red, and his wrinkled clothes were the same ones he had worn the night before.

"I didn't think anyone but this man was going to listen to what really happened last night," Arnold said. "But if you listen, you'll know it's right to help me."

"What did happen?" Jonas asked and immediately sensed he had stepped into a trap.

"That girl rubbing up against me all night." He shook his head sadly. "It wasn't right, I know. I'm not making excuses. I know I gave in to temptation. I shouldn't have gone with her like she wanted. I should have been able to resist. I didn't. But I also want you to know," his voice hardened, "that nothing happened that she didn't want to happen."

"I understand her dress was torn and . . ."

Arnold interrupted. "She probably caught it on a branch. It wasn't torn when I got away from her."

"And she was bleeding . . ."

"What do you expect? She was a virgin." He grinned nervously. Jonas stared, speechless. Arnold dropped his head. "I haven't been perfect," he said. "And I admit it. I yielded to temptation with that girl, but," he lifted his head, "I never did anything she didn't ask for."

"Arnold," Jonas said, "you have a choice. You can face Brawn and the others, or you can face the sheriff."

"What kind of choice is that?" Arnold asked, looking at Jonas with reddened eyes.

"It appears to be about the only choice you have," Jackson said.

Arnold swung toward Jackson and looked down at him. "Now you're turning on me, too?"

"Jonas has just stated the obvious," Jackson said.

"I thought you believed me," pleaded Arnold.

"I never said I believed you. I kept you from the mob last night, and I listened to what you had to say. I don't believe any man ought to be treated like the Indians were treated. Even a rapist."

"Putting me in jail isn't treating me like an Indian?"

"The sheriff's a white man like you," Jackson said.

"What does that mean? I'll still be behind bars."

"It means that you have a chance for justice. Justice is by and for the whites in this country. You'll get a jury of your peers. Even in jail you'll be treated like a white man."

Arnold looked from one to the other. His eyes settled on Jonas. "You're a preacher, right?" Jonas held his head still. He wasn't going to nod agreement to anything Arnold said. Arnold continued, "You're a preacher and you believe in forgiveness." Jonas kept his head still. "You gotta start talking to the people around here about forgiveness. I agree, I get most of the blame for giving into temptation. She's young. And I'm sorry I gave in to her. I didn't get a wink of sleep last night, and I did a lot of praying. God is a God of forgiveness. I asked him to forgive me last night. And he forgave me." He thumped his chest. "I felt it in my heart. So I'm ready to start over new this morning. The first thing I want to do this morning is forgive her for tempting me. While I'm mostly to blame and I have been forgiven, she was anything but pure in the way she came on to me. So I have to forgive her. And I'm ready. Preacher, you go talk to her and tell her that I forgive her. And I'm willing to say that to her face. I forgive her."

Jonas didn't know what to say. He believed in forgiveness, but something didn't seem right with what Arnold was saying.

Arnold continued, becoming more and more animated as he talked. "*Vengeance is mine, I will repay, says the Lord*. That comes right out of the Bible. Vengeance is not Brawn's or anybody else's. It's not yours either, preacher. It's nobody's but God's. I fell into temptation. I know it. And I am ready to throw myself on God's vengeance." He paused. "Or mercy. Whatever he wants to do with me he can. Preacher, you gotta make sure nobody takes vengeance on me but God. I've heard you're a good preacher. People listen to you. Brawn will listen to you. I know you work on Daniel's crew with him sometimes. He'll listen to you. What do you say?"

Brawn won't listen to me after this morning, Jonas thought.

Arnold plunged on. "I admit it," he said, opening his hands, "I need help. I have sinned and got myself into deep trouble. I can't get myself out. I fell into temptation and now I need to be saved. And it looks like God sent the two of you to save me." The tired corners of his mouth tightened into a half-smile. He looked from one to the other. "The Lord heard my prayers. First, this man took me in when I was being hunted like a dog. Now the Lord has sent me my son-in-law, a good Christian preacher. The Lord is taking care of me. I put myself in God's hands and yours."

Jonas turned and headed for the door. Arnold scooted after him. "Where you going, preacher?"

"To talk to somebody."

"You can't turn me over to Brawn," Arnold squawked like a gull.

Jonas turned. "You just said you put yourself in our hands."

"Yours and God's. I am in the hands of the Good Shepherd come to seek and to save that which is lost. He doesn't turn one of his lost lambs over to the wolves now, does he? I'm lost. I admit it. I turned off the path and followed that woman where she led me, right into the wilderness. I admit it. But I was hoping you'd be a true shepherd and save me, instead of throwing me to the wolves."

"I'm going to save you," Jonas said. "I'm going to talk to Daniel to see if he can take you over to the sheriff tonight."

"Wait a minute," Arnold held up his hand, "wait a minute. I don't know if I trust Daniel. He's always hogging the fishing grounds. Him and I have had a run-in or two."

Jonas had heard that Arnold cut Daniel's nets one time.

Arnold never missed a beat but kept talking. "He may not be your best bet. I know he's well respected, but he could easily fall prey to temptation when I'm the one in need. I do agree with the idea of getting me across to the mainland. That's a good idea." He nodded vigorously.

"I trust him," Jonas said.

Arnold said, "Let's keep thinking and see if we can come up with a better idea than Daniel. Can you run his tug?"

"Me?" Jonas asked.

"That's not a problem," Arnold continued. "I can help you run it. You could run me over to the mainland tonight using Daniel's tug."

"I can't steal his tug," protested Jonas.

"I realize you're in a tough spot here," Arnold said. "You have tough decisions to make. Have you had breakfast?"

Jonas blinked. "Yes," he said.

"How about a cup of coffee? I need another cup. Coffee helps thinking and we have some serious thinking to do. I'll get you a cup." He turned and began pouring coffee.

Jonas looked at Jackson who nodded as if to say, Go ahead, you can handle it. "I don't need any coffee. I've made up my mind." He opened the door.

"Wait," Arnold said. "Just a minute. One more quick question. I can see you have your mind made up." He hurried over and shut the door. Jonas let him. He went back and retrieved his coffee. He took a sip. "Okay, you're going to talk to Daniel. What then?"

"If he agrees, we'll take you over on the tug tonight."

"And then what?"

"We'll take you to the sheriff."

Arnold nodded thoughtfully and took another sip of coffee. He eyed Jonas as he blew over the cup of coffee to cool it. He set the cup down and said, "Do you really think that's the Christian thing to do in this situation?"

"Yes."

"I'm not talking about myself now. My life is half over. More than half over. I don't want to spend time in jail, but, if I have to, I have to. But what's going to happen to the young lady if you take me to the sheriff? She's gonna have to go to court and testify. It's gonna be her word against mine. Everybody is gonna hear exactly how she led me on. She's gonna have to live with what happens in that court for the rest of her life, and she's got a lot of life ahead of her. What is the Christian thing to do for her? I'm not in a very good position to answer that question, but you have to. You're the preacher. You have to figure these things out. Like I said a little bit ago, I'm in your hands and God's. Now it occurs to me that that little girl is, too. She's in your hands and you can protect her. You can spear her . . . I mean spare or spare her not. I just hope you do the Christian thing for her."

"Something's wrong with what you're saying," Jonas said.

"I'm hurt," Arnold said. "I know I got carried away by temptation last night, but now I'm trying to think of the Christian thing to do. I'm hurt."

"If you really want to do the Christian thing," Jonas said, "you could go to the sheriff and confess, and Rachel wouldn't have to go to court."

"You make it sound so easy. I've lived a few years and I know life isn't that simple. I know that sounds like a good solution to you, but let's think about it a minute. As soon as I talk to that sheriff, it's out of my hands. Even if I confess, the newspaper reporters are going to get their hands on the story. Oh, they might not print it, but it'll get out. Right now, only the people on the island know. Next week that girl's going back to school on the mainland. I go to the sheriff, and everybody in that school is going to be whispering about her.

Isn't there some way we can spare her that?"

"I'm going to talk to Daniel now," Jonas said, opening the door.

"Think about that little girl," Arnold said, staring after him over his cup of coffee.

Jonas left.

100.

Samantha was sitting on Daniel's lap on the porch listening to a story when they arrived. She was so enthralled that she didn't move until he was done. Then she slid off his lap and jumped into Sally's arms. "Is the honeymoon over?"

"No, honey," Sally said. "Remember I told you I would see you today, and then we would leave for our honeymoon on the boat."

"I was sad this morning. I thought you were gone. Now I can be happy." She bounced up and down in Sally's arms.

"Why don't you run and build some sand castles with your friends," Sally urged.

"I want you to build with me," she said with a pout.

"Jonas and I are going to talk with Daniel a few minutes, and then we'll come and both of us will build a big sand castle with you."

"Goody," squealed Samantha.

After she left, Jonas told Daniel about finding Arnold at Jackson's and recounted the conversations they had. He was holding his Bible and he kept bending the corner, letting the pages riffle under his thumb. When he told about Arnold wanting to spare Rachel, Sally exploded, "That's baloney!"

"Ya," Daniel said when he finished, "you are right, Sally. Arnold tosses words around like a tangle of weeds, but we don't get stuck in them." He paused and adjusted his cap. "Sure. I will take him over in the tug after dark. The two of you might as well come along and catch the midnight train north to the Dells. My brother's expecting you."

They stood on the porch and stared out at the harbor. Jonas could occasionally see the tops of Samantha's and the other kids' heads bob up over the tall grass between them and the beach.

"You do think it's right to turn in Arnold, don't you?" Jonas asked, thumbing the pages of his Bible. "Right for both Arnold and Rachel?"

"Ya, it's the thing to do. Arnold should have been in jail over Sally." He stroked his beard. "And as far as Rachel goes . . . that's a tough one. We have to trust God on that one. Ya, for sure, it's not going to be easy on that girl. If it's splashed all over the place, we'll all have to deal with it. Not just Rachel. It'll be tough . . . " He leaned off the porch, pulled a piece of grass, and started to chew on it. "Life is just a pickle sometimes," he said. He spit out a piece of grass. "I think I better talk to Arnold. Later this afternoon you and I better go over to Jackson's and make sure Arnold understands he should go with us tonight."

"I'll see you at church, right?" Jonas asked. Daniel nodded. "Before then," Jonas continued, "I need to go over the children's story one more time and go over my preaching notes too."

"I promised you and I would build a sand castle for Samantha," Sally reminded him.

"I guess I'll go over the kids' story while I'm doing that."

They stepped off the porch. Jonas turned and waved. "See you in a bit."

Daniel seemed old and sad, standing on the porch, a stem of grass bobbing up and down as he chewed on it. Maybe it's the weather, Jonas thought. It was sweltering already. He looked up at the sky. The white clouds were moving. Maybe the rain would come before church was over.

"Ya, in a bit," Daniel said, giving him a small wave.

101.

In the late afternoon the temperature dropped, the wind picked up, and clouds boiled across the lake from the west. Jonas scooped up Samantha where they had been playing and turned to Sally who was lying on the beach reading. "We better get in," Jonas said. "The rain's going to hit any minute."

Sally closed her book. "I want to go with you and Daniel when you go see Daddy," she said.

He was puzzled. "What for?"

"I want to tell him I'll visit him in jail."

He shrugged. "I think Daniel will think that's okay."

"He's my daddy," she flared.

Jonas motioned at the sky with a tilt of his head. "We better hurry if we're going to beat the rain."

They left Samantha with Alice, after promising to be back for her by supper. It was fine with Daniel for Sally to come with them.

Chased by thunder and lightning, the three of them didn't beat the rain. At the first sprinkle they broke into a run, Jonas and Sally holding hands, heads bent, laughing, while the drops pelted them. Jonas knocked on the door with one hand and opened it at the same time with the other.

"Sorry for knocking and entering at the same time," Jonas said, breathing heavily. "It's raining."

"So I see," Jackson said. "You saved me having to yell for you to come in."

Arnold was sitting in a chair on the far side of the room.

"I'm sorry I don't have much in the way of chairs," Jackson said. "I don't get a lot of visitors all at one time, and I'd have to just keep shoving them out of the way."

"We can stand," Daniel said. They moved into the room; Jonas leaned against a wall, Daniel leaned against a counter, and Sally stayed by the door.

"I did expect company, though, so I do have coffee ready.

Help yourself. Fill mine three-quarters full."

Jonas poured the coffee. Jackson uncorked his bottle and added liquid to his coffee until his cup was full. "Now it should be cool enough. I don't like to burn my mouth on coffee," he said, taking a drink. "Just right."

"Arnold," Daniel began, "I got the radio fixed and the sheriff will have a deputy to meet us when we get to the mainland tonight. You should know, too, that Brawn used the radio this afternoon to get ahold of some cousins of his who have dogs. They're meeting him over at the East Side tonight to sniff your clothes and start searching for you then."

"Dogs?" His eyes opened wide. "Maybe we should leave now."

"There's time to wait until dark so you won't be seen. Brawn's cousins can't leave until after chores."

"Ethyl won't let them in the house."

"She's going to have a hard time stopping them. If anything, Brawn is getting madder."

"How am I supposed to get there without anybody seeing me?" Arnold had been sleeping and he was rubbing his eyes. "If it's still raining, that won't be a problem. But even if it quits, you better figure out a way."

Arnold took a sip of coffee and looked nervously at the people in the room. His eyes settled on Jonas. "I hope you've given some thought about the reputation of this girl. As I was saying, I think something can be worked out to spare her. You did talk to Daniel?"

Daniel answered, "He talked to me."

"As I was saying, I'm not thinking of myself. I do have to pay for my sins. I did give in to her desires. I shouldn't have, but I couldn't help myself. So I should pay. But, really, does she need to pay, too? And if we go to the sheriff, word will get around. I'm concerned for her."

"That's bull!" Sally muttered.

"Watch your language," Arnold said sternly. He softened his voice, "And besides, I'm not finished. I realize that we are in the middle of a difficult situation. Something does need to be done. I do need to be off this island, at least for several days, so I am very willing to go tonight. I'll find a way to get on the *Edna*. But if I'm turned over to the sheriff tonight, what's going to happen to the girl is a foregone conclusion. Let's give it a couple of days. Perhaps the two of you could talk with Brawn. And with the girl. I bet no one has even talked with her about what it means to involve the sheriff. Is anyone really concerned about sparing her?"

"You make me sick!" Sally screamed and threw her coffee at him. The brown liquid arced through the air and slashed across his shins.

"You bitch!" he yelped, leaping out of his chair.

Daniel quickly set his coffee down on the counter, stepped between them, and held up his hand, "Wait a minute, wait a minute." He looked at Sally. "I understand you're angry." He turned to Arnold who leaned over, holding out his pant legs so they didn't touch his skin. "Are you okay?"

"Just burned," he said angrily.

"Jonas, get some cold rags to put on the burns." Jonas got the rags. Arnold, who had rolled up his pant legs, laid the rags on the burns on his shins.

Sally had her hand on the door. Daniel turned to her. "Sally, did you have something to say to your daddy's concern for Rachel?"

"He talks about sparing her," she said. "There is no way to spare her. You raped her, Daddy. It is done. It is final. It happened. You can pretend it didn't happen. This whole island can pretend it didn't happen. She can even pretend it didn't happen, but it happened. There is no sparing her."

"Then you tell her, Sally," Arnold said, "that you, in your almighty wisdom, have decided not to spare her. You tell her."

"Daddy, you did not spare me," she said quietly but intensely. "You did not spare your own daughter. You raped me just like you raped Rachel." It was the first time Jonas had heard her use the word rape.

"Don't bring that up now," Arnold said, throwing up his

hands. "We have enough to deal with."

"You did not spare me, and you and I pretended it didn't happen. You and I pretended, and the whole island joined in the pretense. 'Sally was raped by a stranger. Poor Sally.' Everyone knew it was a lie because there are no strangers on this island. But everyone pretended. I guess they wanted to spare me. What they did was spare themselves the truth. And you know what that did, Daddy? That put me in hell because I could not tell a soul the truth. Because I was sparing this whole fucking island." She started to cry.

"Watch your language," Arnold said.

"Daddy," she kept talking through her tears, "you know what the best thing in my life was? It was this man." She jabbed Jonas. "He didn't keep his mouth shut. He didn't spare me."

"He didn't spare himself," snorted Arnold. "He took one lousy swing and got his holy preacher clock cleaned."

"I didn't know it at the time, but that was the best thing he could have done for me."

"Get his clock cleaned?"

"No, his refusal to act as if it didn't happen," she said, wiping her eyes.

"Put me in jail then," Arnold said.

"Ya, that's the sheriff's job then," said Daniel.

"No, it's the place of my high and mighty daughter."

Sally reached for the door, turned the handle, then looked back at Arnold. "I'll visit you in jail, Daddy," she said.

"Oh, so you can sit and tell me how bad I am."

"No, Jonas and I will visit you because no one deserves to be as alone as I was. Not even you."

She opened the door and walked out. Jonas and Daniel followed her.

It was still thundering and lightning, but there was a lull in the rain. The three of them walked down the path that led to Jackson's house. When they reached Daniel's porch, Daniel stopped and turned to them. "Jonas," he said, "I think you have found a pearl of great price, an honest woman."

"You're not going to tell me to watch my language?" said Sally.

"Arnold's the one who should watch his language. Ya, it's full of dead bones then."

He was about to open the door when Sally said, "Daniel, I want a minute with Jonas before we pick up Samantha." Daniel went in and Sally fell into Jonas' arms, sobbing, "That was so hard." She buried her face in his neck. "I was so scared. It was so hard," she said again and again. Jonas held her, her tears soaking into his neck, the rain picking up.

102.

The rain had stopped and there was a red streak in the west as Jonas and Sally walked with Samantha over to Daniel and Alice's cabin. Samantha skipped ahead of them.

"This will be the longest Samantha and I have been apart," she said.

At Daniel and Alice's she spent a long time holding Samantha, listening to her, telling a bedtime story, and praying with her. Daniel and Jonas visited over a cup of coffee.

And then it was time to go.

The sun had set and a cloud moved long enough for Jonas to see the planet called the Evening Star as they walked back to the cabin. They finished packing and checked to make sure everything was put away.

Arnold was huddled in the cabin of the tug when they boarded. I wonder if he will ever be an honest man? Jonas thought. Arnold didn't acknowledge them, and they didn't say anything to him.

And then Daniel was there, untying the tug, starting the engine, pulling away from the dock, heading out into the cove and then the lake.

The tug plowed through the dark waves, and Sally and Jonas huddled under a slicker at the bow to keep dry from the occasional spray from the rolling waves. Behind them the engine roared. Above them scattered dark clouds scuttled east, as if to catch up with the storm that had passed.

"I meant it when I said I would visit him in jail," she shouted so that he could hear over the engine.

There was a nearly full moon and a sky full of stars. It was then that he remembered the night his mom said, "Stars are known by their families." After his mother told him that, he began to study the stars. He looked at the stars. As the sprays stopped he located Aquila, then Cygnus and Lyra. He could hear his mother's voice: "Stars are known by their families."

Putting his mouth to her ear he said, "I will go with you."

Memories flooded him—meeting Sally, her family, the visit to his family, the wedding, last night . . .

He shivered and put his arm around Sally. He looked at her. By the dim light of the moon he could see the outline of her face. Her face was soft as she looked out over the dark waves.

To speak over the engine he put his mouth to her ear, "Sally, I once heard a story about an old Greek who went around the city with a lantern looking for an honest man. I have found what that old man was looking for. I have found an honest woman." She looked at him. "I just found her by the light of the moon." He could make out her smile in the moonlight.

She put her mouth to his ear, "I thought you were going to tell me that if I had a lantern I would find an honest man next to me." Smiles rose out of each of them.

He put his mouth next to her ear, "When I was a boy my mother said that stars are known by their families. When I was growing up, I always thought that was the family I would be known by. I didn't think about starting a new family."

She put her mouth to his ear, "I like that. I like to think of us as a new family."

He put his mouth to her ear, "I want our family to be known for its honesty."

She nodded. "A family of live bones," she said and leaned against him. The fishing tug plowed through the Lake Michigan night.

About the Author

Rich Foss grew up as one of ten children in northern Minnesota. He graduated from the University of North Dakota. In 1977 he moved to Illinois to become part of Plow Creek Fellowship, a communal Mennonite church, where he is currently an elder. He does public relations and fund raising for an agency that serves people with disabilities. He lives on the Plow Creek farm near Tiskilwa, Illinois, with his wife and three children. He is at work on another novel.